SO VAST THE PRISON

SO VAST
THE PRISON

ASSIA DJEBAR
TRANSLATED BY BETSY WING

Seven Stories Press
New York / Toronto / London

First trade paperback edition, May 2001.

This translation published with the help of a grant from the French Ministry of Culture—
Centre national du livre.

Seven Stories Press
140 Watts Street
New York, NY 10013
http://www.sevenstories.com

In Canada: Hushion House, 36 Northline Road, Toronto, Ontario M4B 3E2, Canada

In the U.K.: Turnaround Publisher Services Ltd., Unit 3, Olympia Trading Estate, Coburg
Road, Wood Green, London N22 6TZ U.K.

Library of Congress Cataloging-in-Publication Data

Djebar, Assia, 1936–
   [Vaste est la prison. English]
   So vast the prison: a novel / Assia Djebar; translated by Betsy Wing.
   p. cm.
   ISBN 1-58322-009-7 (cloth)
   ISBN 1-58322-067-4 (pbk)
   I. Wing, Betsy. II. Title.
PQ3989.2.D57 V3713 1999
843—dc21   99-041329

College professors may order examination copies of Seven Stories Press titles for a free
sixmonth trial period. To order, visit www.sevenstories.com/textbook, or fax on school
letterhead to (212) 226-1411.

9 8 7 6 5 4 3 2

Book design by Cindy LaBreacht
Printed in the U.S.A.

TO SAKINA AND TO JALILA

"So vast the prison crushing me,

Release, where will you come from?"

—BERBER SONG

CONTENTS

The Silence of Writing 11

PART ONE   WHAT IS ERASED IN THE HEART

1   *The Siesta* 19

2   *The Face* 25

3   *Space, Darkness* 37

4   *The Dance* 48

5   *The Absence* 66

6   *Before, After* 87

7   *The Goodbye* 111

PART TWO   ERASED IN STONE

1   *The Slave in Tunis* 123

2   *The Renegade Count* 131

3   *The Archeologist Lord* 135

4   *Destruction* 142

5   *The Secret* 146

6   *The Stele and the Flames* 153

7   *The Deported Writer* 159

ABALESSA 164

PART THREE   A SILENT DESIRE

"FUGITIVE WITHOUT KNOWING IT". 171

Arable Woman I 178
First Movement: Of the Mother as Traveler. 181

Arable Woman II 203
Second Movement: Of the Grandmother as a Young Bride. 207

Arable Woman III. 224
Third Movement: Of the Mother as Little Girl. 230

Arable Woman IV 252
Fourth Movement: Of the Narrator in the French Night 258

Arable Woman V. 278
Fifth Movement: Of the Narrator as an Adolescent. 284

Arable Woman VI 303
Sixth Movement: Of Desire and its Desert. 311

Arable Woman VII 330
Seventh Movement: Shadows of Separation. 334

PART FOUR   THE BLOOD OF WRITING

Yasmina. 353
The Blood of Writing—Final. 356

GLOSSARY. 360

THE SILENCE OF WRITING

FOR A LONG TIME I believed that writing meant dying, slowly dying, groping to unfold a shroud of sand or silk over things that one had felt trembling and pawing the ground. A burst of laughter—frozen. The beginnings of a sob—turned into stone.

Yes, for a long time I wanted to lean against the dike of memory, or against the shadowy light of its other side, to be gradually penetrated by its cold, because as I wrote I recalled myself.

And life dissipates; its living trace dissolves.

Writing about the past, my feet wrapped up in a prayer rug which was not even a jute or horsehair mat tossed down somewhere on the dust of a dawn road or at the foot of a crumbling dune under the immense sky at sunset.

The silence of writing, the desert wind turning its inexorable millstone, while my hand races and the father's language (the language now, moreover, transformed into a father tongue) slowly but surely undoes the wrapping cloths from a dead love; and so many voices spatter into a lingering vertiginous mourning, way behind me the faint murmur of ancestors, the ululations of lament from veiled shadows floating along the horizon—while my hand races on...

For a long time I believed that writing meant getting away, or at the very least, leaping out under this immense sky, into the dust of the road along the foot of the crumbling dunes... For a long time.

During that period, almost fifteen years ago, every Saturday afternoon, I used to go to the *hammam* at the ancient heart of a small Algerian city at the foot of the Atlas Mountains.

I went with my mother-in-law, who would meet her friends there in the mist and the cries of children in the hot steam room. Some of these older women, matrons parading around in their striped tunics, made the bathing ceremony an interminable ritual, with its solemn liturgy and melancholy languor.

There one encountered mothers also, humble, worn out, and surrounded by their brood, and there were sometimes also young, harshly beautiful women (whose behavior the distrustful bourgeois matrons viewed with suspicion). Ostentatiously immodest, they would remove every hair from their bodies but not the heavy gold jewelry that still sparkled around their necks and naked, wet arms... I would wind up being the only one to make polite conversation with them afterward in the large, cold room.

Like many of the women, I felt the pleasure of the baths upon leaving them. Carpeted with mats and mattresses, the antechamber became a haven of delights where you were served peeled oranges, open pomegranates, and barley water to your heart's content. Perfumes mingled above the bodies of sleeping women and engulfed the shivering ones, who slowly dressed as they spun their colorful threads of gossip.

I stretched out, I dozed, I listened. My mother-in-law spread out her satin undergarments and taffeta robes. She kept a motherly watch over me as she greeted this or that neighbor or young beauty passing by. Then in a low voice she would recount for me the details of their ancestry. I surrendered to the hubbub and murmuring warmth. When finally my kinswoman began to unfold her creamy white wool veil and wrap it around herself, I in turn would get ready. The time to leave had come. Then I would play the role of silent companion. No veil, of course, but taciturn. Attentive, while the heavy door in the back opened slightly from time to time to exhale steam and distant sound like breath from a magic lair...

One day an amply endowed lady in the splendor of her fifties, cheeks pink with heat and her forehead crowned with a white taffeta headdress fringed in shades of purple, began the lengthy formulas of farewell.

My mother-in-law, who enjoyed her company, wanted her to stay longer.

"Another fifteen minutes, O light of my heart," she insisted.

The other one, exasperated, made a face and excused herself in a scornful voice. This woman who seemed so expert in affectation ended her list of justifications by letting slip a stark expression.

"Alas, unfortunately"—she sighed dramatically—"I am fettered."

"You, fettered?" her friend exclaimed, filled with admiration, as if she were in the presence of a queen.

"Yes, I am," retorted the lady through her immaculate veil. She then closed the matter by concealing her face entirely with a haughty gesture. "I cannot possibly stay later today. The enemy is at home!"

She left.

"The enemy?" I asked, slowly turning toward my mother-in-law.

The word *l'edou*, resonant in Arabic, had sounded a dissonate note.

My companion helplessly contemplated the complete astonishment that filled my eyes. She forced a half smile; perhaps she felt also at that moment a sort of shame.

"Yes, 'the enemy,'" she whispered. "Don't you know how women in our town talk among themselves?" (My silence continued thick with questions.) "Don't you understand? By enemy, she meant her husband."

"Her husband, the enemy? She doesn't seem so unhappy!"

My naïveté suddenly seemed to irritate my mother-in-law.

"Her husband is no different from any other husband! 'Enemy' is just a manner of speaking. Women, as I said before, have called them that for ages... without the men knowing it. I, of course—"

I interrupted her with a gesture as we stood up. My mother-in-law was a saint: Even had she had a real enemy, she would have called him "my lord." As for her husband, a hard though fair man, she served him with unfailing dignity.

This word, *l'e'dou*, I first heard in this way, in the damp of the vestibule from which women arrived almost naked and left enveloped head to toe. The word *enemy*, uttered in that moist warmth, entered me, strange missile, like an arrow of silence piercing the depths of my then too tender heart. In truth the simple term, bitter in its Arab flesh, bored endlessly into the depths of my soul, and thus into the source of my writing...

Suddenly one language, one tongue, struck the other inside me. The voice of a woman who could have been my maternal aunt came to shake the tree of my hidden hope. My silent quest for light and shade was thrown off balance, as if I had been exiled from the nurturing shore, orphaned.

The word spoken by the older woman in her veil who had been smiling just minutes before, certainly no victim, but comfortable in her role as a city-dweller, peaceable and somewhat affected, this word—not one of hatred, no, rather one of despair long frozen in place between the sexes—this word left in its wake within me a dangerous urge to self-erasure...

This lady from the baths left in a dignified manner. Shortly afterward my mother-in-law and I followed. I, speechless and, as the next few years would show, stripped bare, drowned mourning for things unknown and for hope.

Was that why I began to mistrust writing? It had no shadow? It dried things up so fast? I discarded it.

Those years were not really years of silence or depression: Inside my ear and heart grated the gift of the unknown woman whose voice tormented me. Through her the mother tongue had shown me her teeth, inscribing within me a deadly bitterness... Where was I to find the thick undergrowth within from now on, how was I to open a narrow corridor into the warm, black tenderness, whose glowing secrets and gleaming words piled thick and deep?

Would I not have to beg, plunged into the darkness of the lost language and its hardened heart that I had found at the *hammam* that day?

PART ONE
WHAT IS ERASED
IN THE HEART

"But what is becoming of me now
that makes me dream of you?
As streams bear me along,
there—the end of something,
something unfolding like Asia."

—HÖLDERLIN
En bleu adorable

"Oh, is this your buried treasure?
The light in the heart."

—VIRGINIA WOOLF
A Haunted House

1

THE SIESTA

A SIESTA, A LONG SIESTA, one day in early November... as if this rest came after six, nine months, no, a year, or to be precise thirteen months, thirteen months of soaking—the rising of an insidious flood with moments of inertia, a growing inner swell, swelling in imperceptible vibrations, in prickles. Moments of respite intervene, bright intervals of apathy, a flash of sudden winter sun inside the heart, and once again the fever rises, its exhausted gnawing away, its relaxation of laboring muscles... And the fierce refusals of I don't know what, the repressed trembling, something obscurely digging away inside me, my hard refusal in no way conquering the urgent tide, softly violent, obstinate, an anonymous infiltrating passion carving its design. A mask, that's it. Heroically I manage to keep the mask on. My words are veiled and I can make my laughter—when it's not fake, when it's not afraid to zigzag along—burst out higher up, along some beam of distant light, against the breaking seas of scattered conversations... Yes, after burying everything dug up deep inside me, the darkness of turmoil engulfed in civility, behind my everyday activities and my absent body's comings and goings, after thirteen long, slow months passed in this manner, after all that, a siesta, just one siesta, one November day in the family house—an Andalusian song plays on the radio, a rebec hoarsely accompanying the baritone's voice, and from the kitchen I can hear dishes clattering, the dull thump of cans, then a steady stream of water; they must be washing the tiles, at the door a jingling bell rings, whoever has just arrived stops and stands in the vestibule, a child whines, the polite voices of relatives intertwine their greetings; a moment later, in the room next to me, the rustle of an adolescent girl folding silky underthings, her light laughter cut short as she cautiously closes the nearby door. I doze throughout, my body crumpled in sudden lassitude as if exhausted from a race stretching on for days on end, nonstop, like breathlessness that has reached its limit, and I plunge irrevocably into the blur of a voracious nap.

I am lying on a narrow divan in my father's library; his prayer rug is tossed partly across a nearby chair; the shutters facing me are closed; behind them I feel the presence of the staircase to the little garden with its jasmine and hollyhocks flattened, no doubt, by the not yet fading sun. I can hear the dog outside, chasing flies—and I lose myself, sinking down into sleep inside this house that is also a boat. A two- or three-hour siesta. One sunny day in November. An unadventurous day.

I awake to the layered silence of the house, which suddenly seems deserted. Someone must have thrown a rough wool blanket over me. Astonished, I sit straight up. What's going on? A moment of uncertainty: the light coming through the window is different, not weaker, different. I make an effort to try to understand, then very gradually, uneasily, I sense finally with certainty, something both new and vulnerable, a beginning of something, I don't know what, something strange. Is it color, sound, odor? How can I isolate the sensation? And this "something" is inside me and at the same time it envelops me. I am carrying some change inside me, and it floods through me.

Everything around me, the furniture, the rustic library, the white room, everything seems lit by some pure iridescence. All because in that instant I feel new. I discover an amazing and abrupt revitalization within.

Awake and happy at five in the afternoon. Awake, washed, arisen as if from a long illness. Azure space envelopes me, the air still. The facing window is still there, unchanged, behind it the stone staircase and its jasmine, its hollyhocks. The dog comes back, I hear him again... Life goes on, distant. The world stands still and trembles like some invisible, giant creature about to become a statue; I stare wide-eyed. Space gapes open around me; I sit, still dazed. In front of the shutters a diagonal strip of golden dust sparkles. Everything fits.

Then life takes off once more, flooding; glissando. I feel I grasp its weave, the beating of a secret heart, bursting with darkness... There had been this brief halt to revive me! Here I am, awake now, resuscitated, my body intact and serene, at five in the afternoon.

I get up from the divan. I contemplate the blank day. I make no plans, I move about for the sheer pleasure of it. I dress in order to feel my legs, my arms, my shoulders, my skin beneath the cool cloth. There is no need to look at myself in a full-length mirror. I walk through the other rooms greeting my relatives; I listen to the muffled and politely appropriate things they say. I answer, distant, but not at all absentminded, somewhat ceremonious myself in turn, but really there, satisfied with this conventional present moment yet seeing at the same time its precariousness. The others' façades; they could be simulacra: bizarre projections, moving along and reveling in some ephemeral realm. Nonetheless I join in the usual things, ridiculous though they are, and, overcome by some unwarranted benevolence, I am amused by them. Perhaps we will all be caught up in a whirlwind, some instant dissolution: do we not in fact live on the edge of unforeseeable collapse, under the threat of imminent disaster?

All this time I cannot forget the strangeness, the miracle of my awakening in the library. I gradually learn how to inhabit myself, in the first stages of calm stability: the reassuring density of others floods back, as well as the weight of things. I slowly confirm this for myself as if, before, their physical shape and substance had been their mere obstructions.

One more instant and I might have thought I was the prisoner of some strange, huge picture projected against the void. What if I experimented by rebelling against appearances?

Relief sweeps over me: I am no longer living "before," I am no longer ill, I have left the dream. A thirteen-month-long dream. How comforting it is just to exist: an empty room; the distant voices of the family women; a visitor saying goodbye; outside, the sun setting suddenly, the first lamp glowing. I get dressed; I choose a new blouse; tonight I'm dining at the home of friends. Probably there will be people I don't know: the ordinary events of social life—its reassuring little surprises!

The evening is spent in chatter and smoke, in a lull of laughter and few words, in bursts of music that make you want to dance, and every now and then the vividness of my earlier vision as I emerged from my siesta returns. In this room, amid faces that are indifferent or polite, I can see that, ever since this afternoon's awakening, I am free of influence, I am myself, full of emptiness, available and tranquil, starving for the outside and serene... Not like before! "Before"—what was that like? What was I then, what person? How was I incomplete? What obsession tormented me? What was that uncontrollable quivering of skin, of mouth, the fingers of a hand kept out of sight, the shawl suffocatingly tight... What was that, over and over, at least once a day, or ten times the same day? That was "before": the inner opacity that had to be stifled deep inside and smothered. Before, there was a struggle with neither enemy nor object; before, there was passion fiercely denied, fervor churning through you and the heart reeling.

How good it's going to be to be alive from now on, I think that very first evening—I remember that there was a man I liked, who put me at ease, a man I liked, who leaned toward me and began at that very moment to court me—very cautiously. He spoke slowly, I think; he spoke slowly and I didn't hear him. *It's good to be alive!* I say again to myself, and my whole face is smiling.

It is going to be so delicious to walk, to like walking for the sake of walking, to admire the purplish white of whitewashed façades at the crack of dawn, to listen to the splashing laughter of children as it beads off the balconies, their showers bursting in my face...

To hear and let oneself be carried along by nearby voices, colors, surging impetuously in disorder, gushing, springing! How intoxicating it will be to become a simple spectator once more, with no attachments or particular desire! Everything improvisation, in outbursts or just waiting. How good it will be to prepare oneself really to live, since the process of living is both leaping and standing still simultaneously.

The evening ends in a rumpled dream, gaiety giving way to fatigue. The next morning I experienced all over again a pure, ineffable, eager awakening. An unsullied light enveloped me exactly as it had the day before after my siesta. At daybreak or late midmorning in days to come, the fleeting and certain impression would return that I was coming closer and closer to some secret throb of excitement, freed from convention. The tempo of life: a spring flowing into chiaroscuro and the fullness of silence. Later the rhythm of these days blurred together to establish a beat that lingered stubbornly inside me.

So thirteen months had been exhausted in a long drawn-out battle, harried by a blind-faced passion whose life had dried up. Thirteen months were wiped out in my sleep that November day.

2

THE FACE

NO, THE IMAGE OF THE other will not change. Only his power over me, which I confessed neither to him nor to myself, his charm—in its magical sense—unexpectedly vanished that November afternoon, dissolved into the gray waters of my siesta.

As if sleep were navigation. As if, through the muscles of relaxed limbs—the body at rest, responsive and braced, jumping or tensing in response to some dream, or prone and barely breathing, hardly more than a warm corpse—as if the fibers and nerves of the whole organism were haunted by a memory turned inside out, a coiled animal now stretched out on its back in the half-light, belly offered, eyes blinded and mouth open, grimacing and obscene… Body both overpowered by sleep and overpowering it, in a watchful, sun-drenched brightness filtered through half-closed shutters.

And the siesta unfolded like old lace, its weave uncertain, sheer its whole length. And thus my sleeping woman's body, released and abandoned, rid itself inexorably of the poison instilled inside it for thirteen months.

Must I explain the nature of this clearing away, risking in the process that some powdery spider's web will reemerge, some tangle of silk or dust with its melancholy effect, from memory not yet rotten?

For thirteen months, in this excavation of ruins, the face of the other had seemed irreplaceable to me. He springs back to life before me the moment that I write—probably because I am writing. A face no less pure, its frank honesty still intact, but henceforth stripped of its power over my senses.

Those days it was a matter of inventing ways to parry his influence and not be weak in any way. If I unexpectedly found myself confronted with this man's presence, I was careful to look at him without seeing him.

Looking at him as if he were just anybody. In a split second deciding to see him through a fog. However, if I was in a group or in a crowded room, I would suddenly take pity on myself (I actually was starting to beg from myself), my heart pleading convulsively, I would slip quickly back into a corner and turn around. Suddenly the face of my Beloved would appear as if from some picture frame fated to be there, he would be talking, listening, leaving. I would look at him from a distance, left to the solitude I had chosen, concentrating my burning gaze on him. Just one look so that I could recall everything later ("later" would begin as soon as separation took effect, but it felt a hundred years away)!

Under cover and distant I would note the precise line drawn by his eyebrows, the helix of his ear, his slight Adam's apple, his somewhat projecting upper lip, and how reflected glints of green or blue-green on his jacket, his shirt—it mattered little what—played across his face. I dared move a step closer—then two steps. I lowered my eyes, as if I were thinking about something, which I was, then quickly looked up in an attempt to grasp precisely the texture of his skin, the short scar at one corner of his lips. In a split second I verified things I had seen in a blur earlier: the line of his nose set at right angles but recessed where it met his forehead, the bony planes of his profile, and the deep-set eyes that looked down his nose, creating a distant, proud physiognomy, with the ever so slight imbalance of the face of a bird. This enduring impression from our very first meeting, his particular distant look, made me want to hear the resonate voice that went with it; but his distant gaze had also kept me away from this man any number of times, proving so well the restive caution of bodies, deaf and dumb in their own ways but able to perceive, prior to any contact, the dangerous electricity that will draw two people close or drive them apart.

I had quickly pronounced him "not a very nice man." It took weeks, a party, exceptional circumstances in short, requiring that the scenery and other things were not in their usual order, for me to become aware of something I sensed, something that would make me a prisoner for months: I felt this face harbored a strange peace. In his frail young man's build, in the bright gaze with steely glints flickering across it when he spoke in the broken voice of a drug user (whether music, nostalgia, or hashish was the drug), this man—not yet in his thirties, still wearing hints of his slightly crazy adolescence and the offended air of youth—lay his secret before me. He was offering it to me. I alone would decipher it, share it, without letting on that this would make my heart melt. I would hope that my normally cool, clear vision would come to bear: the devastation within this man, the sense of absence, and the dream of that absence. Later he talked to me, although I was not good in the ambiguous role of confidante; he talked, as if it had been pure chance that I had turned up the moment he felt the need to confide.

I understood, in snatches of his confession, that there was a hidden crack behind this tranquil manner, so openly vulnerable yet proud. His will sharpened into a thin body and features that were too finely chiseled, into disdain for how he looked and dressed. These highly visible signs hid an earlier wound, some suffering that had not yet completely vanished. There was poetry dwelling in this face (too often youth has no connection with poetry).

I recall again how, when I would abruptly find myself in the presence of the Beloved (thinking this word in Arabic do I betray myself?), I would concentrate all my strength so as not to stare at him. For a long time I did this until my will faltered and I would give in to gaze at him for just that last second, at least, with all the violence of a starving woman! Abruptly taking in the features that were already in my heart. (If I went a day or two without meeting him, I would begin to suffer not from his absence so much as from the insidious fog clouding his image in my memory!) Some radiance of impalpable youth haloed the fragility of his appearance... So, no matter how long our encounters lasted, as soon as our separation became imminent, my attention would pounce on the vision of him, which was for me so miraculous. My memory would stock up on its nourishment, all the details, to guarantee the impression would be precise for future memory... It even seemed that, to the extent that every encounter would immediately set the raging mechanism of mnemonics in motion inside me, joy itself, the pure, wonderful joy of savoring the dear presence, would only come later. In the very first seconds of separation the memory-image, thus nourished once again and rekindled, was illuminated in all the exact detail I needed finally to be calm. Lost days when it seemed that his face would always remain!

The earliest days of discovery—still not forgotten... I took a taxi; it was fifteen kilometers from the capital to this village by the sea. The country house, its garden deep in sand... Open rooms, a terrace with mats and straw chairs; a Ping-Pong table and on the ground a game of *boules* lying about; laughter from friends clustered out back under the figtree.

"You're here?"

"Because you invited me!" And I pretended I was just a neighbor on my way somewhere.

He said it again, half muttering, "You're here!" I can still hear his voice, slightly heavy with indolence and a touch of nostalgia. It was as if he recognized something in my manner. What was it—some crazy impulse that I hid beneath nonchalance the moment I crossed the doorstep? Despite my pretense he noticed or recognized this urge because he himself had experienced it before in some other place and time... The saddened, almost disillusioned resonance to his low voice, as if he'd been sick (of course he was probably only drunk on sleepless nights of jazz). The voice of insomnia or fever...

One time when I turned up unexpectedly, he suddenly smiled at me. A broad smile that wiped the dross of this other life and its tension from his angular face. A childish smile clearly addressed to me. I forgot everything; I literally drank in his joy; I registered it inside to make the moment glow with it. It was a princely offering: I had come fifteen kilometers by taxi; but I would have come a hundred to be given this gift.

I said nothing; I didn't move. We stood there face-to-face on the threshold for a moment. Our greetings were awkward, no touching of hands and certainly no warm kiss (in those days I still had the stiffness of a young girl, but that wasn't the only reason that I scorned gestures of familiarity in his presence). Finally, since the house was full as usual, someone came and joined us to talk and socialize. The afternoon was spent playing games in groups, gossiping and walking on the nearby beach.

I left with one guest or another, who took me home in his car. On the way back somebody mentioned the name of our host: standing by the doorway, he had told me goodbye, he had smiled at me sweetly as if I were the only one leaving. Once, in a corner of the garden, he teased me in a patronizing voice and he seemed to be a few years older than I, whereas quite the opposite was true.

"In short, you come, you meet people, and you always leave with them!... It's my friends you come to see, not me!"

I didn't answer. I felt a lassitude that prevented me from keeping up the banter. "You and your friends!" is what I would have exclaimed.

I knew he knew that moments before I had had the urgent need to see him, the need to make sure he was indeed real. I was seized by a violent compulsion to verify his existence in the original and almost that very instant with my own eyes. (At that point I wasn't thinking of the possible pleasure I would get from seeing him, and certainly I had no other feelings beyond this strange anxiety that, if it were to go on, would turn into unbearable torture: *Does he really exist? Didn't I dream him?*) As soon as I stood there in his presence, my fever fell, my anxiety dissipated (*I exist, everything exists, because he is real!*), I became civilized again, cunning, hypocritical, and I said to myself, *I was breathless when I arrived, but now I'd rather die—even for all the gold in the world I wouldn't say that I did this because of you!*

Two or three times at least, when I would show up (in the taxi I held my tongue so as not to say "Hurry, faster!"), I surprised my Beloved alone in his summer house.

He lived in the house year-round, and it was usually filled with friends, foreign visitors, people from the provinces who were passing through; it was like this from June to the end of October. Was it already at the end of autumn or even the beginning of winter that I found him alone—the sun intense, freezing cold, the air translucent and dry before dusk? I have forgotten; the truth is that I had become so distracted during that period—in so many ways. Those thirteen months, I don't think I noticed the seasons, except perhaps, stepping out the door, I would suddenly wrap up or maybe go back mechanically to get a shawl or a raincoat or umbrella. I never even tried to use the reactions of my body, which is sensitive to cold, to locate myself in the yearly cycle—as if, since the story began in the summer, and despite all the external evidence to the contrary, I remained in that season.

My memory, benumbed, registered vaguely a few sighs from other voices in me: *I'm cold! I'm hot! I don't have on enough clothes! Why is it so damp?*

I remember a visit just before winter; I probably imagined it was still the end of September, or at the latest October. As I stepped out of the taxi to see the summer village with its bungalows all closed up and its little streets seeming frozen and abandoned, I was reminded that summer was long gone. "December already," I murmured, paying the driver; suddenly I was at a loss to find some pretext: *How am I going to explain dropping by? I don't even have the excuse of saying that I've come for a swim and thought I'd say hello!*

Of course, in September, I had not used any such pretenses. Even when the adjoining beach was swarming with families who were there to swim, I had not even thought of saying, "I've come for a swim," or, "After my swim, I'll come by to say hello, relax a bit, and then be off again." On the contrary, more than once I even said in an offhand manner, "I thought of you, so I took a taxi, and now here I am with all your friends!"

This time I told myself that I had thought up the most cunning ruse possible. I would tell the truth; without mincing words I would explain my real motivation, the urge that drove me to come in a taxi as fast as possible. Then, precisely because the unadorned truth was revealed, it would be played down, and I would know that my passion was concealed as deeply as possible. The other could not take what I said at face value, because then it would have been a confession! As if I had proclaimed in a faint voice (frail tones, quivering chin, and all the other signs of my soul's secret vibration): *I wanted to see you! I took a taxi. Fifteen kilometers and here I am!*

How easily that passed for a fantastic notion, for the whim of a spoiled woman, flaunting an admittedly capricious desire. In fact at the same time that I was telling everything, or rather the external form of this everything, I was trying to figure it out; it seemed as if I couldn't get over it myself. *How can this be possible? I forget everything just to see your face, to convince myself that you are alive, that I'm not obsessed with a dream, I take a taxi and I come here! What is this weakness in me—and just to check on your existence! The moment I stand in your presence, I see that everything is back in order; I master my underlying fever; I am quite simply no longer suffering, everything is liquid, everything...*

Thus I unveiled myself. Thus I was in search of myself. Thus I attempted to disguise myself from myself.

There were then those two or three occasions when I found this man alone when I got out of the car.

I remember the last visit in detail: The gate was closed. I had to go down toward the beach and walk clumsily through the sand. Since all the shutters were closed now, it was hard to tell the villas apart and decide which was his path and not the neighbors'. ("An ambassador!" he had told me earlier, signs of irony aquiver in the corners of his eyes. "You see, we live right in the bosom of the *nomenklatura!*") From there I could go straight through to the terrace. The shades to the French doors were half down. I tapped on the wood, suddenly intimidated... In a moment he appeared, sleepy-eyed, barefoot, and wearing shorts.

"I'm disturbing you! I'll leave!..." I spluttered.

"Not at all! Come in. I was asleep."

There I was, right next to him in this living room with all its windows shut. Full ashtrays on the couch, a sickly sweet smell of enclosure; the record player on the tiled floor and records out of their sleeves spread around in a circle.

He left the room for a minute to get dressed. He kept on talking from the hallway in explanation:

"You came at the right time! I didn't feel like doing anything, not even listening to music." (He came back and waved in the direction of the records strewn all over the floor and the bulky tape recorder that was still turned on.) "I was sleeping because I was bored."

I gazed at him, dressed now in white pants, thinner than usual, his face still tan as if summer lingered on in his buried-away house, his hair messy (my heart leaped with joy to see the way his beauty retained the carelessness of adolescence). I think I smiled at him, overcome by intense happiness. I went up to him. For the first time I took the initiative:

"Do you know what we're going to do? We'll go out in the backyard and play Ping-Pong!… I told you last time I'd beat you!"

He pouted lazily. Finally forgetting myself entirely, I went to take him by the hand to drag him outdoors.

"Are you sure?" he retorted, "That's what we have to do? Don't you want me to fix you some coffee? I'll bring it to you, I'll serve you… courteously." He smiled. "I'll put some music on for you, whatever you choose. We won't budge!…"

I insisted, pushing and shoving him. Finally (I took him by the hand thinking as I did so: *What I really want is to embrace you, to…!*)

"First a game of Ping-Pong!" I persevered, pleased with my authority. "Whoever loses will fix the coffee."

We went out into the part of the yard where there were plane trees, and a scraggly-looking figtree at the end of a path. The Ping-Pong table was dusty and a little wobbly. We found the paddles thrown in a corner against a border of wildflowers. We began the game.

Even now I can hear the sound of our laughter, my bounding joy, my aliveness... Of course, in the half-lit room inside, what opaqueness awaited us: embraces, silences, two bodies coming together, a tension knotting tighter and tighter that would surrender to the flexing of a neck, to lips seeking each other out, to bites just barely felt, perhaps to the tears of release if I come, will I come?... Soon, a bit later, in the bedroom.

Outside, however, I was not at all in turmoil. Only the present moment existed, hard in its innocence. What was it that was growing imperceptibly inside me and yet apart from me?

In the yard, lit aslant by the pale sun, in the midst of these villas almost all deserted because their occupants had gone back to their offices, their social life, their protocol there in the capital, we two were survivors of summer... My laughter grows louder, my partner lets out a disappointed curse, because I'm winning, I'm triumphant. He goes after the ball; I sing to myself; we start our game again. We are almost equals. I save a shot, I keep up my defense, then I lose ground, I burst out laughing, I'm out of breath, I'm nearly beaten, I don't want that!... He pokes fun, takes the lead, his game turns out to be the steadier, the game seems too long for me, I'm impatient, I...

"How much fun it is, being children together!" I suddenly confess, taken aback by my discovery (with the result that I forget to parry, I lose, pretend to be sorry, I'm so far behind!) My surprise increases: *Am I going to relive a past I never knew? Find myself in childhood with you? Is that the whole mystery?*

I am making this truth glow in the hollows of my body, creeping all up and down my limbs (I run, I prance, my arm stretches high). Casual and carefree and absolutely, perfectly, tranquil watching you be my partner in this lightheartedness—a docile partner, one who is also leaping—I think I am six or ten years old, you are my playmate, this yard becomes the one in the village where I lived as a little girl... Where I might have met you before. No one around us would have found fault. Would you have been a cousin, or better, a paternal first cousin? You would have...

At first I didn't even notice that the age difference (nearly ten years) should have prevented my keeping this fantasy alive: This man could not have been a child when I was! It is only just now that we are meeting! It does not matter: Is every love not a return to the first realm, that Eden? Since I could not have known him before (the prohibitions of my Muslim education having operated in two ways), I savor him as we play these games, in these first days of winter.

What time was it when we went back into the living room? I remember that we spent an hour or two in combined inertia, listening together to several records that I chose, but I refused to get involved in commentary or after-the-fact explanations of my choice. Music—to keep any dreadfully banal strategy from coming into play, we would listen to music, the prelude to our abandon!

I listened. Seated at the other end of the room with my head turned toward the French doors opening onto the vast beach. After quite a while I just stood up all of a sudden; I announced I wanted to leave. Outside, the evening was growing dark, gray and rose.

My Beloved got his car out to take me back. Driving back; night beginning. I was silent for the entire length of the trip; it seemed to me that we were going to drive all night long, to faraway lands.

When we got there, he stopped the engine and turned toward me: Did he have any idea how good I felt? Or share the feeling? His face, his eyes were so close in the intimacy of the car. His eyes shone and he said softly, "Did I disappoint you?"... barely uttering my first name.

"Disappoint me? How?" I replied, uncomprehending, then suddenly I embraced him: "I'll give you a kiss," I said, and I kissed him on his forehead, on his eyes, I stopped, I pulled away, I opened the car door.

He said my name again; I was halfway out and I added, almost cool, "I kissed you because tomorrow I'm taking a plane. I'll be gone ten days or maybe twenty. I'm going to miss you!"

"You're leaving! Where are you going?"

"Canada. Goodbye!"

I fled. Only then did my heart begin to beat uncontrollably. I stood there transfixed after the car left, swallowed up in the garden's shadows; I waited for my breathing to return to its normal rhythm.

In the elevator I shook for the entire ten floors.

It all comes back to me; nothing is forgotten; but the acid of obliteration inexorably does its work anyway. I was thirty-seven at the time; ever since the age of twenty I had experienced a calm, enriching love, full of ambiguities I did not understand; the story, in its own way, could go on. What was the meaning of this great wave, this swell inside me? Why, I wondered, did I have this mad desire to relive childhood, or rather to be finally fully alive?

I thought, in the elevator, that I was shivering with cold, and I said to myself tearfully, *Don't come back from Canada. Go somewhere even farther, flee, get lost, never come back! I don't want to slide into a wretched novel when I return!*

I never pronounced the word *passion*. I didn't dwell on either the word or the idea. I did not even guess that I was in the first stages of this strange illness that, for better or worse, would follow its own course.

3

SPACE, DARKNESS

WHEN I RETURNED, my confusion was gone and I considered the episode laughable, a passing weakness. It turned out I had to work in the same place as the Beloved.

Usually by chance, sometimes out of professional necessity, surrounded by other people, at least once a day we would meet for five minutes or an hour. I could have prolonged our meetings under some pretext but didn't think of it. Working under the same roof together! He was on the sixth floor and I was on the ninth, occupying offices almost identically arranged. I was struck by this, as if our parallel work spaces maintained some complicity between us (and so, in the snares of mutual attraction, the least details swell with exaggerated importance).

I remember how using the office phones made me want to talk to him, my voice low as if he were close by, because he was close by:

"Are you alone?" I would have asked.

"Yes!"

"Let's talk!"

At least once a day, whenever work let up, I had this temptation to speak to him; an urge drilling into my heart. I usually brushed aside this desire. The sun-dazzled love affair that was all in my mind lay in wait deep within, but an inexplicable seriousness was taking shape inside me and gaining the upper hand.

At other times the danger, even though I knew I would not give in to it, was harrowing and persistent; there would be long moments of suffering. I would finally get up and cross my office to open the window, imagining that I could turn into a mermaid swimming in the blue. In just a few strokes I'd be there outside his window, invisible, to spy on him or rather fill my eyes with the image of him... I would return to my chair, and to my work, without enthusiasm.

Sometimes, uncontrollably distracted, I would abruptly stop everything, go out, take the elevator, and leave the building. Flee! Walk fast as far as possible, keep going on and on to lose myself forever, because back there at work, in my thoughts, I had found myself lost.

This upsurge turned into anger at myself, against what, as I rushed down a noisy boulevard, I took to be unacceptable weakness. And my mind, falling into the rhythm of my energetic walk, would be set in motion. What justified my being so stirred up? What was feeding my attraction? What was it about him? What was so extraordinary about this young man who was, after all, ordinary? This world, and this country in particular, were full of driven and inspired adventurers, unknown heroes wrapped in rare humility, this city itself—fifteen years earlier oozing bloodshed and lyricism—still contained at least ten or maybe twenty men, now living anonymous lives, who had shown how exceptional they were in their courage, their altruism, their Roman virtue, their...

Gradually I would grow calmer and get back to work. I did not forget that on the sixth floor an ordinary young man was working—a man whose voice never left me, whose gaze had come from childhood to pursue me. This man had power over me even if I was determined not to give in to it. That same day, a couple of hours later, meeting up with my Beloved in the elevator, I would smile innocently at him, happy to see him without having sought him out, reassured by my earlier victory over myself—something he was never to know about.

Nonetheless, two or three times in the course of these five or six months (I was starting research in musicology in this building whose musical archive was great treasure), I could not resist dialing his office number, feigning casualness in my gay tone of voice. I said, "Let's talk! Let's have recess, like at school!"

"Well, then, come down!"

"I can't. Let's talk on the phone. Whoever gets interrupted will instantly hang up, without saying goodbye. The other will understand."

He agreed. We exchanged small talk, things we had read, bits of the past that came up willy-nilly. He was usually the one to remember: a fragment of adolescence, a walk, a trip. I listened and kept quiet. I felt that the way I listened encouraged him. One evening it seemed to me that his reminiscence was becoming so personal that I began to fear for him; I interrupted, calling him by his first name: "Listen, what if someone is listening on the line?" I ventured.

"You're right!" he admitted; the conversation took off in another direction.

Once we must have talked for more than two hours straight. Finally I had the illusion that we were in the same room, each at a different end of it, settled into the darkness, and in fact we were so oblivious that I hadn't turned on the office lights and night had crept in and swallowed me up. He confessed to the same thing.

I remarked that if one of our colleagues were to come, and hear us speaking softly on the telephone in the dark, what plotting he would suspect! We laughed like two kids on vacation...

"Did you ever know anyone like me? In a village? The sirocco would be blowing outside and all the children had been sent to take a nap and stay there... It seemed to me just now that I was whispering from my corner of the darkened room to my first cousin at the other end!"

He murmured, amused: "So, I'm your first cousin! Pleased to discover the bond!"

I went on, now speaking in Arabic; at the other end of the line I felt a pause or hesitation, so I went back to French: "Could you be my paternal uncle's son? (that is what I had just said in Arabic). No, it's not possible. I've just remembered that my father is the only son, because he lost his adolescent brother in a bus accident a long time ago. You might be the son of my maternal uncle, though! You know that the paternal branch is what counts for inheritance, and consequently, in a marriage for money, whereas the maternal line is, on the other hand, the line of tender emotions, affection, and..."

I was going to add "love," but in this conversation about this and that, the French word would have seemed obscene to me.

"You're teaching me all sorts of things, professor!" he joked.

Taken aback by his ignorance, I dared my first personal question: "Really? Didn't you have an Arab childhood?" Then I added, without thinking, "Maybe your mother is French, or..."

I was ashamed at being so indiscreet.

"No, not French," he replied. "She was Berber, or in any case a speaker of Berber. But she always spoke to me in French, nothing but

French!" He laughed and added somewhat roughly, "Didn't you notice that I only speak French? Not a single Arabic or Berber word comes into my sentences. Nothing, no exception, no asides!" He laughed nervously. "Let's say I talk like a *pied-noir*. I speak English very well if you want variety." Silence; he mused. "I was twelve at Independence... I shut myself off completely from Arabic—'the national language,' as they call it here. And I don't think that I'll develop a taste for the official language. I'm not planning a career!"

I listened to him but I did not retort as I should have: *Those eight or nine years by which I am older than you mark a changing era. When I was fifteen I lived in a country at war! Arabic was the language of flames—not of governmental power, as it is now. When one learned Arabic, outside of school, it was not to have a career but to be willing to die! Oh, how I wanted to go off into the mountains then!*

Instead, after a silence I added in a sad voice, "I'm hanging up! Turning on the lights. Goodbye!"

The lights went on in our two offices simultaneously. An hour later we said goodbye among other colleagues, on the square at the main entrance.

I went home in a whirl, my soul overwhelmed. *What is time?* I thought. *Have I not returned if not to the time of my childhood, at least to my preadolescence? Have I not found my first cousin, the real one, the one I truly love—the other one was brash and insolent; this one would have been affectionate and conspiratorial. We would have shared all the fun and joy of that time with a twinkle in our eyes.*

I went home enriched, magnified. Full of infinite patience for the other life, the life of family awaiting me there. The children's school assignments had to be checked, dinner had to be served. Their father was absorbed in his reading and I ended up in front of the television screen, staring but not seeing or hearing. I stayed up to tuck in my little daughter and kiss my son, but then I was the first to bed, happy to curl up alone at first. A book fell from my hand: books, mere books, so different from my secret life. An invisible stork seemed to step softly toward me, brushing against my eyelids as I sank into a pool of oblivion.

Other times my work would keep me late. I had told them at home not to wait for me. Happy to be working so well at the top of this building at a time when almost all the employees had left, I hardly even wondered if he, on the sixth floor, was as lost in his work as I was. I was deeply absorbed. The temptation to pick up the phone never occurred to me; precisely because of my solitude, I would have felt it was improper.

There was a driver with a company car waiting for me. I could, of course, have figured out some way to let him go (even though it was his regular night schedule). I could have checked with the Beloved—who was, after all, my colleague, whose habit of working late I knew—to see if he could take me home. But the memory of that December evening in his car when I had kissed his forehead, his eyes… *Am I crazy?* I thought, remembering this. *Is there a madwoman inside me who any minute now can surge into my life of flat calm, possessing me and sweeping everything away? Yes, am I a woman possessed?*

Three times I said the name of Allah. That very evening, taking the staircase down, when I got to the sixth floor, I noticed, almost in spite of myself, that the lights were still on in my Beloved's office in the empty corridor. The timed switch suddenly plunged the hall into darkness. I stood rigidly facing the wall, leaning my forehead against the cold wall, and this time I recited the *fatiha* from beginning to end, arming myself against any rash impulse. I groped for the switch and found it, turning the lights back on, and sighed, thinking, *Finally, the danger is gone!* My heart drained. Slowly walking the rest of the way downstairs, leaving a heavy weight up there in the shadows.

The driver was waiting for me. "*Lalla,* Madame, I need some advice."

He went on in Arabic recounting his family troubles to me. His ten-year-old daughter was in school and apparently very intelligent—or in any case that's what the teacher said. But her mother, his wife, kept insisting that this beloved daughter had to stop her schooling: "'She has to help me with the little ones!' is what she says."

He thought for a moment, then added, "Her mother can't take it anymore!" He hesitated, unable to decide in favor of the wife or, as his heart was inclined, protecting his little girl for just a year or two longer.

"Let her have a chance!" I said.

One other evening we returned to this conversation. I lived not far away, but still he had to drive me home because, fifteen years after the war—"after the events," in the amazingly terse expression that people still used—the black night threw a de facto curfew onto the streets of the capital. Fear ripples remained without there really being any fear, maybe just a whiff of insecurity in which the inhabitants seemed to take pleasure. Consequently, being a woman and unable to drive a car, after seven P.M. I could not walk even a hundred meters alone outdoors.

Shortly afterward, standing on my kitchen balcony, I guessed which window was still lit up over there on the sixth story of the tall building. The one to whom I could have gone ten minutes earlier, he to whom, this time, showing up so late, I would let myself go.

I would have said to him, *Let's spend the night together!* And the veiled passivity that I sometimes read in his eyes when he looked at me in my confusion, his hesitation would, I imagine, have triggered my joyful enthusiasm:

Let's go into the city, it doesn't matter where, to a bar, to a dance hall, to a bad place or to your place, there on the beach, open the house up again for me if you have closed it. It doesn't matter where we go, but let's stay together all night long!

Of course I would have phoned home and told the husband, *Don't wait up for me tonight. Tomorrow, at dawn, I'll explain.* The next day I would have revealed everything about the state of my heart. What love does not need an arbiter, and that night, that long night, having finally decided on my judge, I would no longer have been right to keep silent about my inner struggles. Yes, that night I would have surrendered to the violent, patient attraction that I had made myself control up to this point, but then, in a single night, had let carry me away!

I fantasized this sequence of events, like water rushing through an open dam. I experienced it while standing in the darkness, on the balcony.

A while ago I had said the *fatiha*, probably for the first time in my life (I disregard occasions in my childhood or even the time that I was twenty, shaken by a passing mysticism), as if Allah alone, in the darkness of that corridor on the sixth floor, had protected me—or imprisoned me, I didn't know which—I acted as a woman in love who finally has only the magic of religiosity to cure her. The *fatiha* said from beginning to end, forehead against the wall, my hand groping in search of the light switch. I turned on the lights; I went down the stairs.

For the next few months I never let up in my work. Sometimes I would go home at ten o'clock at night. I would sit in silence in the children's bedroom to watch them sleep, gazing at them: My son would grow to be such a handsome young man, with his slender, well-built body; my little daughter, though she was asleep, I could hear her crystal-clear voice: "Mummy, you didn't play the Dussek allegretto." She had left me a note on the piano.

I apologized silently. In my room my husband was sleeping—lights on, newspaper dropped at the foot of the bed next to the ash-tray. Suddenly I had a belated attack of neatness and tidied up. Then I lay down, exhausted.

The early morning, before seven o'clock, still felt the same for the four of us. For me, my balcony wanderings seemed to be part of night dreams not yet entirely dissipated. Through the window I watched the entire city emerge in the reddish glow of dawn.

After the children had gone to school, I hung around the house, left to myself. My mind wrapped itself in ribbons of sound, melodies gathered the night before; I huddled over my tape recorder as my listening resumed its flow. In those days if I had used the word *passion* it would only have been to describe this river inside me; every morning here at home, then at my office, it swept me far away for hours on end into a past of buried sounds.

I either waited for the housekeeper to arrive or I would leave her instructions, because she was supposed to take care of the children after four. Shortly after midday I went out. My work life resumed. The day stretched on for me.

I broke this rhythm. One morning I suddenly quit the research office that had been mine for six months. I felt drawn to field investigation, faces, words. I would store up a wealth of noises and sounds, then try to find some suitable way of using them—radio reports, documentary films, bilingual accounts to be published, etc.—afterward.

Investigation first, forgetting oneself in others, the others who wait. The often silent others. I wanted to discover towns and villages: Oran, Mascara, Sidi-bel-Abb's. Crowded projects, congested public housing full of uprooted rural populations; sometimes, in the old quarters, Moorish houses with a lemon or orange tree in the middle of the patio—a haven.

In Béjaia especially, laughter greets me and there is a hint of escape. The port is a pocket in the hollow curve of the vast, wide-open bay. Taken by the woman who is my guide, a former militant, I happen to go into a house in an aging quarter overhanging the city. There I greet two very young women wearing *sarouels* and embroidered tunics; they are sitting cross-legged on mats stretched out on the floor of faded tiles. Facing them, I squat down as well. At first we speak in Arabic, then in French. I had taken them to be traditional city women: "Two young girls to be married," my companion calls them teasingly, but I discover that they are about to complete their medical degrees in the capital.

"These summer and spring vacations are just a forced return to the harem for us!" the first one says ironically—her vocal outburst almost a hiccough.

Outside, I leave the woman who is taking me around. "I'll find my way back to the hotel alone," I say, and thank her.

I rush down a street of stairs. Happy to be alone, and free, in this city saturated with light. Two young men are standing at the bottom of the hill. One of them approaches almost solemnly, looking me over carefully, to say that he has just made a bet and lost because of me. Seeing me from a distance (with my very short hair, my straight white trousers), he had bet that I was a young man.

Although I am thirty-seven, I probably seem less than thirty: thin hips, a boyish haircut, flat buttocks; that day I was so proud of my androgynous silhouette. The young man had lost. I could do nothing about it, but as I went by, I made a funny face at him. "Sorry!" In that instant I knew I was being provocative.

If he had been there to see it, would the man who never left my thoughts have laughed to see me confused with a boy and flattered by this mistake. I would have flung myself into his arms, for sure: "I really am your age! Let's stay together forever in your house with its open doors, its abandoned yard. Let's spend every night on the sand, if no one comes, perhaps there'll be a storm, whatever the season…"

Precisely because of this frivolous incident, and if my Beloved had been lucky enough to witness it, I would have been ready to surrender to every temptation. I would not have thought I was doing anything unreasonable, but rather that I was racing toward the oasis where we would finally end up, breathless. I had seen those two young girls in their temporary confinement, who one day were going to work as doctors, both of them… Virgins, no doubt, twenty-five or twenty-six at the oldest. Pale faces, diaphanous beauties, as if they were leaving their youth behind, and at the same time still awaiting it.

As for myself, in those days I was virtually returning to my reawakened childhood. If in the past, just once, I had played with a brother or a boy cousin on the roads or in the forest, perhaps this nostalgia would not come back to me like this, like an undertow, magnifying my attraction to this man!

Was I searching for some fever in him, a fever I knew within myself? A fever that, on this sunny day in Béjaia, would have been transformed into a cascade of finally willing happiness.

4

THE DANCE

THERE IS ONE SCENE, or maybe there are two that emerge from the preceding summer as the background to this early winter and this restless autumn. Perhaps my memory, to battle its own insidious, fatal dissolution, is attempting to raise some stele like a mark for "the first time." When was the first time I saw this man, or rather, what is the first image that triggered my first emotion? What events, what light, what words ruled over this disturbance—as if passion disturbed, rather than suddenly put things in order and somehow set the soul straight, restoring to one's impulses their original reactions, their purity. As if any love so blindly experienced—completely swathed in prohibitions, hence unwarranted, hence superfluous, or childish, as it may seem to some people—as if any love, arising like an earthquake of silence or fear, did not lead, as the disintegrating surface order collapsed, to original geology... These vague notions about psychology are, of course, only digressions from the story I am pulling from the ruins more than ten years afterward.

Despite my efforts at remembering, I have only a blurry notion of the specific first day of the first meeting, and whether the encounter was insignificant or important between these two characters I describe. (It is not fiction I desire. I am not driven to unfurl a love story of inexhaustible arabesques.) No, I am only gripped by a paralyzing fear, the actual terror that I shall see this opening in my life permanently disappear. Suppose it were my luck suddenly to have amnesia; suppose tomorrow I were hit by a car; suppose some morning soon I were to die! Hurry! Write everything down, remember the ridiculous and the essential; write it, orderly or muddled, but leave some record of it for ten years from now... ten years after my own forgetting.

There is only one real question that looms for me. When, precisely, did this story, which transpired either inside or outside of me—and I don't know which—when did it take hold? It was summer. A blazing summer with cool dawns, gentle twilights, mild nights. The nights above all were densely populated with echoes: shows and dances, lots of people walking in groups along the unending and often deserted beaches that had recently become fashionable for swimming, an hour from the capital.

Every evening in the large stone theater that had opened recently, concerts were scheduled—light music, jazz or folk from bands coming successively from a number of African countries or countries in the East. To finish off the night, journalists, artists, couples who were friends, vacationers from nearby beaches, young women more westernized than the Westerners, would all get together in groups in various discothèques, while I went with my husband, who was the director of this "cultural complex."

During the months of July and August I drowned myself in the music, the laughter, and the playful conversations of others—as a witness; I would slip lethargically into this or else I would sleep;

during the day I read in the calm apartment whose French doors opened onto steep rocks.

This is how I spent my vacation, gradually aware that, this summer or next winter, despite my slenderness and my inexhaustible appetite for walks and dreams, my youth was coming to an end... No, I told myself drowsily, what people call "youth" can be lived endlessly like a block of motionless years.

I watched my husband directing and making decisions; however, well before all the turmoil, I no longer enjoyed talking with him. We were no longer a couple, just two old friends who no longer knew how to talk to each other. I was happy that, with this new distance (not deserted for me, so much as spacious), there were so many people passing through, so many guests in an evening who would seek us out, and especially so much foreign music surrounding us. So there I was, a spectator, and I thought I was perhaps ready to set out. For the first time also, probably for the first time in my life, I felt I was "visible," not the way I felt during my adolescence, nor after I was twenty, when I would smile at some compliment, some flattery from a man, either a friend or a stranger, thinking then, *It's my semblance, my ghost you are seeing, not myself, not really me ... I myself am in disguise, I wear a veil, you cannot see me.*

Why all of a sudden, did a smile or bit of praise distress me so? ("What a pretty dress," some man would say, his fingers about to touch the cloth, and I would tense up, but hide it. Or: "This hairdo suits you," another poorly timed compliment from someone else— an incongruous familiarity that I blamed on the excitement of the theater atmosphere.) Of course, I avoided any contact whatsoever, but something else disturbed me: *They are really talking about me! I'm ashamed; I smile not to seem prudish, but I'm ashamed. They go so far as to touch me with their fingers!... I can protect myself from it, appear "civilized," and remain elusive. But something else has me disoriented, or makes me sad, I don't know which. It is that they can truly see me!*

But the way I related to the exposure of my exterior self to others is another story.

Back to the young man. Looking at me so intensely. And when I try to remember "the first time, and when it mattered to me," I don't know what to say. One scene comes up, one summer day, no, a night rather. I'll call it the night of the dance.

I did not know right away that this young man, with his almost ordinary appearance, with his words (left hanging sometimes like smoke in the air), his nonchalance and apparent casualness, would ever mean so much to me.

Three men showed up as a group; I took them to be journalists. Although their ages and profiles differed, they had in common a sort of elegance we were not used to seeing in these parts, some reserve in their bearing, and aloofness as well. They were not excessively familiar, which right from the start relaxed me, tempering my habitual defensiveness... The camaraderie established right away between this trio and myself seemed out of the ordinary, a game among old adolescents.

There were two of these three new friends who amused me—the one who seemed the oldest, the other almost a kid at twenty. These two men drank a lot and joked endlessly; I would smile at them when I met them sometimes outside a cafe or beside the pool where they might be any time from morning on, and they would call me over. I laughed with these two accomplices over nothing, or over something funny they would say unexpectedly. Sometimes I felt I was back in the schoolyard. The eldest possessed an encyclopedic knowledge and used it in a snobby manner. I reproached him for his pedantry. In this group, however, the silent one, who was also the most distinguished and well bred, always wore a teasing smile on his face and never spoke unless the discussion came around to the music of upcoming programs.

So I listened to them. We decided right off the bat to stay together, my three companions and me; seated on the highest tier, we watched the evening's show. I don't know how it happened, but after several days I felt as if we were a family. In other days, in school, we would call groups that had mysteriously bonded like this "cliques"; in fact, I had gone through adolescence in boarding school mistrusting the gregarious instinct that drove girls to stick together that way.

Now it was not a need for a group; for me it was, rather, a nostalgia for that lost age: for not having had boys as friends, for having missed that light hearted, disinterested conspiring with the other sex...

After twenty years I finally suppressed the taboo; better late than never. We sat together in the tiers that filled up with families who came down from the capital often in their Sunday best—always in couples with children, sometimes babies (occasionally with a grandmother wearing a turban, a veiled aunt...). When our row became too crowded, we alone, my "three musketeers" I called them (myself the fourth), would leave our row and go to the gallery reserved for the press. We mischievously acted like special guests, privileged spectators!

In the afternoon, as the sun was painting the stone of the theater antique gold, the four of us would watch the star rehearse, usually someone from France here for the performance... And it is true that we hardly ever expressed opinions, either in praise or in doubt; we might only make some vague assumptions about the singer's quality, on how the audience, whose taste was sometimes not very refined, would like him.

I would leave them to go home to dinner, "to be a wife and mother," I would say, as if another role actually awaited me there.

About two hours later I would meet them again as the crowd gradually filled the open theater and night approached.

It was not until a few weeks had passed, it seems to me, that I began suddenly to think about the Beloved separately... Perhaps those evenings (probably twenty or thirty in six or seven weeks), during which the straightforward warmth of the group grew progressively stronger, were my enticement; or perhaps my desire had already awakened and I was unaware of it... In reality, I felt so completely happy to have found three friends. "Writers and artists," I used to call them when, in the afternoon, we would go for a drink and to watch the families; we were always on the lookout for some trivial drama at the swimming pools, another show.

One day the reticent young man must have remarked, "When we go back, back to the university, I mean, you are going to snub us. You won't recognize us anymore! You won't even say hello... madame!"

He was the only one who teased me this way, suddenly ending a sentence with feigned ceremony: "madame." His friends—the very young one who could have been a student and the oldest who could have been my schoolmate—both called me quite naturally by my first name... There was a sort of confident familiarity tying our group together—even though it is true that we conversed only in French, and that I could only imagine using the formal "you" when we spoke, as if that remained a privilege of my age... Was I the eldest? I don't really know. The journalist, whose erudition and affectation I made fun of, looked several years older than me because of his wrinkled face and his leathery neck. Still, that wasn't certain. He was the only one who drank a lot; too much. The few times I would meet up with the group late in the morning, I had to affectionately reproach this "elder" sitting there at the table: "Midday, and already you're drinking straight whiskey!"

"And it's not the first," sharply retorted his friend, the one I suddenly fixed upon as if the echo of his words really took a while to resonate inside me, as if some unusual, strange nuance was getting lost along the way…

So was that the first time I noticed some nervous quiver showing through the cheekbones of this face later so deeply engraved within me? Of course, the remark was revealing of a friend's worry; it was a reproach meant to be discreet… I thought I grasped with difficulty what bound these two companions together, the one who drank so much and the younger man in his thirties. But I was suddenly stymied by something else—as if both by its very transience and by some ineffable sadness, behind the curtain of disquiet lay another face of this man with the vaguely saucy gaze… I turned my attention back to the glass of whiskey and suggested to the man who was letting himself be taken to task, "Pretty please for my beautiful eyes, please, take it half and half with water!"

"For your beautiful eyes, madame!" the journalist exclaimed grandly, his eyes red, and with a sardonic shrug. "Here it is Friday, almost prayer time, and I am drunk already! I'll leave the rest of you and go take a nap so that I can rejoin you tonight, fresh as a rose."

He left, and the twenty-year-old student went with him (I had baptized him "the student" once and for all); then to the third I quietly added, "A student, of course, but beautiful as an angel."

We stayed there alone, the two of us, not particularly wanting to talk, watching the rather ordinary crowd at our leisure…

Definitely I have returned now to the "first scene." To the one that could have begun the logical and well-organized story of the unfolding of this passion. But why would something so blindly experienced be revealed today with no detours, no sidestepping, no desire for a labyrinth?

So, the first time... Not the first time I saw his face, but let us say the first time his presence had reality for me, when he began to "matter." Perhaps also it was when I felt him look at me; when the desire to be looked at by him awoke in me. Let us get back to the facts, because they are in danger of dissolving, fraying into shabby threads.

Everyone looked forward to hearing one star that summer—a poet-singer who later returned three seasons in a row. The posters for his show already covered several walls in the capital, and one morning he arrived.

At four that afternoon I took my seat, alone this time, to watch the rehearsal. I was perched way up high and, though it was unusual, I was the only one watching in this theater that held two thousand. So this is how I saw Leo for the first time, looking down upon him, a robust man in his sixties with a monkey's wrinkled face lit by the sun. On the huge stage, Leo adjusted the mike, talking with the stagehands in a very low voice. Then he tested the acoustics point-blank by calling out to the empty tiers, to the whole village behind and, it suddenly seemed to me, to the whole country, young and clumsy with its thirteen years of independence...

> "*Those eyes that watch you through the night, through the day*
> *Eyes they say fix on numbers and hatred*
> *The forbidden things, the things you crawl toward*
> *That will be yours*
> *When you close*
> *the eyes of oppression!*"

His voice, accustomed to speaking, to lampooning, curled a cappella higher and higher, unfurling the text. Sitting there, I listened. I knew that this night was going to be the event of the summer.

My three "musketeers," it turns out, were standing in the wings. I later learned that they had gone to the airport to meet the singer very early; that they had all had breakfast together. "So Leo was the fourth musketeer that I was waiting for," I said, laughing, when I found them after the rehearsal.

The evening was strange, at least for me. On a sudden whim I had agreed to introduce "Leo who needs no introduction" to the two thousand spectators (there must have been three thousand that night) who had come from the capital... Then I twisted my ankle after having improvised one or two gay sentences of warm introduction. There in front of everyone Leo kissed me on the cheek and I twisted my ankle taking a half-step backward. I took off my shoes with a wave and left the much-too-big stage to rejoin my three friends in the wings. The eldest holding me up by the shoulders, the other two smiling affectionately at me, we stood there, spectators bound together in the darkness, for the whole first part of the concert.

I saw, for the first time, a French poet address three thousand of my compatriots, and for three hours. At intermission I went to perch at the top of the amphitheater to study the audience intently. They all looked alike tonight; everyone seemed to be thirty years old—all had been barely fifteen or twenty during the war, and therefore they had all hummed the same French songs (Brassens, Brel, and Mouloudji, and Montand, and so on.). They had hummed them at the same time as they scanned the newspaper to see how many members of the Resistance had been killed, at the same time as they worried about a cousin arrested and tortured, at the same time as they fell in love, with a "Frenchwoman, a leftist," who believed, it is true, in the future of decolonized peoples, but also in the beauty of the black eyes of her Romeo and his fervent voice!

They had all come together tonight to sing the refrains with Leo, to prompt him with a line when he feigned hesitation, when he stamped impatiently, when he shouted, whenever... Back in the wings, "Is he a ham, or is he a poet of the people, or is he just a real performer?" I asked the young man, the one of all the three who suddenly did not leave me anymore.

He confided that he had known Leo for a year or two, that his work had taken him to Italy to Leo's place "for a two-day marathon interview," and that since then they had exchanged brief notes on a regular basis.

I nodded toward tonight's audience. "All the intellectuals in the country, the old activists of sixty-eight are here!... From who's here tonight we now know that there are three thousand people on our 'left bank,' a majority of them male, and often with a 'girlfriend' who is French. Of course, there are several apparent variations—light or dark skin, straight or curly hair—but all of them are Francophiles tonight."

"Leophiles, rather," my companion corrected, and I do not know if he said anything else or not.

The applause went on and on and the calls for encores became more insistent. The star wanted to appear generous, suddenly feeling younger because this youth of a nostalgic summer bore him along. (Though, perhaps, I was the only one sensitive to this nostalgia).

He was called back two, four, ten times. Leo was sitting on top of the world. He recited another piece; he sang a new song that he warned us would be "short." They finally had to turn off half the spotlights before the amphitheater began slowly to empty out.

At one or two in the morning twenty of us go to dinner in a nearby hotel; Leo presides, drinks, listens... At three in the morning there are four of us who decide not to go home and sleep: my husband, Leo, me, and my Beloved. (At the time I am not yet calling him that, I am sure). An assistant, a secretary, and the driver as well stay with us.

Some of the discothèques stayed open until dawn, and there was one set up not far away under a huge Tuareg tent, with a band made up of four young amateurs who were overjoyed to have a prestigious guest like Leo... A few night owls remained for another hour. Three men (Leo, my husband, and the young man—like Leo's little brother) were seated at a table in the corner; their conversation seemed professional, about the two other concerts they anticipated that weekend. I was with the secretary, a young woman of twenty-five who had already told me all about her marriage, her divorce, and how despite her heavy family responsibilities (a widowed mother, two or three younger sisters who hoped to go to the university), she lived one day at a time. We decided to go from one person to another asking, "Have you been to the concert?" "Will you go back tomorrow?..." People invited us to dance; I declined. I felt I was floating in astonishing exhilaration, in gleefulness free as air; soon the sun would rise, we were never going to sleep ever again. This evening at the theater took place for me outside of any territory; it was neither in France nor in my own country but in an in-between that I was suddenly discovering. Those three or maybe four thousand fans of Leo's had been engrossed in a romanticism that was as much anarchy as French, despite seven years of bloody battles still fresh in our minds. I saw this as the strange end of an era.

I myself was neither here nor there, not seeking my own place, nor even worried about it, but still I could not help feeling there were clouds approaching, storms in the forecast. The country, it seemed to me, was becoming a freighter that had already begun to drift into unknown seas...

Leo's wholehearted success seemed to me enough of a gift from the past, and yet those there were all young men, old young men who had gone somewhere together to reassure themselves. What more could one ask of a true bard, a troubadour, a troublemaker, than to feel for ten minutes, or for an hour, like a family with shared memories, with equal parts irony and nostalgia.

I would have liked to talk about these ideas further with the only one of the trio who was still there, the Beloved. He sat in silence opposite Leo and my husband, listening to them. The young secretary said she was going home and had the driver take her. A few revelers departed, but three or four stayed on along with some foreign tourists; they asked for slow music to dance to.

"No, not a tango," I suddenly said to the nearby musicians. "A pavane, please!"

"A pavane? What's that?" a small fat man exclaimed, not getting my joke. He began to look at me shiftily.

"Any dance," I said, "just not a tango!"

The saxophonist launched into a South American tune and there I was out on the floor. Avoiding the little fat man who wanted to ask me to dance, I insisted, "I always dance alone!"

I must have danced more than an hour without stopping... The rest of the audience was enveloped in a half-light. There were one or two other dancers, and also a couple who joined me in monopolizing the dance floor lit by a dim red light. Then I do not know if they went to sit down or if they left. Whenever I stopped for a moment on the edge of the circle of light, one of the four musicians would make a conspiratorial sign to me and set off again with a new beat that he seemed able to guess in advance would be the rhythm of my body... I was off again, I twirled, time enough to smile at the musicians, my accompanying shadows, my night guides. At the same time, I felt I was alone, suddenly bursting out of a long night and, under these red spotlights, finally reaching shore. The saxophone player, the drummer, the flute player, and the guitarist stood there, lone interdependent ghosts facing me on these fringes—a night quartet.

I danced on. I danced. I feel I have been dancing ever since. Ten years later I am still dancing in my head, within myself, sleeping, working, and always when I am alone.

The dance inside me is interrupted when someone, man or woman, begins to speak, really to speak, relating some joy, some suffering, some glimpse of a hurt. Then the rhythm inside me stops: I listen, surprised or shaken, I listen to bring myself back, suddenly to feel this brush with reality. Sometimes I also listen to ways people have of staying silent... I listen and I try—but I don't know, I never dare—to make the other person, the person who has forgotten himself or herself and spoken, or someone whose silence speaks for them, feel that this imperceptible shock has seeped into my eyes, my hands, my memory. The next instant the dance begins again: under my skin, in my legs, up and down my arms, all along the inertia of my face. Yes, it was that night under the tent that the dance began, in that instant: Leo and my husband chatting in a corner and suddenly the young man coming closer and closer, pulled in by the weak, still reddish lights, drawn perhaps by my dancing body. (I knew then, but only vaguely, of my power over this man, that it was beginning, that it would hover for a long time, that I would let it hover, then fray and dissipate.) So the young man came to the edge of the darkness; he sat down and looked in my direction without really staring at me; he didn't move.

I danced on. I danced. I have been dancing ever since.

In the twenty years that went before, say from when I was sixteen to when I was thirty-six, I had of course played my role within circles of women, guests, neighbors, and cousins, young girls or mature women. There was a protocol to this: Each woman would slowly dance in the manner traditional to the town she came from. When the body was burdened with jewels, belts, tunics embroidered in gold, stiff and sparkling moiré, the dancing was ceremonious. It was frenzied, or I was going to say lustful, when, in special instances, in defiance or the pleasure of showing off, the rhythms were those of a village or from the high plateaus or deep Africa. This often took place when the orchestra was no longer one of established musicians but rather women who were amateurs; with two *derboukas* and a drum, with their rasping voices and brilliant eyes, they would launch into some ancestral refrain.

The urban ritual became more disorganized: Six to ten women would step forward together to see who best showed off her shape, her curvaceous hips, her abundant breasts, her voluminous hindquarters, shaking them frenetically until they hurt, until the ululating, bursting solo voice convulsed.

So I had participated in all those slow, formal ceremonies, even if, when my turn came, I could never keep myself from doing some nervous, hybrid dance, leaping or moving around with only my feet tracing a whimsical choreography, that shook my calves and intertwined my bare arms. Thus I would transform this constraint into a solitary dance, fleeting and "modern"—as the women called it, disappointed by my imagination, which seemed to them a betrayal… Betrayal of what? Without analyzing it, I think that the important thing was the challenge my engulfed body made by expecting to improvise the movements. The important thing was to distance myself as much as possible from the collective frenzy of those women, my relatives—I felt I could not accept for myself the almost funereal joy of their bodies, verging on a fettered despair.

As an adolescent and a young girl I had danced often and long, always in these groups of women and in crowded patios during the traditional festivals that we looked forward to.

Once, at a wedding, one of my female cousins went to get my husband so that he could hide in a window and watch what she called my "personal style of dancing." My heart had pounded from shyness, or some unaccountable distress, as if this man with whom I had been sharing almost everything for ten years had willingly become a voyeur, just because he was a man and had caught me in my dance among women.

Strange theater, the binding of eyes and soul that resulted from the rituals of my childhood.

Of course, traditional though I was, I had ended up seemingly adopting Western dance steps before this summer in the seaside resort: Two or three times, in front of everybody, in the arms of my husband, a waltz or a slow fox trot perhaps had made us just one couple lost in the midst of others. I kept my eyes down, and kept him from holding me tight ("Others can see!"), agreed to none but the lightest touch, and finally, obeying the rhythm all alone, rejected my "escort," in "their" words.

No, despite the fashions I *had* to escape that, I had to avoid being "touched" in such a manner by a man, no matter what man, in a crowd... The secret of the body and its autonomous rhythm, the velvety texture inside the body, and, in the dark, in the emptiness, the music goading me on.

This night, then, I could not stop. I would leap and then suddenly feel like moving more slowly: my feet marking the rhythm unchecked but almost dryly, my hips or my torso applied to stepping back from the excess of this rhythm, playing down the ways it interlaced, transforming its oriental character into figures that were sparing, faithful of course, but neither lyrical nor overabundant. Tonight my arms alone became lianas, drawing arabesques, in the half-light only my bare arms moving now like serpents and now like calligraphy…

I danced for a long time. The saxophone player, eagerly backing me up, sometimes moved one or two steps forward to follow me or bring me back toward him; for a long time I danced. I am still dancing.

I have forgotten if it was the musician who decided it was over or if, just like that, I left the dance floor first. I remember one person sitting there as witness, his eyes toward the light, his eyes turned toward the ephemeral, ever-changing nature of my figures, my Beloved. I remember that I went in the opposite direction, away from his silence.

The spotlights went off under the tent and we left. I was at Leo's side. He took my arm in a friendly manner (Leo, the man I felt was so available this night; he had come such a distance not to give something but to receive… receive some secret—what was it?—from my opaque country that was starting its transformation). My husband came alongside me and it was then that my witness, my young man, left, speaking low to the three of us, "Goodbye. I live just two steps away."

The first light was dawning.

As he went off (I could not help turning my head in his direction… he went along the beach to reach his house, which he had shown me one day was not far!), I finally felt the concentration of his presence vanish as the night drew to a close.

What was this movement simultaneously inside and outside of me that my body, prompted earlier by the sax, seemed to have

released? In what muffled, liquid mystery had he reluctantly introduced himself? I understood, plainly and simply, that I was becoming aware of someone else. Thus a man had watched me dance and I
had been "seen."

And even more than that, I was keenly, consciously, happily
aware of myself (nothing to do with self-love, or narcissistic vanity, or
laughable interest in one's appearance…) as being truly "visible" for
this almost adolescent young man with the wounded gaze.

Visible for him alone? My visibility for him made me visible to
myself.

I lagged behind Leo and my husband on the road. They were still
talking—their voices worn out with exhaustion… I, however, was
blithely ready to tackle the new day. I would never sleep. I would
walk the length of the beach indefinitely. I smiled at the first glim-
mers of light in the sky.

I kissed Leo, who sighed. "How can a person come to your beautiful country and sleep all alone, without a woman!"

Leo was sincere in his protests. Imagine not guaranteeing our
guests, over and above bed and board, a beautiful odalisque!

"You'll find her all by yourself tomorrow!" my husband assured
him. "Don't forget that I'll come to get you in three or four hours!"

The next evening I took my place docilely beside the young man
on our last tier. I was there for Leo's second concert. And once again
I was with two thousand other fans, or the two thousand from the
night before… the young man thoughtful beside me.

At the end, when we rose to go and rejoin Leo in the wings, my
companion said to me quietly, "Tonight, will you dance like yesterday?"

It wasn't quite a request.

"You know," I replied in a deceptively playful tone, "even when it can't be seen, I dance. I dance all the time! I dance in my head!"

Naturally, throughout last night's improvised choreography, it was my passion that was in ferment. I did not yet call it by that name. What else could I say to my Beloved, besides; what could I say to myself?

"I'm going to be good and return to the fold," I whispered without even a trace of sadness.

I smiled at him with the unexplained first stirrings of happiness inside me, like a suddenly gushing spring that took me by surprise.

Standing before the young man like this I was aware in that instant—in a blinding flash, but then it flowed for thirteen months—that he had begun to be the Beloved for me the night before, the intensely Beloved.

5

THE ABSENCE

AFTER MY JOURNEY into the interior of the country, two months went by. I could have resumed my earlier work (listening to sound archives, reflecting on the accumulated material…) in that ninth floor office. But I didn't want to do that. It was now the time for separations, for amputation performed on myself by myself. I had to push forward in a move that I experienced as a painful necessity. I accepted a teaching job again (going three mornings down into the center city, as the sunny winter cleared the dawn skies). That would be another journey for me, a change of scenery that would console me.

It was as if another self rushed through the traffic of the narrow, noisy streets, then spoke in the lecture hall, questioning the students. Afterward I did not go back to our apartment; while I was in my stride, I kept on working, otherwise weakness was imminent.

I would be absorbed for three or four hours straight at the Bibliothèque nationale. I literally went back in time to live the centuries: the various stages in which the Almohades became established in the east and center of North Africa, cavalcades, the displacement of tribes, the toppling of entire regions... The strange and fascinating twelfth century. In the middle of that same century Ibn 'Arabi was born at Murcie, and toward the end of it Averroës, persecuted, was called to Marrakech, where he died.

With these storms inside my head I would walk back up along a raised boulevard that circles the city's amphitheater, its ancient harbor squeezed in down below like a woman's genitals underneath, a sweeping landscape. I had to walk faster; dusk was about to spread the gray or reddish glow of its whiteness. The balconies and terraces in the city radiated for the last time. The long, noisy parade of cars and overcrowded buses turned into a grayish dream scenery; I was the walker, my eyes reflecting only clouds, the architecture hung there in front of the sky, it seemed that I was walking alongside another humanity that was parallel to mine, yet so strange, by its very proximity.

As I returned home and as the century of the Almohades gradually dissipated like the blood-streaked clouds dispersing on the horizon of the setting sun, I felt I was back in my real life, my only life, back, that is, to the wound I felt in those days.

I thought "wound," or sometimes "separation" (and I said to myself that, literally as well as figuratively, I was right at the edge of an endless precipice...), because I had already provided the love story with a brutal ending, whereas, stuck in its preliminaries, it had never even taken place.

I have forgotten exactly when the long, slow, inexorable gnawing of absence began and then, second by second, would not let itself be forgotten. Had my Beloved vanished? Into what void? Was I not the one, rather, who found myself shifted into another reality? I wandered, with this mark on my heart, seeking along the slopes of this boulevard, in the mists of this espaliered city, some ghost… Had the very city itself not split in two in some obvious metamorphosis that everyone saw but me? So my Beloved lived on one shore and I on another, never again would we meet! I would go on seeking him indefinitely; my body longed only to walk and that was the reason; perhaps it would end up by crossing the hidden frontier, finding itself on the other side, in another city—real or unreal, but at least the one in which my Beloved also lived!

I wondered if, at this very moment, he was working there, if he still had the same daily routine. Had time frozen for him as it had for me? Rather, should I not accept that he was laughing, joking, that he came and went, thoughtless and carefree? He must have just barely noticed that his neighbor at work had vanished with no token courtesy, with no goodbye. Yes, obviously, he was laughing, he was alive; he went home to his girlfriend every night.

And this is the moment to talk about the woman he lived with: a young woman whom I had seen two or three times with him; then alone, later rather frequently so. Was she an actress or a musician or the editor of some weekly known for its arts columns? I did not know. I had never asked any questions and no one introduced us to each other. She had not been there all summer or for last season's shows: she must have been away on vacation in France. Later someone or other told me specifically that she had been "living with" the Beloved for two or three years. I gazed at her for a long time, my heart weighed heavily.

Even before knowing this, the aching, sickly air of her bony, not very pleasant face had struck me; it seemed crumpled and shrunk by long illness. And there I was reacting to this physical lack of grace (a sort of shadow, a gray veil enveloping her) by feeling bad myself.

I can see it all again: the first time I caught sight of the couple together, just a few yards from me. I saw him from the back, launching into some animated speech; she was frozen, staring wide-eyed at him. This gaze hit me all at once: She loved him, she loved him and at that moment was devastated by this love. I looked away, I felt bad for her, or for myself, as if I saw at the other end of an invisible chain the results of a passion entirely surrendered to the other... A sense of uneasiness dug the ground from under me: Was this man not just like any other trying awkwardly to shake off some hindrance?

Two or three times after this I ran into the woman and soon knew her first name: Leïla. We looked at each other; I looked down without approaching her.

Once without thinking I asked my journalist friend, my somewhat snobbish cohort, who was always alone when I encountered him this fall, "Was she pretty?"

He and I had never discussed either the preceding summer or our common friend. He was cheerful; he used to invite me to the same comfortable bar whose terrace looked out on a glorious garden, a good place for conversation. This comrade of mine was, of course, courting me ever so slightly, but it cheered me up and was so offhand that the game seemed not to compromise me, just a way to pass the time—I heard myself ask, because Leïla went by in the distance, "Was she pretty?"

"So you are cruel, though not treacherous," the journalist commented. "Cruel since you are the queen."

"Please," I excused myself miserably. "I didn't want to be mean... I'm touched by Leïla; I see she isn't well; is this maybe something recent?"

"She's been like that ever since I've known her!" he retorted. "Some people like to suffer."

Leïla went away. Another time the Beloved had stopped and turned away when I was also there on the square in front of that huge building and I heard him tell someone, "No, it's all over, I'm not coming!" The other kept insisting in a low voice. We had all left the elevator together as a group and were going to part with great formality.

He came back in my direction, I stared at his features: A nervous spasm passed slowly across them—was it just anger? Or was there a trace of pain? I looked away. I felt I was there at a bad moment, and wished I were far away. Why would he absolutely not console her, why…?

I must have turned my back, preparing to leave. Then I heard him call me rather softly by my first name. He was calling me. It was the first time like this. He took a step. I turned around and said warmly, "Finally, I'm no longer 'madame.'"

He stammered. I saw something like a faint wrinkle creasing his features again. For a second I thought he was really present in his gaze, in his thought. He had called me as if calling for help… Being with me would make him forget whatever his lover was begging for, I did not know what, some duty, some obligation.

He said my first name again more softly. Clearly. I think I was filled with a stunning bolt of joy; I lit up, I was about to take his hand: "Let's leave, let's go away!" This would assuage the thin face lifted toward me.

Suddenly a black curtain fell inside me. "Her." Without seeing her I instantly knew she was behind me. Her whole being submerged in sadness. There would be other occasions for us, some other moment; everything between my Beloved and myself had to remain bright and clean. Another day, another century!

"Excuse me," I finally murmured, and slowly turned away.

I felt him not move for a moment, seeing I had pulled back and understanding the reason.

A month later my friend, the journalist, insisted on telling me that Leïla had not been his mistress for at least a year: "After she attempted suicide," he said, "she was still just as desperate!" I interrupted his explanations. Why did I need to know? Let the pain and joy of others be private... I was still filled with thoughts of the Beloved. Not once did I ever ask myself how he was attached to Leïla, if he loved her. I was troubled instead to know that he had such a power over her. As if I felt I was partly responsible, though indirectly, for this woman's torment.

The image of the unhappy lover faded away: something from long ago that preceded my summer of music, dance, and excitement, and had died slowly for lack of air, long before my present suffering began to run its arid course.

Another month taken up by the same uncertainty and its accompanying exhaustion went by. Spring made a chilly start in the city; violent downpours left the landscape sparkling afterward with a translucent light like infinite dawn.

I walked constantly, feeling myself travel from stage to stage of endless insomnia. Every now and then some remark by a friend or a relative would rip through my emptiness:

"Your eyes are glistening!"

"You are sad, thinner!"

"You always seem to be somewhere else!"

I heard myself with my little girl, laughing long and hard the way we did before. We still kept secrets, sometimes at night and sometimes when we took short walks in the nearby park.

But I would suddenly wake up in the middle of the night; a dark, knotty dream—though I could not remember it—kept on dumping me into the swells... To calm down and go back to sleep more peacefully, I told myself, as if I were both the storyteller and the child who needed to be settled down: "Tomorrow, surely, I'll run into him!... and suddenly stopping his car, interrupting my walk through the crowd, he will come up to me politely: 'You are so tired, I'll come with you!' Tomorrow, for sure." And I would go back to sleep feeling sorry for myself, in my constant walking through the city, in my despair. "Tomorrow, for sure!" As I gradually fell back asleep, I thought that I was becoming my own little girl!

I resumed my hours of work at the Bibliothèque nationale. Sometimes I would go there humming the popular laments of Abou Madyan, the saint of Béjaia: melodies that were melancholy and tender, snatches of which, when I was a child, my sweet, sad, maternal aunt used to teach me… Then, as if I were looking for something to give me pain, I would abandon the research I had planned. With my aunt's voice in my ear I would plunge in, seeking some faint secret, some calming water; I ardently went through the chronicles of the luminous Maghrebian and Andalusian twelfth century:

"On that day," I read, "the sheik mounted his horse and ordered me, as well as one of my companions, to follow him to Almontaler, a mountain in the region surrounding Seville. Following the afternoon prayer, the sheik suggested that we return to the city. He mounted his horse and set out while I walked beside him holding on to the stirrup. Along the way he told me about the virtues and miracles of Abou Madyan.

"As for myself, I never took my eyes off him, I was so absorbed by what he was saying that I completely forgot my surroundings. Suddenly he looked at me and smiled; then, spurring on his horse, he quickened the pace and I hastened my step to keep up with him. Finally he stopped and said to me, 'Look what you have left behind you!' Turning around I saw that the entire path we had traversed was nothing but brambles that came half-way up my body."

Gripped by Ibn 'Arabi's tale describing his adolescence and the years of his mystical education in Andalusia, I saw in precise detail his route—lit with passion—as it led him toward Seville. I imagined the sheik Abou Yacoub Youssef, one of Abou Madyan's closest disciples, on horseback, and Mahieddine Ibn 'Arabi running along holding on to the stirrup, and seeing none of the brambles in the path because he was so intoxicated by the account of the saint's graces.

It was this mystical poet from Béjaia whom generations of Maghrebian women—my aunt and my mother its most recent link—passed on with their saddened voices, like a last whiff of the fragrance that was so fresh and green that day, on the road to Seville, where the Sufi master on horseback, despite the thorns on the path, initiated a young man who was already predestined.

I left the library and found myself back on the circular boulevard along the heights of the city. Of all this contemporary metropolis the only thing I kept with me as I set out on my walk was its hum, the faint echo of its roar. I walked and I became the spectator of a day in 1198, probably a spring day, on the outskirts of Béjaia... Sidi Abou Madyan, almost eighty, prepares to leave his city; thousands of the faithful are there, trying in vain to keep him from going. Will they ever see him again? He is so sick. He resigns himself to going to Marrakech, where the Almohade sultan with the fearsome reputation has summoned him.

Surrounded by the sultan's guards who are waiting for the old man to tear himself away from his disciples, he is ready to go; he seems serene. Suddenly he makes a prediction: "Obeying the sultan," he begins, "I obey God, glory be to Him! But I shall not reach the sultan; I shall die along the way, in front of Tlemcen!"

"Then mysteriously, they say, he whispered (was this meant for the ruler of Marrakech? like a statement of the obvious) 'He, moreover, will follow me shortly!'"

I had only been to Tlemcen once. Striding along with the flow of honking automobiles and crowded buses, I kept my face turned toward the espaliered slopes. Small houses from the beginning of the century were interspersed with apartment buildings that were too high and full of people, and here and there a vaguely Byzantine chapel or an ancient mosque stood next to a vacant lot full of garbage but also full of bunches of children tormenting a cat or playing soccer. I skimmed lightly through the shocks of the present. I kept on going, living far back in the past, this time there for the arrival of the saint in the area surrounding Tlemcen. At the entrance of a modest town, Abou Madyan faints, people come running from all over: "The great Abou Madyan is going to die!… He is dying! May the salvation of God…" Decades later, centuries later, the faithful will flock to this place of pilgrimage, and do so still! I feel tired, I look for a public square, a bench, and end up sitting down for five minutes in a men's cafe, just enough time to have some mint tea. I am sad that I have to suspend my daydream because I am no longer walking, because my feet are dragging. Then, suddenly, my torment returns, like an abscess only half anesthetized, erupting now again.

I set off once more. The sun dims; I have to get up there and reach home before nightfall. In vain I look for a taxi.

And along the way I lost the accompanying shadow of the saint of Béjaia, dead at the entrance to Tlemcen and shortly followed, as he predicted, by the sultan who died at the height of his powers… I am no longer protected by my ghosts; they are replaced by my own sense of loss, which crops up again, harsh, pointed, sharpened, this severing I have borne for weeks. It is simultaneously a hardening that bolsters me and the latent danger of falling; how can I just find "him," even at a distance? Even in secret? No, I won't go where he works. I could find a hundred pretexts. No, I won't take any of them! Luck is what I need, and I don't have it. And he, how can he live like this, how has he gotten used to not seeing me anymore, how… Already I am inventing an imaginary argument, a lovers' quarrel, suddenly paying no attention to the fact that nothing has happened, that the attraction has remained implied, scarcely begun, that my cool façade finally seemed to have taken flawless control of me. My eyes search the crowd; I begin to watch all the cars—usually just boxes to me. I am only looking for one color—a particular dirty blue and a chassis rather rarely seen here. Even though I cannot recall any of the makes of cars, I would recognize his immediately, I'm sure of it.

Twice, in a trivial conversation this summer, my Beloved, or his friend, had mentioned the make of the car I was looking for now, whose name at least I was trying to remember; this car that had driven me home two or three nights—if it went by I would recognize it... But then, would he even see me making my way through this crowd of passersby?

The next day at home, stretched out, inactive, I was so devoured by the pain of absence that I did not even feel strong enough to stand up—how much I would have preferred having a toothache, a sneaky, low-level one or the kind that paralyzes your face with its intensity, at least there would be some anesthetic that would do some good! Would I be able to go to my classes tomorrow? Going down into the center city to work for my own pleasure seemed uncalled for, a dismal sham concocted for myself. I ended up hanging around in the empty apartment: like in the theater, where time is suspended while you await a fate decided in advance.

I realized that I was the one who had straight away cut short yesterday's rhythm. Suppose I started working there again, in the place where my Beloved existed, imagining perhaps a necessary breathing space for myself. I was "in withdrawal" from the sight of him. What inquisitor could reproach me for granting myself a slight indulgence? I would make a show of my cool absentmindedness just as I had in the past; there would be a languid quality extending my reserve; he would never suspect I might return for his sake—just to see him, his silhouette leaving the elevator. I promised myself somberly, *No more conspiratorial conversations in the dark on the phone!* I debated this possibility within myself as if bargaining with my conscience and then began to breathe more deeply again; but suddenly I put an end to this future. I killed the temptation; some hidden instinct made me want to act against the fever inside. Had I not foreseen that the painful but exciting gnawing produced by our being together at work was an imperceptible slope down which I would plunge? Did I not fear the fall?

No. I would not go back there again. No, I would not create any such easily discoverable pretext! All the torment that I inflicted on myself by this separation could not weaken my lucidity. The illness possessing me since, at least, the end of summer had taught me something; I could no longer fool myself, I had to keep from slipping into some unpredictable state. No, I concluded with a seriousness that provided a brief burst of new strength, caution was my saving grace and the absence I had imposed the only remedy. I would not go back there again!

I wandered around the house. If only, I thought, groping down the hallways, drinking innumerable glasses of water, abandoned to strange bouts of nausea, if only I could find some short-lived balm! What would console me, besides my walks through the city, my escapes to the sun? What else was left?

I got dressed. I wanted at least to see the car, "his" car; that way I would know if he was there, at work. I remembered the outside parking lot, reserved for technicians, right next to a pine grove. Let me at least go and check on the shadow of a shadow: I would become calmer. I would know he exists, that therefore I exist, my only problem is that I am languishing.

Twice I think, preoccupied in this manner, I go down into the city. Fifteen minutes later I arrive at the ramp above the parking lot. I lean on the railing, pretending to admire the famous view: the sunlit bay, proud as a favored lover; in the distance any number of boats and cargo ships wait because the port is crowded. At my feet, a hundred yards or so down, there is a stretch of parking lot laid out in a small triangle, enough for a few dozen ordinary cars. Eagerly my eye seeks out the characteristic shape and dirty blue of the car I know.

Relief comes over me, relaxation that is almost muscular. "He is definitely there!" Ten minutes away. I could go to the receptionist and have him called. Then suggest that we go sit down in the bar at the luxury hotel across the street. "Let's have coffee together. I was just passing by and wanted to hear how you were doing!" And the whole time I cheerfully spouted these banalities, my eyes, oh yes, and with a hunger whose ardor I would filter out, my eyes would devour his face, his features, the color of his eyes, right down to the defects I would find once more. Perhaps he too had grown thinner, perhaps, on the contrary…

I muse over what I should do. I stare at the blue car—his. I am no longer enduring the acute strain of suffering; now there is only the dull void of separation, that I could do away with in a second. This is so close to where I live… Humbled, after the desert I have crossed, I am enjoying the feeling of pain. I breathe deeply: I almost relish the eternity of this landscape.

It is four P.M. Suddenly I think of the children. *Let's go home!* I tell myself. I walk with a light step. The distractions of motherhood await me. Playing the piano with my daughter.

Late that night, in bed, my eyes open in the darkness, I am confronted again with returning pain; it is not the least bit weaker: *I hurt physically!* I will sleep, despite the nightmares. Tomorrow I will have to invent some other consolations—temporary, I know.

Shortly after these days of confusion, I began to imagine a meeting that would be strange, but possible: to speak to the Beloved's mother.

I could readily have used some easy social strategy to meet women who were cousins of this lady or her relatives by marriage. I could have forced myself to appear on the social scene for a few days, making polite remarks to old friends or relatives. I could end up by asking to be introduced to this person I did not know. She must still be young, certainly beautiful, and with a shy reserve. Yes, I could start a conversation with her: I would show up by chance in some living room or at a party. Even the ambiguity of exchanging banal words with her would bring me pleasure, embarrassment, or at least some new nostalgia. I could hope for some respite from my arid days just because of being close to the woman who could have been but who would never be my mother-in-law. As if because I had at present a very real mother-in-law, one so tender and motherly toward me, whom I loved so much that because of her I could not imagine having to leave her son someday—as if because of this "guilty" love of mine (yes, this is a guilty love for a young man who cannot pose as my husband's rival), a more dangerous rivalry would be generated. This invisible mother whom I wanted to meet (a mother who was Berber, still young, elegant, middle class, from the best part of town) would be pitted against my real mother-in-law, who was so traditional, so aristocratic in manner, full of Islamic gentleness and a goodness that was somewhat severe. She was the friend of the beggar-women of her city, the one who consoled repudiated women, sterile wives, and scapegoat daughters-in-law. Whenever I would visit (I spent at least one night a week at her home, on a mattress on the ground, watching her absorbed in prayer, comforted by her piety which, I was sure, would long protect us, myself and my two children), she would describe in detail the daily wretchedness of the women of this city of invisible lusts and repression. How could I ever have to leave such a friend? Suppose one day I could no longer conceal all this from my husband, he who had begun, with perfect timing, to travel in Europe, Egypt, and even farther away.

There were other temptations that came to mind concerning his family: I remembered that the Beloved's father was a doctor. Once, he happened to mention the neighborhood where he had his office. And I had a distant aunt whom I used to visit from time to time who lived there.

Either apathy or fatigue made me give up on my project of being introduced to the mother. Not only did the very strong presence of my own mother-in-law raise barriers to this vaguely desired scene, but for months now I had been living a solitary life, and leaving to make some slightly risky social rounds would be painful. One morning I decided to go visit my aunt.

Throughout the visit, as I asked her detailed questions about her health, I was asking myself, *Am I going to make an appointment with this doctor at the end of this boulevard? And tell him what? What sickness do I have?* My thinness? My aunt had noticed it when I came in. Of course recently I had been on the verge of fainting several times: My usual hypotension—that's all it was. I told my relative (as if practicing ahead of time for the questioning in the doctor's office) about the last time I had fainted: "Day before yesterday, alone at home, I stood up all at once, to go to the kitchen, I think... Suddenly, blackness. I don't remember anything. It seemed to me that it was a long time later that I found myself lying down on the ground. My hand felt the tile floor. It took me some time to understand: *What am I doing laying on the ground? stretched out?* In fact I had suddenly fainted the minute I stood up. I didn't even get hurt! Not even a lump on the head. Nothing!"

The aunt was worried, then affectionately: "You are not pregnant?"

I burst out laughing. "Certainly not!"

That seemed ludicrous to me. "No, I've had these fainting spells sometimes, but they come on progressively. I will start to feel weak, and lean on something while somebody is talking to me, and then suddenly I'm hearing bells; I keep on smiling at him, but his voice gets far away. Then I sit down, I eat some sugar or chocolate."

"Go to the doctor, the one here on my boulevard," the aunt insisted. "He's the one who takes care of me!"

"Your doctor, what language do you speak to him in?"

She exclaimed, "How do I speak to him? Come, my daughter, in the Prophet's language of course... Are we not independent these days so that at least I can speak my own language to a doctor from my country!... But this doctor, you know, opened his office when the French were in charge, during the war."

I left my kinswoman and went straight to the doctor's office. I sat down in the corner for women and children in the already overcrowded waiting room. In the hallway the doctor briefly made the rounds. One of the women whispered, "That's him!"

I had scarcely time to catch a glimpse of him, a stocky fifty-year-old with red hair. Engrossed in thought, he glanced about as he returned with a lady wearing a veil. When it came to be the turn of the patient ahead of me, I slipped out. What was I doing there? I had no desire at all to answer personal questions. As for my fainting spells, they had lost any interest for me after I described them to my aunt. Above all I was beginning to realize that when I met the doctor— who, in the first place, was "the father"—I would have had to undo my blouse so that he could listen to my breathing and sound my chest. The indecency! He was "the father," not some anonymous man of science.

I took off like a thief. Outside, my heart pounding. For one long moment at least, when I left my aunt's and stupidly came to waste my time in this room full of sick women and wailing children, I had found release from my obsession. I had totally forgotten in those moments the image of the young man… Now, in this crowded, unfamiliar neighborhood, I thought to myself that this stocky, redheaded doctor seemed like an ordinary man with commonplace occupations. His son was a young man who was just as ordinary, the only son of a very quiet, middle-class couple. It was only this cruelly self-imposed separation that was maintaining the aura surrounding this individual! What's more, I said to myself as I walked along, during the preceding months, the summer and the fall, whenever I sought his company and played at being so casual, whenever I repressed my emotion, endowing the young man with so much importance, did this not simply mean that I was distancing myself irreversibly from my husband—the man who for so long had seemed my other self?

I took a taxi to return as quickly as possible to the apartment. I needed the children. I had spent half a day busy with my aunt and then with the temptation of visiting the doctor. I went home, my obsession now a lighter burden. I opened my door; I made some coffee.

But then, going from one bedroom to the other, surrounded by laughter, I stood for a moment on the balcony to recall the pearly gray of the sky, and suddenly the soft voice, the low voice of my Beloved and his slightly ironic look came back to me: obsession renewed. During the evening it pursued me again, despite the fact that the children were preparing to celebrate their father's return the next morning. They asked me what presents I thought he might be bringing them from Egypt; they both offered to read me the poems they had written in his honor.

"Sunday is going to be Father's Day!" the little girl exclaimed.

"That's the new style!" remarked the housekeeper, who was leaving.

The rest of the day was spent singing and telling riddles and finally some fussing and tears.

In my own bed I did not read any more; I turned off the light. In the darkness I lived the summer before all over again—our talking together in the morning, my three friends and I, or myself dancing on an infinite dance floor where my silhouette gradually fades away.

Was it right away, the first evening of my husband's return that I suddenly decided to speak?

Now I know that if I had had a confidante, or a man who was an old friend, or some rediscovered friend from school, perhaps I would have told it just once; with one of them I would have ceded to the temptation and pleasure of hearing myself speak my inner adventure out loud—this slow possession to which I had surrendered at first with delight, but then with pain. After all this I know that the need to speak—to a friend and hence, failing that, to the husband I thought of equally as a friend, since he was no longer a lover—intensified the bitter pleasure of hearing myself, and as a result convinced me of the reality of what preoccupied me, giving it weight and flesh. It would give it thus the reality of words if not the reality of caresses; in fact, before and during the words I spoke, I was racked with desire for that man, a new servitude.

Probably long before this, moreover, and barely even suspected by me (though there was plenty of time afterward, when it was in a sense too late to ask myself about what had gone on before!) there was the ill-timed question: Am I indeed real? Or, in the end, isn't my suffering, the fact that I cannot get used to this separation, the only thing that is real?

That evening I definitely behaved like a raving lunatic. I asked him to listen to me, that we be willing to say "everything" in one night... This "everything" became the weight borne by my dreams, what I denied myself, especially my silent desire, and, above all, my compulsive need to talk about it. A burden of dreams and words resulting from a flirtation that lasted scarcely longer than the games of summer.

I have to see these memories through... My husband returns; my memory wants to swallow up the first evening: He and I in the bedroom, shutting myself up in the bathroom first, almost falling asleep in my bath, which is too hot. He definitely expecting me to come. It is midnight; the lights are out in the children's bedroom. Silence thickens in the house. And I am not alone, I cannot take refuge in my dreams, and...

Everything about me said no. The stubborn pout on my face; my silence. I did not turn off the light. I forced myself to make trivial conversation just to fill the void, to try to forget what I was doing: because, there I was, taking off my dressing gown, climbing into bed in that clinging nightgown, and there was the man who had just returned, watching my every movement. I did not turn off the light.

I was panicked. I just wanted to sleep; my face said it firmly. "Leave me alone! Just leave! Go away!" How could I tell him that out loud, how... A wild obsession, and my stiffness under the covers; a fierce desire to go to the children's room and lie down at the foot of their bed, finding there at least, the only corner where I could let myself go and be protected in sleep... Panic: *If he touches me, if he caresses me, even if I act like I'm dead, the Beloved's name, like a poison flower rooted deep in my waiting, is going to burst out and blossom on my lips. It will happen in spite of me and inevitably at the moment when I come—in the event that I give in out of cowardice!*

I get out of bed and take refuge in the living room, in the dark. My body is shaking. So, I was going to give in to habit. No, but to what? To the husband's silent searching, his hands, his desire, and as for myself, what horrible compassion was going to take hold of me, what apathetic indulgence would bring me to the point of sinking into his arms, his, the other's... I shake. In the darkness, in the living room, I am seized with fury: directed at myself (would there be, therefore, some "female" part in me? anonymous and female?). Ah, if only the children were not there, were not quietly sleeping (which isn't true, the boy is having more and more frequent nightmares), ah, if I were alone with this man who is waiting for me, who thinks I am "his" wife, his lover, who... I am shaken with rage: Break everything! Shatter it all! Here in this apartment—the lamps, the books, the glasses, trash everything together in a pile of ruins, stones, shards! But the children are sleeping. But the boy sighs in his dreams.

I turn on the light in the living room. The husband, completely dressed all of a sudden, joins me there. He opens a bottle of whiskey, helps himself to a glass, and states unequivocally,

"Despite the sleeping pills I took, I intend to drink this whiskey I got at the airport right down to the bottom of the bottle... I'm going to drink, but you are going to talk!"

"I'll talk," I say softly, smiling with relief. "That's all I ask!"

No use describing the bits and pieces of theater—comedic theater, I thought—that went on almost until dawn...

How else describe my confessions, those of a late-blooming young girl? (It is true that I was racked by a sort of blank rapture: Finally I could talk about "him," even faced with the glistening eyes and outraged stare of this listener, this intruder.)

He finished all the whiskey. He stood up. He struck. The large, wide-open French doors behind us (was he the one who opened them earlier? I don't know who did) let in something like the impending danger of a breeze that, I thought, was likely to hurl me at the drop of a hat into that ten-story pit... He struck and I could not take refuge in the back of the room, as if the opening called me straight to it; this man who was large and athletic, with his man's arms would blindly seize me, would fling me so I exploded outside. He struck and I slipped to the floor, an unusually sharp sense of caution on the look-out within me to figure out what was least dangerous.

First he insulted. Then he struck. Protect my eyes. Because his frenzy was proving to be strange: He intended to blind me.

"Adulteress," he muttered, in his hands the whiskey bottle broken in two. All I could think of were my eyes and the danger represented by the too-wide-open window.

Then I heard him, as if echoing from within a prison cell in which he found himself, in which he wrestled, in which he was trying to keep me. From inside this nightmare space, inside this bodily fear, my eyes closed, and hidden under my arms, under my lifted elbows, under my already bloody hands, I heard and I would almost have answered with a laugh, not a madwoman's laugh nor one of tearfulness, but the laugh of a woman who was relieved and struggling to free herself. "Adulteress!" he repeated, "Anywhere, except this city of iniquity, you would deserve to be stoned!"

"Eyes, light," I sighed two or three days later as I lay there at my parents' home, my face swollen, my hands in bandages, my body broken.

The image of man has eyes, but the moon, she has light. I would have liked to be able to repeat this line from Hölderlin in its original German.

Throughout my convalescence, for seven days, I no longer knew I was in Algiers. No. Rediscovering the old books I used to have at my bedside in this house, I plunged into *Sylvie* by Gérard de Nerval. I imagined wandering with the poet all over Europe; I fled to the Orient, to Cairo, where I suddenly dreamed of becoming the captive slave that the poet bought in the market, who got in his way so badly!

6

BEFORE, AFTER

BEFORE THIS WAS ALL ERASED, even before the torment of the absence, there was one time when my Beloved confided in me. One time when I found him alone, when we chose to sit on the beach, in the sand.

He did the talking; I contemplated the vast sky. I studied its drifting, fleecy clouds, whose pink stripes would become streaked with blood before the purple of nightfall. The air was punctuated with short cries: a seagull crossed the azure before vanishing; and not one person walking on the beach. Turning my head halfway, I could just catch sight of two or three of the village women's colored veils as they left their jobs at the tourist's hotel to hurry in the direction of their hamlet, behind the hills. Silence floated around us and we would soon be submerged by the night.

My Beloved spoke—steady streams. Then he stopped. I did not speak up; I did not look at him. The dusk grew redder and redder. The voice of the man confiding in me began again.

Toward the end, cautiously turning toward him, I must have asked him one or two questions. I remember his profile—the tic like lightning twitching his cheek. It was only later that I thought to myself, with cool astonishment, that he was talking to me and coming alive again at the same time. He told me the story of a former love—he was specific right from the start that "it was five years ago"—but he had only begun to feel its pain in the present. Later, I, too, found his story moving, not because it was infectious, or even out of compassion. No. The disturbance in me came from seeing him taken from me by these recollections to some other place totally foreign to the two of us, sucked back to that other place. So he was there in front of me without being there; I no longer existed for him. He vanished into the shadow of this stranger whom he described without naming; with me present he was once again living with her, and I suffered—not as I listened to him on the beach, but later, in a sort of amazement.

Then not far from us a group of three or four women, Europeans, walked by. One of them seemed to recognize me and greeted me. I replied absentmindedly, without getting up. She said something to the women with her and one of them looked back once or twice. The group moved away.

"Wives of Belgian volunteers who live near you year-round, at the yacht basin," I said.

I explained that the preceding week I had been at a party with my husband and several of his colleagues and had met that woman there.

"She said she has been living here for two years, and asked me all sorts of questions about myself and my work. I wondered why. Finally she admitted, 'Ever since I've lived here, always at the hotel, the only examples of women from this country that I have met are the village women who clean house. They don't speak French…'"

My sense of the irony began to stir in the moment of silence that followed, as I thought of that party, and I added, somewhat wearily, "She didn't even realize that nine miles away thousands of women come and go in the city, working outside their homes, teaching, nursing… She asked skeptically if I taught at the university."

And I shrugged my shoulders, resigned before so much ignorance; the passersby had disappeared.

After this digression the Beloved went back to how his story had concluded three years earlier. As if he knew I didn't want to question this "before," letting it spill out however he let it flow, according to the rhythm of his memories… As if, I thought to myself, the Belgian women taking a walk were, after all, a ghost, while the reality passed before him on the beach, sometimes smiling, sometimes melancholy, a shadow—the foreign woman whom, for at least an hour, he had been bringing back to life.

Yes, remembering his confessions, my disquiet returns, bearable while he spoke of her in my presence—"her," this foreign woman from five years before, three years before—he would immediately plunge once again into the days of worry, excitement, or hope. (Whereas, for my part, I would scarcely find myself face-to-face with him when everything would disappear for me, my everyday life, my family attachments, my ordinary turmoil.) And he described them so well, those stormy, tormented moments, that, hearing him, I was completely inside that time as it passed, in those emotions: I was "she," I was he.

Then he was silent. The last gleams of the setting sun had been extinguished just as suddenly a few moments before. We stood up in the darkness. A few yards behind us the door of his house was still open, the lights inside seemed to beckon.

I remember that once I was standing, I had felt some sort of weight on my shoulders. Tired. Infinitely tired: of the passion of others and because, in fact, it was the passion of others! I bent down swiftly and, with one hand, picked up the pair of espadrilles I had thrown on the damp sand. At the same moment he also bent down toward me.

"I'm cold!" I said quickly. "I need to go back to the city!"

He kept his face raised toward me as I was leaning down like that for a moment. As if, in spite of the diffuse twilight, with the reflection from the water behind us, he finally discovered I was present. His face seemed to me so close; it seemed outside all those memories that were finally dissipating. A childish smile lit up his features and he stared at me.

I reached out my hand to him. I just barely managed to stop the words on the tip of my tongue: "Take me home, or else I'll never leave again!"

As if he were becoming close kin to me, an almost incestuous brother, I had that tender thought. I was on the verge of calling him "my darling" in Arabic, or anyway in the dialect of my maternal tribe—he would not have understood, he would not have guessed its emotional weight.

Pressed against me, he took my arm (my body, my sides, my torso arched, and became cautious, rebellious, immobile):

"Of course, I'll take you home!" he said unequivocally. "We have just time enough to have a drink of something, then I'll get the car from the garage."

With his fingers he brushed my hand that was carrying the pair of espadrilles.

"Warm yourself up! You're cold!"

"That's it!" I said in a half-joking tone. "Warm me up with a bowl of hot milk, look after me! Afterward we'll take our time going back!"

Next to him in his messy kitchen, sitting on a stool and putting on my shoes, accepting one of his big wool sweaters for my shoulders, in this nocturnal intimacy, I softened. However, I did not forget how he had taken me shortly before into his past, and I let him wait on me—as if reproaching him indirectly for the distance set up by his confiding in me.

He waited on me, he smiled; he became a more than thoughtful host. Probably he was expecting that after those ambiguous moments on the beach, after the things he had said that had made me both more distant and oddly more close to him, probably he hoped some impulse would finally be released in me. It is true that my gestures, maybe even my voice, seemed different that evening. Yes, that is what I think, now that I write it down for myself, after it was all erased, after the twists and turns of separation; I think that he saw into me better than I did myself, that he was foretelling the emotional demonstration that was imminent, that he was preparing for it.

The kitchen, half-lit; the little yaps of a dog outside; some neighbor's child singing. And he and I there, occupied with almost ordinary things, the smell of the warm milk that nearly boils over: he watches me intently, my sheer pleasure as I drink. He reaches out to hand me a napkin; laughing, I wipe my lips. He is standing so close. I pull off the heavy sweater—of good red angora—I want to give it back to him. He insists I should keep it on in the car. He puts it back on my shoulders. He becomes protective; he seems affectionate. In a flash I see him clearly with "the other," the foreigner he loved so much: but the vision does not trouble me. His attentions warm me more than this angora wool.

"Let's go!" I whisper, in a final gesture of caution.

I follow him to the garage, I sit down next to him, and I think once again that the trip will last all night long; that we are leaving, that's all. That nothing will be over.

Together we two return in a silence that envelops everything, even the engine's purr. In the middle of the trip, to have some music, I push a button.

"John Coltrane! 'Naïma'!" I say as the music plays, becoming the only reality we have.

The car stops in front of the second door of the building where I live, near the tall palm and the ash trees. The concierge and his two grown boys, squatting on a step: their stares bore into me, the lady who at ten in the evening has herself calmly brought back home where, upstairs, the husband and children, already in bed are waiting. "Today the order of things is upside-down!" the fierce doorkeeper will say behind my back, and one of his strapping youths will spit to the side. At the moment the concierge is standing ceremoniously erect and waiting for the car to leave.

Though conscious of the hostility of these guardians of suspicion, up to the last minute I remain absorbed only by the presence of the man at the steering wheel, who is smiling at me. His eyes glisten. Our fingers brush together in the car; not one word is murmured before we part. I know that he is amazed now that, during the entire evening, as well as during the time we sat there before the twilight on the beach, *nothing, in the end, happened between us!*

Does he really say these ordinary words? Or did he just think it in the abstract? I feel it vaguely in the somewhat amused, indulgent look he gives me and a diffuse tenderness—which has nothing to do with the changeable fabric of the turmoil I am managing to hide.

So I smile at him at the last minute, happy to strengthen our secret bond, our mutual attraction whose rhythm is so different for each of us. I am afraid of the wave that might sweep me away, hence preoccupied with building a dam against it. He—I understand in this moment of goodbye—nonchalantly letting the things that began to be detected between us sweep over him: the comings and goings of my capricious dance around him, his house, the days of respite, the lazy days. He is, in short, passively preparing to wait for me. "When, finally, will you really be close? I wanted to dispose of yesterday's tumult and reveal my history to you just so you would know that everyone has a turn at experiencing intoxication and passion, no matter how he or she resists. Everyone goes through the mill. Everyone, even you! Let yourself go! Come, come softly! I'm making no demands and I'm not pushing you; I'm simply waiting for you!"

Was this what he was preparing to tell me when he was done confiding on the beach? I put all this together—or invented it—after I left him, after his car took off, and after I had been followed by the stares of the concierge and his two sons, the watchmen of bourgeois respectability.

In the elevator, my eyes shut, I say to myself, *He gave me that slightly surprised look, as if I were his younger sister, always behind, still paralyzed by taboos.* Yet it was a tender look, and I got his message: *I'm waiting for you! You'll take the time you need. I'm waiting!*

But then I did not take the time. No.

His love for this Frenchwoman, five years earlier.

"I was settling down in this country again, after studying in England. My father paid for that, one advantage of being an only son!" he said, half apologizing. "I still wasn't doing much; I was twenty-five, without a girlfriend or even a fiancée in reserve for me among the cousins of the tribe... I remember my hunger for traveling the country: December spent in the Mzab, the next months in the Sahara, summer preferably on the beaches in the west... And again, the oases, the ones in the east: escaping the new society," and he laughed. "There," he said, nodding his head toward his house behind us, "there is where I found them again, the people I was running away from. I couldn't do anything else! Ah," he went on, "those wonderful years of living single, as a nomad."

He stopped. Then he described their meeting. A woman a few years older than him. With a ten-year-old child, and a husband.

"A major," he sneered, then, more lenient, he smiled. "Of course, when she met him, he was a mathematics or physics student taking courses in her own provincial city, in Alsace, I think."

I mused over the many couples I knew. The romanticism of yesterday's nationalist war was not over yet. It still created an aura around love affairs between Algerian men and French women. But it was not long before the former "fighter" was "promoted," becoming a director of some ministry, or a diplomat, or in this case a high-ranking military officer.

"She was bored at home. We fell in love... And after that it was nothing but catastrophe, one long summer of catastrophe! First happiness: she left her husband and son. We hid ourselves away in a mountain village in the Aurès. We lived in a summer cottage loaned by a friend..." He paused, steeling himself. "We should have escaped to Europe, right from the beginning! But she was afraid of permanently losing custody of her child."

She was afraid, I thought. *Imagine living happiness this way, streaked with fear!*

He went on: "The major used all his connections to find us: the chief of police, a director of the interior, who knows?... But however he did it, they showed up one morning very early, with the police. They handcuffed me like a criminal to take me away. And then this husband, so certain of his rights, slapped her right there in front of me! And my hands were in shackles!"

He broke off his story. Was that when the Belgian ladies passed us on the beach and I told him about them? To let the present dissipate the miasmas of the past nightmare.

He went on, not describing the crisis, but rather the days that followed. "Almost a year!" he said. And the young woman ended up being expelled, stripped of her rights "for loose behavior."

Now, I thought to myself, the major is remarried to some young native-born woman "from a good family," of course.

"As for me," he went on, "I spent three days in jail."

He suddenly guffawed. "You should have heard my mother when she arrived with a lawyer from the family; her passionate diatribe against what she said was tyranny. In addition, she said, the crime of bride theft is not provided for in the Constitution!

He asked me how you say "bride thief" in Arabic. I told him and merrily recounted the fantasies that we children used to find so exciting when we attended weddings. They would shut the bride away, concealing her from everyone's gaze. Even on the threshold of the bedroom an old woman stood guard to see that she was not left alone for a single second until her husband entered; until he tremulously lifted the silk veil covering her precious face. Because "the thief" is still there, he is hiding, endowed with every evil power, to gather her to himself and take her off into the forest! Some of these brides were waiting, I knew, their hearts pounding, for this *khettaf el-arais*. Many of them would have preferred this thief with all the beauty of the devil to the appointed groom!

He listened to me, this man who would not be my "thief," and we returned to his past. He had lost his passport for almost a year. Finally he was able to locate Genevieve in France—only now, toward the end of his story did he call her by name. "Then, over there, more than a year later, not far from her parents, I had to acknowledge that we could no longer be happy... Not like before. She constantly felt guilty that her son had been taken away. She had joined a group of foreign mothers who, like her, are actively undertaking a legal battle. It was all over for the two of us."

I would have liked to interrupt him: *Why? Does it only take you a year to forget? Isn't it rather that while you were apart, you were bent on keeping her so close but, face-to-face, you found she was different, matured, sorrowful? Stripped of her child, expelled from the land of sunshine in which your love flourished? Was the magic gone for her too? Shouldn't you have persevered, stayed together to thumb your nose at the major—former member of the Resistance, former husband, former who knows what?*

I no longer remember how these confidences came to an end… Genevieve, image of the sacrificed woman whom I would never know, whom I already imagined as some new, distant relative.

I remember, on the other hand, that he kept saying that he couldn't live in France "for more than a month," that he had quickly returned home, that his mother had turned over their summer house to him, and that he liked it there, staying put like a hermit, especially during the winter and spring. The flood of people from the capital having not yet arrived, he routinely spent time with the men from the nearby hamlet.

Afterward, I say to myself—no longer knowing whether by that I mean "after making a final break with my Beloved," or after the scene I then lived through with my husband the night I made my ridiculous confession. The consequences of this outrageous event I, of course, imposed in haughty silence upon my confused parents, who naïvely saw this brutality and conjugal havoc as either a remnant of the old ways of doing things or else as the result of some corrupt modernism. And—one of my cousins reported to me what they had said, while all I could do was hold my tongue—they trusted my "upright" character.

Afterward… This incredible thing, I can't quite understand why I did it! In fact two or three weeks after this breakup, I agreed, yes, agreed to return to my life as a wife—only not in the usual apartment, as if that were the only place still retaining the poisons of the recent chaos. I went back to the seashore, to the house my husband had there near the now-deserted open theater. The harshness of the rocks it overlooked agreed with me.

I accepted, yes. I see once again the sequence of my return unfolding and—now that it is all over, now that all connections are broken, my passion evaporated—disintegrating.

In short, hardly had I bandaged the wounds on my body when I instantly returned to my prison—why? how? I am trying now to discover what temptation could move me to say to myself, *You are going back to where the danger lies, to understand, or rather to confirm: Is it really dangerous there—at the point of delirium, during that night of violence, when the husband meant to blind you?*

It is true that I had barely escaped his rage when I had stated categorically to myself, *It's my fault! Not that I meant him to do it, but I was wrong not to have foreseen his jealousy!* As if the confession I laid out before him to lessen my own torment had triggered an almost legitimate husband's rage. *My fault!* I kept repeating, afterward.

Still I wanted to be sure: Was my obsession with the image of my Beloved an inner madness isolating me, or was there more to it, something ambiguous in its complexity? Did my husband's violence deprive him of any significance for me, even though in the gesticulations of a hyperbolic passion whose real sense escaped me, he forced his way back into the foreground?

Yes, I went back to prison.

Before... an evening spent in the restaurant of one of the best hotels—my son who for the past few weeks has insisted on staying with his father has come to find me and then to convince me to come to dinner. A touching messenger. So there the three of us are. Then child slips away at dessert. And I find myself listening to a long plea—not really listening actually, but registering with astonishment that this man who is pleading with me, who, as soon as he is alone with me, begs me to return, this man whose face I am not even focused on is speaking to me from another shore.

Is this really the man I lived with for thirteen, fourteen years straight, sharing innumerable nights of love I thought I carried within me, invisible treasures that, as I imagined for so long, made me glow secretly? With this man, really?

I tried to listen to him. I kept my eyes downcast: concerned about how my mother would greet me shortly—she had been worried seeing me leave. How could I tell this man, "It is not a matter of pardoning or forgetting... Perhaps it really is my fault!" I was tempted to say that.

In fact, after less than three weeks of convalescence, I found it comforting to have only one struggle to face from then on: the fight over my possession by the other, the Beloved I mean. My passion was again looking for a chance to quickly take over the void that had settled into my life. Would this, then, be the final struggle or, on the contrary, the prelude to a likely and licit surrender? For me these were the only important questions. I could not keep my mind on any others.

But then, on the other side of the table, there was the husband from whom I was separating (I was considering the formalities of divorce—I even told him, "So that it will go faster, and since the law is on your side, well, then just repudiate me! The important thing is to straighten it all out as quickly as possible!"). This man who was pleading with me spoke from the other side of a gaping rift.

At the most, in a final weak moment, I should have thought of this gulf between us with nostalgia: "fate," I later would say, "time" alone caused it!

And all of a sudden…

All of a sudden I listened to him—this man who, a moment earlier seemed almost irreversibly a stranger.

He was talking about his day today: in his old parents' small town. In the morning his father, an *imam* of the *hanéfite* rites—rarely practiced in the region—had expounded a long moral discourse: recommendations of justice and fairness. With no beating around the bush he had, in the presence of his son, spoken of his daughter-in-law's "qualities as a woman," the confidence he had in her feminine lineage. "What is essential," he said—it was one of his leitmotivs—"is what affects the education of the children and the future of the couple," and so on. I, of course was his daughter-in-law, and "my feminine pedigree" had been carefully examined at the beginning of our union. We had found it amusing in those days. So he was harking back to something said earlier, that was all—not offering advice or suggesting direct intervention in his son's present life. He then returned to his little old mosque in the old city. It was a Friday.

"And the upshot," said the son of this stern *imam*, "was that I had a great urge to take the baths!"

He had then asked his mother to prepare his linens for him. He had hurried to the baths "as if before a feast day," he added in an eager voice. I tried not to look at him but to pay attention and listen carefully.

He described how he had gone into the warm room, how he had tended to his body, how he had asked the most experienced masseur for the longest massage. He even added—remember, our son was now gone and we were alone—that he had wanted to have all the hair removed from his entire body, that he had perfumed himself with

musk and jasmine, that he had rested there for half an hour, enough
time to sweat abundantly, and then he had dressed himself in the cold
room.

He had gone home in a taxi. His mother had, as usual, fixed him
the sugared beignets that he loved; there were pomegranates, some of
them with the seeds plucked out, others simply parted, awaiting him
on the low table. It was five in the afternoon. One of his sisters, married and living in the city, had just arrived; she had taken off her veils
intending to make herself comfortable beside him.

He stayed there barely long enough to drink the coffee that had
been prepared and inquire after his sister's children and husband,
but did not sit down. His mother was praying in the back room
when he left.

He could not wait, he said. He decided to return to the capital
and ordered his son, who was playing in the courtyard with the
neighbors' children, to accompany him.

He drove very fast, too fast, and in an hour the car had swallowed
up the miles.

When he left the baths, he said in conclusion, he felt sure he could
convince me—to return to our life together, to speak no more of the
past. To start all over again, like a young couple!… Had he not gone
to the baths in preparation for our next night, a new wedding night?

Finally I looked at him: I faced up to his passion, his eyes of
desire, the trembling of his fingers.

This, then, is how he loved me, or simply desired me. This, then,
is how he came alive again, in my presence.

But for my part?… Verging on somewhat fearful respect, I had
listened to his story. I almost envied him for having experienced this
fever, for hoping this way. I would have liked to be in his place: decid-

ing, as he did, to go to the baths, plunging myself into the mists of the steam room, burning myself in the heat and the cold, shivering, removing all the hair from my body, my naked body smudged with the greenish mud, then returned to its translucent ivory. Then I would have liked to perfume all the hollows and joints before receiving the blessings of the bathers at the first door, I would have liked to wrap myself in any number of towels at the second door, entwining my hair with garlands of jasmine and roses at the third door, dressing myself and brushing my hair, my cheekbones pink and head enturbaned with sequined taffeta to cross the last threshold! I, too, would have liked to be welcomed home by oranges, half-opened pomegranates, and steaming tea for everyone on a low table. I would have liked, after these long hours of relaxation for my body and muscles, to fall asleep, without speaking, with caresses, in the arms of my Beloved.

The arms of my Beloved, of course!

And I lowered my eyes there before the husband. I heard myself say then, "Yes. I'll come back!" He did not move. I still did not fix my eyes upon him; I went on:

"Not tonight, however! I have to tell my parents! And make them understand. I will join you tomorrow with my daughter on one condition—that we not return to the apartment for a long time but live in your house at the seashore."

He accompanied me to my parents' house, and when we reached it, his face was bright and he wanted to embrace me. I surrendered my hands, my shoulders, my closed eyes to him.

Silently, without saying anything to him, and because once again I could not understand my decision at all (what contagion from his fever was I seeking?), I asked him for forgiveness.

And thus I returned to prison.

Long winter weeks, or spring beginning but too cold. The children would be off early with the chauffeur to the distant city while I stayed idly at home—usually stretched out on a mattress on the floor of my little girl's room (as if to tell the truth that I was once again merely a guest passing through!). It fascinated me to contemplate the gray sky; belatedly I realized that I had unintentionally become my Beloved's neighbor again, that I shared this sky with him closely enough to be aroused by the proximity, that he knew none of this but that I knew it for both of us. That I was snared again like a bird in a net but that it gave me a feeling like euphoria… This is how I would conquer the time, and the absurdity of the situation into which I had once again fallen, waiting for what? Fording what? Across to where? To what unknown? The stillness of my days seemed deceptive; to aggravate the point even further, I sent word to the university that I was ill. Besides, was I not really ill? Or rather "quarantined"—I was coming to understand myself as a "quarantined woman," the way wives who were repudiated and yet not freed formerly were in Kabyle villages!

One night scene from this period stands out, luminous and dreamlike, a still scene whose sound, for no reason, I had cut off— leaving wide-open mouths in the masks of the protagonists, amplifying their passionate gestures, emphasizing the silent density of their angry gaze.

First a burst of temper. Rage from the husband, whom I had finally agreed to go out with one night, to one of the dance halls where a few young, amateur musicians performed in the off season.

I agreed, but I grumbled: "If there is music I like and the band is not too loud, I am going to dance! I'll dance as I please!… Too bad," I announced, confronting the look of impotent annoyance he shot in my direction, "too bad if the others think that because I'm the 'wife of the director,' I shouldn't make a spectacle of myself or dance. As for you," I went on to add, "now you know the despair and fire that I keep buried and silent within me! If the music pleases me, how can I not seek to give my body, at least, some relief?"

I dressed. I kept on my jeans from the morning; I put on a loose-fitting blouse of gauze or silk, and I took a big scarf in case the night was cold.

I went out with my husband. The only time during this period after what had happened. The only night.

A scene from a bad dream, frozen in a wan light.

A scene from a melodrama whose sound I cut deliberately.

The Beloved, practically back from the dead, actually reappeared in this night space, into the depths of boundless despair I was struggling to bear, believing this to be my fate—this raw pain, this expectancy opening onto nothing, opening onto the impasse of this life I had chosen for myself.

He turned up in that cabaret.

I was dancing alone. The dance floor was rather small, the band a student quintet. I was smiling at the trumpeter.

Not many clients this weeknight. The cabaret manager and two or three of his assistants quickly focused their attention on my husband. As much for the sake of avoiding this party as because I was happy to see that the place looked almost deserted, I decided to dance. Only the musicians existed, only the trumpet solo whose flow would carry me along.

I paid no attention either to the first group or to the second when they came through the rear doors. I was still dancing when I heard a diffuse murmur swell and spread. One of the musicians signaled unobtrusively to me; I turned to look toward the far end of the room.

My husband was standing surrounded by his four companions; facing them was the trio composed of my three summer friends. I was completing a dance figure when it slowly dawned on me that the Beloved—whom I had not seen for three or four months—was there, very present! No doubt he had glanced at the dance floor and lingered for a second to see me move (as he had in the height of summer, that first night when Leo came). No doubt.

Loud voices in the back. I had stopped; I took one step, then two. I cannot remember what came next. Except what was at the bottom of it all. Except the moment of open rupture.

My husband: his mask of rage. He seemed to have spoken out loud... For me his mask was silent. A gesture. The mask: eyes huge and almost bloody. Then an arm shot out, a hand: to strike or curse. The mask is upright, very tall. The faces around are stunned, frozen or sucked into a kind of vertigo, a great, unexpected blast.

My gaze settled upon "him": his silhouette, his body, a collection of vertical lines but on an angle, a poplar on the verge of bending to the storm, just before bowing, before breaking, just before.

Then I looked straight at his back. I mean the back of the man who occupied my soul, who for months and months had been clawing at my heart. A fleeing back.

And I, petrified, defeated. What shame! *How could I ever have been attracted that way to someone whose back I am seeing now? Because he is running away, is it possible? Because he is leaving, he is afraid, can this be true?*

I looked at his back. Then I turned to look at the other. Only then, behind me, did the trumpeter suddenly stop his melody. He alone had accompanied me in this desert, he alone tacitly asked, "When, now, will you ever have the heart to dance?"

And so I continued to see this back after it had vanished. Inside me a colorless voice: *I loved a child, an adolescent, a young brother, a cousin, not a man. I did not know it yet.* The voice spun out clear and hard; it did not speak in French or Arabic or Berber but in some language from the hereafter spoken by women who had vanished before me and into me. The voice of my grandmother who died a week after independence and who vehemently addressed me from the depths of my raging, my astonishment:

He did not face up, the voice went on, *not even for me! He could have turned toward me. Faced with my husband seeking out his ridiculous duel, I would have made a lightning decision: I would have gone to you, you, Beloved of my heart, I would have gone toward your hesitation and even your fear, in front of everyone I would have held out my hand to you. "Let's go! Let's leave!" I would have said without question.*

And he, the young man who was not quite a man, would have found the courage. Past the shrieking and the insults and the silence of others, we would have left.

My husband, his face full of hatred, would have stepped forward of course. He would have wanted to strike. He would have struck: he, who was larger, more athletic, more threatening than you the fragile, high-strung, sharp one, you next to me, myself trembling but steady, my husband more threatening than both of us together—but us together!... He would have hit the young man; he would have spared me, tried to pull me by the hand to put me back in the cage.

Myself with the loser. Resolute. Myself going away with the man being beaten by my husband and the other men.

An hour later I collapsed in my daughter's room. Onto the mattress on the floor. Alone. I was not leaving this place anymore. One day, maybe two, I lay there. I was staring at my Beloved's back before me—and because I had seen his back, I said to myself he was "my formerly Beloved."

At the time I was still my grandmother's grandchild—though she had been dead for fifteen years.

"What is a man?" her harsh and, toward the end, somewhat sepulchral voice used to exclaim, her hoarseness caused by occasional fits of coughing. The women of the town, the young girls and the little ones, used to wait for her pulse and breath to become regular again. Lying there on her sick bed, later her deathbed, she breathed with a death rattle that would become freer toward the end. She would fix her gaze on us one after the other, and, with unspeakable bitterness but also undeniable pride—as if, throughout the eventful journey of her life, she and she alone in our ancient city had had the rare privilege of having married, after all, "only men"—she would say it again: "What is a man?" Then, a ragged breath would tear through her that was even worse than her spasmodic coughing and she would say, "A man is someone whose back one does not see!" Then she would repeat it, staring especially at the granddaughters whose wedding day she would never see—"Someone," she went on more specifically, "whose back the enemy never sees!"

Thus, at the age of forty, lying there like a vulnerable and shamefully enamored adolescent, I could not stop hearing my grandmother gasping for breath before me, stubbornly harassing me, fifteen years later. *Maybe it is fate, maybe on this earth we women who know "what a man should be" have to bear this as our curse: We are no longer able to find any men!*

She spoke to me. She said "we" because she continued to carry on within me. Because she was living through my defeat. As for myself, I was trying to free myself from her. I was no longer seeking liberation from the husband with his melodramatic mask, but trying to get away from the virile grandmother, away, at least, from this bitter, virile woman, and I wanted to retort, *You speak of "our present lot, no longer being able to find any men! No longer having anything to do with men!"… But as for me, that is not my problem: myself, I love. I love and I did not think that I was guilty; I thought I was sick. Not at all because there was the husband from whom I had to distance myself, from whom in fact I discovered that I had long been distant. No, I thought that I loved and that it was itself a strange illness! He was so young, at least he was younger than me, a sort of young brother or cousin from my maternal line whom I discovered too late… And yet he is the one, in an awful moment, my Beloved* (silently: my Beloved) *whose back I saw!*

I am trying, because of you, thanks to you, to get out of this mess, and at the same time perhaps to free myself from the spell of my obsession. Help me, grandmother, but not with your bitterness or harshness. No! Speak to me, confess the passions you felt as a young girl, your emotions: Was it the second husband, or the third, my grandfather, whom you loved every night?… My grandfather, I have always known, never showed his back to anyone, either in battle or in any sort of confrontation—only the murderer saw his back when he shot him from behind the day the grandfather invited him into his orchard and served him with his own hands each dish, receiving him as a guest at his meal. My forty-year-old grandfather's back, in the orchard: the murderer took dead aim, then disappeared forever.

Who is the murderer for me? Shooting my silent passion, my hope, in the back? Today is it my own eyes that cannot stop seeing the young man, not quite a man, run away?

If it is not from your bitterness, then, is it from this languishing after him, O grandmother, that I must recover, you whose face lies deep in the earth, there where someday I hope to meet you again?… (Even though, in fact, I am desperately seeking the lover, to make love night after night beside him, but above all, when all is said and done, seeking to die beside him, before or after him, to meet him again in the earth, to lie within him for eternity.) O grandmother, whose face is buried in the earth, most likely I shall meet you again for want of this final love, this passion to the point of death that I seek. Because there is no Isolde in Islam, because there is only sexual ecstasy in the instant, in the ephemeral present, because Muslim death, no matter what they say, is masculine. Because to die, like my grandmother and like so many other women who know instinctively, through their struggles and torments, what is a man, one "whose back one never sees," is to die like a man. In Islam all these women, the only ones who are alive right up to the moment they die—in a monotonous transmutation that I am beginning to regret grievously— the dead women become men!

In this sense death, in Islam, is masculine. In this sense, love, because it is only celebrated in sensual delights, disappears as soon as the first steps of heralded death are danced. This first approach to the sakina, *that is to full and pure serenity, is feminine moreover. But after this introduction, which is light as a woman's breath, death seizes the living, living men and women, to plunge them as equals—and suddenly all of them masculine—into the abysses inhabited by souls "obedient to God."*

Yes, of course, O grandmother, Muslim death is masculine. But then, as for myself, I want still to be loving with my last sigh; yes, I want to feel, even when borne off on the shoulders of funerary bearers, on that plank, I want to feel myself going toward the other, I want still to love the other in my decay and my ashes. I want to sleep, I want to die in the arms of the other, the other corpse who will go before me or who will follow me, who will welcome me. I want.

Why, after what happened in the cabaret, do I talk to the grand-mother for so long?... The film of what happened that night loops over and over again, as I lie there in full daylight: I am trying to forget the gasps of the old and formidable dying woman—she who did not love me, who preferred the daughter of her only son. I see also, and again, the face of the husband twisted in hatred—suddenly I remember that he is from the city, where married women, even in a harmonious marriage or one, in any case, with no apparent conflict, secretly call any husband "the enemy." Women speaking among women.

Thus the husband finally returned to the role that for generations he had been assigned by the memory of the city. In his renewed rage, and because I was deliberately turning off the sound, he played the role of enemy even more easily. "My enemy." I sighed, because enemy of my Beloved.

The young man, the formerly loved, had made an anguished gesture before the enemy standing there; a gesture that meant "screw you!" (Of course, I now grasped it: for him, this threatening husband was in the same category as the major from the mountain village who had slapped Genevieve.) He turned for a moment toward his friend the journalist; then he left.

On the third day I got up. A cold late spring dawn.

The solution obsessing me during my nights of turmoil demanded that its words be heard—French words, bizarrely wrapped in the harsh and passionate voice of the grandmother, the fearsome dead woman: *Put up a door between the husband and myself. Now. Forever!*

I surprised myself by concluding with a solemn oath: "In the name of God and his Prophet!" These words, in Arabic, were mine and at the same time my grandmother's (I tell myself that I was spontaneously rediscovering the first Koranic tradition whereby women also repudiated their men!)

I quietly made a suggestion to my little girl, who had not gone to school this morning: "Get dressed and let's go walk on the beach; would you like that?"

I went out first. Outdoors I saw that I was not wearing enough clothes. I whispered to the child who joined me: "Sweetie, I'm cold! And... I can't go back to the house." (I was fervently thinking, *The oath is already spoken!*)

"I'll go get you a coat," she said.

"The white coat! And bring what you need for the day!"

We walked for a long time along the sunny beach, beside a limpid sea. Was I running away, was I setting myself free?

After an hour or so, almost tired, I saw a tourist hotel perched on a hill not far away. In the hallway I asked a boy who recognized me if they could call us a taxi.

The little girl, her face all rosy, was already grinning over this escapade. I gave my old aunt's address in her noisy working-class neighborhood; I thought especially about her balcony over the city and the scent of old jasmine that hung heavy from morning on.

In the midst of all her hugs and kisses I murmured to my relative, "I've come to stay with you for a few days!"

7

THE GOODBYE

THERE IS ALWAYS A GOODBYE, when the story or the stories have too much in them, are woven together with several wefts, are full to bursting with too many dreams, with excess. There is always a good-bye in a true love story. Leaving it to hang among the breezes, under the ample sky of memory.

Yes, there is always a goodbye—but never in a plot with a con-torted and disfigured side to it, where its progress is jammed; or in the hyperbole of a deceptively lyrical jealousy, with its swollen hatred; or when the desire for the other is death-dealing, killing the other's laughter, taking the other's life. So, frequently, in what is ordinarily called a love story (often only a story of abduction where it is never really decided who is the thief and who is the one taken), the ending is settled by exhaustion, or asphyxiation. There is never the disinter-ested elegance of an explicit goodbye, or a goodbye blown like a kiss, sent like mercy or a gift.

Long after the day of the siesta that was my salvation, of course, and after the return to my usual lightheartedness, there was a good-bye. I said goodbye. And I smiled tenderly at my Beloved.

I remember leaving a concert of Berber music in Paris. I was standing there, part of a group, with friends. "Where shall we go and dance now?" That is always the way: seeking in vain for someplace to have a party at midnight, some empty apartment, a terrace over-looking the river.

In the crush of people leaving: a man's face close by. In spite of the crowd's rush the stranger stops; he is like a dam. I am getting impatient: his eyes are smiling. "You don't recognize me anymore?"

His voice came to me first. My formerly "beloved," a year later, I thought, a century. What was different about him, other than his voice? I bumped into his shoulders because of the crowd. We went out together.

"The singer tonight, he's your best friend... I should have remembered." And I went on with my banalities: "Do you live here... or are you just passing through?"

He did not answer. He smiled the same smile, studying me almost mischievously. I kept on talking, and talking: "I live here now, did you know that! Some of us live that way, destined to be tethered to two cities all our lives: split between Algiers and Paris..."

The singer, accompanied by several musicians, arrived. Once again there was a crowd. I studied the Beloved—no longer so young. Without a trace of melancholy I noticed that something about him had changed.

The star singer insisted that I join them at the brasserie across the street. The Beloved stood facing me as if he were just some friend passing through, without saying anything. He was waiting.

"Goodbye!" I said, almost merrily.

And I went serenely back home to my place, or really, our place—the place I shared with a poet who loved me.

Subsequently, in other briefer, perhaps denser stories—relationships that were if not passionate, at least based on attraction, games of ups and downs or friendships verging on tenderness, self-reliant, self-protective—there were other goodbyes. Pauses in an inner music, never to be forgotten.

And I think of Julien. Back then, when he was introduced to me for the first time in the southern capital, he bowed, his tall silhouette that of an expatriate Viking: "Julien!" I exclaimed, repeating his first name. "Were your parents Stendhal scholars?"

He was an extremely thoughtful comrade throughout the months I was working with the peasant women of my maternal tribe. Julien wanted to be the photographer in order to accompany us, myself and the ten or so technicians, in our research and my wanderings. So, often I liked to go off with him at dawn. He was always silent as he drove, and we liked "looking at things together." I would tell the others we were "looking for locations"!

Julien and I worked with the same rhythm and our searches for settings were extremely fruitful. We would return like conspirators with bundles of images between us.

On days of rest, in the inn where just a few of us were lodged, far from the tourist hotels, Julien got up a little before dawn to go with the cook and her children to the nearby sanctuary: It was Friday.

So there was Julien—such affectionate company, so unassuming with me and two or three others around me!... One day when I was in despair—this time it was in Paris—over some rough patch or misunderstanding with others (a male blunder, a proposition whose vulgar haste had struck me dumb at first), one day when finally alone in his car I burst into tears—sitting in the backseat and hiccuping: "Julien, just drive straight ahead! I'll calm down!" he drove the whole length of the shining black river. Then, dropping me off at the hotel and opening the car door for me, he silently kissed both my hands. I was no longer crying; I went in.

The next day he came back early and said in no uncertain terms that he was going to take me out to eat. It was sunny.

On the Place des Vosges we talked for a long time about the sanctuary where he used to take the cook every Friday. Back home!

Julien who, shortly afterward, fell painfully in love with my closest friend... Julien who, six months later, set out on his third trip to Tibet. A new trail had been opened on the peaks of the Himalayas. He went with two mountain-climbing friends.

"Take care of yourself!" I told him suddenly, finally using the intimate form of address.

Although I was used to seeing him as vigorous and invulnerable, I let myself be gripped by some vague apprehension.

"I'm entrusting you with all the photos I took when we were looking for locations last summer," he replied.

I kissed him.

That was not yet goodbye.

Two or three weeks later I had a card from him: a photograph he had taken of a young woman seated on the slope of a hill in front of her tumble-down house and playing with her baby, in light that was iridescent... On the other side Julien had written a few lines: In this village where he had studied scenes like this all day long, he thought about me, about the spring before when we had worked, "had looked," he wrote, so well. And at the end he said: *Tomorrow it's the Himalayas and the new trail. I'm happy. See you later, boss!*

That was goodbye. For the first time in our friendship, he used this ironically polite tone with me: "boss."

It would be a while before I knew that, as I read his card, as I admired the young Tibetan mother he had watched one sunny afternoon, Julien already lay inside an infinity of snow where, three days after writing me, he and his companions were brought by a sudden avalanche. His goodbye? My friend is not dead. He is sleeping beneath the depths of eternal snow. One day I know someone will go to look for his body and will bring it back. Then they can call me finally to contemplate his unchanged beauty, the expatriate Viking, and then, only then will I weep for him.

I remarried.

Feeling young again and free of worry, I rediscovered the streets of Paris.

Each day I would dream, wandering two or three hours daily: alone or paired. The austerity of my material life expressed the relief I felt. Suddenly I went back to writing: what was the shade I sought? Back and forth in what in-between place?

Three or perhaps four years living the carefree life of a couple. At almost forty I was once again twenty years old: sometimes the days stretched out in a kind of purifying vacation and sometimes they were overburdened with work… then this joint rhythm unraveled. Conflicts and unhappiness—or rather, anger. One evening just as night descended, emerging from depression, I rediscovered what might have been the equilibrium of my age: my face hard, I stated unequivocally, "I will not have you in my room anymore!"

But to myself—only to myself—I spoke vehemently: *You love to share things, you want to discover things and laugh and die in a couple, so are you not carrying your own prison along with you?*

A few months went by. Paris was a desert, but happily I still had my wanderings and all they reaped. And there was also work, making one deaf, deaf and dumb, in the richness of absence.

Once in the middle of the night my husband opened my door, letting the light from the hallway filter in. He quietly slipped in to look for a book on the shelves opposite my bed.

I kept my eyes closed. I was not pretending to be asleep: I felt asleep and conscious at the same time. I heard him come in, take a book, some guidebook or dictionary, then go to leave and shut the door again. He stopped. He came back, close to my low bed placed on a rug from the Aurès Mountains. I felt him right next to me.

Leaning down, he brushed a light kiss across my forehead. Stepped away. Closed the door carefully.

In the total darkness I opened my eyes. The obvious became clear: *His last kiss. That is really goodbye!*

I fell asleep again rather quickly. A bit later he left the house. He had left it almost lovingly when he imparted what he thought was a secret kiss that night.

The Beloved—really, "the formerly beloved"—and I had yet another encounter. On a vast stage, as if our coming face-to-face were something arranged secretly in advance by a magician.

It was the middle of summer, I think, after the vacationers had all left the city en masse. I can see the esplanade of the new Montparnasse station at the beginning of a rather hot afternoon. Few strollers; the rare tourist; one or two groups of young people sitting on benches or on the ground.

Myself emerging into that space. I was in no rush. I was on my way to my sister's, not far from there; in short I moved like someone used to being there, at ease. Probably because I was hurrying off to celebrate my nephew's birthday, I was feeling at home, despite the fact that I was in Paris.

At the far end of the station, leaving it: the silhouette of a traveler, bag in hand or on his shoulder. I myself was heading diagonally toward this isolated shadow clearly outlined against the sunlight.

Almost blinding light this afternoon. Not a sound: none from any bus behind me, none from any crowd—the people were sparsely scattered.

So that summer day I was walking along, strolling unhurriedly, and my heart, I remember, was filled with peace, or, as it so frequently is, gently submerged in the mere joy of existing. Halfway to where I was going I recognized him: It was he, the passionately Beloved, *the Beloved*, I thought, *not "the formerly beloved."* While the man who loved me, to whom I blithely returned every evening, was waiting for me somewhere else in the city.

So I recognized him; and he, changing pace, came quickly to meet me. No visible surprise, either on his part or on mine.

I shook his hand; hesitated before kissing him in a friendly way. He kept hold of my hand for a moment. We looked at each other.

Full of a new affection, I looked at him calmly: his face was heavier; his cheeks were tanned. He had gotten larger; his shoulders seemed wider.

Have two years really gone by? I wondered. *In any case, he has become a handsome man!*

He told me that he had just returned that very day from a distant country: "A year," he said, "working in an exchange program abroad—in New Zealand!"

I was somewhat distracted and now I wonder whether he didn't say Australia instead.

I smiled, my heart quickening again. *So,* I began my internal dialogue with him, as I had before, using the familiar form of address in my silence—*you have been to the ends of the earth and the day you return, I show up at the exit of this Paris station to welcome you back!*

I was not surprised. I believed in the miracle of some invisible master of ceremonies summoned to bring us together this final time.

This time I gazed unabashedly at my formerly beloved. Suddenly, then I was aware—unless rather, it was only after I left him that I understood this—that seeing him thus grown into a vigorous and seductive man my heart was filling with love that was really maternal! I felt he was happy and ready, at that moment, to take the time to tell me about his life in Australia… *I love him,* I said to myself, *like a young mother! As if, even though he was far away, I had contributed to transforming him, to bringing him to this mature state!*

Consequently my silent love, formerly so hard to control, changed in nature; it was still there within me, still secret, but it no longer had the fragility that had troubled me for so long. The young man stood there before me, radiant in his new beauty.

He asked for my phone number. I wrote it down for him and said something friendly. Then I just said, "We'll see each other again!"

That was the goodbye. I knew that right away as I walked off.

I go back to those days before the siesta, to those thirteen months. I do not know why I have drained these springs of self, with so many convolutions, in a disorder that is willfully not chronological, when I should have let them wither on the vine, or at least kept their growth in check.

And that man, who was neither foreign to me nor someone inside me, as if I had suddenly given birth to him, almost an adult; me suddenly trembling against his chest, me curled up between his shirt and his skin, me all of me close against the profile of his face tanned by the sun, me his voice vibrant within my neck, me his fingers on my face, me gazed upon by him and immediately afterward going to look at myself to see me through his eyes in the mirror, trying to catch sight of the face he had just seen, as he saw it, this "me" a stranger and another, becoming me for the first time in that very instant, precisely because of this translation through the vision of the other. He, neither foreign to me nor inside me, but so close, as close as possible to me, without touching me, but still wanting to reach me and taking the risk of touching me, the man became my closest relative, he moved into the primary vacancy laid waste around me by the women of the tribe, from the days of my childhood and before I reached nubility, while I took the first shaky step of my freedom.

Him, the one closest to me; my Beloved.

PART TWO
ERASED IN STONE

"I had buried the alphabet, perhaps. In the depths of I do not know what darkness. Its gravel crunched underfoot. An alphabet that I did not use to think or to write, but to cross borders…"

—CH. DOBZYNSKI
Prologue à Alphabase

1

THE SLAVE IN TUNIS

GOOD OLD THOMAS D'ARCOS! He is more than sixty years old and up to this point has led a rather pleasant life: Born in the somewhat troubled times of 1565 in La Ciotat, near Marseilles, when he is very young, he goes up to Paris, where he becomes secretary to the cardinal de Joyeuse, brother of the favorite of Henry III.

Suddenly, who knows why, he quits high society, returns to his sunny Provence, travels, learns languages, is seized with literary or scholarly ambitions: research on the history of Africa, a project to chronicle Ottoman customs (written in Spanish), as well as commentaries on Turkish and Moorish music. He is full of unmethodical but unflagging curiosity. He seduces women, of course, when he is young, then he straightens up and marries a local beauty in Sardinia. Does he mean to settle down there or in Marseilles, or in Carpentras?

Good old Thomas d'Arcos! Guess what! More than sixty years old and pirates from Tunis capture him aboard a sailboat. Thus in 1628 he finds himself in that city, a slave of the Turks.

Despite adversity he has unflagging energy. Does he not like oriental languages, antique coins and medals, rare objects, old books? He succeeds—no one knows how, probably by cashing in on his knowledge and gifts as an interpretor—yes, in two or three years he succeeds in putting together enough for his ransom. Free now, will he return to Marseilles or to the home of his wife in Sardinia? No; he settles in Tunis, where he will die.

That is when the story begins for us—after 1630. From Tunis he writes to a magistrate, an important local personage named Peiresc, who serves as counselor to the king at the parliament of Provence in Aix. (The famous Gassendi will later write a biography of this notable who was his friend.) He also corresponds with M. Aycard, a royal equerry and a friend of Peiresc's as well, but above all a scholar living in Toulon, where, thanks to traffic with Smyrna, Constantinople, all of the Levant, and Barbary, he is the recipient of manuscripts, antique medals, cameos, foodstuffs, and exotic things.

Thomas d'Arcos goes back and forth throughout the Regency, the Muslim states of northwest Africa, and he seems happy. He must be engaging in trade or barter to live well; no doubt he likes this life in the sun, probably easier and less expensive!... Has his wife not forgotten him, as his friends at the court of France, the nobility of Joyeuse, had done before?

He must admit to himself that, as far as his peace and pleasure are concerned, he is better off among the "Turks," the infidels, finishing this *Relation de l'Afrique*, his most important project, and after that his volume in Spanish. He is learning a lot here. He roams about and, even though he suffers from bad eyesight, he also writes. He teaches himself other languages. He is a scholar in Tunis, and certainly among the lower classes and perhaps among the notables, the foreign traders, the dragomans and celebrities who pass through, Thomas, good old Thomas d'Arcos, commands some respect here, enjoys some honors.

It is through his correspondence with Peiresc and Aycard that we can see into his days in Tunis: his schemes, his ambitions, his comfort, his pleasures as a well-read man, and sometimes his fears.

Then, gradually, quietly, a real drama unfolds for him. Persuaded that he will remain permanently, he complains about his bad eyesight to Peiresc; he can never find any eyeglasses that suit him and he would pay their "weight in gold" to have some. Then he adds sadly, "For more than five years I have been unable to read by candlelight with my regular ones!" To pay for them, he sends his correspondent some very warm slippers for both the magistrate and his wife, as well as couscous and the skins of vultures!

But one can guess that the ongoing drama that is causing his two correspondences to be interrupted is still brewing. Drama? Call it a passage, a shift—no, not a new passion for women or boys, nor for other realms of knowledge that might have opened up for him. Call it "an experience."

Thomas, good old Thomas d'Arcos, sixty-two or sixty-three years old, with failing eyesight, but still energetic and full of bounce, leaving Tunis for the nearby villages, then adventuring east, far into the interior—Thomas, the former prisoner who has been free for some time, feeling he has been accepted by everyone and resigned to dying in Tunis—Thomas decides to become a Muslim!

A conversion in due form: first the circumcision, then the words of the *chahadda* and the assuming of an Islamic name. Thomas becomes Osmann.

This takes place apparently around 1631 or the beginning of 1632. No sooner has he "turned" than he is "renounced." (He is not

the only one to make this turnaround, or, one might say, this accom-
modation. Several of his friends who are younger and with different
perspectives manage the transformation. There is a Provençal man
like him who will take the name Chaabane, a young Fleming who
will call himself Soliman, a very young Greek boy who will be
Mami.) But as soon as he feels he is a "renegade," he begins to doubt
and suffer, and to think about his friends to the north.

In fact Peiresc waits more than a year before showing any signs of
life. Thomas complains to Aycard, "The early characteristic of salvation given me by the Church will never be erased from my soul
although my habit may be changed!" He goes on to conclude philo-
sophically, "God sometimes allows evil so that he can draw some
greater good from it."

There he is, a middle-class man firmly attached to Tunis: he
could almost hope to find some rather mature Tunisian lady with a
warm heart and hospitable fortune to cuddle with in his old age!
There he is, borrowing Islam—at least that is how he describes it to
his friends in Provence, because, in the end, he refers to a double
faith: the faith of necessity and the faith that, he assures them, he has
never really denied, the faith of the faithful. But in Aix, Peiresc refuses to communicate, sits in judgment, and does not write.

Thomas-Osmann has sent him his finished book about Africa
and expects some criticism and observations; in this way he will
indeed continue to exist, if only in his writings, on the shores he has
left behind for good. If Peiresc considers his book to be serious and
of value, it may be that he, Thomas-Osmann will not to be forgotten
back there… Though he remains in the sun on the outskirts of Tunis,
his heart and his mind are journeying off with the book he sent to
Peiresc.

Repudiated, but trying to make Peiresc forgive his new faith, he turns to his other friend, Aycard, telling him about further presents he feels obliged to send each of them.

That is when he sends the gift, a really nice gift, of a gazelle—the *alzaron* he calls it. It is the end of 1633; in January 1634 he writes that this gazelle was caught in Nubia, that "it has a wonderful way of running," that he bought it from a great *marabout* in the city, and that someone else wanted it for the duke of Tuscany.

It will take several months for Peiresc to reply. Thomas, who meant to send him some little chameleons as well but got them too late to do so, inquires about his *Relation de l'Afrique*. In the end he confesses, "I admit that your long silence has caused me extreme pain and actually I attribute its cause to my sins..."

Gassendi, writing later about Peiresc, mentions the Nubian gazelle sent by Thomas and describes it. We know through him that it ended up in Rome at the estate of Cardinal Barberini.

The correspondence between Thomas-Osmann and his two friends comes to an end in 1636. Peiresc dies the following year and Aycard soon after. No further trace of Thomas d'Arcos, the renegade of Tunis.

However, it is neither the gazelle, which lives from this point on with the famous Cardinal Barberini in Rome, nor the scholarly work sent to Peiresc that makes this shadowfigure—a freed prisoner who became a Muslim—a silhouette that is inseparable from "our" story, from the shores of the Atlantic to the beaches lining the gulfs of Libya and Tunis, and all the way to the desert of Fezzan.

It was that Thomas was present, alone, in this first half of the seventeenth century traveling back and forth around Tunis or farther to the east with his truly ravenous gaze! Just before his conversion (sincere or strategic), he took a trip to the border between the two regencies, Tunis and Algeria. In a letter to Aycard, he mentions that Sanson Napollon, a knight of the king's order and governor of the Bastion of France, is now before Tabarka, that he wants to capture Cape Nègre and abandon the Bastion for it. (Things would definitely be easier with the Tunisian powers than with the rulers of Algeria.)

In this atmosphere Thomas embarked on an archeological expedition to a nearby spot, the ruins in Dougga—which he calls Thugga. It is now the autumn of 1631.

He must have been amazed at the fields of columns standing or lying about, the disorder of the marble objects in the midst of luxuriant vegetation, and never tired of describing and drawing them. Two or three poor villages are spread out nearby. Then suddenly he finds something wonderful!

In the middle of this plain, an imposing monument, not a simple triumphal arch but a majestic, harmonious, even strange mausoleum. Thomas studies the sculptures, the inscriptions. All day long he does not leave it.

In the slowly setting sun, some children from the village come to bring him flatbread, eggs, and sheep's-milk cheese—he knows there is only one thing for him to do. The most unusual and unexpected thing about this whole mausoleum is certainly this inscription on two parallel but not similar faces; he will copy it down meticulously. He studies the letters for a long time and corrects himself: "Two inscriptions, two scripts," because he finally understands that the magnificent stele is composed of a bilingual text.

He is not sure he will be able to return soon; a year earlier in his first letter to Aycard, he reported that he had been in the entourage of his then "patron" four leagues from Tunis, at La Calle, "where ancient Utica lay." He had been drawn there by his curiosity about the Roman past.

Even though he is unable to read any of the signs, he suspects that one of the scripts on the two faces of the stele is Punic. For a moment he muses over the final moments of the Carthaginian presence: he tells himself with tears in his eyes that what he is copying down dates at least from the second century before Christ! So this space, these stones, these signs that he cannot understand, have remained inviolate in this place for more than eighteen centuries!

If one speech, one solemn declaration is inscribed there in the Phoenician language, before (or after) Carthage was abandoned to the flames, the other side would bear the same declaration, but in what language? The language of the Vandals? No. Or that of some other vanished population?

He asks himself no more questions. He sits down. Although his tired eyes are weeping now from the strain, he works away at copying these mysterious signs!

Three days later, back in Tunis, his mind still smarts from the fire of this new enthusiasm. He had no witness, not a single confidant in his entourage, and he feels frustrated. Who will there be to come back to this after him? Who will be able to decipher the strange characters?

He spends days copying the double inscription several times over. He decides to send a copy to Peiresc, who does not respond. His curiosity, or his instinct, faced with the mystery, begins to lapse when he hears no echo. Neither Peiresc nor Aycard seem to think his discovery of any value…

It is then, during the following months, that Thomas's desire for apostasy occurs: as if, drawn by an obscure call from something far back in time, something unknown and as far back and ancient as these stones in Dougga, his soul regained a sort of equilibrium thanks to this conversion—which he referred to as "a shift."

In June 1633 a learned man, a Maronite, came through Tunis; he was a scholar of oriental languages and, writes Thomas, "highly respected in Rome" by the pope. His name is Abraham Echellen, and the reason for his being in Tunis is to negotiate the buying back of Christian slaves.

In great excitement, Thomas (from now on Osmann), with the text from Dougga in hand, introduces himself to Echellen. *He will be able to read it!* he thinks eagerly, and waits there respectfully with lowered eyes.

The Levantine studies the copied characters with a magnifying glass for a moment: "This is neither Syrian nor Chaldean," he asserts. "Perhaps certain characters bear a sort of resemblance to some ancient Egyptian! I shall have to study them at length once I am back in Rome. I shall work at identifying them if you let me have this copy!"

He promises to send Osmann in Tunis the results of what he discovers.

Thus, well before the gazelle reached Cardinal Barberini, this paper with the double inscription, copied by the former slave, ends up in Vatican City. Is put away in the paper archives. Lies dormant there.

As for Peiresc, he will not know what to do with these "hieroglyphs." Later Glassendi will describe the gazelle from Nubia at length but will disregard these drawings sent by "the Provençal renegade."

Thomas, good old Thomas d'Arcos, we do not know how or where he dies, whether as a Christian or as a Muslim. Thomas, between two shores, between two beliefs, will be the first person to transmit a bilingual inscription whose mystery will lie dormant for two more centuries.

2

THE RENEGADE COUNT

THE YEAR 1815 is the year Napoleon fell from power. The man feared by all the thrones of Europe is locked up for good. The Ancien Régime—its monarchies brought back out of the cupboard, its emigrés back in their châteaus and estates—is reestablished after Waterloo.

1815, or the return of the previous century: in Paris first, but also in Naples where Joachim Murat, king of Italy and brother-in-law of the "Ogre," has just been shot by firing squad.

In Naples where, as it happens, Countess Adelaide was feeling all alone: Adelaide, wife of Count Borgia, never leaves her dwelling, a veritable museum, the palace of the Borgia family. Her husband, Camille Borgia, the forty-one-year-old son of General Giovanni Paolo Borgia and the nephew of Cardinal Stefano Borgia, has had to choose exile as a precautionary measure, because in his youthful ardor as a sympathizer with the "revolutionaries" of earlier years he had enlisted in Murat's army as an officer. Then, rather rapidly, he had been promoted to the rank of general.

Having been born in a museum, Camille Borgia wrote, he had, so to speak, *suckled a passion for antiquities with his milk.* In his current difficulties, he decides to cross the Mediterranean to explore the ruins of Carthage around Tunis—to reflect, among the stones of antiquity, upon the destruction of the empires of this world and finally to fulfill what he believes to be his true vocation, becoming an archeologist.

As 1815 comes to an end and throughout 1816, Countess Adelaide will do her best to make something of her forced solitude. She regularly invites her circle of friends to the ancestral palace to read the chronicle that the count regularly sends her of his "scientific travels." Had Borgia "fled" to the land of the Moors? No, this was rather more of a stroll, drawing pencil in hand, with a mind inclined to wax philosophical in the midst of ruins, in search of monuments, some of which had been standing intact or nearly so for more than twenty centuries...

And this is how the renegade Neapolitan count will end up following in the footsteps of the Provençal slave of earlier times, Thomas-Osmann d'Arcos!

The count arrives in Tunis on 19 August 1815, carrying a Danish passport: He did in fact have the title of king's chamberlain in Denmark. Welcomed by the Danish consul in Tunis he is introduced to the bey's ministers and the diplomatic circle... He sets himself up in the Imperial, the only hotel in the capital with European amenities, and at the same time immediately begins his first archeological tours in the countryside around Tunis. He becomes the friend of a Dutch engineer, J. E. Humbert, who is an officer in the corps of engineers sent there long before and on good terms with several dignitaries serving the Tunisian sovereign.

In December 1815 Count Borgia and Humbert decide to make an excursion to study the origins of the aqueduct of Carthage in the Zaghouan plateau. Together they make discoveries that escaped several travelers and explorers of the previous century (Peysonnel, Shaw, Bruce, and so on). Not long after, when his Dutch friend manages to join the entourage of Mohammed Khodja, one of the bey's ministers, Count Borgia undertakes a journey to Le Kef with them. On their return he stops and spends four days in Dougga.

Was he, like the Provençal slave before him, struck with passionate amazement so that he spent his days there drawing everything in sight? As soon as he is back in Tunis, he writes a long letter describing everything he saw, specifically the strange three-story mausoleum. While there, he made numerous pencil sketches, some of which he later traces over with ink. He methodically reproduces each of the monument's façades as well as numerous plans of the inner chambers on all three levels. Finally, he copies down the bilingual inscription— in the notes he wrote in Italian to accompany the reproduction he mentions two types of lettering, mistakenly referring to them as *punico e punico-ispanico*.

Thus it is not the mystery of the unknown writing that strikes him, although he senses something strange about the cenotaph, which he attributes to its architectural style, a mixture of Hellenistic inspiration and oriental archaism. He reproduces the Ionic columns with their capitals whose volutes are in the shape of lotus blossoms, and on each level the horizontal stone layer with the architrave and an Egyptian neck. He asks himself questions about the funerary functions of the whole: Had there been small funeral urns in the empty niches of the inner chambers?

Borgia spends all of 1816 exploring other sites in coastal and northern Tunisia; his accounts are regularly sent to the countess, where they are read to a circle of scholars and enthusiasts. In Naples, Borgia the military man is forgotten in favor of Borgia the archeologist. He finally returns to his country in January 1817 with the intention of publishing as quickly as possible the chronicle of his wonderful journey that so inspired him. A well-known engraver is already at work on a series of plates based on Borgia's wash drawings; among them is an engraving of the Libyco-Punic mausoleum of Dougga.

Alas, Borgia dies suddenly at the end of 1817. His widow assembles all his papers, the *Borgiana* (harvest of her husband's travels), and sells them to a French enthusiast, who promises to publish them quickly, but he in turn sells them to the national museum in Leyden ,which also acquires Humbert's papers. This entire unpublished body of work will remain dormant, unpublished, until… 1959.

Meanwhile, in a scholarly review in 1867 the traveler's son will lament the fact that the Dutch government did not keep its promise to make known his father's work. Meanwhile, luckily, several scholars will go to copy from this voluminous file at least the mysterious writing of the bilingual inscription of Dougga.

Years go by after Borgia: The strange alphabet keeps its mystery and the mausoleum stands intact—how long?—in the space and ruins of ex-Thugga.

3

THE ARCHEOLOGIST LORD

~~~~~

AT THE BEGINNING of the summer of 1832 in Algiers, the painter Delacroix, returning from a visit to Morocco, stops and spends three days painting at the home of a former *raïs*. On June 22 he departs once more, carrying in his sketches and in his memory the elements of the composition that several years later will become the masterpiece *Women of Algiers in Their Apartment*—a lighthouse on the outposts of the colonial darkness represented by Algerian history. Thus placed so suddenly and prominently on display for the public to see, the feminine Algeria will henceforth make itself invisible in its heart of darkness and iridescence for generations to come.

Delacroix left at the end of June, and on July 5 a British lord, Sir Granville Temple, who is a fanatic about archeology, lands in Algiers. Accompanied by his wife, his sister, a couple of English friends, and a young French artist, whose job it is to draw views and landscapes, Lord Temple stays with the English consul, St. John, who had witnessed the capture of Algiers by the French.

They launch into a fashionable social life "with the charming daughters of the duchess of Rovigo," and they attend the very brilliant ball given by the governor on July 29 (at which the former bey of Médéa appears, dazzling the foreigners with his oriental elegance). Ecstatic over the beauty of the countryside, which he explores from Algiers to Bouzareah, Sir Temple also has time to visit the American consul, discover the city, and note the price of merchandise at the market of Algiers, as well the number of schools (twenty-six Koranic, three Christian, and eight Jewish).

He leaves Algiers to return to the city of Bône, which, on March 28 of that same year, had been conquered by Colonel Yousouf. From there he sets off again by sea and has his presence announced to the English consul in Tunis when he arrives there on August 19.

The consul, Sir Thomas Reade, greets Lord Granville Temple and his family and friends at their boat and accompanies them to La Goulette; from there he takes them to his property at La Marsa. But Granville is dying to do just one thing.

The next morning I was going to walk on the site of great Carthage, he writes. It is the ultimate goal of his *Excursions en Méditerranée,* the collection that he will publish shortly after his return to London.

In it he recounts how, after having visited Monastir, Mahdia, and Jem, he wants to travel farther into the interior but is kept in Tunis by the incessant rains of January 1833. Finally, on the first day of Ramadan, he sets out on his ride eastward, which will take him, in four days, to the site of Dougga.

The next day at dawn Granville Temple begins to look around the area. He remarks that Doctor Shaw, who in the middle of the preceding century left a description of his travels in this region as well as in Algeria, never visited this city, although it must have been "remarkable and thriving with many beautiful buildings." The first of these that he admires is a temple of Jupiter with a dedication allowing him to date it back to the reign of Hadrian.

Lord Temple is drawn above all by how beautiful and well preserved the mausoleum standing in the center of an olive grove is. He notes its dimensions and describes the two stories and what remains of a third, the stepped foundations of the pyramid where a beautiful statue and other ornaments remain—one of them a quadriga with a warrior and a chariot driver. He also notes a statue of a draped woman, already damaged by bad weather.

On the east face a double inscription catches his eye and he is fascinated by it: One of the scripts is Punic—he quickly recognizes it. The other has unknown letters, probably "some form of old African," he says to himself. He supposes therefore that this mausoleum dates from the last years of Punic Carthage—shortly before its disappearance, in 146 B.C.E.—or after?

He in turn copies down the double inscription and in all good faith believes himself the first foreigner to do so. In any event, when his account, *Excursions en Méditerranée*, appears in London in 1835, this version of the bilingual inscription will be reproduced by the scholar Gésénius. Learned researchers will follow him in attempting to decipher the mysterious writing: Honneger, *Étienne Quatremère* (who had already published work on Punic inscriptions), but also de Saulcy and A. C. Judas (a specialist in the study of the Libyan language).

Lord Temple presses on with his journey into the regency of Tunis, where he takes notes both about the ancient past and its stones and about everyday life in the present. Before leaving the country he makes friends with a Dane, Falbe, who has lived near Tunis for eleven years and who has just published a topographical map of the ruins of Carthage.

These two amateurs will meet up again in Paris in 1837 in an archeological association established by eighteen members of high society (among them a prince, a duke, two counts, but also the painter Chassériau) to undertake "digs at Carthage and other ancient cities in the regencies of Barbary." Sir Temple and Falbe, because of their shared passion and their knowledge of the region, agree to go to the area themselves as volunteers in charge of directing the first excavations.

Summer 1837: To make up for the stinging failure of the siege of Constantine the previous autumn, the French government is actively preparing its revenge against the Algerians with the son of the king, the duke de Nemours, as one of the leaders of this campaign.

They decide on a military landing in Bône, attempting once again to take Constantine, where the bey Ahmed still rules.

Following behind the French army, Sir Temple and Falbe meet in Bône in September, where General Valée has promised to help the two archeologists by creating a scientific commission. The two take advantage of the occasion by identifying the ruins of Hippone, and they hope soon to locate those of Cirta, once the city has been captured.

Thus our two friends become witnesses, from an unexpected—apparently "scholarly"—perspective, to the siege and capture of Constantine in all its dramatic and murderous detail. Cirta, an eagle's nest that only on rare occasions over the centuries had been made to submit!

The siege begins 6 October 1837. It will be trying for both armies: Torrential rain falls without break until 12 October and Lord Temple is already dreaming a little less ardently of discovering the tomb of Masinissa! For six nights in succession it is the work of the engineer corps to move the artillery cannons, which sometimes tip over into the ravines despite all the efforts of sappers and zouaves. They flounder in the mud and the sticky earth clings to the feet of both men and horses.

Everything is told from the point of view of those laying siege, sometimes in vividly realistic detail: "happy were the men who had tents!" to rest in, says the narrator with a sigh. In the cemeteries of Koudier Aly, soldiers break open the sides of tombs and "took out the remains of the dead so that they could lie down in their place."

On the morning of the twelfth, good weather returns. Making a tour of inspection on horseback to study the area with his telescope, Damremont, head of the command post, is struck down by a cannon. He dies on the spot and is followed in turn by General Perrégaux, also fatally shot.

That very day the city is surrounded. The bey Ahmed, who thought it was impregnable ("nature has made it a second Gibraltar," writes Lord Temple) had only provided for weak fortifications. On the evening of the two French generals' death, the city is breached. On 13 October, at four in the morning, the attack is on, led by the Lamoricière's column.

Hand-to-hand combat, house by house, street by street, alley by alley; the battle is made even more relentless by the explosion of a munitions depot belonging to the resistants, many of whom are killed there. The defenders begin to withdraw into the Casbah. Lord Temple gives a rather brief account of one episode: the death of hundreds upon hundreds of the people of the city as they try to flee through the ravine of el-Medjerday. "They descend the precipice using ropes" that give way under the weight; "they are all dragged down onto each other as they fall." The next day, hundreds of bodies that have not been removed will be counted.

At the end of the morning of the fourteenth ("the night of 13–14 October there is a total eclipse of the moon between nine in the evening and two in the morning," adds the witness), the Casbah is taken: the tricolor flag floats over the city.

During the night, thanks to this eclipse perhaps, the bey Ahmed and most of his cavalry are able to reach the nearby mountains. As for the survivors, the civilian population either unable to or not wishing to flee, almost sixteen thousand of them remain, holed up in their tile-roofed houses. They begin the experience of French occupation: provisions of wheat and barley are requisitioned from each home to fill the needs of the conquering army. The city dwellers huddle over their memory, their patios, the invisibility of their women.

Gustave Flaubert, who will visit the city almost twenty years later—before heading east, like our archeologists, to Carthage—will have as his guide the grandson of the great Salah Bey (a legendary figure from the beginning of the century, a hero of the resistance, and martyred by the Turkish rulers). And now his descendent is a mere secretary of some French officer! Going down into the Rummel Gorge, the great writer recalls the fall of hundreds of unfortunate people attempting to flee—a scene from the past that was now the subject of a currently popular painting. At the bridge of el-Kantara, the great novelist muses over the wild scene: "this is a place that is both enchanting and satanic." Flaubert concludes magnificently: "I think of Jugurtha; the place resembles him. Constantine, moreover, is a true city in the ancient sense."

Let us return to October 1837 and to our two friends, Sir Temple and Falbe, living in the captured city. Doctor Shaw's English account in hand, they list the ancient monuments still in good repair twenty years earlier. Many have been demolished, but the underground cisterns are there; the fountain of Aïn el-Safsaf ("the poplar spring") described by Leon the African at the beginning of the sixteenth century is still there, but without the hieroglyphic characters, no trace of which remains.

In the Casbah, an old Byzantine church is almost intact. As for the famous bridge, when one enters through Bab el-Kantara, it is visible with its two rows of vaults and the "remarkable structure," about which Edrisi had already exclaimed. Our two tourists resume their calculations, locating various sites, then Sir Temple admires a statue of a woman with two elephants that Shaw had drawn. With two hands she lifts up to her belt the cape that she is wrapped in; the dress underneath fits closely. She is nodding her head—the features of her face are erased—to one side: her braided hair is down to her shoulders. At her feet there are little elephants that have lost their trunks.

The beautiful unknown woman in stone materializes: an immutable pagan idol, preserved because it was placed down low, set way down against the ravine. Although rage and death on the move spread out now above her head in these October days, the two foreigners, the Englishman and the Dane, have come only for the past. These men are only concerned with her, the unknown woman whose face has been eroded by the centuries, foreshadowing for them what if not destruction from now on?

4

DESTRUCTION

THE DESTRUCTION OF Cirta's freedom sounded the deathknell for Algerian independence, for any last bursts it made after 1830.

The bey Ahmed, who took the resistance off into the Aurès Mountains, becomes the head of an underground movement and will hold on for ten years more. To the west the emir Abd el-Kader continues to wage war; he will not be conquered until nine years later.

The year of Constantine's fall, the son of Hamdane Khodja, an important dignitary from Algiers, is in Paris. His reaction to the news of the disaster is to write an account of a journey he made earlier with his father who had to cross Kabylia—still undefeated—to meet with the bey Ahmed. During the negotiations with the tribal chiefs that were necessary in order to gain *anaia*, that is, the host's protection— the young Ali Effendi served as interpreter for his father in the Berber language.

Ali ben Hamdane Khodja had his text translated into French, and printed, by the orientalist de Saulcy. The latter had known Hamdane

Khodja, who spoke English and French fluently as well as Arabic and Turkish and had correspondents in several capitals of Europe. Hamdane Khodja tried in vain, after the surrender of the *dey* of Algiers, to save what could be saved, but rapidly became the leader of a peaceful opposition—a position that was hardly tenable. He was attacked for his wealth; he was pushed to the limit.

He came to Paris, where he had plenty of friends who supported a French presence that would respect individual Algerian freedoms. He wrote a book, *Le Miroir*, in which he denounced the encroachments by French soldiers in Algiers, thus becoming the first essayist on the subject of this servitude now beginning.

In 1836 he throws in the towel. Leaving his son in Paris and escorted by sixty friends and relations, he takes the road to Constantinople, where the sultan provides him with a pension. There he hopes to use Ottoman power to sway the politics of the Maghreb, not abandoning Ahmed Bey to his own forces alone. He corresponds with the latter in the name of the sultan, writing in code.

After his defeat and the conquest of his city, Ahmed Bey, in a letter to the sultan demanded that cannons and four thousand soldiers be sent. Now here in Constantinople, faced with the unrest breaking out in the Tripolitaine, Ahmed Bey is expected to be named the pasha of Libya. But the Turkish powers go back and forth for a long time, despite the warnings of Hamdane Khodja: "The French," he said, "are going to occupy Constantine; next they will infiltrate Tunis and Tripoli and carry their ambitions all the way into Egypt, I have no doubts. Tomorrow it will be too late!"

The statue of the Constantine woman prefigured another destruction for Lord Temple and Falbe—in such a rush were they to get to the ruins of Carthage, there was so much to do in this year of 1837!

Of course, ever since Napoleon's expedition in Egypt, there had been treasure there, inexhaustible treasure, giving rise to trafficking, theft and irreparable loss: Ancient objects (including mummies and papyruses) are easily negotiable and enrich the intermediaries. Rivalries become intense among states and consular agents in Cairo.

The consul general of England in Tunis, Thomas Reade, the same man who welcomed Lord Temple and his friends in 1833, sees by Temple's second trip that there is increased interest in Carthaginian archeology. Knowing the extent to which his colleagues from every nation are rivals in this lucrative commerce in Egypt, he goes for the bilingual stele at Dougga. He decides to take it and sell it to the British Museum. He counts on getting at least fifteen hundred pounds for it.

In 1842 he goes to Dougga and hires there a team of workers to pull down the monument and bring back the stele! He has probably obtained some authorization from an official of the bey's government, it being a well-known fact that the bureaucracies of Muslim countries are more often than not indifferent to this remembering of antiquity... Reade has the entire façade bearing the engraved stele demolished, and the stele is sawed in two to make it easier to transport.

The local workers hired on the spot lack the technical means to detach this stele carefully. The other blocks of stone stacked on each other should have been pulled away to get to the block on which the inscription fit. They throw down the top blocks by lifting them with heavy levers. Thus the bilingual stele carried off to Tunis leaves a field full of ruins behind it!

A French visitor, Victor Guérin, who was there more than ten years later, described the scene: "In the jumbled heap I caught sight of the trunk of a statue of a winged woman (but with no head, arms or legs). On one of the remaining blocks a chariot pulled by four horses can be seen; the driver of it is mutilated, as is a second statue of a winged woman..."

Earlier an Englishman, Nathan Davis, had even more fiercely denounced "the shameless demolition" resulting from "the avarice of Europeans driven only by money matters." He, too, described this mausoleum broken apart "barbarously," and called his compatriot's plundering a "crime."

In a sad irony he reports that the consul indeed sold the stele to the British Museum, but not for the fifteen hundred pounds he had counted on—for a mere five pounds!

Time goes by and Tunisia is now a protectorate of French.

The field of ruins, Punic as well as Roman, becomes an area reserved for French archeologists. One of them, C. L. Poinsot, attempts to reconstruct the cenotaph of Dougga, making use of the sketches made in 1765 by J. Bruce in his travels.

Shortly after 1900 they begin the careful work of reconstructing the monument, making initial use of the stones still there, reconstituting the sculptures of the winged women, the quadriga, and the chariot driver. In 1910, with the exception of the bilingual inscription, which is still in London, the mausoleum is once again standing, almost intact, but stripped of its double writing.

Fifty years later C. L. Poinsot will devote himself to studying the papers of Count Borgia, forgotten in Leyden. Reconstituting a portion of the stele's secret, he will prove that at Dougga there were, in fact, two steles, and that the second—probably the most important—of these had been partially erased.

Thus, even if the funerary monument has regained its hybrid—half Greek, half oriental—elegance, some mystery still seems to hang over Dougga, over the lapidary writing, the words in stone that were desecrated and carried off but also those words, victims of erosion, that have almost entirely vanished.

5

THE SECRET

THE WRITING AT DOUGGA began to raise interesting questions starting with the scholar Gésénius, who outlines several conjectures after learning about it through the copy published in 1835 by Lord Temple. In Paris, de Saulcy does detailed research, then Honegger visits the site, but it is Célestin Judas, especially, who, during the years from 1846 through the 1860s, clarifies the meaning of the seven lines in Libyan and succeeds in listing the twenty-three characters of the alphabet.

A work begun at the end of the preceding century had just appeared. The author, Venture de Paradis, had compiled a French-Berber dictionary that was published, with a preface by Champollion, in 1838. Célestin Judas will base his work on numerous remarks made by Venture de Paradis, who had persistently questioned the Kabylians of Algeria about the structure of their dialect.

Throughout the nineteenth century all the questions asked about the stele of Dougga focused on some vanished alphabet, some lost language—one as ancient as the elegant figures of African princes who paid visits to the pharaohs and were melancholically rendered on Egyptian frescos.

Paleographers, following the example of Champollian, felt they were penetrating into a cavern of images and scripts that were indeed exciting but from the past.

Now comes a trickle of doubt: What if this "old African," which in North Africa the indigenous people themselves consider to be merely an oral dialect, what if this "barbarous" speech, before being accepted as "Berber," used to be written? What if it was a written language, was the same as Libyan, whose shadows loom throughout the seven centuries of Carthaginian power, yes, what if this archaic alphabet had preceded the Phoenician culture and survived long after it?

Then suppose this strange writing came alive, was a voice in the present, was spoken out loud, was sung. Suppose this so-called dialect of men who spoke by turn Punic with Carthage, Latin with the Romans and the romanized until Augustine's time, and Greek, then Arab for thirteen centuries, continued, generation after generation, kept alive for endogamic use (mainly with their mothers, their wives, and their daughters). Suppose this speech, this language—the one in which Jugurtha expressed his insurmountable energy as he fought and died, the very one Masinissa spoke throughout his sixty-year reign—went back even farther! Suppose, even longer ago, the Barbarians/Berbers, the great pharaohs' guests and sometimes their friends or rivals, mentioned by Herodotus of Halicarnassus—suppose those ancestors, who apparently sometimes surrendered to peoples from the east or north and sometimes rose up, struggling until they were put down—yes, suppose these first men and these first women had written this alphabet on skins, shards, stone, on their horses' and camels' flanks—same signs, same symbols—which then became indecipherable until the mid-nineteenth century, in short until a stele with seven lines on it was carried to the British Museum, leaving in its wake a field of broken statues and felled columns.

And leaving scholars in their studies to seek and study and listen and suppose... always with the thought that they are on a quest for some lost meaning—underground echoes.

And yet the writing was alive. Its sonority, its music, its rhythms still reeled on around them, around the travelers and their followers going back and forth between Dougga and Cirta. It traveled into conquered Constantine and onto the Kabylian mountains, still rebellious fifteen years after the fall of Constantine, and then, beyond the dunes and sands of the Sahara, it went all the way to the heart of the desert itself! For there, from the Fezzan to Mauritania, among the nomads who thought they had forgotten the Numidians, Libyan letters from earlier times have stealthily slipped in ever since. Perhaps they came in the days of the Garamantes—who gave up their horses for the newly introduced camels, who let the herds of ostriches disappear from their lands until only their silhouettes, in a dancing, animated crowd, remained, engraved on the walls of caves a thousand years old.

The Libyan letters, however they did it, escaped all together, curled up as far away as possible in the reddish dunes as if propelled by some immobile god. They went off to hide in the palms of noble women—the queens, the wives, the lovers of the Veiled Men.

The writing of the sun, fertile secret of the past!

This lost writing was resurrected in various stages over the course of several decades and once more with an Anglo-French rivalry as their basis.

In 1822, after traveling from Alexandria to the Tripolitan regency, a man named Scholz brings various unfamiliar characters to the attention of the public. He believes some of these signs found on old, ancient monuments as well as on Arab buildings, to have been carved several centuries earlier while others, in contrast, seem of rather recent origin.

In 1827 another traveler—his name is Pacho, and he is from Cyrenaica—notices other odd signs on buildings and rocks; he also sees the same signs written by nomads on their camels' flanks. He reaches the rapid conclusion that this is not an alphabet of some lost language but utilitarian signs the shepherds use.

Before Pacho, however, during the years 1822 and 1823, Walter Oudney, a medical doctor returning from an expedition, brought back nineteen characters that he had seen traced on a Roman monument at Germa and then on rocks in the deserts between Tripoli and the Fezzan, places frequented by the Tuaregs. He determines that some of the signs are several centuries old and others were made more recently. Oudney, publishing his account, is quite clear: In Germa the inhabitants are unable to read most of the inscriptions. But, pushing beyond their borders, the traveler meets up with the Tuaregs and learns to understand their writing: "We discovered for the first time that the characters traced on the rocks were Tuareg!"

This English account is available in Paris in 1836, where first de Saulcy and then Célestin Judas learn about it. The mystery begins to split open: They finally say to themselves, what if this writing that is so ancient were still being written?

So, at the same moment, in Paris, Ali Effendi ben Hamdane Khodja is telling de Saulcy about his stay with the Kabylians when he was traveling with his father. De Saulcy translates this account into French. To thank him, Ali Effendi agrees to lend one or two letters that he still has from the correspondence between his father and the bey Ahmed.

The Parisian scholar is confronted by the following puzzle: The main text is in Arab; but, running along the sides, the bey Ahmed has written several lines of a secret writing: just simple code, de Saulcy thinks. Plagued by curiosity, however, he gets the idea overnight to compare these signs with the ones copied by Dr. Oudney in Cyrenaica. Then, to decipher the first line, de Saulcy remembers that any letter written between Muslims begins with the sacred formula: "In the name of God the Merciful, the Forgiving!..."

Suddenly the Frenchman understands: and what if the bey Ahmed, who could obviously speak Chaoui Berber, has learned—thanks to Saharan nomads passing through Constantine—this mysterious writing and used it as a code, thinking that this alphabet, now so rare, is the only thing that can ward off the danger of interception?

In short, de Saulcy concludes in amazement, contrary to what Venture de Paradis believed when he made a point of learning Berber but thought it normal to write it in Arabic characters, in short, what if Berber had always been a written language? Was still written? Since the dawn of time?

First in Constantine, then after having been driven from his city, the bey Ahmed keeps up a political and military correspondence using this script, whereas, the majority of the population at that time—in the middle of the nineteenth century—have almost entirely lost the ancient alphabet. The resisting leader uses it to write dangerous things, actually to ward off danger!

He will surrender in 1847, a year after the emir Abd el-Kader. There is no mention of the language in which he signs his surrender; moreover, did he sign anything at all on this occasion? In 1830, when the dey of Algiers, without really putting up a fight, writes his capitulation, it is in Turkish—the official language of the time—that he hands himself over to the invader.

After the defeat of the bey Ahmed, the Tuaregs will remain free for seventy more years. As if the ancestral writing, maintained outside of any state of submission, went hand in hand with the intractability and mobility of a people who, in a gesture of supreme elegance, let their women preserve the writing while their men wage war in the sun or dance before the fires at night...

Finally then, Célestin Judas, returning to the inscriptions that English travelers brought back from the Fezzan and Cyrenaica, and aware of de Saulcy's intuitions, sees the solution—clear as day: Whether Libyan or Berber, for thousands of years this has been the same writing with a few variations: ancient and neo-Libyan.

This is the 1850s. It is during this period that Gustave Flaubert visits Constantine and mentions the grandson of Salah Bey, as well as his French superior, Captain Boissonnet, who is in correspondence with de Saulcy. Boissonnet has a highly valued informant, el Hadj Abd el-Kader, the secretary of the sheik of Touggourt, who traveled in the past with nomad caravanners. Boissonnet gets "a small example of tifinagh writing" from el-Kader and sends it to the orientalist in Paris. "I was struck by the similarity between these written characters and the ones on the Libyan inscription from Dougga," he says in conclusion.

Of course, this informant has not visited his country for six or seven years, so his memory must not be completely reliable. Captain Boissonnet manages to convince him to resume his contacts with the nomads, maybe even to undertake another trip himself—his seventeenth!—to the Touat.

Will el Hadj Abd el-Kader of Touggourt risk such a thing? The fact remains that, the next year, he sends Captain Boissonnet of Constantine a second list, this time more complete, of the signs currently in use among the Veiled Men.

Once again Célestin Judas provides a meticulous account, comparing the signs on the stele from Dougga, the characters brought back by the Englishmen from Cyrenaica, and those sent to Paris by the captain in Constantine. The same signs are on the stone and on the rocks of the Fezzan and written on their camels' flanks by Tuareg warriors.

It is 1857—just before the English and French travelers to Dougga discover to their despair the "barbarous crime" committed by Consul Reade against the bilingual stele. But in this same moment the meaning itself—and the music and the throbbing orality—of this alphabet comes back to life, no longer stifled!

Thus, during the 1860s, the stirring course of a very ancient civilization is restored. Though its memory had, indeed, preserved the language in all its toughness and bitter-sweetness, the letters now return to their source, seek to be written again, and by everyone!

While the secret is revealed, how many women and men are there still, from the oasis of Siwa in Egypt to the Atlantic and even beyond—to the Canary Islands, how many of them—how many of us still—all singing, weeping, ululating, but also loving or rather being in a position where it is impossible to love—yes, how many of us are there who, although the heirs of the bey Ahmed, the Tuaregs and the last century and the *aediles,* bilingual Roman magistrates in charge of the monument of Dougga, feel exiled from their first writing?

6

THE STELE AND THE FLAMES

DOUGGA. IT IS THE SPRING of the year 138 B.C.E. The city notables are presenting, therefore, a magnificent cenotaph to commemorate the tenth anniversary of the death of the great Masinissa. After reigning sixty years as king of all Numidia, he had died at the age of ninety. It was he who made it possible for the Romans to take Carthage for the last time, conquering it completely.

It has been eight years since Hannibal's age-old capital went up in flames after a siege lasting almost five years. What astonishing, unflagging energy and desperate resistance on the part of the Carthaginians! How amazingly the Romans pulled together following their senate's implacable decree: *"Delenda Carthago!"* And in the end—those April days in 146 B.C.E.

Masinissa saw the siege begin and saw the glorious capital gradually suffocate. But before Carthage will die, consumed by tortures and fire, he dies of old age.

Masinissa died before he could see his dogged enemy vanish. His son, Micipsa, who is present at this commemoration at Dougga, witnessed the tragedy; his other son, Gulussa, with his thousands of fearless, mounted soldiers, took part in the event, but on Scipio's side, the side of the conquerors.

When the carnage begins, Scipio Emilien (who has summoned from Rome his teacher of Greek literature, the writer Polybe, who was thus fated to be the chronicler of the fall of Carthage), this Scipio—adopted grandson of Hannibal's rival, Scipio the Great, decides to save some part of the splendor of Carthage.

Of course, the ancient treasure taken from the Syracusans was returned to them; of course, fifty thousand survivors were spared and left as slaves; but what could he preserve of Carthage, other than its writing—its books?

Everything is burning, everything vanishes into dust and ashes: sanctuaries, palaces, the magnificent statues of Baal. In a few days the beauty and munificence of a society that has endured for seven centuries disappears.

Scipio—with his old master standing behind him—raises his hand to intervene: "Save them! Save the books!"

Then with a condescending smile he announces that he does not do this with the intention of carrying the books off to Rome! No. Romans do not care about Carthaginian heritage. Quite the contrary: they will seed the land with salt to give notice that it must become sterile.

"Save the books!" Someone who has heard what Scipio said repeats it: "Not for us, not for us to carry off to Rome! Save the books to give to our allies!"

"Our allies?"

"The Berber kings!"

And so, just barely rescued from the flames already eating into the walls of the most important library, the Carthaginian books are safely set aside and carried away in copper-studded metal boxes.

They will be delivered a few hours later to the tent of King Micipsa once the general gives the order. Micipsa is not surprised and thanks no one. He commands them to carry this booty to Cirta, the lofty capital. *We'll see what happens there,* he thinks, and it is as if the memory of his father's arrogant enemies were rising intact, over the flames.

Micipsa is thinking, in fact, about these books as he stands there, his calm, heavy silhouette that of a man in his fifties, the one they respectfully call the Life of the Living. The important men of Dougga form a circle around the steles engraved with their double alphabet.

"Bilingual," the head of the technical team, a man named Atban, makes clear: "We wanted the inscriptions to be bilingual."

No one present forgets that Masinissa formerly declared Carthaginian to be the official language in his kingdom, but how comforting to be there among themselves finally, speaking their ancestral language that is carved equal with the other, this time in stone!

The town notables speak: "May the great Masinissa and the Life of the Living both be praised throughout future generations. Do we not owe to their fighting and their vigilance the fact that we were not dragged into the ruin of Carthage or under the Roman yoke that is going to grow stronger and more burdensome!" In Dougga, the peace-loving city, where we still live...

Micipsa goes up to the steles. He checks each inscription and thanks the carpenters, the stone-carvers as well as the decorator and the sculptor; the statues of the winged goddesses are magnificent.

"So," he says without solemnity but as if talking to himself, "at the height of my powers I was granted the sight of the destruction of the greatest metropolis on earth!"

Two or three representatives of the municipality of Dougga begin to make speeches. The first one speaks in Carthaginian, showing off his fluency; obviously he has studied in Carthage and is still proud of it. The second, a stockier man, makes his speech in Berber, with something like the rediscovered comfort of relaxing in the warmth of being "among one's own." And the third man, the youngest but the most gaudily dressed, brings it all to a quick conclusion—in Latin, *the language of the future,* he must have thought.

Micipsa, who has been listening patiently, raises his arm; he begins by thanking the orators for the eulogies that, one after the other, they have made to his father, Masinissa. "I would like, before you all, to ask a favor of my young nephew! It was not ten years ago that he saw, as did we, our enemy vanish as if in a nightmare. Now he reminds me that he is one of the people who speaks yesterday's language best! May he then read for us all, and in both scripts, the stele dedicated to my father and the one bearing the names of the skilled artisans! My dear nephew!" he insists before everyone.

And Jugurtha steps forward.

In a very clear voice resounding through the respectful silence, he begins with "the Others' language," as he calls it, and his Carthaginian rises in praise of the great Masinissa, his ancestors, and his three sons. Then he calls out the names of the team from Atban in the same manner.

He takes a breath for a moment, a brief moment, and in the intensifying heat the chatter of a cicada is heard; he begins to read again, this time in, he says emphatically, "the language of our ancestors."

All present reply with rounds of applause. The young Berber prince stands erect and unsmiling there for a moment before the elegant monument. Soon he moves away under the olive trees.

To leave! envisions Jugurtha who is not yet eighteen.

He uses up his days hunting and in battle practice with his fellow students. He studies, at least when he is living in Cirta, law texts and historical chronicles in Carthaginian—the family library enriched, so much enriched, by so many new books, the booty of Carthage...

Jugurtha has read the account of earlier wars between Rome and Carthage, but it is neither the ghost of Hasdrubal the Great nor even the ghost of glorious Hannibal, triumphant in Rome and many other Italian cities, that haunts him. No. He dreams more about the indomitable enemy of these two heroes: great Scipio.

Because the young man remembers: He was barely seven years old, he was standing there, frozen, at the gates of the palace of Cirta, above the cliffs, when a Roman named Scipio, a leader who was scarcely thirty, said to have been the adopted grandson of Scipio Africanus in Rome, dismounted first, at the head of his troops.

The child Jugurtha stared at him with fiery eyes. Listened to what they were saying in Latin. Micipsa introduced himself and greeted the Roman guest in the proper manner: "My father," he said, "died scarcely two hours ago! Certainly we have awaited your arrival for the burial. The women who come to weep, and his wives as well, are now at the place where he lies!"

Then, as was customary, he wrapped the general in a spotless woolen toga so that he could cross the first threshold.

At the entrance to the vestibule the child appeared, standing bare-chested and holding himself proudly, his hands together and ready to make the offering. He offered the general the cup of goat's milk and three dates soaked in acacia honey.

Jugurtha raised his hands high. The general lowered his weatherbeaten face, weighed down by his helmet. He smiled with his eyes and his mouth at the same time as the child-prince slowly spoke the

words of hospitality in Libyan which his uncle, Micipsa, scrupu-
lously translated. "He is welcoming you in our language: 'May the
mourning,' he says, 'be eased because of your arrival, O friend!'"

Before drinking, Scipio Emilien studied the child's face for a long
time. He asked his name.

"Yougourtha," the child replied in his sharp voice.

7

THE DEPORTED WRITER

WHAT JUGURTHA DID will not be recorded in Berber: the letters of this alphabet, scattered on the ground like the bas-relief Roman chariots, the quadrigas, and the winged goddesses from the dismantled monument of Dougga, seem to have fled by themselves, going all the way to the desert of the Garamantes to slip into the sands and settle onto the immemorial rocks.

Jugurtha and his passion for battle will not be inscribed in the Punic alphabet either. Carthage is no longer there, even if Caesar will attempt to make it rise again on the high plain that the Romans made sterile. Carthage is no longer there, but its language is still current on the lips of both the educated and the uneducated in the cities that fell but were not yet romanized. The language, in fact, like a current, runs freely on, never becoming fixed. The Carthaginian language dances and quivers for five or six centuries to come. Freed of the soldiers of Carthage, of the priests of Carthage, of the sacrifice of the children of Carthage, Carthaginian speech, free and unsettled, transmutes and transports with vivid poetry the spirits of the Numidians who yesterday made war on Carthage. Now they will understand that they were almost making violent, bitter love to it—wanting to desecrate it.

Later and elsewhere, in the first century B.C.E., the same sort of ferment and the same inability to record its outbreaks of resistance will be seen in Gaul as it fights for its independence. Here, too, the task of writing about the defeated Vercingetorix will fall to the conqueror, Caesar. Later.

When Jugurtha reads the double inscription at the request of Micipsa on this spring day at Dougga, however, Polybe, "the greatest mind of the time," who will soon be seventy, writes.

He records the destruction of Carthage. Before him rise the heroes of the tragedy of the blaze that for six days and six nights and for weeks to come seems to burn and redden the four corners of the known Mediterranean. Houses endlessly collapse in the streets of Byrsa, bodies living and dead of women, children, and old people mingle, and the horses of Roman and Numidian soldiers trample them, splitting human brains into this mud mixed with cries. Nine hundred desperate people shut themselves up in the temple of Aesculapius. In their midst on the roof the wife of Hasdrubal, the Carthaginian leader who is now a suppliant kneeling at the feet of the Roman general, holds his children by the hand, improvises a lyric of scorn, and shouts it at him; she refuses to have her life or the lives of her little ones saved and then leaps with them into the crackling fire... Little by little, a line of slaves leaves the city and its ruins; in sudden magnanimity Scipio Emilien has spared these survivors. And this Scipio, deeply shaken by a metaphysical nostalgia, declaims the verses of the *Iliad* describing the fall of Troy and the end of empires.

Old Polybe was present for the literary musings of his disciple Scipio who, once it is all decided, at the height of his complete and deadly victory, becomes elegantly sorrowful.

Polybe of Megalopolis, the man deported from the Peloponnesus sixteen years ago, his spirit now full of the flames of Carthage, full of the delirium of proud souls struck down and the thousands of trampled bodies, as well as images of despair and flight, prepares to write about the destruction; destruction is his point of departure.

Before he returns home to Greece, he makes a request to see the Atlantic Ocean, to look at the coast from the land of the Moors (present-day Morocco) to the Mauritanian shores: he is passionate about geography, as if now truly tired of history—too heavy, too somber. He wants instead to see the physical world, landscapes, animals ("as for the quantity and power of the elephants, the lions and panthers, the beauty of the ostriches," he writes, "there is absolutely nothing of the sort in Europe, but Africa is filled with these species").

Once back in his own country, in the autumn of the same year, Polybe must then bear the sight of the sack of Corinth, "pearl of Attica." He would try to act as a negotiator and arrange better terms for his people, but a second time he is present, helplessly, at an irreversible fall of Achaean autonomy beneath the boots and brutality of savage Roman soldiers. He watches the light of Greece suddenly flickering out; he accepts it and writes.

But I, today's humble narrator, a woman, say that whereas Jugurtha at Dougga reads in the ancestral language for the last time, the writing of Polybe is nourished by all this simultaneous destruction. (He witnesses first the razing of Carthage, then the statues of Corinth, knocked down or carried away in shards, and, to finish it all off, he soon will have to contemplate the burning of Numantia and the dead Spaniards convulsed in their grandiose heroism.) I say that his writing, composed in a language that was, of course, maternal, but espoused by the cultivated minds of the West at that time, runs freely over the tablets and is polygamous!

As if, giving an account of death—the death of men, the death of ancient cities, and especially the death of the spirit of light that had shone through the darkness—Polybe, writing in this third alphabet the account of his life—his political deportation, his observation of the seat of power in Rome, his journeys, as well as the sight of these immense ruins at the very moment that they come crashing down—Polybe, almost in spite of himself, turned the coat of mail worn by all resistance inside out, the one implied by a language of poetry.

In fact for him the writing of history is writing first of all. Into the deadly reality that he describes he instills some obscure germ of life. This man who should be faithful to his own people justifies, consoles, and tries to console, himself. We see him, especially, confusing points of view. In the destruction his writing sets itself at the very center of a strange triangle, in a neutral zone that he discovers, though he did not expect it or seek it out.

We see him, far from Carthage, but also far from nearby Corinth, writing neither as a loyalist nor as a collaborator. The mere fact of his history somewhere else nourishes his astonishing "realism."

Polybe the historian—who did not merely set out to give an account of civil war's fatal effects like his fiery predecessor, Thucydides—Polybe the deported writer, returning in the twilight of his life to his native land, sees that he no longer has a land or even a country (the latter enslaved and in chains). All that he has is a language whose beauty warms him and that he uses to enlighten the enemies of yesterday who are now his allies.

He writes. And his language, his hand, his memory, and all his powers just before they fade, contribute to this untimely, yet necessary transmission. Is that why his work, like the stele of Dougga, after having fed the appetite for knowledge and the curiosity of his successors for several centuries, all at once, unexpectedly and in great slabs, is erased?

Because Polybe's accounts of Carthage, of Corinth, and of Numantia, exist henceforth only in scattered scraps, only in bits of relfections in the mirrors held up by imitators, those writers of lesser stature, Appien, Diodorus of Sicily, and a few others.

As if this literary ascendance exuded some danger, some acceleration toward its own erasure that would prove inevitable!

Abalessa

"Departures departures departures
In these anchorages
A wind to loosen trees
Spins around its chains"

—MALEK ALLOULA
"Rêveurs/Sépultures"
(Dreamers/Burials)

Let me finally turn my musings to the royal Tin Hinan, the ancestor of the noble Tuaregs of Hoggar. Her history had long been told like a dream wreathed in legends, a fleeting silhouette as evanescent as smoke, or a ghost, or a myth, an imaginary figure. She suddenly became solid thanks to archeological discoveries by a French-American team in 1925. Tin Hinan existed. Her so moving mortal remains (the skeleton of a woman closely related to the pharaonic type) were taken from the necropolis of Abalessa and carried away to the museum of Algiers.

Yes, let me dream about Tin Hinan, the fugitive princess, who made her way into the very heart of the desert of deserts!

She was born in the north: in the Tafilalt, in the fourth century C.E.,
just after the reign of Constantine. What young girl's reason could have
made her decide to flee this northern Berber land in the company of her
attendant, Takamat, and a group of servants? What reason, private or
political, made her decide to abandon everything—despite her youth and
the fact that she was perhaps to be the ruler—and push on beyond the
oases of the Sahara? Was it because freedom—her freedom or her family's
or her group's—was threatened?

The Tuaregs ever since that time like to tell of her expedition: Tin
Hinan, riding a white female camel, is accompanied by faithful Takamat
and a caravan composed mostly of women, young girls, white and black
intermingled. From their country they carry with them dates and millet,
rare and precious objects, the royal jewels of course, as well as the vases
and urns required by the pagan religion they practice.

The route to Hoggar was long. In the final stages food became scarce.
The situation became critical: to die of hunger in the desert!

Takamat on her dromedary or Tin Hinan mounted high on her
mount—the story does not decide which of the two friends—sees the lit-
tle mounds on the ground formed by anthills. Takamat, with the help of
the servants, sets about gathering, grain by grain, the harvest of the hard-
working ants! Thanks to her patience Tin Hinan and her cortège are able
to continue their journey. Finally Hoggar is close, a green and fertile val-
ley opens up before them. Saved!

They settle there west of Tamanrasset: Abalessa was a site of pilgrim-
age even before the mausoleum of the princess was discovered there.

One day in 1925 the Frenchman Reygasse and the American Prorok
enter the chamber of the dead princess, seventeen centuries after she was
placed there in the center of a vast necropolis containing eleven other

burial places. Around it a road was laid out for the religious processions that fervently circled the dead women!

This funerary grouping, for its dimensions, its complex organization,. the thickness of its walls, and its basalt stones, is the most imposing pre-Islamic necropolis in the region.

I find that I am always dreaming about the day that Tin Hinan was laid to rest at Abalessa. They stretched her out on a bed of sculptured wood. Her thin body, pointed east and covered with cloth and large leather ornaments, lay on its back with its arms and legs slightly bent under.

Tin Hinan—as the two archeologists verify by studying her skeleton—wears seven silver and seven gold bracelets on her left wrist and a single silver bracelet on her right; a string of antimony beads circles her right ankle. Precious and exquisite pearls cover her breast.

Near her, dates and fruits had been placed in baskets; nothing remains of them but pits and seeds. Facing the recumbent body there is a stylized statuette of a woman (her portrait?) that has not completely vanished, as well as some pottery, fragments of which remain.

A gold coin stamped with the likeness of the Emperor Constantine is still there; in a nearby room a Roman lamp from the third century is preserved. So, despite the distance of centuries, the chronological date of the tomb can be fixed.

But there is something especially troubling to my stubborn dream in its attempts to reassemble the ashes of time, to hold on to the traces around these miraculously preserved tombs. Especially troubling (even though I am just as disturbed by Tin Hinan's removal to Algiers) are the tifinagh *inscriptions found here. They are very ancient in origin and they can also be found on the walls of the neighboring chambers (the* chouchatts*), where each of the princess's friends was buried in turn.*

Libyan writings. Earlier even than the writing at Dougga, they are in Libyan script, no longer understood by the Tuaregs, who respectfully followed the archeologists into the tomb, then averted their gaze when faced with the recumbent Tin Hinan.

And so I imagine the princess of the Hoggar who, when she fled in the past, carried with her the archaic alphabet, then confided the characters to her friends just before she died.

Thus, more than four centuries after the resistance and dramatic defeat of Yougourtha in the north, also four centuries before the grandiose defeat of la Kahina—the Berber queen who will resist the Arab conquest—Tin Hinan of the sands, almost obliterated, leaves us an inheritance—and does so despite her bones that, alas, have now been disturbed. Our most secret writing, as ancient as Etruscan or the writing of the runes, but unlike these a writing still noisy with the sounds and breath of today, is indeed the legacy of a woman in the deepest desert.

Tin Hinan buried in the belly of Africa!

PART THREE
A SILENT DESIRE

"Confession is nothing,
knowledge is everything."

—HERMANN BROCH
Hoffmansthäl et son temps

"Fugitive Without Knowing It"

There are four of them, and when the message hanging from the end of a reed comes out through the closed window, it is only intended for the fourth man…

The four are captives and probably a sorry sight—all except this fourth man receiving the missive in Arabic (a language that is a mystery to him) that comes with a tidy sum of gold. This writing in the native language, translated for him by a renegade who is in on the secret, comes from a mysterious woman of noble birth, the beloved only daughter of her wealthy father.

That is the story of the Captive and Zoraidé from Don Quixote. *I imagine (and why not?) that this entrance of the Algerian woman into the first great novel of modern times actually took place in Algiers between 1575 and 1579. Somewhere beneath a blind window this note of alarm was sent by a woman who was perhaps not necessarily the most beautiful nor the wealthiest nor the sole heir of her father, no, but certainly she was a woman who was locked away.*

Because she has been secretly spying on the wretched world of the convicts doing their hard labor in prison but out of doors, the unknown woman boldly dares to initiate the dialogue from her enclosed and gilded prison.

The dialogue with the other: not particularly because he is this other, not at all, but because she is able to discern the true nobility and worthiness (that of the hero of Lepanto) beneath the tatters indicating this man's temporary loss of place in the world. A voyeur, with her lynx-like gaze, like a madwoman, relishing the danger, she offers herself as the liberator of the person who will venture with her to make the ultimate transgression. Even as she plots the course, does she have any premonition that, at the end of the journey, she will find herself the wife of this Christian or perhaps some other, but that above all she will find herself a foreigner, a stranger in the language of Cervantes?

Of course, right from the start the fugitive woman will recognize the images of Marie-Mériem in the church. However, in return for making this eventful trip with a whole group of people among whom she shines like a jewel, in the end she will see herself reduced to the role of stunningly beautiful deaf-mute—but then she will write no more.

Freeing the slave-hero from the dungeons of Algiers, she sets herself free from the father who has given her everything except freedom, leaving him behind on the shores of Africa, and he will curse her for her betrayal. She exchanges her gilded cage (the richest house in Algiers, where she was queen) for an elsewhere that is boundless but uncertain.

Her writing is erased. No one can read it, so now it is useless. She is indeed the first Algerian woman to write—Zoraidé who meets, if not with Don Miguel, then at least with Don Quixote's captive. The writing of a fugitive: a writing whose very essence is ephemeral. And the Knight of the Sad Countenance will be her first witness in the Christian world, while the language buzzing or written all around her will, for the present, allow her only a silent gaze. Which is, consequently, the end of the initial dialogue, if not of the dazzled, then of the dazzling, presence of the traveler.

All up and down the Mediterranean this is the way the first exchange takes place: a portentous intermingling of the sexes—first of languages, then gazes, before the bodies collapse into each other. An ambiguous transmutation of roles: the woman free and the man a slave, the first image of the couple in this shift in worlds, that will—after numerous fluctuations, including a twofold and simultaneous servitude—result in a different equilibrium. The couple will be composed of the strange, foreign, Moorish woman—a Christian wife who is neither free nor a slave—and the soldier freed from his chains, but not at all from wretchedness and uncertainty...

From the start the dominant theme of this loosely connected tale concerns a woman writing in Arabic, writing that on several occasions takes on weight by the addition of a gift of gold. The woman who writes is the one who pays, but she is also the thief and traitor in the eyes of her father and her family. She is the woman who, in the country garden in the Sahel of Algiers, dreams up the plot and sets it in motion, then, in the middle of the night, collapses in the arms of the stranger, and yet persists in her wish to run away. The journey she began wearing a gown studded with diamonds will end with her in the clothes of a pauper; her face veiled as it had been at home, she will make her way riding on the back of a donkey: and so exoticism creates a backwash.

Zoraidé's story, told, with her present but silent, by the former captive to the guests at a country inn where Don Quixote and Sancho Panza are staying, is indeed the metaphor for Algerian women writing today—among them myself.

My family's city, the former Caesarea, was repopulated by hundreds of Moriscos, the people who were expelled en masse in Cervantes's time, in

*a final and profound bloodletting inflicted by Spain on itself at the begin-
ning of the seventeenth century. They found refuge in the cities of the
northern Maghreb, one of which was my very ancient little city, the
romanized ex-capital.*

*These families, therefore, made Zoraidé's journey, but in the opposite
direction, bringing with them the Mohammedan faith that for three or
four generations, since 1492, they had been practicing in secret. Amid the
general pushing and shoving of the exoduses and sea adventures, they in
turn will look like renegades...*

*The women of my city in those days, these refugee women, in the
modest patios of impoverished houses, make jasmine and lemon trees
bloom again, while their men, when they do not choose to cultivate trees
on the surrounding mountainous slopes, return to the sea for expeditions
of revenge and pillage, as new pirates...*

*Three centuries after these journeys from which they will never
return, just before the 1920s, my mother was born there, in the midst of
these families who, with a naïve pride, still displayed the keys to their lost
houses in Córdoba and Grenada. What was this legacy that she inherited and what did she transmit to me of this memory already covered in
sand? A few details about the embroidery of women's costumes, some
residual accent distorting the local dialect, Arabic-Andalusian speech kept
as long as possible... Above all, the music known as* andalouse *that was
called "classical," the music that simple artisans—Muslim and Jewish
cobblers, barbers or tailors—practiced conscientiously whenever they
gathered in the evening. At the same time, among the groups of women,
the cantilenas of women musicians with their graceful, languorous
rhythms maintained rhetorical figures, an old-fashioned prettiness, and
the sweetness that masked the pain of the glorious epoch created by the
intermingling of races, languages, and knowledge back there.*

Thus I spent the summers of my early childhood surrounded by women who sang or embroidered. These odalisques young or old of a city closed in upon itself, where only the lute could complain out loud, passed on to me this still flickering light from the women's Andalusia that still provided us with a little nourishment across the centuries.

My mother, accompanying my father, who taught French in one of the new villages of colonization, found herself isolated as a citydweller. Among all the articles of her trousseau, the velvet caftans, the ancient jewels, the rare boxes, my mother set the greatest store by her books of music. Though she could not write French, only later learning to speak but not write it from the Frenchwomen who were her neighbors and later from her children, she would open these notebooks where, as an adolescent, she had written down the poetry of the noubas *of Andalusia. She knew the couplets by heart, and could read and write them in Arabic, so she could not be classified as illiterate, though otherwise she might have been so in our circle.*

During the years of the Algerian war this writing would prove to have a meaningful destiny! One summer, a summer of journeys for my mother, who had removed her traditional veil to visit her only son in France, where he was imprisoned in Lorraine, French soldiers broke into our apartment (shut down while she was gone), to search the place. At the height of the wanton destruction usual in such cases, they ripped up the books of Andalusian music, interpreting this writing that they found mysterious as the message of some nationalist complicity...

In the first days of independence my mother told me with tears in her eyes the grief she felt over the violent attack on this writing. Her sorrow might have seemed incongruous during those days when all around us so many women were weeping—some for a son, others for a brother. Nevertheless because this writing had come so far, navigating from beyond the centuries and shores, having been transmitted from woman to woman, some of whom were in flight, the others locked up, I in turn felt my heart in a stranglehold.

"You knew those texts by heart," I said faintly.

"But I had written them." She sighed. "I was fifteen at the time; I cared more about them than about my jewels!"

My mother, who wrote Arabic but had shifted to oral French, probably saw herself as no longer able to write the language of her learned culture with as sure a hand. Although she no longer wore the veil, either on her face or on her body, and although she had traveled from one end to the other of France to visit its prisons, my mother, the bearer of this ancestral legacy, suddenly saw the legacy erased and felt an ineffable sadness.

The end of a woman's writing, as if, as her body begins to move, no longer wearing her grandparents' veil, her writing hand then lost both its passion and its sense of its own destiny! Zoraidé has thus returned, but in the opposite direction; with a new tale of the Captive that could have been about the son freed from yesterday's French prisons but which becomes the tale of the daughter taking on the mother's status...

Fugitive without knowing it, or rather without knowing it yet. At least up to this precise instant in which I am relating these comings and goings of women in flight from the long–ago or recent past. Up to the moment in which I become conscious of my permanent condition as a fugitive—I would even say: as someone rooted in flight—just because I am writing and so that I write.

I do not record, alas, the words from noubas. The language is too scholarly for me to write, but I remember them. Wherever I go, a persistent voice, either a sweet baritone or a reckless soprano, sings them inside my head while I stroll through the streets of some city in Europe, or even in the first few steps into the first street of Algiers, where I am immediately aware of every prison, whether open to the sky or closed.

I write in the shadow of my mother, returned from her wartime travels, while I pursue my own travels in this obscure peace composed of silent internal warfare, divisions within, riots, and tumult in my native land.

I write to clear my secret path. I write in the language of the French pirates who, in the Captive's tale, stripped Zoraidé of her diamond-studded gown, yes, I am becoming more and more a renegade in the so-called foreign language. Like Zoraidé, stripped. Like her I have lost the wealth I began with—in my case, my maternal heritage—and I have gained only the simple mobility of the bare body, only freedom.

A fugitive therefore, without knowing it. Because knowing this too well would make me silent, and the ink of my writing would dry too soon.

Arable Woman I

ON DECEMBER 18 of that year, I filmed the first shot of my life: A man sitting in a wheelchair has stopped at the entrance to a room; he is watching his wife sleep inside. He is unable to enter: The two steps up to the room are impassable for his wheelchair. Room like a cave, hot, so near and yet so far: the bed is big and low, surrounded by numerous white sheepskins that soften the harshness of the high walls of this peasant's house. The sleeping woman has wrapped her hair the old way, tightly in a red scarf. The immobilized husband watches from a distance. His torso moves; his hand rests on the door-frame for a second, and that is the end of the first shot.

The next three are from the man's point of view (he is an actor with sad blue eyes). The camera pans slowly, very slowly around the bed: in my mind, and later in the soundtrack, a low-pitched music curls and spirals. The gaze of the paralyzed man: This is the dance of impotent desire.

The Arab woman seems asleep, an almost traditional image of her wearing a red scarf, an elusive image. The first "shots" of my work show a clear defeat for the man. I said: "Action." I was gripped by an emotion. As if all the women of all the harems had whispered "action" with me. Their complicity excites me. Only what their eyes see matters to me from now on. Resting on these images that I assemble with the help of their invisible presence over my shoulder.

This gaze, I claim it as mine. I see it as "ours." A single gaze piercing the walls of past centuries, escaping beyond the tomb-houses of today, concentrated, seeking a place to alight. Giving pause to the rhythm of things, slowing its pace.

My elation persists. "Action!" My voice neutral. Around me is a crew of nineteen people, fourteen of them technicians. Two, besides me, are women: the one who does makeup and the script girl. Julien, the friend who is supposed to be my photographer, will shoot some pictures of the set during the next break. It is dark, it is cold amid all the commotion of getting started, and I could feel alone. But no. The man is looking at his wife, a distant image, as she sleeps, and I look at him look at her.

Community of women shut away yesterday and today, an image-symbol that is the true action, the drive behind this hunt for images that is beginning. A female body completely veiled in white cloth, her face completely concealed, only a hole left free for her eyes. Ghost who, reversing appearances, is rendered even more sexual by prohibition; shadowy shape that has strolled along for centuries, never screaming that we were enshrouded, never tearing off the veil and even our skin with it if required. This image is the reality of my childhood, and the childhood of my mother and my aunts, and my girl cousins who were sometimes the same age as me. Suddenly this scandal that I experienced as normal looms at the beginning of this quest: a single silhouette of a woman gathering in the folds of this shroud, her linen veil, the five hundred million or so segregated women in the

Muslim world. Suddenly she is the one looking, but from behind the camera, she is the one devouring the world through a hole left in the concealment of a face.

This hole is the only lance she has to throw out toward space. For me the eye, questioning from behind and in spite of all the screens, was no longer there just so that the wretched woman could see her way: just a bit of light, a gleam to see where to go and how to escape, as she walked away from man's gaze.

"Because they spy, they watch, they search, they snoop! Smothered this way you go to the market, the hospital, the office, the workplace. You hurry; you try to make yourself invisible. You know that they have learned to make out your hips or your shoulders through the cloth, that they are judging your ankles, that in case the wind lifts your veil, they hope to see your hair, your neck, your leg. You cannot exist outside: the street is theirs, the world is theirs. Theoretically you have the right to equality, but shut up 'inside,' confined. Incarcerated."

This artificial gaze that they have left you, smaller, a hundred, a thousand times more restricted than the one given you by Allah at birth, this strange slit that the tourists photograph because they think it is picturesque to have a little black triangle where the eye should be, this miniature gaze will henceforth be my camera. All of us from the world of the shadow women, reversing the process: We are the ones finally who are looking, who are beginning.

FIRST MOVEMENT:
OF THE MOTHER AS TRAVELER

FOR A LITTLE OVER three months they had not heard a thing from Salim: no postcard from some little town in France—with that same illegible writing describing the weather or what he seemed to be studying; nothing, not even a telephone call like ones they had had two or three times, late at night, when a stranger's voice said, in Arabic: "He is all right, he wants you to be told not to worry." Nothing: silence from the mails, silence from the phones.

Though our mother was thinking about it, she did not dare discuss it with her husband. Every morning she would watch him go out very early for a few minutes and return with the two local newspapers. Anxiously he would skim them and she would end up by calmly asking, while she served him, "Nothing new?" They were both at that moment thinking of their son. The father was silent and then calmly replied, "Nothing!" He would, of course, discuss yesterday's attempted assassinations, the military operations, or how the press assessed what was going on with his colleagues. She, however, would

181

soon leave for the market there in the basement, under the housing project where they lived. They and two other families were the only native-born teachers living there among the hundred Europeans. She would take the occasion to visit with her French friend, the woman who ran the pharmacy next to the market—just taking the time between two clients to smile and say hello to her. That would reassure the mother!

Three months and more had gone by with no sign at all from Salim, from France. Eastern France, the father assumed, the one time he opened up about it in front of his wife and his brother-in-law who was visiting: "Yes, we are telling the neighbors, or at least the Europeans, when they make polite inquiries, that, yes, he is at university in Paris. But we know perfectly well that he is not in Paris anymore, or going to classes, even though he needs his student-identification papers for military deferment and to move around! We know… well, really, what can we know these days about our sons, about ourselves!"

He stopped; he had never revealed his worries at such length, but his wife's brother was also his best friend; with him he was moved to speak up and thus confess his fears, especially relating to his son, things he usually did not even reveal to himself, or to his wife…

The mother stood bolt upright and left the room, left the two men alone; she went into the little bathroom, washed her face with great splashes of cold water, looked at her features—those of a woman who had just turned forty. Her face in the mirror became stiff, with a sort of gasp her cheeks tightened: she would not cry, she had decided. Comfort her husband before herself! As for her unspeakable anguish, she usually chased it away by talking endlessly with a few old women. The cleaning woman would come every Monday to do the laundry, and there were one or two other women in the market who sold herbs or eggs—in short, she would talk about it with anybody who told her she was lucky that her son was far away (of course he was her only son, "the apple of her eye," "the promise of her future," and so on) in France or somewhere else, but not here, left to the risks of retaliation, searches, interrogation, or… After listening to the whispers of the vendors or the washerwoman's murmurs every Monday, the mother would breathe deeply and feel almost lucky. She would think that someday, returning to the city of her childhood, she would do what her old mother had done before her. She would go to the sanctuary near the sea, take tallow and wax candles, hard-boiled eggs and brioches for the poor, and give thanks to the dead saint. She would beg for blessings—you had to pay for them of course—from the heirs of this saint, and she would do this without breathing a word of it to her husband, who would be annoyed at her rituals!

Leaving the bathroom, she calmed herself, momentarily persuading herself that she would have the luck in this endless war to remain a mother. After all she had only one son, which was rather rare here, God would be kind to her…

Over three months with no news, the banality of days, the banality of fate!

She took the occasion of the end of Ramadan—also the fact that their daughter, their youngest, who was thirteen, had a holiday from school—to ask if she could go and spend the whole day in their city, in Caesarea.

They had barely arrived, but after dinner she and her sister-in-law excused themselves to visit an aunt who was very ill. They did, in fact, pay her a quick visit, then on their return (as they had planned from the start) they trotted along in their silk veils, each wearing the little stiff veil of embroidered organza across the bridge of her nose, leaving only two large eyes visible. Half anonymously, they thus visited the woman who was a seer and who, ever since her recent pilgrimage to Mecca, no longer sold magic potions or read the cards but lived on alms and her savings, which became more and more depleted by her devotions: Lla Rkia. All the matrons of the city knew her name.

As soon as the mother arrived that morning, she had confided in her sister-in-law, "If this silence from Salim continues, I won't be able to exist without showing anything, I won't be able to put on a strong face for my husband and my little daughter, for..." and her voice fell.

"You and I will go to see Lla Rkia. Her visions are often of comfort... Still, she has to agree to it. Now that she has made the pilgrimage to Mecca and is a *hadja*, it is not certain that she will! Maybe for our family."

After two messages sent via the little girl next door, the woman sent word that she would be expecting both of them at coffee time and that she was doing this "only to give thanks to God and his Prophet!" The sister-in-law had explained that this was the expression she used to let them know in advance that she would not accept any money because of remaining faithful to her vow. Nothing, however, prevented their being armed in advance with some special present, perfume from Paris or a silk scarf... So now they were walking along the low wall separating the old, antique theater and its ruins from the high road; they came to the little house tucked back into a dark corner.

The mother tapped on the carved iron "hand of Fatima." They went in and crossed a patio that was small but dazzling with an almost purple light that seemed to flow from a heavenly fountain... Blinking still, her veil slipping off her hair, the mother quickly removed her face veil and bent over the venerable woman seated on a deep divan awaiting them. After the kisses and customary compliments the mother stood close to her sister-in-law and waited, her heart in a tumult.

It was the sister-in-law who spoke about Salim, almost calmly, in her soft, almost dreamy voice, as if he were there, as if in a second he would enter this room, bend down because he was too tall, half smile his sidelong smile… The mother, listening, accepted this nearby and not completely unreal presence.

Silence. The servant had just had a *kanoun* full of burning coals brought in without the mother noticing, and then slipped away. The silence stretched on but seemed translucent. In the shadows of the small, cool room, the mother saw the mask of Lla Rkia, her tawny scarf with black fringes. Beneath her half-lowered eyes, beneath her long, thin, arrogant nose, her thin, almost completely erased lips were murmuring in this no longer total silence: The old woman was uttering scattered, disconnected scraps of *sura*. Finally, they could hear the language of the Koran as if it were pouring from the mouth of a woman half dead: this time the mother waited without emotion. The sorceress swiftly threw a powder, or some herbs or a little sac of medicine, into the *kanoun* without having it brought closer to her. All at once whitish, then almost green smoke rose up, and for a moment the acrid smell made the two visitors cough. Inscrutable, the old woman waited, then when the smoke had dissipated and the women were calm, she asked in a haughty voice, "What month was he born, your prince?"

The mother hesitated and then said, "In the month of *Rdjeb*. The twenty-seventh, I believe."

Once again, the fear in her causing panic (her wind a storm inside her). She hunched over, bent her head over her breast, tried to find the breath left hanging; finally she thought that she herself might say the beginning of a *sura*, the one everyone said, the *fatiha*. She repeated the first lines two or three times and regained her calm. She watched the lips of the soothsayer, whose eyelids were lowered in concentration.

The silence settled in the room. The sister-in-law seemed invisible, or dead. You could not even hear her breath, thought the mother, who was patient now and confident. If Salim knew, she said to herself, he would surely make fun of her! But if he saw her now, full of confidence, he would smile at her indulgently. Imagining this, this sort of tacit affection for her that he had expressed ever since puberty, was a comfort to her.

The old woman coughed. Then she began:

"Do not worry about the youth! The protection of Sid el-Berkani,"—the mother was grateful that she had not forgotten the hallowed ancestor up in the nearby mountains—"is upon him."

She went on, speaking more softly, as if the vision were written down already and she only said what was there: "Do not worry about him. He will have a destiny... one greater than his father's!" she finished off pompously.

The sister-in-law gently put her hand on the arm of her companion, who had started unknowingly.

After a sigh, almost a death rattle, the voice of Lla Rkia said loudly in triumphant tones, "I see him... I see him..." She hesitated then: "I see him walking on the road to Verdun!"

This last French word, which she pronounced rolling the *r*, surprised them. The two visitors looked at each other despite the half-light. They both knew old pensioners, veterans of the other war, who were called, even in Arabic, *"the men of Verdun"*—always with a rolled *r*. So what did the other war, the one from which only old men remained, have to do with this one, "our war"? the women wondered. Could it be that old Rkia in turn, despite her magic potions and her recent pilgrimage, was slipping into some disturbing senility?

"I will admit," said the sister-in-law from under her veil on their return trip, "I thought, 'She is rambling; she no longer can see the way she could before!' But you see, she was firm when she said 'Selim is in good health.' Where he is does not matter!"

"She did relieve my anxiety a little," the mother acknowledged.

They went home, where they found the others; of course it was only with the women, young and old, that they talked about Lla Rkia's verdict. Some of them embraced our mother warmly and she thought to herself that this was one of the reasons she had come on this second day of *Aïd*—to share in the almost childish buzz of excitement and spontaneity.

That same night she went back to their apartment in the capital with her daughter, who was her youngest child, and her husband.

The following nights she slept peacefully.

Ten days later a letter from the court in Metz, in Lorraine, arrived. The prison administration informed the father that his son, aged less than twenty-one, had been arrested, that he was being indicted for "criminal association" and other equally pompous charges. The mother did not feel that these were as serious as the charges made against Salim when he had been arrested at seventeen in his own country. She remained silent, looked gravely at her husband, and breathed deeply, thinking excitedly, *What is essential is that he is alive. He is safe. All the prisons in the world don't matter! He'll get out!* Then finally she asked softly, "Metz, in Lorraine—isn't that near... Verdun?"

"Verdun?" the father repeated, surprised.

"The seer, the one in our town..."

Stammering then in confusion but at the same time calm again, she explained, or rather admitted, that the last time she and her daughter had visited their town, she had met with Lla Rkia, who had "seen" Salim "on the road to Verdun," she repeated almost triumphantly. So the news of the arrest of their son did not really arouse either anxiety or alarm—at least not for the mother.

Shortly afterward the two of them left for the village to visit their old nurse. She herself had a son in prison in the south, "in the Sahara" she said. They could tell from her silences that her two youngest sons (though without sighing she said rather proudly that she had not heard anything from them) had very probably "gone up" into the nearby mountain, in short, joined the Resistance.

The nurse who was nearly sixty was ill: a weak heart and chronic diabetes at the same time. In bed, in the half darkness of her cool shack, she was informed of Salim's arrest in Lorraine and that they had to stop worrying about him from now on (prisons in France were less harsh than the ones here), or rather muster their patience until things finally worked themselves out! She listened to the news from her bed of pain; in the old days she used to say she loved Salim as much as two of her sons put together!

"I'm getting old," she finally murmured. "Prison. Provided he doesn't stay there for years. Provided I can see him standing before me someday…" She stopped, musing, then finished her sentence, "and free! Oh yes, Lord and gentle Prophet, free, the son of my heart!"

The mother listened, showed no emotion, asked about life in the village. She delivered the medicine they had brought, took care of making another list, and then located her husband so that they could return to the capital.

Late that evening in the kitchen she silently decided, for herself (she then would talk to her almost adolescent daughter about it before laying the groundwork for getting the husband's permission), yes, she made a firm and irrevocable decision. If her son had to remain in jail for years, well then, she would go there "even alone if necessary!" because her husband, who had just left teaching, would be less free than before over summer vacation. The next evening, finishing up the dishes, and this time with the young girl there, she repeated, "I will go alone, unveiled—now I know that I will—alone into every one of the prisons they put him into!"

"You'll take me with you!" the daughter interrupted, hardly surprised at her mother's resolution.

And so, for the mother, the news of Salim's imprisonment meant that she could anticipate the beginning of an adventure…

She slept peacefully when they returned from the village. After market the next day she talked about it with her only friend, the woman who ran the pharmacy. She bought some aspirin and began tentatively to study the different models of sunglasses. (It would be summer when she went, and it felt easier to think of herself suddenly off the boat, taking the train, without her veil now but with her face blocked at least by dark glasses.) The Frenchwoman left the last customers with her assistant and showed the mother into the back of the shop. The news of the son's arrest was reported, explained. "So," said the mother, "I'm right not to be too worried?" and she watched the expression on the pharmacist's face. Then, without waiting, she came out with her prepared sentence: "My son is a political prisoner!" She repeated the last words, trying them out, and watched for any little reaction in the woman she was talking to, who, of course, remained friendly; to be a "political prisoner" was noble, not shameful. Would the Europeans who were less well disposed have the same reaction as her friend?

She would have liked to talk about her projects, just to be encouraged. Would her husband, if he could not get away and go to France for a holiday, let her travel alone, in short, in his stead? But she did not talk about it anymore this time. On her next visit in three or four days there would be fewer customers. Then she would mention it. She would explain that she felt strong. She would seek some comforting reassurance.

That evening, in the kitchen when she and her daughter finished putting everything away, she whispered to her a little impishly, with a knowing smile, "Find us a map for the city of Metz. Because I've had an idea. We'll go to Alsace for 'rest and relaxation'! That's not far away, is it? Your father will let us, I'm sure!"

She went to sleep imagining the high façade of the prison in Metz: not gray, not black, a tall building, of course, but with a gracious air, a bit like a deluxe hotel where her son was staying, where she would cheerfully go…

When mid-July arrived in 1959, the father, emotional over letting them go on such a long trip alone, accompanied the mother and his daughter to the boat. During the crossing in their second-class cabin the mother watched over her daughter, the daughter watched over her mother—she was elegant and seemed so young. *The* piedsnoirs *passengers, especially,* thought the adolescent, *would never guess that this lady in a flowered summer suit just a few weeks earlier, in Caesarea, had been just as elegant but in a different way. Reigning in the first rank of guests seated like gods around the musicians as they celebrated the seventh day after the birth of her youngest nephew, she was an Andalusian Moorish woman! In which place are we playing a role? Is it there among the family or here on this boat among these passengers who think we are tourists like themselves?* And the mother, who stayed in the cabin, absolutely convinced that she was going to be seasick despite the sea's being clear and so calm, the mother advised her young daughter, who wanted to go up on deck, "Be careful! Don't talk to strangers, but if it becomes unavoidable then don't mention the real reason for our trip, that is, your brother! Not that you should be ashamed, to the contrary! We are proud of it! But you never know. We are two women alone, and among 'them' they might take us for what they call *fellaghas!* Remember, we are going for our health to a treatment center in the Vosges, and besides, it's really the truth!" She delivered her advice in Arabic, then lay down. It had been bound to happen: Unable to sleep, nauseated, she would not doze off until they took the train from Marseilles the next day. Her daughter acquiesced and went up on deck, where she stayed alone for hours, filling her eyes full of the night that made the waves sparkle.

Two days later, silent, united, and so weary, they arrived at the clinic at Trois-Épis. They expected to spend three weeks there. The first week they expected the letter from Metz. It came.

Salim had written them (in his splotchy handwriting, stamped over here and there by the prison censor) advising them not to come see him. He was well; he said so two or three times. But he explained that the present conditions of detention were very harsh, that his "brothers" (that was his word, just before something deleted by the censor), "forty of them" he said after the crossed-out word, which his young sister finally read or guessed at, "are organizing!"

"Yes, I'm sure that what he wrote is that they are organizing, and those men, the administration, crossed out the word!"

"Which means?" the mother asked, and her daughter tentatively explained that probably the prisoners were going on strike, they must be demanding political rights or even just a better quality of life.

"I don't know," she said. "It's not that he doesn't want to see us, it's because this is a bad time! It's just the way it is—even in prison they are still part of the struggle!"

Then the mother collapsed on the bed in the room they shared and cried. She sobbed. Right before the startled eyes of her youngest daughter she let herself go. Then she pulled herself together, dried her face, and apologized. After a while, feeling guilty for her weakness, she proposed that they take an excursion this next Sunday: "We'll even go to Germany if you'd like, and we'll send your brother a post-card from there!"

The visit ended on a sad note. They decided not to go through Paris and spend the three days they had planned with friends, an emi-grant family. They sent everything they had brought for Salim in sev-eral packages, including the things his girl cousins had knitted for him. As for the money, the pastries, and food from home that they should have carried him "in our hands," moaned the mother softly, they sent all of that the day after they received the letter from Salim that was so disappointing.

A year went by in Algiers: the everyday life of war baring its teeth in the countryside, in the mountains set on fire with napalm where the resistants were hanging on in caves, where the peasants were brought down from the mountains and placed in camps under super-vision. In the capital fear was a diffuse, gray fog, and it stayed that way for a long time, until later, somewhat later, one exuberant December. (The days of barricades on which, among the children and women who fell beneath the bullets, they flew the new flag, and its red and its green…) Later!

Before all of that the father kept up a regular correspondence with his son's lawyer, and this time the mother looked as if she were resigned. She only talked about Salim when she was in Caesarea among women, her friends, who knew that she would not, certainly not, give up on making the trip to see her only son. The son who was "safe," she called it, rather than "imprisoned," because as months went by, how many young people around her, how many grown men would leave, disappear, be abducted! Even her brother (her half brother through her father), M'Hamed, her favorite because of his kind heart and his beauty. One day the French army searched the bus he had taken between Caesarea and Hadjout. They pulled him off the bus and took him and two other men, like him in their forties, into the nearby forest! Their bodies were never found; the lawyer assigned to the case had searched for some trace in all the prisons around. After six months there was still nothing! Our mother regularly went to Hadjout to see her sister-in-law and her four little ones—all of the relatives there certainly considered her a widow with orphans already. But the hardest thing was this: You could not weep for M'Hamed openly; he had no right to the ritual, even if his body was departed! "No," her husband declared, "we have to hope for M'Hamed, we have to keep on searching!"

They came home from Hadjout, or from Caesarea, and there was a letter from Salim waiting for them with news that seemed banal, nothing unusual. He thanked them for the packages; he mentioned, as always, that he shared everything with his comrades. *We pool everything we have*, he wrote—and at least that was something, said the young sister when she came home from lycée and read the message in her turn—the fact that the usual censorship had left them those comments!

The mother no longer said anything—except in her regular conversations with the pharmacist, who sometimes came upstairs at tea time. The mother said nothing for that entire year; she endured patiently until finally the summer of 1960 arrived.

The mother left again in July, for the same treatment center, this time alone—her fourteen-year-old daughter had been sent to a summer camp for adolescent girls in the Pyrenees.

As soon as the traveler checked in at the Trois-Épis, she informed the housekeeping staff that she would leave the following Saturday, that she would return after the weekend, and that while she was away she would be in Metz. She took the train, then at the station she asked for the bus "to the prison." She spoke now with no accent; her light chestnut-colored hair and her clothing from the most elegant shop in Algiers made people think not so much that she was a Frenchwoman (at forty, she seemed at least ten years younger, looking chic and a little tense) but rather a bourgeois from northern Italy or a frenchified Spaniard.

She arrived at the gates to the prison. Paying no attention to the posted schedules, she rang the bell and waited, her heart pounding. The caretaker behind his glassed-in station greeted her with surprise: "What about the schedule? What about visiting days?" Despite her ladylike appearance that led one to believe she was a teacher, a lawyer's or magistrate's wife, she explained in a voice that was almost a little girl's (she was working so hard in this language), "I have come a long distance! From farther away than Strasbourg! I traveled yesterday and all this morning. I want to see my son."

She gave Salim's name.

"Your papers!" the guardian demanded, loud and gruff.

Somewhat disconcerted by the Arab name because he recognized it as belonging to one of the "agitators," he could not understand: This lady seemed so well-mannered! *Her, the mother? This almost-blond young woman who looks…*

He watched her in silence, beginning to feel spiteful. She waited, forcing her face to reveal little of the agitation the wait was causing her: *A fiancée*, the suspicious man thought vaguely. *She doesn't look like a mother, not one from over there!*

He ended up by telephoning to explain that there was a young lady there who claimed to have been traveling since the day before… She said she was "'the mother of Salim,' the young ringleader." These prison inmates had spent the last year in a struggle for their status as "political prisoners," which they ended up getting. They had even begun to set up courses in Arabic. "They're pretentious on top of it all!" muttered the man awaiting his instructions, his eye on the visitor. The answer was not long in coming.

"Go through there," he said to the mother. "They want to see you first. I don't know if you will get to see your son! But you can go in…"

Then, confronted by the silhouette of the visitor passing through the second doorway, he suddenly felt vicious and angry.

They took away all of the mother's packages. "What do you think, that we'd let you bring in delicacies like this, what you call your regional cakes, dates!" But there were more than sixty of them there, including the ten old ones from the most important crackdown in Lorraine (among them Salim, "the student"), and the collective atmosphere was permeated with tension. From here on in, everyone had to be on his guard. Until when? Who knows… It was that Salim who was responsible for the literacy courses. Of course, of course!

Up to that point, as she went down the half-lit corridors, she could hear the two guards in front of her talking to each other. She knew it was about her. She could not be sure of their tone: warning or grudging, perhaps to prepare her for the final refusal! She listened with an empty heart. One single apprehension filled her: *to see him, just to see him, God help me and don't abandon me! Not like last year!* And her two guides went on with their chronicle, but their voices were lower: a hum, maybe not so hostile, preceding her.

One last door opened and suddenly there was light, brilliant and intense; it was the warden's office. The other men vanished, but it was as if some recrimination on the part of everyone, guards, attendants, the janitor, awaited her on the other side.

A man stood there in front of her and examined her. She remained standing, empty-handed, her leather bag hanging from her shoulder. *They will give me back my packages when I leave,* she thought, not knowing what to do with her hands, and she still did not look at the stranger, just at his office and at this light that she was finally getting used to.

"Have a seat, madame," said the very polite voice.

She sat immediately in the leather armchair facing the large desk. She waited, her hands resting on her knees. *My son... Will he let me...?* she agonized, as she now had the warden himself seated facing her.

The warden spoke... She did not hear everything. She tried to understand from his features, his delivery, his tone: Was he going to let her see Salim? Would they agree to it? She peered as if through a fog at the face of this man and she thought of all of them, the crowd of others, other men, an army... Faced with all of them (suddenly, through the open window a sound rose, outbursts of voices, giving brief commands...), she must try to remain dignified, to speak French correctly when she answered, so that they would see that she was perhaps a mother like mothers in "their country," that...

The warden repeats a question: "Did you come a long way? From Strasbourg?"

She nodded in the affirmative. Not waiting, he went on, not really hostile, she thought, beginning to hope.

"He is young, the youngest one here... He is intelligent and has character, too."

Silence. Suddenly she thinks she is in a classroom; this man observing her discreetly through his eyeglasses could be one of her husband's colleagues, the head not of a prison but of a school.

She knows what the conclusion will be just before he says it: "You shall see him! But here, in my office, just this once. Briefly. You have gone to a lot of trouble!"

It is true that she has come a great distance. A sudden weakness comes over her. She turns her head and would like to go to the open window, but dares not move. She breathes to overcome the faintness she begins to feel. Sounds at the door. Three silhouettes: The two guards stand there motionless, with "him" between them. Salim. Long and thin. Thinner than usual. And that strange beret like a plate on top of his head.

He looks at her. Without a word. Turns his head toward the warden. Says nothing. Waits, then hesitates and takes a step in her direction.

She has stood up. Sentences jumble together, rushing around inside her, in her throat. Strangling her. She cannot breathe. Sentences in Arabic.

"I will leave the two of you for fifteen minutes, or a bit longer!" says the warden in a loud voice, then, gesturing pompously but awkwardly, he speaks to Salim: "Embrace your mother!" He starts to add something but thinks better of it. He stands up, makes a sign to the guards. All three leave.

Finally, all at once, the sentences held back inside her, the Arabic words, tender, loving words, come out, burst out. Mixed with choked-back sobs and giggles.

Salim in her arms. He does not give himself over completely, he holds onto himself—and he is surprised (later, in his cell, he will think about it again) at her girlish exuberance. Which is what he had thought at first in the harsh light of the director's office: *So young, my mother, they must have thought that themselves! And even doubted!* Later he would say to himself, *When she dresses that way, like a Parisian, with gestures that are almost awkward because of her clothes, those short sleeves, the schoolgirl's collar, all those colors, lilac, rose, fuchsia, she turns into a young girl!*

She has calmed down, his mother. And now she is sitting, her serenity regained despite where they are. Maybe because, once alone with him, she had been able to let herself go in words that were Arabic. Which gradually restored her armor and decorum… Her appearance, her tone of voice, right down to the gestures of the traditional North African city-woman (*her household gestures*, Salim thought gently), they all returned despite the way the French clothes looked, making her brittle, making her beautiful of course, but also exposing her…

She asked him questions: about his meals, how much time he spent in the courtyard, when the doctor visited. ("Since you haven't grown any more, if you look taller, it is because you have gotten thinner!") Does he sleep alone in… she says "your room"? He gives a sidelong smile.

"No," he answers. "There are three of us."

She asks what region the others are from. Kabylia? "Not from home!" she says.

He corrects her: "The whole country is 'home'!"

"Of course," she says, but she would feel less worried if her son, who is so young, were with men who were, if not from his town, at least from the surrounding area, some neighboring town… He is slightly annoyed, slightly ironic. She sees it, apologizes, stops talking, then considers the strange headgear, the beret that is too flat, too round, and flat as a plate.

"Can't you take it off?"

She laughs: she thinks he looks, not exactly like a bandit or a hoodlum but, really, in the end—a prisoner. She says "prisoner" again in Arabic, then, with a sigh, "Prison!"

She reaches her arm out, hesitates, then, determined, she takes off this headgear, this... She runs her fingers through his short, curly hair.

Salim blinks. He sits down to face her but only when she focuses on his prisoner's beret. He tells her, in a low voice, in Arabic, "They have left the door open!"

His voice sounds wary. If the director comes in behind him, he shouldn't find the two of them confiding and talking like this in Arabic. He quickly asks for news of his father and his sisters.

She, in turn, starts talking again, but in French; he notices her careful enunciation, how much progress she has made. *She speaks correct French now and almost without an accent!* He could tell her this; he knows it would please her, this young mother who has come from so far away. He feels touched, but he says nothing. He smiles with his eyes. He listens to her.

She has launched in; she does not stop.

"Back at the Trois-Épis, I told the man in charge, you know, that I would just take one afternoon a week to go to Strasbourg! Now I have to go see my son in Metz. I need two days! This time and one other!" Then she says in a lower voice, as if it were a secret, some funny, harmless incident, "I added, naturally, 'My son is a prisoner!'" Then she went on, louder and almost gaily, "A political prisoner!"

The warden stood there at the door. Salim stood up at once. His hand quickly replaced the beret on his curly hair.

The mother, who abruptly cut short what she was saying, looked up at her son. He looked now like a stranger again, like a young man wrapped, she felt, in a lack of respectability, some peasantlike and willful clumsiness. This boy, she thought to herself later, who was so stylish and elegant in adolescence—maybe it is the "politics," or to make himself older, he is trying to look like a "real Arab," like one of his cousins just barely out of the mountain *zaouia!*

Her face is twitching with sorrow; she does not notice it. She looks at the warden coming toward them.

Salim says softly in Arabic, "Goodbye, mother."

He does not even bend toward her to embrace her. He will not embrace her in front of the warden and the guards behind him.

He studies the face of his mother. Clouded with a delicate sadness. He assumes an air of severity: "Be calm!" he seems to say, "in front of them. Them!"

She understands. She is unable to say a word. She does not even smile. The warden says in a voice that means to be understanding: "You have to tell your son goodbye, madame!… you will have to wait for visiting hours next time."

Salim turns partway around. His mother stands up right next to him: she comes up to his face. He does not look at her. Just a gesture of his hands, touching her lightly on her shoulders. "Goodbye," he repeats in secret, in Arabic.

Then abruptly he turns his back on her. He goes toward the guards. He disappears.

She, standing, empty arms dangling by her side. The warden sits down, watches her as he had in the beginning: almost the way an ethnologist watches, *A Moorish woman? This young woman who is so well dressed?* Those are the words he thinks as he stares at her.

She listens carefully to the information about visiting, thanks him, takes a sheet of paper with the schedule on it. She murmurs goodbye.

She shuts the door, follows the two guards who have reappeared so close to her down the gray corridors. The hubbub all around her: *Like at the* hammam, she thinks, and this persistent odor of dampness, her son stuck here for good! She hardens herself, keeps going at her own pace, goes past the attendant, who hands her back her original packages. She starts to refuse them, then takes them: She will mail them. Of course they will open them, but at least they will give him the underwear. She and her son have agreed that for spending money she will send him a money order; he'll have it to buy his cigarettes.

She finds herself outside again, takes a few steps into the sunlight at the foot of the high wall; then, finally, a little farther along, like a little girl, she lets her silent tears slowly fall.

She will see nothing of the city; she returns directly to the station. She drinks a cafe au lait and eats a piece of fruitcake at the snack bar while she waits for the next train. It is almost night when she arrives in Strasbourg. And there, in the little hotel room near the station, she finally feels herself collapsing, there, lying on the narrow bed, she hears all over again the stir of the prison.

So she only saw her son for fifteen, maybe twenty minutes, and that was after a year and a half of waiting and several months of anxiety. All alone, huddled in the cold bed (she has stomach cramps because she hasn't eaten, she was not brave enough to go into a restaurant alone so late), she turns out the light—she listens to the hubbub of the prison that follows her and suddenly reassures her. Does it not bring back the moment he was present, *my little boy*— suddenly she thinks of Salim in those words.

The light is out now, and completely dressed, in the dark, she cries: gently, with stifled sobs, then in gasps that tear at her for a long time, and again in floods of soft tears… The pain does not stop, glows like blood she is losing, or milk… Like sadness going away? No, enveloping her, invading the half-light of the anonymous room, mingling with the hubbub-memory of Metz…

Gasps, sobs that she still tries to hold back. Can't let go. How long she has been standing up, such a long time, up and standing, and firm! But she is alone and lying down and lost in a strange city. Still no.

"Little boy," she repeats. Then there is no more Salim, the noise of the prison in Metz has faded and the darkness of the hotel room, and her own goings and comings (the bus, the train, the boat) in this France of theirs, where the prisons are full of her son's friends... No, everything goes, comes unraveled, recedes, but she cries, the tears flow, the moans now form one long, single, formless howl, and it is such a long sorrow, but one without origins. "My little boy," she repeats, before sinking into loosely woven sleep where the spaces between the threads grow larger, bending and curving as if on a screen of beige and mauve, of many harmonious nuances intermingling.

She does not understand, she does not want to understand, that she is merely reliving another sorrow from the past, that she is pouring out other women's tears that have never flowed. She knows it, she will know it, but no, she sinks, soft, weary, completely given over this time to smooth, unruffled sleep carrying her off to the shores of the next day.

Arable Woman II

～

THE FIRST SHOT: Lila is sleeping. A face with perfect features, a red scarf knotted over her forehead in the traditional manner... The actress, my friend, squatting on the carpet in front of the big copper mirror (brought for this purpose from my mother's house—it had belonged to my grandmother in Caesarea), had earlier tied the scarf slowly over her forehead to hide her hair.

I took a wide-angle shot as she did so; lit by several candles, her blue-flowered Kabylian dress stood out against the half-light. I watched her gesture from behind—the gesture of all the women in the too-full houses of my childhood, in the midst of their brood, the shrieks, the steam from couscous cooking, and the sighs, my God, the sighs... The gesture of their raised arms to make the scarf as tight as possible across the brow. ("I bind up my head, I bind up my misfortune!" No use speaking. When one is out of patience, tightening this red cloth is like clenching one's teeth.)

Now Lila sleeps in the bed, watched by Ali, her husband, who will try to get out of his wheelchair on crutches, will try to make it over the steps at the threshold, will fall back down into his chair...

The point of view has changed. At the other end of the room, the camera is now the voyeur following the man as he stands up at this

impossible threshold. An actor from the theater, he mimes the muscular effort, he hoists himself, he rests his head on the cold door-
frame, he... I tell him to fall back into his chair. And we do several
takes: the first fall, the second...

Gradually I begin to come closer and closer to Ali's body to direct
his fall. Yes, with his crutch he has to feel for the best spot to support
himself as he gets up... Yes, let him be figuring out where he will balance best as he tries to stand upright. In fact it is not with one's features that suffering is expressed, but always with subtle movements of
the shoulder, the torso, the way one holds one's head. The actor who
plays Ali is patient, I want to have all the patience in the world, as
together we discover the way to map these gestures hidden in shadows.

Before this working dialogue begins, I am aware, as I reflect for a
moment, that I am directing silently and humbly; I am happy to be
working with a natural actor, and I direct him by being an accomplice.

Yes, for a moment, noticing this, I am happy and regal. I have a
calm power that comes from my sense of being forty (the age when
every day one lives all the ages; the age of political majority, according to the Romans; the age for verbal prophecy, thought the Arabs;
and for me, as it happened, the age when I entered into filmmaking,
"realizing" through image and sound). I "direct," therefore the way
that, in bed, I would show the motions of love to someone, whose
inexperience I would pardon, happy to lead him because I feel secure
in the kingdom of fluidity. What strange work, what peace!

All the technicians are on the set. The generators that power the
projectors deafen us with their constant rumbling. Silence inside me.
I seem cold, neutral; just barely friendly. In any case, the others think
of me as an "intellectual." I know they are disoriented, of course,
because for the first time a woman is "boss."

But that is not where the distance between them and me lies.
There is no one here who suspects that, after the months of prepara-

tion as I thought about this work, now, at the moment of "filming"—
that is, of creating some new space—I am working as a woman. My
quest is immersed in my physical rhythm, and listens to my ever
more subtle sensations. What does "filming" mean for me if not trying to look every time with the first look, listen with the first listening? "Filming": that is, first closing the eyes to hear better in the dark,
and then opening them again only for the flickering instant of birth.

Two or three months before starting this work, I heard the news
of Pasolini's death on the radio. I was getting ready for a voluptuous
siesta one Sunday afternoon after an excursion into the Sahel of
Algiers along the blue-gray November roads. Pasolini dead. Instantly
this bed was a place of confinement.

Ax stroke in my personal history (admittedly, the previous few
months had been lived in conjugal blur… *No!* I thought to myself, if
only the man I loved so much, who loved me so much, had made
some gesture, a word, an impulse: *Yes, Pasolini is dead and I am going
to love you,*—if he had kissed my eyelids as he murmured, *Yes, Pasolini is dead.* Grief-stricken, I told myself again, *Good Lord, even couples
have brotherly shadows, or else, what is the use? We would just see ourselves turn into the two sides of an oyster that closes! No, not my personal history! Never again the dream that lets its light drain away.*

It may seem ridiculous that an Arab woman, one in love and
loved too long—alas beloved and cursed with loving—one day
decides, *No, I will no longer make love this way because I have just
learned that Pasolini was murdered! I do not care, they can make fun,
you can make fun of me and say, "An Italian homosexual filmmaker has
been murdered and you think you have somehow been the one hit…"* I
went on: *Because they are going to rush to spit on his corpse: they killed
him and they will aim to smear him. The fine moral order spreading its
display all over the world!…*

That is how it was. From that moment on I wanted one way or another to break the glass panes behind which I had too long been coiled.

Why Pasolini? That is how it was, there is no more to it than that... I, an Arab woman, writing classical Arabic poorly, loving and suffering in my mother's dialect, knowing that I have to recapture the deep song strangled in the throat of my people, finding it again with images, with the murmur beneath images, I tell myself henceforth, *I am beginning (or I am ending) because in a bed where I was preparing for love, I felt— twenty-four hours later and with the whole Mediterranean Sea between us—the death of Pasolini like a scream, an open-ended scream.*

I also remember how, ten months later, my mother wept over the death of an Andalusian singer who was popular in Algiers: Dahmane Ben Achour. It was the twenty-seventh day of Ramadan. As the news was announced on the radio, a few minutes before the breaking of the fast, she simply wept, sitting up straight at the table, and we ate our dinner in the silence... I knew then, because of my mother's long pedigree, that an artist does not die, not on the day of his death. Afterward, perhaps, after the mud and violence of others... My mother wept while the others broke the fast. And I wanted to hold on to the tears of my suddenly younger mother. I wanted to delve into the song... but how, with what unreal choreography: images of women's bodies floating across patios, in the air trembling between marble statues, with the modulations of the baritone voice of the man who had just died!

I am really moving toward the work of image and sound. My eyes closed, I grope in the dark, seeking the lost echo of the lamentations that made tears of love flow, back at home. I seek this rhythm in my head... Only afterward will I try to take the gaze inward, see the essence, the structures, what takes flight beneath matter.

SECOND MOVEMENT:
OF THE GRANDMOTHER
AS A YOUNG BRIDE

~~~~~

OF THE GRANDMOTHER as a young bride: At fourteen she is given in marriage by her father—who was scarcely more than forty—to an old man, the city's wealthiest man, and she becomes his fourth wife... Was she a little girl? Not at all. For four years she has been nubile. She lived up in the mountain hamlet near the most ancient sanctuary in the region, the one honoring Saint Ahmed or Saint Abdallah, the most firmly entrenched saint in local history. Her father is his descendent and is therefore the *mokkadem*, the man whose religious *baraka* is respected and who administers it naturally, petty nobility of the region, proud, stubborn, and calculating. Coming down into the city from her hamlet, she is proud as can be to be wearing the veil worn by city-women of the day, the veil that swallows up shoulders, bust, hips, on a body already wearing wide, puffed-out pants, obliterating the outline of the legs, the ones they call the "going-out *sarouel*."

Wool on wool, the wide pleats that slowly fall and that take so long to prepare just before one goes out across the thresholds: wool on wool, even in summer. Silk and moiré will only replace rough and opaque wool twenty or thirty years later, at the end of the First World War!

So the little girl Fatima is like a normal adolescent as she comes to the city. It is 1896 and barely fifty years since the little city (called Caesarea, because it was formerly "Caesar's city," destroyed and brought back to life several times) became French, with a community of colonists from Provence and a small population of fishermen from Malta who live separately and are just barely beginning to put down roots. Ferhani, her father, has property, sharecroppers on the nearby hills, but a rather ordinary house in the ancient heart of the Arab quarter, sheltered by the ancient wall around it. He does not live there, except when he comes down on market day and spends just one night in the city. It makes him unhappy not to have a home in the city that is worthy of his rank. The people there (so many of them upstarts in these oppressive times) have absolutely no idea that up in the hills—that is, throughout the Dahra all the way to Miliana in the south and Ténès in the west—anyone who knows anything (naturally not the vagabonds and starving people wandering more and more along the roads, alas) recognizes him as the son of his father and of his father's father and so on all the way back to the thirteenth-century saint, Ahmed or Abdallah! Consequently they kiss his hand; consequently they pay him rent when they come to the cradle of the family at the *zaouia*. As for Fatima, even as a young girl she had inherited a bit of her father's pride, a less ostentatious version: timidity mixed with aloofness.

So Ferhani gave his second daughter, who was just fourteen, to an old man who was...

"Sixty-two?" I asked.

"Oh no," my aunt replied. "They said he was a hundred!"

"No," I retort. "That's not possible! And besides, would he have married again?"

The aunt insists.

"Soliman's grandsons already had beards! They say he had just lost his third wife, whom he had married very young, a virgin from a modest family who was fifteen or sixteen while he was already more than sixty-five, I'm sure of it! At that third marriage his oldest sons had already sulked, especially the first one, who was a highly regarded man of law in another city, Koléa, I think. And Soliman had been prudent this time in not requesting the daughter of a family of notables, but one from modest people who must have felt themselves honored all the same!...

"Well, this wife had given him four or five more children, three of whom were living. She died suddenly, giving birth once again, this time to a premature child, who took his first breaths of air, that blessing from God, and moaned once, then a second time, and was silent forever. And the unfortunate woman suffered for a whole day, despite the expertise of the old midwife, losing almost all her blood.

"Scarcely was the burial over when apparently old Soliman went into his bedroom—the most beautiful one, on the main floor and open to the west, and he wept there—great, long sobs... His daughters-in-law, or at least the second one, the one who dared speak in his presence and sometimes stood up to him, and therefore was his favorite, came to him and chided him: 'Lean on God's mercy, rely on his patience! Don't despair and don't weep so for the poor orphans! They have brothers and sisters who are men and women! They can count on them. I myself promise that if you wish I will suckle the youngest. I will be a mother for him!...'

"She had a big heart, this Halima, and thought to console him this way. But Soliman had always spoken his mind, and now that he was older, this habit was even more pronounced, and do you know what his reply was?

'It is not for the orphans that I am weeping. No! They are little and know nothing about life! But I, I, am I going to end my life all alone?'

"In short, you see, ten years after people thought he was too old to marry a virgin, he was complaining. He was afraid of how cold his bed would be! He wanted a woman…"

My aunt sighs, gets up to serve the tea, then, after a thoughtful silence she goes on, her head bent into the all-absorbing past: "Of course, one could imagine that being so old (eighty, or a hundred, tell me, what is the difference?), he would at least be looking for a widow, a lady unable to have children anymore, just because his bed is cold every night and also, as they say at home, "so she can carry him," him and his old bones! That could have seemed normal. Aren't men after all, and especially when they get older, big egotistical children!" Suddenly she briskly recovered: "Except, may Allah forgive me, our Prophet so sweet to our heart. He and the Mourashidien, the four well-guided *imams*, especially Sid Ali, the Prophet's son-in-law, his cousin, and—" her pious murmur became lost in a long list that her tears made incomprehensible.

"Soliman," she went on, calmer now. "Think especially how this would have affected his sons—there were at least ten of them alone—and his daughters, at least five or six, two of whom, the widow and the one who was repudiated, had returned to their father's house! Not only did the old man not die (and you must not forget that he was a tough businessman, who looked after his own interests, with his heirs even more than with strangers) but he got married for the fourth time, with your grandmother, who was so young!"

"Explain to me, Lalla, how the girl's father—this Ferhani, this forty-year-old who was, you say, a *mokkadem,* makes the decision to give his daughter, who was so very young, to a man who could be older than his own father!"

"It's true." She sighs. "If old Soliman had not had so many sons, you might think that the father, Ferhani, had reasoned that if his daughter were widowed young, he would stand to gain something himself. But in this case he knew very well that he would get very little. And besides, Fatima, who did in fact become a widow after three years of being there in the big house, had only a daughter and not a son!"

The aunt hesitates for just a moment; she stops, gets her breath, and then starts in again, this time speaking more dispassionately: "I must say, though—why should I hide this from you, after all, he is my maternal grandfather, even if I did not know him—that this father Ferhani had a reputation for being greedy."

My mind went elsewhere: I was having absolutely no success at imagining this grandparent now emerging for me from the darkness. In my childhood the only genealogy that had counted for me, through my mother's father, who was therefore my grandmother's third husband, had been that of this third husband. The important genealogy had been only through the father of the father of the mother, and going back, only the fathers of the preceding fathers, as if one single branch had been glorious, prestigious, heroic. Perhaps that was simply because it was the only one recorded in writing! Yet now my grandmother's father was making an appearance, an unexpected figure, in what my aunt was saying.

"When the father Ferhani gave his daughter in this manner, he in turn asked old Soliman for his own daughter, and obtained her, the most beloved Amna, daughter of Soliman's second wife. She was a beauty who was twenty years old, of course, but above all she was also very wealthy through her mother—the only daughter of a *caïd*. This young woman was nicknamed the Golden Woman, and she had been widowed recently. A widow and with no children! So that was what had really happened: Old Soliman agreed to give the beautiful Amna to Ferhani, who, though already married, with several children, was, in short, remarrying this time for pleasure and for esteem. At the same time that he sacrificed his little girl, he became the son-in-law of the wealthy Soliman and found himself the father-in-law of the old man as well! I don't know how they thought up this exchange. Perhaps Ferhani was the initiator of it after hearing the women talk at such length about how the old man pitied himself rather than his youngest children, who were now motherless! Probably Ferhani was already ogling Amna's beauty and surely her wealth. In any case, at first the barter between the two men was almost secret, but shortly before your grandmother's wedding, the town gossips discussed every detail on the terraces and in the far corners of courtyards. Yet no one became indignant. They let the little fourteen-year-old girl be carried off to spend her wedding night in the arms of the man…" The aunt hesitated, then added bluntly, "In the cold arms of a near-corpse!"

Suddenly, decades and decades later, she seemed to be suffering in Fatima's place as the virgin began her wedding night. Listening to my aunt chronicling the past, I felt fascinated—but also offended— I do not know why, by this more than sixty-year-old woman who was talking about her mother, dead now for fifteen years. She was delving three-quarters of a century back into her mother's life to become, instead of a tender and bitter daughter, just one woman facing up to another woman and attempting to live through the stings and nettles in her place, to relive the ordeals of this first destiny!

Once alone, near the balcony where the aunt takes such good care of her slender but profusely blooming jasmines, I try to imagine

Fatima's entrance into the house in Caesarea that I know so well: the most magnificent Arab residence in the city.

In 1896, when the nuptial procession arrives (barouches and people on foot, the bride entirely swallowed up beneath her father's flowing woolen cloak, riding on the ceremonial mule, and the line of women and children bearing candelabras, a group of black musicians walking ahead of them and keeping rhythm with their cymbals to the mournful songs, then the crowd proceeding down the very narrow streets next to the Roman theater, whose ruins had recently been excavated), Fatima descends from her mount and is carried to the first vestibule. From there she is led slowly to the main floor into the jostling crowd filling the marble and mosaic staircase—all the way to Soliman's chamber of honor. It was a summer day, or rather night, in the last century; and yet now I myself hear the pounding heart of the *mokkadem*'s daughter. She sees nothing of the women and children of the house where she is going to live. She knows she is going to sit in state (they close the shutters made of priceless cedar on the door, they give her a cup of lemonade to drink, they sprinkle perfumes from Mecca over her, an old woman intones a very shrill litany). Yes, she will live there as the mistress, as the infanta, in Caesarea's richest dwelling.

She will be able to look around tomorrow—or rather, not until after the seven days of interminable protocol. She will examine the banisters with their columns and arches crimped with copper, running all around the galleries of the main floor that overlook the patio below with its basin, and its floor tiled in turquoise blue and sea green. She will go down. In the reflection of the basin she will contemplate the overturned sky of the city. She will climb up to the terraces at dusk or early at night when the moon is full. From there she and the young girls of the family will spy on the neighboring terraces; she will try her hand at the game women play where messages are mimed just with moving fingers, or their bare forearms. She had already been told about this wordless language in her mountain *zaouia*. Apparently it is unique to the city-women, a language that, according to some, was supposed to have been brought from Andalusia, so that now the baker's daughter, Aouicha, who is simple-minded and mute, easily understood it and participated with sudden bursts of laughter in the nocturnal conversation floating in the sky from roof to roof among the women thus set free…

Yes, under her wedding veil, her hands and feet brilliantly stained with henna, her face wearing the traditional makeup with sequins glued between her eyebrows and the glistening triangles on the top of her cheekbones, yes, Fatima, her eyes downcast, expects that in a moment the "prince" will enter! Fatima imagines the whole heart, the whole body of the house, a sort of small palace, where, as mistress of the premises she is supposed to reign starting tomorrow… She knows that it is Soliman, her husband, who oversaw its entire construction a long long time ago, providing lodging for the best craftsmen in the country. He had marble brought from Italy, crockery from Morocco, maybe even from Holland. Then he inaugurated this house when he celebrated his second marriage and went on to celebrate his third there as well… Little Fatima suddenly felt how little she was, how isolated: her mother did not come, stayed behind in the hills to weep. But her proud, rough aunts, with their countrywomen's tawny scarves are there, coldly studying the copper and marble, all this luxury, and trying not to seem impressed. The crowd of women speed up their excited, spasmodic moaning: *ululu.*

Is the prince going to come in? Is the bridegroom going to lift the curtain? Fatima begins—even though the old woman guarding her as if she were an idol squats there on the threshold, keeping an eye on her (or at least on the small, silk veil half masking the girl's face)—

she begins to hope. Like so many young girl brides, she hopes, not daring to hope, that the "bride thief" will intervene. He is the one who will come in, the Adonis. Invisible to all the other women, he will slip in. He is the one who will lift the gauze veiling her face, will brush her lips, will reach out his fingers to make her stand up, and all of a sudden, two ghosts, they will float out to the vestibule where they will easily find the stairway to the terrace. They will take refuge there: facing the whole city and its port and the sea in the distance, its reflected glints of onyx.

Motionless, Fatima is dreaming when the curtain is raised. Her old guardian's voice intones the conventional good wishes: "May happiness be upon you, O Soliman!"

And taking in her hand his generous contribution, she slips outside, letting the curtain fall as the two cedar panels close softly behind it. Fatima feels her heart stop, her body suddenly grow cold. She keeps her eyes cast down when the man—her master—raises the light veil with his fingers and brings his gray face close to the young bride's eyes… His hand gropes, brushes Fatima's cheekbones, her eyes, and slowly, finally, she looks at him.

Humbly, Soliman murmurs in a voice full of emotion, "A gift from God, my daughter! From God!"

Then, as is customary, he goes to the corner of the long room to begin his prayer: trembling, praying that God grant him the potency, the power—he repeats the word at the end of his invocation— "the power to enjoy the gifts of God!"

On my aunt's balcony, beneath the jasmine and not quite a century later, I wonder if the old man in his seventies was able to deflower the virgin that first night. There is no doubt that was what everyone wanted to know the next day: the women of the extended family, young and old, and the waiting heirs: the sons, the sons' sons, the sons-in-law, the brothers-in-law… In the morning Soliman was the first to enter his private *hammam:* "For ablutions," he said, his head held high and looking proud.

Did some mystery remain at the end of this wedding celebration: Was the old man "potent" from the first night on or only after several nights of effort? By spying on the bride, the women were unable to guess, as they usually could, whether her face radiated some secret contentment, some passive or serene acceptance, or bitterness not properly kept in control… The fourth wife seemed so young, and, it must be said, so reserved, whereas the daughters-in-law and the daughters all knew that this daughter of the *mokkadem* of Saint Ahmed, or Abdallah, grew up in the country, free no doubt, and cherished and laughing… The day after her wedding she stood up straight and mysterious, neither bitter nor beaming with fulfillment: nor was she closed and withdrawn; she put on no airs; she concealed nothing. There, confronted with so many matrons, and heiresses, and wives of heirs, was she already facing up to the future days of mute rivalry, spying, and complicity? No. She remained the *mokkadem's* daughter, calmly accustomed to the homage of peasant men and women in her hamlet up there, thanks to the *baraka* entrusted to her as well.

Did she almost think of herself as old Soliman's daughter, or granddaughter? Did he, as the gossips imagined, all night long caress her naked body, the blossoms of her breasts, the face she offered? She said nothing. She confessed nothing. Nor did she seem to regret anything either.

Even after the next day in the *hammam,* when she would only tolerate bathing with her young aunt and her younger sister, she did not listen to the murmurs afterward as the wedding sheet, spattered with a long streak of crimson, passed from hand to hand among the

oldest ladies seated on the deep mattresses of the reception hall facing the bedroom of the master of the house.

I stayed there, living with my aunt, the only one of my mother's
sisters still alive, although quite old, pious and gentle, and I felt
fussed over. She guessed that these are transitional days in my life and
was worried about it. ("So, like your grandmother you, too—but she,
she does it later, for the youngest child, the third, a boy—you are
leaving the man, you flee, you abandon the unlocked house to him?
Is that the law, are you at least retaining your rights?… Alas, where
are our rights, whether we are illiterate or educated, all of us, all
women? It is as bad today as yesterday." That is what she whispered
that evening as we stood looking out over the twilight, while the
sounds of the crowded street rose up to the balcony.)

Why, I mused, still dreaming about the grandmother, does feminine memory tirelessly return in concentric circles to the fathers and
leave in the shadows (naturally in the silence of the unwritten as well)
the real crises, the blacking out, the fall of a woman? As if that were
too much, as if it undermined the very roots of strength and hope, of
the future! Too much…

For example, back to father Ferhani! The man who married off
his fourteen-year-old daughter but who shortly afterward hastily
remarried, forcing his first wife to be present for this wedding,
responsible for the meals, the proper reception of the guests, and the
necessary organization of the festivities… And he required particularly (a husband's ambiguous and strange cruelty) that she look at the
bride who was younger, of course, though already widowed, and
especially more fortunate because she was "the Golden Woman." She,
the wife who reigned in the other wife's room—and who had waited
beneath the candles for the husband on the verge of entering, wearing his white ceremonial cloak, dipping his shoulder at the door and

smiling with happiness to the sounds of ululation—she was the first wife! But now her hands were in the butter, her face red as she bent over the bouillon for couscous in the steamy kitchen, and she watched from her own place, watching the husband repeat his entrance into the bedroom, fifteen years after her own marriage.

It had only taken fifteen years for her to change roles, for her to cease being the one set up like an idol who waited, her heart pounding. Only fifteen years for her to become the servant, the cook at the hot stove. Yes, on the same evening, the same smile from the man, making the same entrance as today, and suddenly—suddenly a long cry, followed by silence from all the women (too late, the bridegroom has already closed the door on his marriage). And she, the first wife, falls flat on the ground, right on the threshold of the pantry... All the women of the family run to her and sprinkle her face and palms with cool water, they make her sit up like a floppy doll, they repeat verses for her, they pass the ewers around and orange-flower water. But still, a week later, they carried her off, dead: "With a swollen belly," my aunt tells me today.

"What did she have?" I feel touched, and I add, "What did the doctor say?"

"Was there a doctor for women then? No... In those days, never, not even for childbirth, would we have entered a French hospital! The women who told me about it (no, not your grandmother, she never said anything about this wedding, but instead her young sister, my aunt, whom you knew, the mother of the "great fighter" in the resistance), these women all thought that it was livid, powerless jealousy that "made her blood go bad."

And so, father Ferhani had hardly remarried when he found himself a widower. It must be said that "the Golden Woman," his newlywed, turned out to have a big heart: She went back down to the city and moved into one of the houses her mother had inherited. There she regularly received her husband when he would come down, dressed in white, even more sumptuously than before, like a *caïd* or a *bachagha*. Afterward, she remained barren, but she dealt generously with her husband's children as their stepmother.

"He died honored by all men and all women?" I asked tongue-in-cheek. "This Ferhani who," I stressed, "was the one responsible for the death of his wife!"

"Oh!" My aunt was surprised. "In those days men were naturally harsh! Often without even being aware of it… And others, of course—Moh', your mother's half brother, comes to mind, and M'hamed, the younger half brother—others keep their hearts untarnished. Sometimes they even love just one woman in their lifetime! Ferhani died in the sanctuary. I remember hearing the news of his sudden death; I was a little girl. As for the saint's tomb, what is left of it? Nothing, only ruins, the result of the war of liberation! Today's "people in high places," as you well know, make fun of our *marabouts*… Because they themselves have no lineage." She muttered in displeasure, shrugged her shoulders, then was silent.

Now, during the week following the final breakup of my first marriage, as I plunged into the maze of my genealogy—the genealogy of my mother and of the grandmother whom I used to feel was so terrifying—I reconstruct this memory.

I wanted to conjure up the grandmother when, just before 1900, old Soliman died: What was the day like when the seventeen-year-old widow left this house that later would be so familiar to me?

The entire extended family, numbering so many, is there after the third day of the funeral. The women have returned from the rustic cemetery, the one overlooking the city and close enough to the

Roman baths on the west that the dead of recent generations are getting in the way of the digs that scientists from the capital consider necessary!

Soliman's sons, his daughters, and his grandsons respect the standard custom, keeping the house (which, for many, during these times of deprivation, seems the last remaining little Arabian palace) in joint ownership and favoring the eldest along with the most energetic (or at least the least lethargic) of the younger ones. Oddly, several of Soliman's sons, unlike the founding father, will prove to be dreamers and given to pleasure, frequenting musical evenings or spending their time in the company of fishermen in secluded inlets. So "the most capable" are allowed to manage the surrounding farms and orchards.

The hierarchy of the heirs was visible in the new division of the domestic quarters: The second floor, the most splendid (because the father lived there), with its four long, deep bedrooms each of which had its separate kitchen and "Turkish" toilet, and galleries covered by luminous mosaics, with banisters whose twisted columns were made of cedar and pine from Aleppo, was reserved for the sons of the first marriage, or at least the ones who remained in the city. The rooms on the ground floor were more numerous but more shady, wide open to the patio, with its basin and fountain rippling their tiny, honeyed music. These were reserved, half for the daughters (the repudiated one and several grandchildren, adolescent girls) and half for the two younger sons who remained bachelors... (I imagine them from puberty on feeling vaguely disgusted, or merely uncomfortable, with the "vitality"—in marriages and descendants—of their omnipresent father!)

This new division of the space must have been made easier when Fatima, the young widow, had let them know—either through one of the old women (one of those poor relations living there two or three months at a time before finding shelter somewhere else, in another of the "great houses" of the city) or telling the eldest daughter-in-law directly—her decision. "I shall not remain with you. You are my family of course. But I have sent for my father to come for me and my little daughter."

The daughter-in-law replied, "This house is your house, O Lalla." Because even if the young widow was not yet twenty, she was still the only widow of old Soliman and had a sizable share in the inheritance.

Fatima looked at Halima for a long time, Halima, always the most eloquent one in the sadness of these restricted days: "I thank you, O Halima. This house will be a haven for my daughter, Khadidja; she will be well off here among you, among her brothers and sisters. There are many of them, thanks be to God! But please, tell your husband that I have sent for my father. Because tomorrow I want to return home with him."

Halima emotionally kissed the widow's hand and cheeks. She had had the opportunity to confirm Fatima's character and maturity. ("Just sixteen!" Halima thought to herself. "If only the dead man's sons, the ones who are already forty, had the lucidity of this adolescent!")

Father Ferhani, adorned in his two togas, the one of Tlemcen wool and the heavy woolen one from Fez, arrived that very evening. He bore regretfully a message from his wife (whether he admired or loved her I do not know; perhaps he was also afraid of her): Amna the Golden Woman, made known to her half brothers that she would not take part in the discussions concerning the inheritance, that they should inform the *cadi* of this. Allah had assured her—thanks to her mother's wealth alone. which her father, it is true, had luckily made profitable—of a comfortable and peaceful life. She was content with that. She had no descendants. Her husband, thanks be to God, was noble and "beloved of God." Consequently his house and "the *caïd's* orchards" (the most beautiful olive trees on the hillsides as well as an orange grove at *oued* el-Mellah) were enough for him: for his comfort and for the alms that she would now give increasingly. She would take care of the youngest of her sisters, Khadidja, who was scarcely two, the daughter of Fatima, and, by lucky accident, the grand-daughter of her husband whom she so much respected... Let Fatima come to her home and live there, where she would be surrounded by peace and serenity!

And so Fatima packed her bags: three willow trunks lined with pink satin, several others that were wooden and painted in the Algerian style, her gowns, and above all her jewels, the ones from her marriage and the ones that Soliman liked to buy her almost every month, because toward the end he had become more and more extravagant with his young wife.

Fatima takes her little daughter in her arms, even though she is as heavily veiled as when she arrived for the wedding night three years before.

During the three years that she lived there, she left the big house regularly once a week on the eve of Friday to go to her father and her stepmother's house. From the beginning she had told Soliman, "My father is used to having me be the one to bring him the copper cup for his ablutions and then the towels every Friday morning, and having me unfold his antique rug from Fez for him. I do this for his dawn prayer because the second prayer he makes in public, though not like his father. In earlier days his father would descend from the *zaouia* just to pray at the great and venerable mosque, the mosque "with a hundred columns" and built of green marble—alas, this sacred place was turned into a common hospital by the French! But my father goes now to the oldest remaining mosque, the one most people go to."

Soliman, in the bedroom—this was around the tenth day after the wedding and already Fatima knew how to make her desires known—had listened to his child wife's wish: "Oh, I wouldn't like for my father, the *mokkadem*, not to have me there at dawn every Friday!" Then Soliman, to everyone's astonishment, agreed, with the excuse that Fatima was descended from *mokkadems* (and thus blessed). Every Thursday evening she went to spend the night in Amna's house with her father; she stood there at her father's bedside at dawn, even before the faintest voice from the most distant *muezzin* could be heard.

So this time, accompanied by her daughter, she went back to her father's home. She stayed there until the next day, Friday. Saw to Ferhani's prayer... Then, seven days and seven nights later, she heard herself say to him as well as to his wife who sat beside him, radiant, "Forgive me, both of you! As God is my witness I would like to live my whole life beside you! And you are my daughter's true guardians! But..."

And she stopped, intimidated.

"What do you want, then, daughter?" father Ferhani exclaimed in a gruff voice, giving his wife who was just as surprised, a questioning look.

"I miss the mountains, and I like being at the *zaouia* so much! I want to go back up there and probably live there!" She sighed.

Soon afterward, Fatima, her daughter in her arms, left the city in a *barouche*.

Arable Woman III

A MONTH BEFORE filming began, after two days of looking for locations, I got out of the car with the assistant director and went toward the farm: sheds and solidly built houses, all buried, however, behind any number of reed hedges. It was a beautiful day.

I went around the main house. Behind it and beyond a hedge of Barbary figs a large wasteland went down to the sea on the other side. There, among the pebbles and red rocks, a panorama of Chenoua mountain met one's eyes: a wide view with the isolated mountain jutting out like a gigantic ship over the deep bay. Nobility of lines, majesty, with a sort of modesty to its various colors, and on the left, hills fading off toward the interior plain: Chenoua—a screen, almost like one in a theater, standing in front of my family's mountains, where I have been traveling now for four months already.

I wanted this flat, open stretch to be like a balcony out over the calm and everyday countryside that the couple in the film story could see. Luckily from here one cannot make out the new patch of white, the tourist village built ten years ago.

Up behind me, surrounded by peasants, the chauffeur and the assistant director are waiting for me. It is four in the afternoon: alone here, my rendezvous is with this space. It is the space of my childhood and of something else… perhaps the space of this fiction to be created. Four o'clock in the afternoon: not even Camus and his *étranger* come to mind.

Alone I walk across this shelf. I hide my excitement by walking athletically, in sudden great strides (I am glad I have long legs for walking energetically while everything inside me churns and boils).

On this November day the air is soft and the end of autumn takes on intense hues, almost those of spring, and I am happy. I neither hide it nor show it. Not yet. I neither burst out into dancing nor yeild to the violent desire to dissolve, to fly away and disappear. Oh, these months of fierce chastity (just as fierce as were my years of sensual love)!

And thus it all began. Not the first period of quiet investigation: the endless whispering conversations with the old women of my tribe, the questions that were misleadingly banal, the words of my childhood language.

Everything really began this first day on the farm, everything. Because as I found my everyday space, this film's existence became no longer theoretical but present. Though you might not think so, this freedom.

This space, in actual fact, is like me. So, I think, begin a film story, when the space that is right for it is really found. Go all around this space. The way they used to make the walls of the city first and then—an hour later, a day later—build the city in the middle.

So this November day my own city—that is, the house in which my three characters, Lila, Ali, and their daughter Aïcha will live—is founded.

I went back up to the hedge of fig trees encircling the main house. Hamid, the assistant director, is in lively negotiations with the people living there, fishermen or peasants from the nearby cooperative, in case I intend to shoot on location. I leave them. I say that the view is beautiful. I go to a door in the back. Silhouettes of women staring at us between two reed hedges. Greetings. They invite me in. Then I have my second flash of inspiration, just as secret, not very expansive.

Three women in rooms without electricity. An infant cries sporadically. And I, feeling my way around until I get used to it.

The mother, who is probably forty, looks to be fifty or older. Stern, with well-balanced features, tall; her smiling manner has a touch of reserve. She seems attentive to whatever might happen at the edge of her gaze. Two other women, a young girl—sixteen years old, with plump cheeks, named Saïda, who later will be Djamila in the film, the couple's friendly neighbor—and another woman, whose beauty would strike any visitor.

I never knew her name. I will call her "the unknown woman at the farm," or "the Madonna." She was scarcely more than twenty; her balanced features were disturbing, with such a pure bloom, yet seeming, at the same time, tarnished with shadow... a half smile, not aware herself of her own sadness. The Madonna: whenever I saw her after this she was holding a baby in her arms, a sickly baby. How can I portray her first appearance, how it extended into each of the forty days spent at the farm? Forty times as I came or went through a side door (a door only I was allowed to use) between the rooms rented for the film and the rest of the house, I would see again the slender silhouette. She held herself up straight, with only her shoulders a bit sunken as if the threat of tuberculosis hung over her. The Madonna.

Sometimes with her breast out, her baby whimpering (the baby I did not look at but whose illness I felt, I heard), she would smile at me. Forty times I looked at the dazzling purity of her face, her clear gaze, her cheeks still rosy with youth, and that hollow between her shoulders.

I lingered over the Madonna. Perhaps because, several days before we started filming, I knew for sure that she would not figure in the film. By chance I had come upon a family willing to collaborate with the image and the machinery we brought, whether out of economic interest or out of a real openness (a rather rare event in the new rural world). Afterward I wondered to what extent the mother was the dominant influence. She had guessed, confident in herself and her authority over her family, that she could extract some profit from us with no moral damage. I also think that the mother had instinctively judged me and the new role I represented for them, the threat I was in a position to keep in check...

So I quickly knew that the Madonna would only exist for me, outside the "shot," that her image could not be bought... It was as if, right from the start, she held on to her integrity for two reasons, as if her beauty concentrating the family secret had to remain inaccessible to us... There was no violent refusal when this happened, not even the Islamic prohibition that one might have expected would be aggressive. "No." It was a calm no that the mother would put to me, and the only reason she gave seemed obvious: "No, because her husband, my son, works in the capital and is not here."

I did not insist. I knew instantly that no would be no. Even though, during this period of cold heat prior to shooting the film, I knew that I would get everything ("everything" in my hunt for images). I was persuaded that insistence, friendliness, and solidarity, an appeal to reasonable interest, would work, and "any method" seemed honorable to me. But the crux of my confidence lay finally in this drive to make the film concrete; all the thankless or exalting work consisted of putting the documentary materials into shape. More precisely, rediscovering its original form and thus redoing mine.

I go back to the Madonna of the shadows, to her baby who nurses but is sick. She could have been the first to say, with that shy smile she gives me, "I represent all the women here that your machines will not define. I am the fringe of what is forbidden, and I like you."

She made coffee for me every time I would come in tense and wanting to feel I was somewhere else. She was the somewhere else— and by the same token all my feminine past. Now I understand: Starting from the moment when taking her picture was denied me, precisely because of the proximity both of her beauty and of the half-light in which she constantly lived, her presence was an extension, the background that made those in the film uncertain. She evoked the persistence of things enduring back in time forever…

And I stitched it together with the women of my childhood. Drawing a parallel between the Madonna and the wife of my maternal uncle, this aunt who died at twenty in childbirth and whom I must have just barely known, and yet—because of a faded photograph (she was seated, her long face, her evanescent body, in the huge armchair of a Syrian salon whose pearly luxury intimidated me for years afterward), in my child dreams she took on a poetic, haunting presence. She was dead, they told me. I was expecting to find her again in the back of some scene; suddenly the reality would come unraveled into shadows.

And so the Madonna, during the course of this project, represented for me the grace to secretly question it. *I, elusive, invisible, if I decided suddenly to appear, your moving pictures would reveal their bloodless, embryonic nature.*

If I decided... I came and went from shadow to reality, from the stage to the wings, from the spotlights to the Madonna's candle. The obvious fact that crystallized in spurts within me was that it was the others: brothers, husband, neighbors, and most of all the all-powerful mother, who maintained the barrier between the two spaces. *If I decided...*

The Madonna could have put her sick baby down just like that on a sheepskin or at her feet and take one step, just one step. I would open the door for her, she would have nothing to do for the cameramen, maybe just a hint of movement, her fingers pulling the neck of her gown shut, just a few steps.

Abruptly the need for this work of sounds and images would dissolve; there would be no point to the fiction because, wonder of wonders, suddenly every woman on this earth would be able to come and go.

"Finally, there are no more spying looks," my character, Lila, says. Lila, beneath the spotlights, would reach out toward the Madonna; Lila would gradually move backward to the rear of the scene, the spotlights would go out, eyes would open wider and wider and from them the real light would finally well up as the Madonna would slip out, smiling. *If I decided...*

THIRD MOVEMENT:
OF THE MOTHER AS LITTLE GIRL

TWENTY YEARS LATER, Fatima, daughter of the *mokkadem* of Saint Ahmed or Abdallah, goes back down to the city, this time for good.

During these two decades she has lived her fate as the wife of three successive husbands. (The third was my grandfather, from whom that year, 1920, she officially separated, asking the *cadi* for autonomy, according to Muslim law, to manage her own wealth alone.) It was also her fate to be a mother. She returns to Caesarea where her stepmother, Amna, a widow now for ten years and a devoted friend, had welcomed her in her home before.) She is accompanied by all her children, except Khadidja, her first, who at the age of sixteen was married in a nearby hamlet. Khadidja was expecting a child at the time—finally a son who will live, O merciful Allah, not like the first three, all boys as well, who each died after a few days!

Fatima: from now on everyone will call her Lla Fatima, though I, like all my cousins, call her *mamané*, hinting with this word at the affection that her strict bearing kept us from showing her. Lla Fatima has with her for this first move her only son. He is just barely ten, it is true, but so extraordinarily beautiful; this son, from now on, according to her will be "her only future." And she has her three daughters, two adolescents, and the youngest child, who is two years old, the only child of the husband she is leaving. This little girl turning her back on the mountain (and leaving the Berber language) is my mother.

Of my mother as a little girl? She never spoke of this day from her early childhood when she entered the first house in Caesarea. Does she even remember it? She probably does not want to, why recall the sharpness of the separation? The country house they had left behind whose many low rooms were painted in purplish-blue whitewash every spring, that had two yards and a row of fig trees and, in the middle, two very majestic zen oaks. There were children scattered everywhere. A separation from laughter and the vast horizon… Without transition there they were living in town, in a high building with imposing walls; at the bottom one huge, bleak bedroom into which they all squeezed. The mother is endlesly conferring. To begin with, she is given some advice by an old cleric connected with the family. Soon afterward she sells all her jewels to buy an old house a little higher up and not far from the walls, still in the Arab quarter. Consequently Lla Fatima will be almost Amna's neighbor, in the neighborhood of her former home where Soliman lived. His daughters, moreover, who are older now, some of them already grandmothers, come to visit her and congratulate her on her move: She is the model of feminine decisiveness and intelligence. They call her aunt or *amti*, that is, "paternal aunt." Out of respect.

Lla Fatima, finally in her own home, surrounded by her son— who attends the French school—and her three daughters, begins her new life. She is not yet forty.

Little Bahia, a little more than two, almost three now, explores the new place: four deep rooms, the patio with just one tree, an orange tree (with the bitter oranges so much sought after for preserves) spreading its low, dense foliage. Way in the back is the edge of a well and right next to it a staircase leading to a broad, low terrace from which there is a view of the mountainous slopes of the southern part of the city.

Bahia squats all alone in the back near the edge of the well. When they call her, she runs away; she climbs the staircase and makes a place for herself on the terrace with her cat, in a hidden corner where she has put down a mat. She stretches out, contemplates the mountain: she can hear noise from the nearby houses, smell the coffee roasting or the paprika cooking, hear the scattered voices of the gossips shouting, laughing. One voice of an unknown woman, in the evening, just before the prayer at sunset, sings, naked and alone, always singing the same lament...

Lying there on her back, Bahia fills her eyes with the blue of the sky and dreams: She would like to be far from the city. (Below, in the reception hall, the endless stream of ladies still comes to congratulate Lla Fatima.) She imagines herself at her father's house at the *zaouia* of the Beni Menacers.

Bahia's father is the man Lla Fatima has left. One afternoon a week he comes. One hour after the Friday public prayer he knocks at the front door. The meal awaits him; he comes in. Afterward he shuts himself up with his wife in her room.

When Hassan, Lla Fatima's son, returns from school to discover that "the other man," the one not his father, is trying to bring Lla Fatima back to her senses (or submission?), he climbs up to the terrace, where he finds little Bahia. To calm his displeasure, he says mockingly, "You, why don't you go with your father? That's your father, isn't it?"

"That's my father!" answers the child.

"Go do it! When he comes out, go and tell him to take you!"

Bahia would like that. She would like to take her father's hand when he crosses the patio, she would like him to call her joyfully in his clear, musical voice, she would like to stay with him… She bursts out crying; she weeps in silence, but how could she defy the big brother?

A fifteen-year-old girl appears; her long hair is light brown and her somewhat wide-set eyes are the color of honey. Catching them in this childish conversation, she scolds Hassan roundly: "Why are you jealous of her? And what will she do without us?"

Bahia takes refuge in the skirts of her favorite sister, Chérifa. She cries even harder, this time for the pleasure of being comforted, of wallowing in Chérifa's sweetness, her warm voice, her almost motherly caresses.

The brother shrugs his shoulders, implying that he knows what is going on.

"You think I don't know! *Mma* brought us all down here so she can hang on to her wealth. Her wealth comes from my father. And that man there," he says, waving angrily toward the couple's room, "was the one profiting from it up to now!"

"You're not even ten years old and you're already looking after grown people's business!" Chérifa says sarcastically, finished now with consoling the little girl.

"What kind of authority will my brother have over me and my sisters and my mother when my Lord Brother"—she says it in Arabic, *"Sidi Khouya"*—"is a grown man!" Chérifa, jaunty and teasing, bursts into laughter.

Even now, three-quarters of a century later, I, Isma, the narrator, the descendant through the youngest daughter, do not know if Lla Fatima ("*mamané*") loved her two successive husbands afterward, or one rather than the other, or one more than the other... Surely I am the only one who wonders about dead people this way!

"The two mountain husbands," I call them for short. The mountain is the Dahra—etymologically the mountain of the "back" or "that turns its back" on the city of Caesar. Despite the way it looks, in these ravines at the beginning of this century called by some "the colonial night," right in with these rocks and eroded slopes, at the bottom of half-dried-up wadis, some rebellious individuals hung on and kept alive and resisted. They felt they were still "aristocrats"; even though all that remained of their property was dust, still there was a dark deposit springing inside them, the memory of former battles (against the Turks in the old days, against the French yesterday).

Was it for this oxygen that Fatima, widowed at seventeen, furrowed with pride and sensing the acrid taste of freedom, left the city and went back up into the mountains? She raised her little girl, Khadidja, alone for several years and only returned to Caesarea once a year for the great feast of Abraham, to show her first child to the crowd of half brothers and half sisters. Was it for this air?

When Khadidja is six, Fatima, taking the advice of her father the *mokkadem*, agrees to marry an honorable suitor from the region: Si Larbi, one of the descendants of another saint, twenty or so miles from here, on the slope that faces Miliana. This saint's religious reputation is greater than Saint Ahmed or Abdallah's.

Si Larbi is not young, but he is still not an old man. He is "in the prime of life," or at least that is how Ferhani describes him to Fatima through his wife Amna, "the Golden Woman." In the spring Amna goes up to the *zaouia* for a few days. She sees Fatima, at twenty-four, acting as mistress of the house for the entire little community: servants, dependent families, tenants... Fatima, first one up at four in the morning, taking care of the animals in the darkness first then awakening the little shepherds and farm girls. Not stopping there, smiling, sturdy and radiant, taking hardly any rest when it is time for the siesta and then receiving the usual women come to visit; they will bring her the detailed chronicle that makes its way through the valleys, from the hills and tiny hamlets. On the other hand, she will listen somewhat absentmindedly to the news Amna brings from the city: the scattering of Soliman's family, the weddings, the funerals, the newly wealthy...

Amna mentions the Berkanis, the prestigious family to which the suitor belongs. She does not say that she understands perfectly well what Ferhani is up to. Up to this point he has been setting in play a whole strategy against the heirs of the two Berkani saints (father and son, buried side by side in two mausoleums), men of exalted faith who had only arrived two centuries before. Some said, predictably, that they came from Seguiat el-Hamra, on the borders of Mauritania, the cradle of almost all the sacred genealogies. Others preferred to say they were Andalusian exiles come through the usual places: Tétouan, then Fez and Tlemcen, then the mountains neighboring Médéa, at the moment when Algiers was a modest village (a little hideout for pirates trapped by the Spanish fortifications on Peñón). Finally, at the beginning of the eighteenth century, they would have reached this *zaouia* of the Beni Menacers that the oh so "glorious" General de Saint-Arnaud would come to pillage from top to bottom, burning the olive trees and all the orchards...

So, as the *mokkadem* Ferhani sees it in his schemes and ruminations, Algeria at the turn of the century apparently is still at war with itself. One dead saint vies with another dead saint, one *koubba*, that is, tomb and sanctuary, vies with another *koubba*, another sanctuary—just as elsewhere, in other places, one bell tower would be the rival of another. A phantom Algeria where the living, who think they are living for themselves, continue in spite of themselves to settle the accounts of dead men who are not quite dead and who keep right on devouring each other...

Amna talks to the young Fatima and convinces her to marry Si Larbi, the descendant of Saint Berkani, this saint who is considered to be a "modernist" because one of his grandsons (in fact, a great-grandnephew) chose, right from the outset, to side with emir Abd el-Kader against the protégés of the French. Aïssa el-Berkani, one of the emir's five caliphates, lost almost the entire Berkani patrimony as a result, but increased its prestige considerably. Si Larbi, who thus became Fatima's second husband, after a stormy life, much of which was spent in exile in the west, seems to have been a beloved, perhaps loving, spouse—in any case one who was sensible and with a tranquil spirit. Long after his death, forgetting herself, Lla Fatima, throughout her austere old age would mention and even sometimes quote Si Larbi.

Her first child by him was Chérifa, the great beauty, and next Malika, two years younger. (This is the aunt who now welcomes and cherishes me during these days I spend resting there, probably because she has always been sad that she had only boys and not even one girl of her own.) Then finally came the beloved son. Soon afterward, Si Larbi, always lovingly responsible for the eldest child, Khadidja, gave Fatima some advice concerning her marriage. Then he fell sick; for a whole year Fatima cared for him.

Dealers in ancient medicine came from every hill, from even the most modest and humble sanctuary, from as far away as the Sahel around the capital, sellers of potions and rare herbs: but any *roumi*, even a learned doctor, the sick man would have refused. Fatima knew that no Christian would cross the threshold of the Beni Menacer family, and regretted it. A second time she found herself a widow. This time, I imagine, she wept.

When, two years later, she married Malek el-Berkani's cousin (she was thirty, or a little older; he was practically the same age, though some say he was probably two or three years younger), it came as a surprise to the people around her. They expected her to take solace in solitude and piety. No.

Was it a marriage for love this time? No one will ever know... The bitter and cynical version of the "other man's" son sometimes seems to be right: Yes, Fatima's wealth was primarily Si Larbi's, hence it was also the property of her son and her two adolescent daughters... And now the cousin, having remarried into the same household, started any number of new projects: modernizing the arboriculture and buying agricultural equipment never seen before in the mountains... Up to this point no "native" farmer had dared to imitate the European colonists of the plains!

In the off-season the young husband, who had been so busy and energetic, became unruly! He liked the itinerant bands of musicians and supported them. Sometimes he would not show up until dawn after evenings spent far away in the company, people said, of dancers... News of this was reported any number of times to Fatima, who, with her children, remained near the sanctuary. Did she regret the days when, she, all alone in her father's *zaouia*, knew just as well as this man how to inject enthusiasm into everything, or did the shadow of the dancers inhabit the sleepless hours of her lonely evenings? She was of two minds.

Then Malek would settle down and devote himself entirely to overseeing the crops. Everyone called him the *chatter*, the man who is energetic and unflagging, throughout the region.

The little girl that Fatima had by him, Bahia, was two, the same age as her eldest daughter, when Fatima was widowed for the first time and decided to return to these "back" mountains—the Dahra. She muttered this word: *dahra;* ancient revolts had taken place on this site, and it was also, she thought: "the site of women's bitterness" (as if, suddenly, the image of her mother who died so tragically, had the upper hand)! In the end she decided upon the separation of property that is provided for in Islamic law.

"To protect my son's future!" she would say on the day that she and almost all her children rode in the barouche back down to Caesarea for good.

Two or three years later she is just barely getting used to her new house. She learns that her husband, Malek, whose weekly visits have become less and less frequent, has now taken action. Lla Fatima did not plan to live in the mountains again (using the excuse of her son's French education). Lla Fatima does not want to come back and moreover does not let him manage the land. So he will remarry. He sends her the letter of repudiation… Is it on this black day that she starts going into her dramatic trances? No, I think not.

Misfortunes continue even though she has just bought another house. It is near the European quarter, just behind the church built like an ancient temple; this building is larger, its huge rooms have windows and balconies facing the street on the first floor, but they also look out onto Moorish galleries opening toward the sea and the port. So it is in a modern, mixed style (she is already imagining her son's wedding that will be celebrated here in ten years)! She does not yet live there. She leaves one of the apartments on the ground floor rented to the city's former rabbi and his family, whom she knows. She will live on the main floor and meet with her sharecroppers in the unoccupied rooms downstairs... She thinks about how she will move when autumn comes.

And yet misfortune (or probably "the evil eye") continues: This is 1924 and there is an epidemic of typhoid fever in the city—it occurs first in the surrounding regions, but no one pays any attention, then it quickly reaches the Arab quarter.

Just before summer Lla Fatima realized that almost all her children were infected. Only Malika remained healthy, and took care of Chérifa, who took to bed first, then Bahia, the little one, who became dangerously delirious as a result of her raging fever. When it was Hassan's turn to become tortured by constant vomiting, Lla Fatima lost heart. She was alone: Her father had been dead for ten years, her younger sister had long ago married in a distant city, and Amna was now practically paralyzed by the rheumatism of old age.

Aided by Malika—who was just thirteen but a hard worker, silent and energetic—Lla Fatima coped with it all. She decided that she would even call a doctor—yes, the French doctor, why not: she was the first Arab "lady" in the city who dared do so. The physician, a gruff man of fifty who could speak a few words of the local dialect, came to the house, curtly sounded "the hand of Fatima" at the heavy door, crossed the patio, went into the first room, where the son had lain, almost unconscious, for three days. He listened to his chest, wrote out a prescription, then asked to see the daughters who were ill. He spent more time over Chérifa, who smiled at him sadly (it was only at that moment that her mother became aware of how thin the adolescent had become: she never complained, she was sweet and passive in her illness, her narrow eyes looking at you from far away, so far away, and always this smile!…). Bahia, the baby, also seemed to worry the Frenchman. Without consultation he administered some lotions he carried in his heavy satchel; he wrote out a second prescription and said he would come back in two days' time.

While he was washing his hands and wrists—Malika poured the water for him from a ewer by the edge of the well—he remarked that he was an object of curiosity for the anonymous women watching from the neighboring terraces. He did not even smile: Fatima's children were on his mind, and Fatima understood this and was grateful for it. So a Frenchman could be her ally. She gave him her sincere blessings in thanks and asked how to "pay him"; he answered briefly in Arabic: "Afterward," and he left.

This created a small revolution in the city. The old families took note of the fact that Lla Fatima (who was nonetheless descended, both through her father and through her two last husbands, from the men who had formerly resisted the occupying forces) had not thought twice about having her children treated "in France."

Hassan, moreover, was the first to get well, and it seemed to his mother that the first noose had been untied. Bahia was still lethargic and hardly spoke at all. She hardly ever left the bedside of Chérifa, whom she adored, in whose arms she had loved to fall asleep so often—Chérifa, who did not get well.

Lamentations of women… The little girl crouched at the head of the young dead woman.

The little girl sits dry-eyed before the crowd of women in white all seated in a circle around Chérifa, swallowed up beneath the shroud, only her face still visible, pale, a mask. The little girl who is looking at it does not speak, will not speak, not tomorrow, nor still at the end of the week.

The kinswomen are touched; one of them comes and tries to take hold of Bahia, to make her sit on her knees: "A six-year-old child, in state like that at the head of a dead woman!" "Beware of the evil eye!" warns another, and the third: "Chérifa, may God have mercy on her, was in fact like a mother to her youngest sister! As if she had a premonition, poor girl, that she would never have children, that she would die first!" "Orphaned by her sister, that is the most awful thing!" moaned another, a woman they did not know. She was from the capital, recently married, and her beauty was a little wild, which made her somewhat feared and respected by her sisters-in-law.

"The loss of the sister, awful?" exclaimed an old woman with an inquisitive look. "It is the mother, when one loses a mother, that leaves you with an open wound!"

"I am sure," continued the stranger (they called her this because she did not speak her dialect with a Caesarean accent), "that losing a sister is the worst!" Then, without getting up, she recited in a louder voice and in learned language:

"O my other self, my shadow, my one so like me,
You are gone, you have deserted me, left me arable,
Your pain, a plowshare, turned me over and seeded me with tears."

At these last words, rhyming in ancient Arabic, a woman suddenly shrieked. She stood up, tall and thin; she tore her scarf with one hand, and the fingers of her other opened to tear slowly at her left cheek.

The poet crouched there and was silent; Bahia stood up, her mouth gaping and her eyes growing larger at the sight of the bloody face of the weeping woman. Another woman gently tried to draw the little girl to her. The one who screamed just that once now was casually wiping her cheek, then suddenly she had something like a spasm, her torso shaken as if with a sort of laughter. To everyone's astonishment, she cried out: the strange language that most of these city-women did not understand or that they had forgotten and greeted now as the improvisation went on by making faces that showed their embarrassment mixed with condescension. The Berber language ran rapidly on as if pawing the ground, stamping, as one woman whispered to another, "That is the dead girl's cousin who has come down from the *zaouia*; she often improvises like this in their mountain language!"

So the cousin, her cheek dry now, with just the pink traces of scratches showing, beat out:

> *"Seg gwasmi yebda useggwas*
> *Wer nezhi yiggwas!"*

And she cried out the last two lines in a more piercing voice:

> *"Meqqwer lhebs iy inyan*
> *Ans'ara el ferreg felli!"*

And Malika, the dead girl's sister, who did not weep but remained standing, motionless, near the doorway, then said in her metallic voice,

"Oh bless you, my uncle's daughter, come so far to share our grief!"

Then, speaking to the women who had apparently not liked hearing this "mountain" speech, she went on, "For those of you who do not understand the language of our ancestors, this is what my uncle's daughter has said; this is what she sang for my sister, who is not forgotten."

Malika stepped out into the middle of the crowd of white veils before she continued, to make sure that her mother, Lla Fatima, was not there. But Lla Fatima still lay unconscious as she had since morning, driven almost mad after spending a long time in trances, carried away by despair. Finally Malika translated for the city-women who only cared to understand in the dialect of the city:

"Since the first day of the year
We have not had one single day of celebration!"

… … … … … … … … … … …

"So vast the prison crushing me
Release, where will you come from?"

At these words, little Bahia, who had stood up, went back to the dead girl and sat down by her head all alone, absolutely determined to stay there, since the men who would carry the funerary board had not yet come…

Bahia, motionless. And even when some kinswoman sprinkled her forehead or her hands with eau de cologne, it was like blessing someone not there. Deep inside, Bahia, mute, face dry, repeated to herself the Berber lament of the cousin who tore her face…

"So vast the prison," *"Meqqwer lhebs."* Two or three words, sometimes in Arabic and sometimes in Berber, were singing inside her, slowly, a sort of rough march, jolting, but also calming—which made it possible for her to watch peacefully as Chérifa, with her face suddenly enwrapped in the swallowing shroud, was carried away.

In the days that followed and then the weeks, then the months and seasons, one after the other, Bahia did not speak. Did not smile. Did not sing.

This is how she lived, cool and calm, but how could they know whether she was in pain or indifferent? Until she was seven.

On the anniversary of Chérifa's death, or shortly afterward, Lla Fatima agreed to put her youngest child in the hands of a local sorceress. She was told the sorceress knew how to free someone possessed, kidnapped by a beloved now among the dead who held on to this person "despite the will of God."

It was difficult, but she let her little girl go with an old neighbor, the woman who gave her the advice. "It will be near the beach, in an isolated inlet where the woman lives as a recluse… You will see, with the will and protection of the saints of your lineage, Ahmed or Abdallah and the two Berkanis, father and son, she will succeed!"

Bahia returned that evening silent. The next morning, the last Friday before the month of fasting, just after her mother and big sister completed their prayer, Bahia spoke softly, as if things had always been the way they were now, without sadness: just a few words about the cool breeze and the brightness of the light.

Lla Fatima gave alms every morning for the next week.

Twelve years later Bahia is nineteen. She was eighteen when she had me.

At nineteen, just thirteen months after my birth (because she nursed me only for the first month; she had no more milk after that; she had grown thinner and felt ill. Her lethargy and sadness faded when this blessed pregnancy arrives a few weeks later to renew her energy and make her bloom), she finally has her son. Her first.

So beautiful. A big baby who made her suffer giving birth. But how happy she was afterward hearing the women's compliments when they came to visit: "White, fat, and so blond, so blond…"

"He has blue eyes, you are lucky, he will be a real lord! A bridegroom!…

"He has his father's eyes, his lineage is paternal!"

"The women are mountain Berbers," another whispered, all sweetness.

But Lla Fatima, my mother's mother, retorted calmly, "It's true! On our side the men have black eyes and long lashes! They are all dark and handsome at home." She sighed, thinking nostalgically of her son whom France kept in the Sahara as a soldier, so far away!

The endless talk of the visitors creates a warm babble of sound close by. It is Bahia's third day after the birth; she will leave her bed before the seventh day for the celebration—what a stroke of luck that after all she delivered her son in the city, and in her mother's beautiful house, she will enjoy the ritual cermony. A great many women will come as guests; an orchestra of women musicians will provide the music. Lla Fatima attends to it all, as she did when this her youngest child was married (the most beautiful wedding in the city, the one that all the women will talk about for a long time. The bride, after having arrayed herself in the traditional caftan, then was so proudly the first in the city to wear the white gown of European brides: according to the wishes of the bridegroom, the brother's friend, just out of teachers' training...).

Consequently Bahia does not worry. As the seventh day unfolds her serenity and contentment will grow in this soothing, new sweetness.

When she bore her daughter a year earlier, it was quite the opposite: Everything had been done hastily and far away, at the first teaching post assigned to the husband, in the mountains north of Bou Saada. As if she had had her first child in exile! On that last day of classes, the baby coming a week too early, whereas they had both expected to leave the next day (in the corners half-open suitcases needed only to be closed). Summer vacation was beginning, her mother had prepared her room for her in the city, the bed, the sheets and the provisions for the celebration with all the women arriving to visit... Now the birth was going to take place in the middle of the mountains! They were going to have to get through it with the midwife, an extremely old peasant woman; she was experienced of course, with a jolly, soothing face, but still, she did not even speak Arabic, except the words to invoke God and to call for patience, just a few expressions from the Koran sprinkled over her chatter. It sounded like some foreign idiom to the woman giving birth as she tried to surmount her pain.

The old woman had wanted to get a rope ready to hang from the ceiling so that the woman in labor could hang on it and help herself by pulling with her arms raised over her head... Bahia refused: She knew that was a peasant custom. No. In the city all they did was tilt the bed... The boiling water was ready, and while the future mother suffered, she recited verses from the Koran... As a last resort they might call the French doctor. Lla Fatima would be determined: he would come, even at midnight, he knew the family... And Bahia, waiting to give birth for the first time, would have been tranquilized. Instead, now, faced with this old peasant woman who came running from the nearby *douar*, my mother had to suffer, first in silence and then with harsh rattling breaths that became more and more rhythmic—until finally I burst into the light of day.

The old woman set to work with a great laugh. She cut the cord. Turned me quickly upside down. Waited for my first cry. Then she spouted a long sentence that my mother in her weakness heard but did not understand.

Lla Fatima arrived in haste four or five days later (taking the bus to Bou Saada, then as far as the road was passable in a car, after that she asked for a mare, a mule, anything at all, and there before the surprised peasants she proudly straddled her mount). She was impatient to see her youngest daughter safe and sound, even though she had been abandoned to the customs of the past. When my grandmother found herself there with the midwife (whom she brought a remnant of cloth from the city for her *séroual*, perfumes from Mecca, and a string of beads that were blessed as well), the two women plunged immediately deep into a conversation that lasted the entire evening.

Even though she was able to get up after the third day and take a few steps before lying down again, my mother was lying there on her bed and heard them laughing. She thought, *How long it has been since I heard my mother laugh, she is such a stern woman! They seem to get along well!*

Finally the midwife left, spreading a great flood of blessings. Lla Fatima said to her daughter, "Do you know how she greeted the arrival of your first child, when the baby uttered its first cry?"

"I heard her give some long speech," said my mother, "but I didn't understand any of it."

"Luckily her version of Berber and mine, the one I spoke as a child, are rather close: we talked together like two cousins!"

She began laughing all over again, long, soft laughter, almost inaudible, but it shook her entire torso. Bahia, still surprised, watched her until finally she took a breath, and went back to what she was saying. "The midwife greeted the child, when your pains finally came to an end: 'Hail to thee, daughter of the mountain. You were born in haste, you emerge thirsty for the light of day: you will be a traveler, a nomad whose journey started at this mountain to go far, and then farther still!'"

The young mother, Bahia, said nothing.

"So much talk for a girl!" She sighed.

"You will have a boy the next time!" retorted the grandmother.

The second delivery took place as Bahia had hoped. She did not necessarily expect such radiant beauty in a newborn.

The blue eyes, of course, that was ancestry on his father's side— whereas her daughter had hazel eyes; she had noticed this but not mentioned it to anyone. They were the honey color of Chérifa's eyes, the sister she had lost as a child, for whom she had never wept.

When she was just slightly more than nineteen, Bahia savored the joy of entering the realm of the mothers. For a month, as if to make up for the fact that the firstborn, the daughter born a "mountain girl," had not been entitled to the usual honors, women poured into Lla Fatima's house to pay their visits.

"A prince! You have been granted a prince, you, your mother's princess!" the closest neighbor exclaimed, the one people considered the most eloquent both on happy occasions and for bereavements.

Two months later Bahia carried the baby in her arms as she left. Enveloped in a silk veil, she took the bus with her husband to the Sahel village where my father had just been named the "teacher of a class for natives."

Where was I during this first trip? I certainly have no idea. My mother has no memory of it. It seems most likely that my father carried his little girl in his arms.

"Unless you walked at eleven months. Then you would have trotted along beside us to the bus stop."

My mother does remember how much care she took to protect the baby in her arms: hiding his face, keeping him safe from the dust!

"Also from the evil eye!" the grandmother had advised her.

That is how the four of us entered the French apartment where I lived until I was ten, except for summers and the winter and spring vacations. Then we used to take the bus (later we would go in our own car) to the old city. To us, my mother and me, it seemed a haven, a cocoon: and my magical child's memory turned it into a place of constant celebrations where gentle, languid women seemed to laze around.

When we lived in the apartment, we felt we were "among the French."

"That is," my mother explained to her friends when we would go back, "French people from France!" The teachers' families all come from France. They say hello to us; I even learn a few words from our neighbors… (*What an experience!* the friends think, curious) "But the others, the Europeans who live in the village, it's like here: They have their world and we have ours!"

So, in the apartment building meant for teachers with families, we touched the fringes of another realm that was entirely strange for people from Caesarea: "the French from France." Needless to say, in that village, we, my mother and I, were within a hair's breadth of touching almost another planet.

"I have two languages," says the mother orphaned for twenty years.

"Orphaned" that is, having lost her first son.

I hear this moan later, many years later: "I have two languages!" Twenty years after it happens the mother travels across France. In Strasbourg, in the hotel where she sleeps, where she cries herself to sleep, she awakens in the middle of the night. Does not turn on the lights. Opens her eyes and looks. Remembers? So far away from her imprisoned son whom she only saw for an hour, far from the Algeria she left in reckless daring, looks back on her days in the distant past, looks.

The baby in the apartment: when she crossed the threshold, her first son in her arms, under all her numerous veils. And she talks; she talks to me:

"He was six months old... In the village, it was just before the beginning of the holidays when we would leave for Caesarea. My mother-in-law lived with us, she was rather shy, and even uncommunicative; she knew so well how to rock him at night before he dozed off and very early in the morning, to let us sleep. She leaned over the cradle.

"I still hear the baby's prattling; he had burst into a long bird cooing and then a chirping. The grandmother burst out laughing; I had never seen her that way, so excited. 'Do you hear, my daughter: He just spoke in Berber!'

"And seeing my doubt, she insisted, 'I promise it's true! Of course, words just one after the other, almost bits and pieces. No one constant meaning… but it was Berber!'

"I shrugged my shoulders. I left the room. I regret doing so now, because he is not here anymore—the six-month-old baby (how could he have spoken Berber, not a syllable of it was spoken in our home… As for the village nurse, she came to us when my second son was born). And I feel remorse because of her, my mother-in-law; because she is now dead and because, except for this scene, I do not believe there was any point at which I failed her… she was sweet. When I was brusque with her that day, it must have hurt her.

"So we went to spend the vacation in Caesarea. In the middle of the worst dog days of this scorching summer he became sick, my baby; one Friday night… And before the end of the next morning he was dead. In just a few hours he had become completely dehydrated… The French doctor muttered, 'You should have awakened me during the night!' Dead and buried the same day, my baby! The language was smothered with him, I know. He went into the earth with his mouth open; fingers spread wide on his hands, and his eyes… His eyes, I still wake up at night and see them, I stare into their blue!"

My mother did not want to go to his grave. Even after the third day. She would not go back to the cemetery except for the funeral of Lla Fatima, her mother, who died a week after independence!

Salim, the son still living, has only just gotten out of the French prisons. First, however, he has to spend some time in a sanatorium—his lungs weakened in his last prison in Rouen, where he spent too much time in solitary confinement. (The only memory I share with my mother of her many trips to the French prisons: a day in 1961 when, the three of us, my mother, my young sister, and I, all went to the prison. The director, who received us in his office, his cold gaze fixed on this lady flanked by her two young daughters, told us that Salim would remain "in solitary" after his failed attempt to escape).

No, even in the summer of 1962, when we are all going to spend some time in prayer—"the day of women," always on the third—at the grandmother's grave, even then the mother does not go to where the dead child lies. She will not come with us and admire the view of the whole city spread out quadrilaterally above its ancient port, now half under water, marked by its easily identifiable lighthouse, because she does not want to believe he is buried—buried since 1938. He would be twenty-four, fifteen months older than Salim.

Why go back over this sterile, blackish crust of a bereavement she formerly refused? Probably because before and along with the six-month-old baby taken away too soon, as if cruelly kidnapped, she first buried the language above all. She first buried the language that, for that first son, could have been a wreath of orange blossoms!

Unless this forgetting, this refusal, this denial had already come once long before when, at the age of six, she lost her voice when Chérifa, the all-beautiful, died. Unless, in this autism that went on so long, in the paralysis of her mouth, her throat, her vocal cords that reached even as far as the throbbing of her lungs—breathing in, breathing out—the language vanished into thin air. The language of the father who preferred to remain at the *zaouia* up in the mountains, the language of the sharecroppers who used to come with their accounts to the woman in charge, Lla Fatima, this language the little girl had wanted to turn away from, all at once was gone—within her, around her.

And the dead child remained entombed in her memory forever, the sleeping child.

Arable Woman IV

～

SECOND DAY OF FILMING... Up to this point I have only discussed the location, the farm, and its queen who was absent for the nineteen members of the crew: the Madonna.

This is the day we move on to the final zoom: the camera circles the woman whose sleep now seems disturbed. The problem of the child's bed in the background comes up: The head of the little girl sleeping there shows, but Ferial, the child intended to play the part, will only arrive from the capital the next day.

I go into the peasants' house, where the children are still all excited about our beginning to shoot the film. The first house, we are told, belongs to the "widow"; I go inside and quickly choose a dark-headed little girl about Ferial's age. I explain that all she has to do is sleep for maybe two or three hours in a child's bed that is all prepared. All that will be seen in the picture is a tuft of black hair. I take little Aichoucha by the hand and lead her onto the set. The work goes faster, the technicians bustle around, it is ten o'clock, we are going to work until midnight; outside there is mud and cold, but the scene inside the brilliant spotlights is one of a sweetness that is half crudely unpolished and half carefully chosen, a feminine childhood intimacy.

I do not let go of the kid's hand and, in spite of all the noise, talk to her softly. Near the little bed (one brought from my mother's house, the bed in which her three children slept), I take off Aichoucha's shoes, which the widow had insisted she wear. Her feet, alas, are still covered with mud, too bad! There is no time for us to wash them for her (whereas maybe that, in fact, would be the real poetry, the shepherdess with muddy feet washed under the spotlights).

I pick up Aichoucha, put her down in the bed with the white sheets that will now get stained; forget that detail, the child's eyes fill me with emotion, I stroke her and whisper to her that she should really go to sleep, we only need her dark curls on the pillow. The shot begins.

Aichoucha, an eight-year-old shepherdess, the other indisputable beauty of this place. I met two queens here: the absent Madonna and the little shepherdess who is our first extra. Later she will become more and more present, but in silhouette, running after her sheep.

I return to my abrupt entrance into the cabin that night. Nine o'clock: no oil lamp, no candle; somebody brings a light. I catch sight of the mother's face, still young, with huge eyes, and a swarm of children hanging on to the folds of her baggy pants. Aichoucha, whom I take with me, has the same eyes as her mother: large, slightly round, fastening you with their slow, ceaseless gaze...

The next day I insisted on going back so that they would offer me coffee and I could sit in the midst of the little family and spend some time with them.

The widow is thirty-two or thirty-three, maybe less, she does not know her exact age. Because she is tired and worn out, she seems already old, but her brow, her gaze, are those of an adolescent.

Despite the morning sun outside, the cabin is immersed in shadow; the furniture is rudimentary: a Berber chest, a few pieces of pottery, a charcoal-burning *kanoun*, a few sheepskins, and yet also two scraggy, Western-style chairs that are too high. Seated on one of them while the children scattered on the mat stare at me, I drink the coffee; I protest that they should not have begun to make bread on my account; above all I listen. Moments later, warm bread in my hands, Aichoucha like a cat at my feet, I listen to the mother's story.

She relives the day her husband died: he was in charge of maintaining the machines at the cooperative. She describes the cause of the accident—a truck, apparently, whose brakes failed; she tells me how she got the news, shouted over the fields. She gives the details, the weeping, the family, the neighbors; there is only one essential word of comfort after all that: insurance.

This key word—spoken like a Frenchwoman—is still her hope and her despair: The formalities have dragged on for almost three years. The five children are growing up; the eldest, a fourteen-year-old boy, is the only one who goes to school, but their misfortune has made him the head of the family. He is employed as an apprentice from time to time, his daily salary, at half-pay, provides some income in addition to the meager support paid by the cooperative while they wait for the insurance to come through.

It surprises me to learn that none of the other children goes to school: The farm and its neighboring cabins are on the border between two districts. For our project we dealt with the community council in Tipasa: They have an active president and have energetically attacked the problems of schooling in the remote mountain hamlets that are geographically dependent on this district. All the children, including girls up to the age of fourteen (the real revolution in this rural society), are able to take the school bus free of charge.

But these houses, just two kilometers away from this district, are in an area where no such public service is guaranteed. With the very concrete result: This widow, whose resources are pathetic, is unable to pay two dinars a day per child for the bus that would take them to school. In other places, I will find out, the transportation fees can be waived for boys; for the girls there are only a few families, and not necessarily the most well-to-do peasants, who can bring themselves to pay.

Aichoucha consequently does not go to school. *What is the point of our being here?* I suddenly say to myself this morning. *Are we just going to move in for as long as it takes to expose enough film footage?*

I hear myself explaining the modest pay for extras provided for in our estimates, but why not use the boy, the "head of the family," as an assistant? I take some more coffee and say nothing more. Did I really come last night like a shadow thief for this child with the eyes of a doll and muddy feet?

Two days later I find out by chance that the technical crew has taken up a collection to cover part of this period while the widow waits for the insurance, and that she insisted on making couscous for them for the lunch break. I only learned the details of this exchange of favors by accident when someone kept insisting that I taste this couscous that, he said, "was a good sign."

Ambiguity, my problems make me look the other way... I see, in what the crew did, the usual altruism of the beginnings of a shoot (as if we were mindful of placing ourselves under favorable auspices), but also the technicians' indirect way of somehow thanking me. They learned of the crisis through my conversation and they were vaguely beginning to forgive my rhythm of work, whose apparent improvisation astonished them.

Ambiguity, I said... That would be the real story: darkness in the

humble lodging; myself, entering at night to take away the little girl
with her dirty feet and her hands red with henna, the mother overburdened but saying nothing, the next day an ordinary conversation... Then, behind the hedge and because they are affected by this
story, the nineteen members of the technical crew (seventeen of them
men) would create their own scenario to deal with this long, hard
wait for the insurance.

Suddenly this bothers me: Why is it that all these intentions,
obviously born of collective generosity, do not result in social aid?

Whereas we, nineteen other people and myself, are coming with
a camera, that is, a gaze, that is, "the" Gaze. Whereas what must be
caught is the first wrinkle, the whispering at the moment when, like
the Ogress in legends, I come to take away the little girl, the beauty
with innocent eyes. Whereas the camera must catch the gaze of the
widow when, in the morning, she tells about the accident, the husband who no longer provides protection, the boy-child who can only
be a temporary defense. The camera has to record the silence of my
pupils: when one has nothing to say in the face of misfortune, it is
hard not to turn a blind eye oneself when confronted with the other
who is blinded by misfortune.

Yet the camera takes nothing. The nineteen people, who should
know that they are nineteen facets of the spying eye, feel rather that
they are endowed with a kind heart. Like everybody, they have a clear
conscience when the widow offers them this "couscous of the sun"
with her blessings.

I do not feel my conscience is clear.

Aichoucha, during the next two months, became a smiling dream
friend. I frequently caught myself gazing at her, dividing her time as
she did between coming to see us work and then dashing off immediately after one of her animals that had strayed. She came and went

but stuck to her job of keeping the sheep, observing us afterward without real curiosity but rather with fond indulgence.

She seemed, however, to flit lightly about over us, protectively. Sometimes I wanted her to think of me as one of the sheep; I wanted to feel that it was her responsibility as the shepherdess to look after me when my enthusiasm would go drifting off toward so many different rivers... Aichoucha, the illiterate shepherdess, eight years old, scandalous in today's Algeria—and this was only seventy kilometers from Algiers. In actual fact Aichoucha is the real outsider in these regions where I think I see the future dawning imperceptibly...

FOURTH MOVEMENT:
OF THE NARRATOR
IN THE FRENCH NIGHT

THERE IS ONE NIGHT during the World War—I do not know what year it was—that I want to tell about. Not to begin my memories of earliest childhood, no, this was a night that caused some imperceptible shift in me at the age of three. As if, because of belonging irrevocably to the family community in a colonized country, one consequently split in two, there would be some sort of alarm set off in the consciousness of this entirely Arab little girl. It was only decades later that I would become aware of its subterranean swell.

Let us locate the facts first: I remember this World War as just beginning. Bombing of North Africa by the German air force. Any textbook about this period would give me the precise date, of course—what month in 1940 or 1941, perhaps even later… But I shall rely only on this child's memory. The scene I want to describe—revive, pass beneath the spotlights, dimmed or blinding, of my sudden new curiosity—this scene takes place in the parents' room, in this modest apartment in the building where the teachers lived in a village in the Sahel of Algiers.

My bed was also in this bedroom—a deep, narrow bed of wrought iron, which I would later use for the bedroom of the heroine of my film. That is where I slept, at least until my brother was born, the second one, the one who is not dead, younger than I by three years and three months. After that I went back to my paternal grandmother's bed to be lulled to sleep every evening in her arms, to have my feet warmed in her hands. I know that having been wrapped for several years this way in maternal warmth was like a second birth for me.

The strange night, or rather the almost uncanny way I woke up during this night that I am trying to resurrect, comes therefore before that second period.

There was war, and bombing; I have to have been less than three years and three months old. This gentle, humble grandmother whispering affectionately in the night shadows becomes for me a sort of motionless statue (a female version of one of the lares), standing guard outside of this first memory with its dragging undertow.

There were many bombings earlier during the tumultuous nights of this period: probably ten nights or so over about three months... In the center of the village, between the easy-to-spot church and the bandstand in the public square, not far from the teachers' apartments—where we were the only "native" family alongside five or six households of French teachers—some bomb shelters had been dug. I can see us all heading for these shelters, a line of about twenty people, in the dark of night barely pierced by the glow of a few candles.

These few expeditions left a cheerful impression on me. Not only was it fun when we had to race to this place close by (because they had dug the trenches in a nearby park) but it was especially so when we were all seated more or less in a circle, finally safe, awaiting the return to calm outside. There was a scattering of other children there; we must have been all wound up because of the completely incongruous protocol that we saw perniciously take hold among the adults. What did we expect other than that the danger would pass? Our village was at the foot of the mountains of the Algiers Tell, the main target of enemy planes for I do not know what strategic installation. My father and two or three other teachers used to remind us of this during the attacks, probably to reassure the ladies. When we left the trenches, it was highly unlikely that we would find our houses destroyed, the village devastated, or that any of the people not, like us, in shelters would be dead...

This line of reasoning, spun out to fill the time as we waited, remains for me a sort of sound sculpture... However, the relations among the adults in this shelter shifts subtly, uneasily in my memory. So I am not absolutely sure whether my mother (then about twenty-one or twenty-two), who at the time wore the veil in the style of city-women, was there dressed in European or Moorish fashion. I have no memory of this detail; writing now, all I would have to do is ask her—she would repair or correct that forgetfulness... I am not doing so because I am trying to discover how it was that I sensed a change, some disorientation in this minisociety.

These parents were seated side by side in couples in a circle. Most of them looked up at the ceiling when there was a pounding dull rumble or the wail of some distant siren.

Snuggled up next to my father, I watched the scene as if it were some sort of suspended theater, noting the presence of my grandmother (she was certainly wrapped entirely in her veils), silent as usual, and my mother, who was so young. Her cautious voice comes through to me clearly. She is speaking to one of the French wives, making conversation, and it is as if I were hearing, for the first time, French words—hesitant, careful, uttered somewhat haphazardly one after the other—as if, in this general swell of fear, what the others felt was in no way comparable to what my mother must have experienced when, through the force of circumstances, she conversed in a language that was not yet familiar and did so to maintain her "social rank."

On the nearby mountain German planes were bombing a point strategic to the French army, and my mother took advantage of this to take her first steps in the "others'" language. Maybe the way her voice trembled, the slightly labored tone to her words, would go unnoticed when one French lady—one of the ones who usually stayed home—or some other—a teacher this time—gasped *oh*s and *ah*s every time there was a whistle outside, or a bursting shell's repercussions echoed all the way to where we were...

There was all this ruckus; and in the midst of it, like an invisible ripple in the heart of the subterranean silence, there was my mother's emotion. She had dared break in, slipping into the talk of the others—the neighbors, other mothers—but also the language of the school world, her husband's usual realm.

I saw that: not the disproportionate levels of exhilaration, but this gap and the rosy color my mother's timidity brought to her cheek before we returned to the surface and confirmed that in fact the village had survived, the houses were intact, the everyday world was safe and sound...

A few hours later, curled up in my little bed, I hear in the living room next to me the voice of my hesitant mother: She is asking my father whether or not, in the few sentences she spoke out loud with Mme. Carbonel, she made any very bad mistakes... I hear her questions again, the slight quaver in her voice: bits and pieces of conjugal dialogue—they have left the door ajar and think I am asleep. Their voices mingle in the shushing tones of the Arab dialect peculiar to our city that was once resettled by Andalusians… In that language my mother recovers her ceremonial habits, I would almost say her haughtiness, her elegance. That she might have displayed some sort of awkwardness just because she ventured into "their" language seemed to me then almost too much to bear. My heart was pounding. Looking back, I felt afraid: Could my mother, a woman so purely bred, of such distinction, have seemed otherwise to the other women?

Asking her questions now, and once again possessed of the warmth both of her own home and of her idiom, she regained her confidence—as if she had, indeed, been afraid, but needlessly. And now she seemed to give in more to an urge to flirt with her young husband.

Of course I remember none of what the father answered; maybe I did not really hear it. I only recall my brief feeling of helplessness about my mother's words. Was there a danger that they ("them," all the others who were earlier in the shelter, lit solely by a makeshift, overhead light) had an entirely different image of her than I did, who saw her wreathed in all her graces (her subtlety, her slight arrogance, her ease)?

Them: the foreigners, and not just the adults—men, women, and children equally—our neighbors in the building at the time; the more they brushed against us as we came and went every day, the more they seemed to me creatures from some other shore, floating in an ether that was not ours… Foreigners, whose language I was beginning to stutter, hardly less awkwardly than my idealized mother, complete foreigners for the resolutely silent grandmother (who, for six months every year, in almost total silence and out of love for the son, put up with living with the "others," whom she found unpleasant). They seemed foreign to me: But am I sure I really thought they were entirely?

It should be recalled that the foreigner, during this period of collective servitude, did not merely seem different. No, if not always seen as "the enemy," he was still at all times the *roumi*. (The native Jews were excluded from this category in our eyes, especially when the women, the old people, had kept "our" language, which was of course theirs as well, that they spoke in a "broken" accent that was their own.) But in very rare exceptions the foreigner was perceived as, was received as, the "nonfriend," an impossible familiar with whom one associated only by force of circumstances. A dense though invisible silence, a blank neutrality like a criminal sentence, surrounded him, separated us. I was obviously too young to analyze or understand this impossible passage, but the fact remains that these teachers, their wives, their children, whom we mostly thought of as "the French from France," seemed like unreal beings—they very rarely entered our home; we did not cross their thresholds; we made do with polite greetings in the stairway or the courtyard. When my father alluded to his day's work to my mother, or reported some dialogue with a colleague, this person would appear on the scene as if he were a walk-on from some other place. And yet that night...

I have great difficulty approaching this first memory, this night when I was three, in my parents' bedroom. Is it a knot that I am only now going to disentangle? Is it a welt, a crack, a definitive break that I immediately tried to erase on that night when these "French from France" did not seem to me (how strange this is) completely foreign?

Nights of early childhood. The ocher-colored bed of wrought iron is set just behind the door: it seems deep to me, so deep that I sink into it and I still have a vague memory of waking up in the morning and sometimes wanting to stand up—only my head showed above the bed.

In the beginning I sleep alone in the room; through the door left ajar I hear the sounds of voices: My father has to correct his students' papers, it is my mother who is talking quietly with my paternal grandmother. The apartment is rather cramped.

I slowly fall asleep, reassured by snatches of adult voices. Across from me the window looks out on the village square and its bandstand. The windowpanes are covered with newspaper; this is wartime. Lying there, I stare at this newspaper. Was it during this period that I began to be fascinated by the same photograph, a French military man with a mustache, rather elegant, who stared at me at length in the triangle of light carved by the open door? A certain General Weygand, but I only knew that later.

So I slowly went to sleep under the general's gaze. When I would wake up just before dawn, I would look first for my parents' bed: Probably my mother, already up, was just leaving the room... On Sundays, it seems to me, I would ask if I could jump into that great big bed, to be there next to my father, or between them, in the hollow of their complicity... Laughter and chatter: the outbursts of these lazy mornings have faded irreparably (no, they came back to me vividly thirty years later, when my own little girl seeks out the same spot, on those lazy mornings, between father and mother!).

I still remember an unexpected awakening from this part of my childhood.

Wartime it was and in this village the siren often pierced our evenings or nights. When it howled, it seemed to me that I heard its endless spiral bore into my flesh: the alarm emanated from the town hall across from the teachers' apartments. Consequently the first thing I would do was run to the bedroom window, and from it try to focus on the façade of the town hall. But it was already night. Everything had to be closed to make sure that not even the thinnest line of light would show. My mother and my grandmother went from one window to the next, one room to the next... I sometimes preferred to sink deep into my bed almost voluptuously, feeling I was the only one sheltered (the alarm, the airplanes—all that was up on the mountain and we could not even see the spectacle), but at the same time savoring the anxiety that was so exhilarating, so deliciously exhilarating.

It was only later that we began to leave the building and go in frightened groups to the hastily constructed trenches in the surrounding parks...

For the time being I am still in these first dark nights of mine: I am not budging from my bed; I am watched by the General Weygand of windowpane and newspaper—asleep like so many times before. But one morning I woke up just before dawn; everything around me, everything inside me reeled slowly.

Probably during the night there had been some vague turmoil of which I was barely aware, but it had not awakened me. Probably my sleep this time was not clear and limpid but rather jerky and uneven, in fits and starts. In the distance voices, torn but still dangerously blanketing me; suddenly a white light over my head, over my closed eyes, then abruptly turned off; a few whispers in the dark, maybe other people. Or had I rather dreamed some new voice, the soft tones of a foreign woman and—(but it was only long afterward that I would not piece together what I heard that was not part of my usual sleep) a "French" sound. It was as if the parents' bedroom had shift-

ed horizontally, was half open to the village square, and there, where
I still slept in my baby's bed, where I still kept my eyes shut on purpose, I and my relatives standing around me were exposed to the four
winds in front of everybody, in front of "the others." And so France
was for me simply the outside.

Finally I opened my eyes; nothing in the room had moved.
However, right away, in the half dawn it seemed to me that there
was no denying, because of the strange night sounds but also
because of a certain stillness around the beds, it was obvious: I was
waking up somewhere else, in a room that seemed the same but was
totally different.

Bright daylight, gleaming gray-blue transparent lights, lit the
imposing mahogany armoire whose tall mirrors had beveled edges,
the one that stood there, on show and impenetrable, across from us.
Tick-tock. Regularly, from the clock on the other side of the room.

Where was I? I did not move. My heart was pounding. Where
were my parents hiding? I did not sit up. I did not look beside me.
And still there was this absurd impression of being both there and
somewhere else: the sound, the sound of breathing was different; a
different silence inhabited the big bed. Then I greedily studied that
hollow in the bed to discover whose imperceptible breathing was covered by the sheets… My father, my mother, where were they? In the
blur of the night I heard their voices in the turmoil, or in my dream.
My heart was pounding wildly.

It did not take long for me to determine that they were not sleeping nearby; the window grew bright. A woman's hand, not my mother's, a fat, white hand emerged from the sheets, lit the lamp, a different voice, not my mother's, murmured.

Murmured what? Some question. I must not have understood.
But I recognized the French language: I was definitely waking up in
the home of foreigners!

I open my eyes, in the lamplight and the gray light of dawn. I look. In the parents' bed our next-door neighbor—a teacher who is widowed or divorced, I do not know which—is sleeping. And what is more, beside her is her son—stretched out in "our" bed. "Ours," I thought as if this were the final, irreparable breaking and entering in the night—occupied by the teacher's son, a boy who was ten or twelve, Maurice. It is only just now his name comes to me intact.

So there they lay in my parents' place, "them," the French mother and her son, our neighbors… That night there had been sirens and German bombing in the nearby hills. In this terror the neighbor who was alone had panicked: she had come and knocked on our door. To reassure her, my parents had invited her in and had, quite naturally, given her their room. They made do themselves with a mattress on the floor in the dining room: just everyday Arab hospitality… he was, poor thing, a woman alone.

There, right next to me, as I lay motionless in my bed, a new couple were stretched out: the mother and her son… The boy was sleeping: I only saw his silky light brown hair. The teacher was sitting up in bed. She was wearing a nightgown, her ample bosom, her blond hair loose on her round shoulders, and on her chubby face a smile that was almost a little girl's, sweet and half surprised, was turned to me. She looked at me, as if asking to be forgiven, then glanced tenderly at her still-sleeping son.

"Maurice," she began, then she turned back to me, because, probably, I was staring at her fixedly, as if demanding some explanation for this intrusion.

I did not get out of bed. I no longer stared at the neighbor. I felt this boy there right next to me, a boy who in those days must have seemed to me a sort of hero, one close but faraway. For me this was the height of disruption—"he" was in my house, in the most secret part of "my house," of "our house," and he kept right on sleeping as if nothing had happened!

That night when the tumult was unable to wake me up completely, that night became one of transmutation. The mother and her boy, the "French," were of course neighbors on the same floor but also the closest representatives of "the other world" for me; "they," this couple sprung from the dark and stretched out there in the open for me to see, had taken my parents' place!

Substitution: I must have spent long minutes thinking it was irrevocable, that my parents had vanished into the wings of the scenery, that this pair of recumbent forms, mother and son, were taking their place. Was I not going to become different all of a sudden? In the slow shifts of this astonishing night was I not going to remain like this: simultaneously in the bedroom of my parents (perhaps they had even chosen different roles themselves, in some other people's house, in some other French apartment?) and discovering I was in the opposite camp?

No, I would not move from my bed, my only haven. I stayed, open-eyed, frozen. So many years later I am relocating the ineradicable minutes of this awakening, trying to relive inside myself: what did I feel, what made me worry?

The fear that one might have expected from a little three-year-old girl who imagines for an instant that she has lost her parents—this is not a fear I recognize… The excitement of an unknown world, a new mother (the neighbor did of course seem older, more of a "matron" than my mother, who was then scarcely more than twenty), no, that is not familiar either. The nearness of this twelve-year-old boy, however, this boy with whom I would sometimes play in the afternoon in the park and who seemed to me a young man, this unexpected familiarity provided an ambiguity and keen pleasure that I can deal with more readily.

So there I stayed: neither frightened nor particularly excited by the adventure. I relive the awakening. For a few seconds I imagine I am a little Arab girl (myself, my bed, with my silent, gentle grandmother close by) and yet suddenly all decked out with French parents: this widowed (or divorced) lady with her hair down who is casually waking up next to me.

I do not smile. I make no move to get up. Finally my mother appears at the door. The neighbor rises and sincerely begs to be forgiven for her night fears.

I closed my eyes. I did not want to see anybody. I felt I was at the border, but which one? One moment I was going to have a French mother, a "brother" and not "a brother"; her son stretched out close by, in this great big bed into which I liked to leap and curl up between my father and my mother. I closed my eyes. I am sure I must have dreamed that I was going to jump into this big bed again, back in my old Sunday ways, squeeze up next to the "lady," between her and her son, next to Maurice, between mother and son, who were my parents, speaking French, breathing French... That is the moment I experienced at the age of three.

That was perhaps a year or more before I began school. This waking up, the only one from my early childhood, is still unexpectedly the most vivid. (It is oblique, its mobility establishing its fragile equilibrium.)

What were my games like then? In the courtyard of the apartment building, my voice sings the usual counting rhymes tirelessly, while with the other little girls I throw the ball against a high wall painted white. Then we play hopscotch or on the swings... I don't wander off into the village; my father set limits on where I can go: the courtyard and the garden in front, never the street.

I think of myself as being happy in the garden to this house, with a sort of inexpressible excitement in my heart... A few trees, lemon trees, and a medlar tree in the midst of weeds; a corner where someone must have grown salad greens... We reach it through a rickety gate whose squeaking made us laugh.

It is only in this garden that I see myself playing with Maurice, the twelve-year-old boy who woke up one morning in my bedroom, next to me.

"Playing" with this boy: the voices of our dialogue have vanished. Of the scenes that come back, there is only one of these two child's bodies clinging to the tallest lemon tree—Maurice, full of energy, manages to perch on the highest branch. He waves to me to come. His wave suggests that I climb up to where he is.

I stay clinging to the bottom branch. Strangely I refuse; I stay where I am. I am afraid of the contact. As if reaching the same branch, squatting there beside him, seemed to me in some vague way utterly sinful. My heart pounds. I am full of guilt, prickles of anxiety: In just a second my father, I am sure, is going to appear, stand there before the garden gate whose squeak I can already hear. My mother, at the kitchen window, must have watched me from the heights of her lookout post: she would watch powerless the scene in which my father would catch us at something, needless to say, I was doing wrong. I stay on my branch, immobilized. Maurice invites me up again; I can still see his mocking face. Not suspecting anything, not imagining that my fierce refusal could be anything other than a mere lack of physical daring, he insists; then I see him jump all at once into the grass on the ground, sing to himself, climb back up to the highest branch... He was probably sorry that I was not joining in this athletic competition!

The strangest thing is not so much that I refused, that my reluctance was as burdensome as if I had already come of age. The most incomprehensible thing about my memory is that I remember this scene of the tree stripped of words, with nothing at all uttered by myself. It is accompanied by no sound: no laughter, no exclamation, not the slightest word exchanged... So I did not yet speak French; so this boy seemed handsome to me—his energy, his smiling face, his beautiful straight brown hair that fell across his forehead, his air of an only son whose every last personal detail is wrapped in maternal solicitude.

In this aura in which Maurice moved, he was very near me and yet almost unreal because he was behind a frontier. He belonged "to the world of the others," and there is no doubt that this frozen state of voices is what gives the picture of the boy its clarity, its immutable presence.

So I did not yet speak French. And the look I sent up toward the top of the tree, at the face of the boy with brown hair and mocking smile, was the gaze of a silent, formless desire, utterly powerless because it had no language, not even the crudest, into which to flow.

Maurice was neither close to me nor a stranger: he was first of all the one my eyes, through the branches of the tree, were filled with while my voice drained away, its laughter, its shouts, its words suddenly gone dry.

In that silence of childhood, the image of childish temptation, the first garden, the first forbidden thing—takes shape. Intense but paralyzing dawns.

This scene comes, I think, almost immediately after I awoke that night in a room that had suddenly become "French."

I was not yet attending school. All these memories are set earlier than my fourth year, before the autumn in which my father decides to take me to nursery school.

The girls' school and the boys' school were separated only by wire fencing down the middle of the large central courtyard. Just about 330 feet separated the apartment building in which we lived from the elementary school. I crossed them, at least for the first two years, hand in hand with my father, who was the only Arab teacher of French, and also the only one proudly wearing a dark red Turkish fez of felt perfectly straight above his sparkling eyes.

He had a "native" class: During this period, at least for boys, school segregation was justified in this colonial village by the fact that little Arab boys, because they did not speak French in the family, needed "remedial" teaching. And for native pupils—a native teacher. But also these children, who were for the most part the sons of farm workers, had to spend two years studying a curriculum the others did in one. My father fought against this discrimination. He would have several levels of teaching in the same class and, in an attempt to repair this vocationally unjust pattern, he became a hard teacher to the point of being uncompromising with his pupils.

My teacher-father's reputation for extreme strictness comes back to me now that I have recently rediscovered the first group photograph in which I appeared. (The only little girl, there I was in my father's class, caught sitting in the middle of forty or more boys of different ages but all of whom were native). Thanks to this picture, I remember now those first days at school: Seated in the back row, I used to wait in my father's classroom while he finished teaching his class.

Silent observer in this class of boys, I remember the collective respect, maybe even fear, in the concentrated attention of these children listening to the lesson. The teacher standing there, stick in hand, leads them through it from his desk on the platform, making them repeat a sentence, a word, several times, speaking sharply to a recalcitrant boy, giving extra homework.

His authoritarian voice, intransigent but patient, is raised. It goes up; it goes down. He is tall. He wears a black coat that he will take off when school is over. He never abandons his role, not for a minute—but is it a role? He is filled with an impassioned wish to urge these children, these minds, forward... He seems inflexible. Forty pairs of eyes of little boys of various ages say so.

Even though I am sitting in the back, I, too, share this kind of terror of the schoolmaster; master who dominates in every sense. I, too, am afraid, even though I am the "master's daughter." I must not move. I must not disturb this function.

I only see the boys from the back. Sometimes one of them, called on by the master, stands up and mumbles what is written on the blackboard. The master repeats it, he is merciless especially regarding pronunciation, elocution: he imposes some punishment... I am in the grip of anxiety, as if I were the child up there whose diction is deficient, but I also think I am invisible.

From time to time the master walks around, goes up and down the rows. When he comes abreast of me, he does not speak to me; he does not even give me a knowing glance. I must have a book before me, or more likely a slate. But I am so fascinated by my father's class that I turn myself into a sort of peering shadow, passionate but powerless.

I see them all from the back. I do not remember any one in particular. I never speak to them of course, neither before nor after. Not one word: they are boys. Despite being so very young I must sense what is forbidden.

When class is over, when the shrill sound of the siren marks the end of study hour (because we are now in study hall and the reason for my still being there is that I am too young to go home alone: I am waiting for my father to go back to our apartment), all the boys must stare at me.

For them I must signify some privileged image of "the teacher's daughter." Their sisters, obviously, do not go to the French school.

My father, at the podium, erases the blackboard, takes off his black coat that is full of chalk dust. He puts his things away meticulously; he places the pupils' exercise books into his briefcase.

I go up to him. He is father again. In the chalky dust, in front of the open windows—the cleaning women are already coming in to wash the floor and wipe off the tables—the father and the little girl return to sweet, friendly conversation.

Hand in hand with my father, I walk through the village. I am going home with the Arab teacher. A tall man, wearing a Turkish fez above his green eyes, his handsome face, he takes me home. A little girl who is four, then five.

I remember nothing about sitting for the school photograph; at least for that first photograph in which I appear, right there, in this class of boys.

Today, so long afterward, I look at it. My father is less than thirty and I see him there: he poses in a dignified manner in his role, or his mission, as the village's native teacher, but despite his stiff appearance, he seems a handsome man to me. And only today do I look these boys in the face, one by one.

They put me in the middle, on the front row: little girl with a rounded forehead, her black hair cut short, her gaze perhaps resolute, although I cannot really characterize it. On the slate held by a boy sitting in my row, written in chalk, is the date of the school year: 1940.

Now I look questioningly at each of the boys, who are seven to ten years old... They are *yaouleds*, the sons of workers, people who have been dispossessed, in this village in the Sahel where the richest farms of colonial Algeria lie... A few of the pupils, however, seem less working-class: the son of the grocer (who will later attend secondary school, who will become a student), the son of the barber, and among the faces that look serious, almost worried, there are two boys who are the sons of the *caïd*. Sons of the most important personage of the village—this *caïd* who wore traditional robes (a silk coat and woolen cloak and an impressive Bedouin headdress), an old-fashioned Arab chief. Their father always seemed to me to be an old man because, when I would be in his home visiting his daughters and stood close to him, I was afraid of his hand, which trembled.

Yes, I am staring at the pupils in my father's class. What have they become fifteen or twenty years later—that is, during the war for independence?

The majority must have gone back up into the mountains, which, at the time of this photo, watched them, seemed to expect them. More than half died there: in the ditches, under a hail of gun-fire, or in hand-to-hand combat... a minority—probably three or four—returned as survivors, as triumphant victors perhaps. Later, one of them must have been elected mayor of the village, which would later become a big agricultural town. Another probably enjoyed some important local position, sent as representative or allied, through marriage or business, with important officials in the nearby city... Yet another must be a policeman.

The yellowed photo is in my fingers: how can I know who these anonymous boys are, have I dreamed of them before? What reality have I entered, here in this class of my father's?

The strange thing is that I so completely forgot the photo session itself. The photographer? Every year, toward the end of the year, there was a photographer who made us pose in our respective classes. This was the very first time, and so I was in my father's class.

Reconstructing the moment it was taken: My father made all his pupils sit down, outdoors, in front of the door, the little ones who were shorter or younger in front, seated in two rows, the tallest standing behind. He must have checked the state of their clothes so that they would not seem too seedy. Then he went and stood beside them: They are all ready for the shutter to click.

And I? I would have waited there, docile and silent, at a slight distance, off to the side. It was the first time: no one had explained to me the etiquette of class photos. Suddenly… Suddenly, how did my father get so carried away? He looked at me, he saw me alone, waiting, intimidated as usual. What came over him? Some sudden affection? Some vague sense of injustice at seeing me alone, isolated from these children, as if excluded? For a second he forgot that I was a girl and thus, for his boy pupils, someone separate from them… He came to get me, he took my hand; he made the boys in the front row back away and had me sit in the middle facing the photographer… Then he went back to the side in his position as vigilant master. So there I was as if enthroned, the unexpected queen in the midst of these future warriors! Enthroned and unaware.

For the master now everything is fine, just before the click: he holds himself straight and tall, he is waiting beside the boys he teaches. He is posing for the others—the whole village, including the little colonial society that he scoffs at in his pride and his egalitarian demands. He poses, proud of the forty boys he is educating not just in how to speak French, and he is proud at the same time of his oldest child—she is a girl and so he put her in the middle like this.

She stands there, the little girl, leaning forward slightly, her face tense. The look in her eyes is probably too serious for her age—four, but she might as well be almost forty. She can tell, but in such a vague way, that she is out of place: Anywhere else putting a little girl all alone in the midst of those forty boys—and furthermore, older boys—is something that should not be done. She does not know that they are intimidated by her; she feels them as a single presence, respectful but mistrustful if not hostile. The little girl looks at the photographer. On one side her father, like the others, is waiting for the click.

That was the first photograph taken of me. One school day at the beginning of the World War in a village in the Algerian Sahel.

Arable Woman V

AICHOUCHA, LITERALLY "little life," thus entered the house where we film at night—into one of the two rooms packed with technicians, spotlights, and stage props. I turn the child over to someone at first; I forget her; I plunge into the world of the artificial.

An hour later, just as we zoom in for the final close-up that curves in to embrace Lila sleeping, I remember the child's bed in the background. Aichoucha? She has hardly budged. There, in the bright lights, she stares into my eyes and I take in her face, with the fleeting charm of a doll's, and at the same time her silence.

She has contemplated everything that has gone on over the past hour: our bustling around, the people all concerned about different things. She has probably listened to some of the trivial conversations about the mud outside, the price some drink costs at the village bar… She has watched me rehearsing with the actor who plays the husband immobilized in his wheelchair; she looked at me, not understanding what I, a woman, was doing there.

I took her by the hand again. I led her firmly away to rescue her from it all, from the others. Alone with her in a poorly lit room, I provided a brief rundown, whispering to explain things: "You are going to be photographed sleeping! All I need you to do is sleep… All they will see is your hair… okay? Tomorrow you will meet another little girl. We are waiting for her to come from Algiers… She is the one it will be hard for…"

She smiles at me confidently. I begin to undress her… I feel my hands move softly and caressingly the way they moved in the past with my own daughter, when I spent a year entirely alone with her… a year of joyful motherhood.

Going back in time like this, I undress Aichoucha. That is what this story in images and sound is, an attempt to navigate as smoothly as possible back through the stream of my memory and the memory of several other women.

The little girl is smiling when we return to the world of spotlights. She still holds my hand. The next few days we will save flashes of her working daily as a shepherdess in the background. But tonight this is the first time, and she takes off her shoes next to the child's bed. I chide her very softly for having left all that mud on her feet when she put her shoes on. Nonetheless I refuse to have them washed; everything is ready…

I pick the little girl up and put her down between the white sheets. I tuck her in and softly whisper a word or two. She will be able to try to sleep now for an hour, and when we decide to stop at midnight, just before turning off the spotlights, it is true that we will wake her up.

This is how—eyes in the darkness and in the dazzling lights—she stole in among us… And it was also how I approached the work of images and sound. First with my eyes shut, to grasp the rhythm, the noises from submerged depths believed lost, then rising back to the surface again where finally, eyes washed clean, I see everything lit by dawn.

Four days later, full of fire, Ferial, the daughter of a colleague at the university, came on the set. (Aichoucha had preceded her the night before like her lady's maid.) A prodigal child, a super-sophisticated child of the studio with all the ease, naturalness, vitality, and instinctual intelligence… She was truly the "star" in this fictional universe that in these first days was stumbling forward in an attempt to come to terms with itself, a miraculous "star" in the eyes of the inhabitants of the farm. For them Ferial became the child-king.

She strongly believed in "cinema," and the sweet pride that she showed made it impossible that the artificial nature of the fiction—magnified like this through the brilliance of a child's dream—be reduced to the cramped measurements and under-developed technique that was otherwise unavoidable.

And so, I thought calmly, when this child steps onto the scene in this room, the trio becomes balanced: Lila—my friend—radiates true poetry, the actor husband has good instincts, now finally here is the glowing, magical exuberance of their child. Aicha, nonetheless, still represents the real life, showing us the heels of the future in the frozen present of the couple exposed thus before us.

The first scene was acted by the mother in bed with the child. The director of photography, whose impressive bearing gave him the nickname "John Wayne of Belcourt," was tall and kind-hearted, but impatient, father of five children himself, but impatient, this photo director whose lights had been ready for some time, now mutters a question to me: "How old is that child?"

"Five, Sheik."

"By the time we get through this scene, she will certainly be twelve!"

"You have to be patient, Sheik!"

I am delighted. Ferial is not only the first one to play the star but, in her own way, also the first to put "feminism" into practice.

"Your film is about women?" she asks me.

"Of course," I say... "You have your mother, really your pretend mother; you two are in bed and you play together... whatever you want to play!"

That suits her, but it does not suit her to get undressed in front of the others. I take her somewhere else—into the room of the Madonna, who smiles at her in silence.

"Is that your friend?"

"That is my friend."

She makes an appearance in a fancy nightgown... Okay, it suits her to cavort about and play on the bed with Lila and listen to stories, okay. I watch first the pretend mother, then the real one who is watching somewhat anxiously not far away.

"Leave!" Ferial says firmly, speaking to the technical crew (I can feel that she is about to add "They are men," as if all of a sudden we had returned to a traditional childhood of marble patios and fountains...) "Tell them all to leave!"

"Leave!" I said, feigning resignation.

They leave.

"Even me?" asks Sheik, who this time must have adopted some vaguely Valentino-style manner.

Ferial, the flirt, says, "Okay, you, you stay..."

Once she begins her cavorting about, some of the technical crew will be able to sneak back onto the set. The child-king plays, laughs, imagines her present as she goes along, in spite of the spotlights, and now, despite the people watching. Lila, with her caresses, begins to be the element of stability in this exuberance. Ferial laughs.

The camera, ravenous, catches it.

"Ferial, go closer to your mother!"

I almost destroy the spell.

"Not my mother," shouts Ferial instantly in a temper, "my pretend mother. My mother is right there next to you!"

And I, made patient by the little game, I say "Yes," of course, "your pretend mother." Why not play games when one is happy? Real life is also an illusion, the illusion of childhood given free rein…

Ferial expends great energy, Ferial jumps, Ferial is always on the move. The camera, poor thing, dragging its crew behind it, has trouble keeping up with the expression of so much life.

It resembles a dance. Lila, like a good partner, picks things up when they die down, keeps the bursts of rhythm contained. Flares of laughter spark and soar. Ferial is in charge, she knows she is in charge. Suddenly she does not care that the whole technical crew is there, congregated as if to watch the show. She knows she is the star, she can do whatever she wants, she does whatever she wants, and it is still grace and pure joy, and life, unrestricted, following its life line. But the camera is no longer following…

"We're filming! We're still filming…"

Now film Ferial's fatigue, let her laze around on the big bed: she knows she is sleepy; she would rather have her real mother beside her. I beg her and try to trick her too. "They will forget about you…"

"I'm sleepy," she pouts.

"What about this bed?"

"No, I want my own bed."

I argue with her, discovering great stores of diplomacy within myself: "No, not your bed in Algiers; very soon you will be sleeping with me in my hotel room, we agreed on that, didn't we?" She agrees. "Now rest a little, no one will pay any attention to you now." Finally I get what I was vaguely after: her languid, indolent movements—

the little girl lying on her back and the slender leg bending, raising. The camera takes the last pictures of the night: childish sensuality, within a hair's breadth of entering the secret kingdom, that we will leave in shadow for the young mother of the story.

FIFTH MOVEMENT:
OF THE NARRATOR AS
AN ADOLESCENT

THE DANCE ON THE PATIO: I was slightly more than thirteen, not yet fourteen... Why does this wedding of my first cousin, the third of them, come back to me? Perhaps because of a summer dress: I remember perfectly the black fabric sprinkled with purple flowers. I had dared ask the seamstress to make it so that my back, as well as my arms and shoulders, were left completely bare.

"In short, practically a beach dress," the lady remarked as she smilingly listened to me insist on an extraordinarily full skirt.

I was happily surprised to find that my mother agreed, on condition that the seamstress add a bolero with little sleeves that would cover me up when I went outside.

"For a wedding, just among women," she said, "why should she not have a low-cut dress?"

Still it seemed to me that my mother was suddenly allowing an astonishing bit of daring—"because among women!"

Was it because I wore this dress that I still remember with something of an adolescent's strong sense of style my first real dress, that I had the courage to accept the invitation? At the height of the festivities, deep inside the house where Soliman's daughters lived, a house full to bursting with a crowd of guests, in front of the band composed of the town's women musicians, yes, I agreed to stand up. And then in a few minutes forgetting myself, right in front of everyone, my back and arms bare, I was riding astride the rhythm and discovering the new pleasure of my body, despite the spectators and their eyes, in this most ancient of homes where long ago the grandmother made her entrance as a young bride (while I accentuate the twists and turns of my hips, my shoulders, and the fluid freedom of my arms like vines), yes, disregarding the kinswomen, all those spectators turning into a single multiple being, voracious, buzzing...

My mother smiled at the compliments elicited by the black dress baring the girl. Well, but there it is, the twirling, irrepressible body quivers all over before the women on the alert. Too bad if two or three boys with even perhaps, a young man among them, are hidden away in some closed room where they become voyeurs behind half-open shutters.

I dance. A few others are dancing as well, mature women. Gradually, in spite of themselves, they are dancing their grief and their need to get out, to fling themselves into the distance, into the beating sun. And I, I wheel around with my eyes closed (beginning to feel dizzy), offering who knows what image to these sequestered women, the ones crouched there, already prepared to repudiate me.

"She goes out, she reads, she goes to the cities like that, naked, her father, bizarre, lets her... She goes into the homes of those other people there and walks around like that in the enemies' world, well, in fact, the free world, but far away, so far away! She makes her way

around in it—her poor parents when they find out that she will never
come back! What good is the caravel that sails far out to sea after
whatever riches and brings none of them back? What good is the caravan out beyond the deserts that takes the wrong road home and
becomes lost in the sands? Oh what reckless parents this girl has!

"Look how her face is stiff because she is both timid and too
ardent; she dances, but too vigorously, her manner is too lively. How
should one put it? She dances blithely! She has not yet understood
and never will understand because she will never be part of our houses, our prisons, she will be spared the confinement and as a result our
warmth also and our company! She will never know that when the
lute and high-pitched voice of the blind mourner make us get up and
almost go into a trance, it is because our grief makes us mourn, our
hidden grief.

"She dances, and is dancing for us, that is true; before us, well
but there it is, she is expressing her joy in life. How strange that is.
Where does she come from, just where has she been? Really, she is not
one of us!"

"And yet," said one of the matrons, the wealthiest, very high and
mighty, "if her father put her back in her place… really, if he made
her wear the veil, and sent her back into the darkness and protection
of our homes, I would not hesitate to ask for her in marriage for my
eldest son! I would describe her to my son just the way she is now,
her waist, her bearing, and all the fire in her eyes! Definitely! I would
ask for her and I know my son would be happy I did!"

Someone reported what was said to the girl's mother, and told her
who said it. The mother made a little face. The woman, who would
have liked to present herself as future mother-in-law (on the condition, it is true, that the father lead his daughter back to strict Muslim
orthodoxy), well, the narrator's mother did not consider her station
to be high enough for them. "Them," that is herself, her mother, her

paternal lineage with the saint in the mountains, who was so much a presence for them all, men and women. How could she even think of making an alliance with this bourgeois woman who was so "high and mighty"? And out of her depth!

"Besides," one of the mother's friends said ironically (evidence, it is true, of her cramped conformity), "a forty-year-old woman, looking at a thirteen-year-old girl and wanting to describe her to her son herself. Is that proper?"

"She would do that herself?" the mother exclaimed in innocent amazement.

As if everyone did not know that any mother, especially a young mother, would also be modest in the presence of her eldest son, or any of her sons as soon as they entered the world of their father!

"That is not how we do things!" replied the other.

The mother would have been inclined to think that the woman's remark was rather pleasant because she had been thinking about the happiness of her son, and before he yet desired it, she wished him to have a beautiful girl "with fire in her eyes"!

Suddenly she had doubts. She had to ask the neighbor who was friendly and knew more than she about how people said things, "My daughter, my eldest daughter, how would you describe her eyes?"

The neighbor used the typical terms and metaphors to praise the adolescent girl's features, her eyes, her hair.

At which point the mother stopped the conversation: "In any case, the father will let his daughter complete her studies. Tell that lady to look somewhere else for a daughter-in-law!"

Once back in the village the mother boasted about this possibility of arranging her first child's marriage while she was still so young. She talked about it with the only family she received in her home or whom she herself would visit: the *caïd*'s.

He was a widower; the eldest of his three daughters who was divorced did not want to remarry because she wanted to attend to her very young sisters and two brothers. The last of the orphan girls had just finished elementary school and, as was customary, was now cloistered at home awaiting some future suitor.

The *caïd*'s eldest daughter was the mother's only friend. Upon her return from the city, Bahia described her niece's wedding to this somewhat rural audience with discreet satisfaction. These womanly conversations, especially when they took place in the *caïd*'s house, looking out upon a deep orchard on the outskirts of the village, would end with musical sessions. One of the women brought a derbouka, a little girl had a tambourine, and the rather unpolished, somewhat nasal repertory of la Mitidja, could be heard beneath the trees, close to a hedgerow of almond trees—hostesses and guests all sitting on carpets laid out on the grass, the children all around, in the background some animals: a rooster and a peacock, kids, some very skinny cats, and even a rather terrifying wolf-dog that frightened the mother, a city-woman...

At nightfall my father came to get us in a Citroën that he and the Kabylian baker had bought together. The baker used it all week, but when he was not at work, he agreed to chauffeur my father, who was incapable of driving it.

The baker had closed up shop. He arrived accompanied by my impassive father. The car was parked. One of the little boys came and told us they were here. We climbed in back: my mother engulfed beneath her veils; myself at thirteen, stiff because I was on display; and my very little sister.

My father then signaled to his chauffeur partner (or perhaps they had decided between them to do this long before) that they had to go the long way around in the car. It was "apéritif time" (my father's phrase seemed mysterious to me, I never asked what the words meant). The two large cafes in the center of the village would be filled with men who were *pieds-noirs*, while on benches just across the way the native men, Kabylians and Arabs, congregated in angry, silent confrontation.

Consequently, even with two men in the front, we could not drive there. A wife would immediately be the focus of all eyes: As if my mother, a lady who was of course veiled in silk, with embroidered organza over her nose masking almost her entire face, must not, because of her very worthiness, be thus exposed to the gaze of such spectators.

A double public gaze, exclusively masculine: Europeans gathered on the terraces for their apéritifs and seasonal workers, whom hostility bound together to contemplate the leisure time of others.

It would have been unthinkable for my father to permit "a lady" from where we came from to parade past, even rapidly! These potential gawkers would be incapable of seeing the innate distinctions: This masked figure, made mysterious because of her very sophisticated veils, in the Caesarean style, had to be imagined as extremely beautiful in theory even though they could not see her! Why do them the honor, even for the five minutes it would take the Citroën to drive around the little square and arrive in front of our apartment building?

After all, the wealthiest settler of the plains, an all-powerful colonial master—with his farms, his hundreds of acres of vineyards, his army of workers—the man who decided the mayor's election, who chose local elected officials, to whom one bowed very low on those rare occasions that he deigned to show himself, this secret master kept his wife and daughters hidden. He spared them the need to go through the village, just as a jealous sultan would have done.

Of course it was not a matter either of male jealousy or of prohibition, merely disdain. The lady of the manor—or "the queen," as she was called by the Europeans playing bowls and the natives play-ing dominos—stayed invisible, except...

"Except on August fifteenth," the baker at the wheel reminded him in a low voice, as he took us on a big detour to the south, then along the far eastern side, to return by the alley that was almost empty at this time of day, passing one side of the church and ending up, finally, in front of where we lived.

As we drove home, through all the detours, I heard my father muttering, as if in a duel with the all-powerful settler whom so many visitors from Belgium, from northern lands and even farther away, came to see. (They came to admire the highly technical nature of his farms, his sowing by helicopter, his mechanized vineyards. They never, however, ventured into the innermost recesses, into the hidden corners they were unaware of, where ramshackle huts were reserved for his serfs.) "Because he does treat them like serfs!" my father remarked, furiously, there next to the baker. I think now that it was for my benefit that he would let fly this way in his usual diatribe against the local despot...

As if, right at the beginning of my adolescence, he called me as a witness: "Your mother, my wife, has a special status, at least equal to 'their' lady of the manor, and it is as it should be that all those men— the 'others' and ours—do not deserve to see her go by. And I"—(this is the father speaking as I imagine it later)—"following the example of 'their' master, will not expose my wife either—the very heart of myself. She is of course entirely wrapped in her stiff and immaculate veils, and following our customary ways, she remains silent outside, her eyes lowered beneath the face veil! And I am just a schoolmaster. The only native schoolmaster for native boys. Pretty stiff and inflex-ible I am, too, and tough-minded under my fez. When I was a young man, I admired Atatürk because with a leader like him we certainly would not have been colonized—in our own country without being in our own country. Then, your mother, like the Turkish ladies of the former aristocracy, could have taken off the Islamic veil and worn Paris skirts. She might even have been able to drive the Citroën herself, as breezily as any sportswoman—because it is clear I will never be able to drive a vehicle! In that case, well then, she would deserve to be photographed!

"Here women would have emulated the ladies in Turkey, but also the ladies of Damascus or Egypt, Cairo and Alexandria, the first emancipated Muslim women." (My father was thinking then of how many of his friends, doctors, teachers, lawyers, who, like him, had dreamed ten or fifteen years too soon of "unveiling" their wives, traveling with them!)

But we were living in a colonized country. Sétif, Tébessa, Guelma, tumultuous cities—thousands of men dead, then thousands imprisoned on May 8, 1945—that was two or three years earlier… Algeria at war, thank God, had other matters of urgency. It was perhaps even a stroke of luck that in these little ancient cities the families were huddled together like this, and the women of the city were trembling but safe in the warmth of women's apartments.

We returned to our apartment.

By this time my paternal grandmother, who had lived with us, was dead. Only her ghost remained of her, nostalgically floating through the rooms… It was the period in which my sister, the youngest, about six years old, was just beginning to feel unwell—a long illness that made her weak for over a year. I remember the next summer, spent in a verdant mountain city so that the fresh air would make her get well soon.

How exactly did I pass from my childhood to my preadolescence? It was before I was thirteen, or rather before I was ten, when I left for boarding school in the nearby city. ("The city of roses," André Gide called it fifty years before I arrived. But he was there fifty years after the painter Fromentin, the first one to write a French account of this Arab city.) I see myself still half submerged in the mists of innocent childhood while all that surrounds my coming of age—the unknown, the ambiguous—marked by an ardor with no words to express it in an Islamic land, was making itself known to me.

What were the early scenes, experienced with the passivity of blind innocence, during which I partly left the family cocoon, the warm protection assured me by the affection of a group of women (an affection not without its acrid moments)? "Coming of age": this term applied to women, to girls who reached physical maturity, is in the maternal dialect laden with threats. In the masculine plural, however, the *kharidjines*, the men said to be "of age," are dissidents, indeed bearers of a religious freedom that occasionally turns out to be a cause of war, but the beginning of a collective adventure that starts a new phase... In the feminine singular, the girl "coming of age" promises only pure danger, sometimes reduced to a gratuitous fuss and bother. When did I, then, come of age out of limbo?

The *caïd* had three daughters: This triad is at the heart of my village memories.

My usual playmate is the youngest of these sisters, a year or two older than me. Our confederacy is reinforced every Thursday or Sunday in the back of their rustling garden by frequent disputes with her brothers, one in particular who was about ten. He used to climb the trees and trap birds. With a cruel grin, he would bring us their trembling, wounded bodies. "I am going to slit their throats according to the ritual right now and fix them for you to eat. You'll be licking your fingers when they're plucked and grilled, you'll see!" His teasing eyes stared right at me; his calm cruelty made me uncomfortable... I stood stock-still; his sister never let up berating him.

Before all this teasing, before our screaming—little girls scandalized by this boy we used to call a hoodlum—there is a sense of disquiet that remains and comes back to me, indelible.

Was I six then, or was I seven? I think I had left nursery school. The youngest of the *caïd*'s daughters, following my example, was also now being sent to the French school. Whenever I visited, her sisters, who were oddly inquisitive about me, would pounce and trap me in a corner. There they would lift up my skirt or my dress to examine— my slip! It was a piece of lingerie they had never seen before. My mother was so style conscious that she insisted on buying me European clothes for little girls from a young Spanish woman who used to travel the length and breadth of the plains in her small truck selling underwear and various fineries to the village women shut up in their homes or living in isolated places.

The *caïd*'s daughters, who were dressed in traditional clothing, did not dare speak openly to my mother of their compulsive curiosity. But no sooner would I find myself delivered to them in their house than, in a great state of excitement, they were immediately compelled to feel the satin slip I was wearing, even its embroidery if possible. I struggled. I had the feeling that what they were so eager to know through this feminine underwear was French womanhood itself. Because I went to school and was therefore disguised as a little French girl, they would have liked to caress, and feel through me, the whole body belonging to these distant ladies who seemed to them arrogant but so precious. "To know," they exclaimed as they encircled me without seeing me, "to know what they wear, how they doll themselves up, underneath!" The fervent sigh that went with *underneath* made me want to throw up.

I got away. I pulled their youngest sister with me. The two of us ran off together to the far end of the orchard. Being touched in this way was an assault that brought tears to my eyes. My friend was surprised at how strongly I reacted and in the end I said I was not going to come back alone to see her.

I told my mother why, and must even have wept. I think this experience still makes me instinctively back away, restive and anxious, when faced with the slightest physical contact in the most ordinary social situations (except in love. No, on the contrary, in love, too, which requires such a long preamble before I reach it)... Later on, when I was about twenty or thirty in fact, I discovered Western customs: coeducation, where the sexes mixed in apparent neutrality; the exchange of kisses on the cheek that no longer meant anything more than an easy, often immediate familiarity. The same is true of unrestrained public shows of affection between a boy and his girlfriend that other people pretend not to watch. Later I will approach this language of bodies, their display, sometimes their flaunting, with the eyes of a primitive. So often, I will find myself forced to turn away, in a reaction that made it look like I was a prude when in fact I was just "oriental"; that is, my bared eyes were sensitive, desiring above all to drink in the world as it truly revealed itself: secret, lit by the beauty of beginnings.

I return to my conversation with my mother: "I won't go to their house alone again! Even to play... I don't want them to touch me!" I screamed. "I don't want to be touched!"

My mother came to an unexpected conclusion. Still in charge of my getting dressed every morning, she decided to take off my amulets (two squares and one triangle of silk, a present from my paternal grandmother, now dead). I wore them underneath my dress or pullover; I remember the thread braided in the old-fashioned way, more precious to me than any simple hidden necklace. I recall some classes vividly precisely because, while my attention was turned to the blackboard or to the teacher sitting beside it, I was in the habit of touching these squares or triangles of magical writing I wore on my chest. ("These amulets will protect you from the envy of others!" my grandmother told me, imagining that the world of the French school was hostile.) At night I would proudly wear these ornaments, finally on display, on my nightgown.

Did these night jewels still connect me to my grandmother, who was so sweet, a second mother to me? Probably, as she had said many times, I was convinced that these silk adornments, with their dull colors, gray, dark blue and black, were "protecting" me... I would go to sleep feeling safe, as if the grandmother were still there beside me. And throughout the day, without any of my schoolmates knowing, and in spite of them, I was under a second protection: an invisible and ancient eye that looked lovingly down upon me from afar...

But now my mother decided—I do not remember if it was in the morning or in the evening, all I remember is the room where I stood, undressed, maybe in my nightgown or maybe in the process of preparing for school—yes, she decided to strip me of them: she must have argued and explained. She said it was because the doctor was going to visit the school sometime in the next few days. How would I look, what would I say, parading these magical squares and triangles in front of the other girls, foreigners?

"But still! It's the writing of the Koran!" I must have protested.

But had I yet discovered the argument of legitimization? I do not know: I must have talked about the gold crosses that they wore, the other girls—not hidden like my amulets! It was clear to my mother that the ridicule I might experience would be far more serious than wearing these holy writings, which was, she said, not particularly orthodox. They would call me a pagan, me, the one who was native, there with all the French girls, me the Muslim!

I must have given in. I was stripped, I might as well have been naked. And it was my mother who, caught up in a fit of rationality, took this first writing away from me.

During this same period, however, when the elementary school let out, I attended Koranic school. My mother liked to have a party with the nurse and the *caïd*'s family to mark each level I achieved in learning the Sacred Book—three *suras*, then ten others, then twenty more. My walnut tablet, decorated by the sheik with numerous examples of calligraphy, was conspicuously displayed to all the women. How beautiful, the guests would exclaim! They claimed that this tablet was so elegant that it was a foreshadowing of "my wedding dress" that would come later!

My mother enthusiastically brought us pastries and recited the verses with me. The celebration—with the *caïd*'s daughters all there, in our house this time—ended with musical improvisations.

I have only lamented one death, that of my paternal grandmother, the silent one; I mourned her, screaming and shouting in the oldest street of Caesarea. I ran down this street, leading down from the humble house where my father was a child and where his married sister who was always sick lived, until, sobbing, I arrived at the maternal family's wealthy and half-European dwelling (with its windows and balconies on the main floor). I arrived where "they" lived, thinking this somewhat spitefully, because at that moment I was only the daughter of the woman who had held me when it was cold and dark, who had embraced me silently, who had not dared speak in front of the Frenchwomen who were our neighbors in the village. I am, first of all, the daughter of this mute affection, she, the grandmother that I saw as humble (why did this grieve me?)—humble and modest…

I cry, I weep (willing these tears to fall endlessly in protest), and my mourning, galloping at the same time as I race through space, becomes exacerbated and then splits in shreds like the great tapestry of my rebellion itself. It ends up vanishing because the women, all wearing white headdresses and squatting on carpets—the neighbor women have come to pay their respects—finally take me onto their laps.

Two, three years later, during the same period that I lose my amulets, I see my mother, merry as a child, chatting conspiratorially with the woman we called "the nurse" who, ever since her second son was born, worked for us as housekeeper. In the village everyone, right down to those in the poorest hovels, referred to her by the imposing title "the general's wife." Her husband, who was very old and never left his bed anymore, must have been some sort of handyman, the caretaker of equipment in the army, or perhaps the navy… Someone must have called him the "general caretaker," and the term, at first said jokingly, in fun, stuck to him. Decades later he bore this nickname with not a trace of self-consciousness; sometimes, seeing the nurse and hearing her nickname, someone would ask, "Was her husband a sergeant? Sergeant general?" Nobody knew anything more about it. The "general's wife" was a dark-skinned villager in her fifties with a face that radiated jovial kindness (despite the huge, ugly wart on one cheekbone that, upon the insistence of my mother, she allowed our family doctor to remove using local anesthesia).

I see my mother, on a Thursday afternoon, sitting recovering from the fatigue resulting from her weekly session at the Turkish baths. The nurse, the general's wife, has made fritters the way I like them. The warmth of the house after the cold of the cold room at the *hammam,* where we had been offered pomegranates, oranges, and clementines already peeled and sectioned. At home the nurse's thoughtful welcome…

I remember that particular Thursday. And my mother, in league with the nurse, suddenly asking me, "Yesterday you were in our room, sitting on the floor at the foot of our bed: you were reading that library book you had just brought home. Then, from the kitchen, I heard you crying… You were sobbing, but softly, a bit as if you were singing! I sneaked in to see, to understand." In fact she was talking for the benefit of the village woman. "Explain this to me, my daughter. I think there is something mysterious going on. I read the words to the old songs in Arab, I sing them and sometimes weep to them in my heart… But still I am singing!

"But you, I was fascinated watching you from a distance: your little hands turning page after page, you stopped crying for a moment; then suddenly, after a second, your voice—or, it was almost like the voice of someone else—began to moan. Moan? No, sob, but softly, a sort of lament!" She turned once again toward the nurse, who was smiling doubtfully. "You understand, it wasn't because she sang and cried at the same time, no, it was that she never stopped reading, and when she wept that way, she seemed to be enjoying it. Isn't that strange?"

She admitted a little later, disturbed, "You made me regret I cannot read French! It is good that I'm learning to speak it now, but what I would like is to read it like that! One is never alone then, I think…"

The nurse listened, then, in her tranquil way, spoke, her eyes first on one (my mother), then on the other (her little girl): "Come now, what are you saying, Lla Bahia! Human beings are never alone. God is always looking down upon them, isn't he!"

"Of course," my mother murmured sadly, turning her attention toward me, apparently discouraged by the village woman's remark. And also, perhaps, by her unshakable calm.

Scattered scenes from a childhood I left behind at the age of ten to become a boarder at a school in the nearby city.

The year I was thirteen, soon to turn fourteen, how distant the day seemed when I was seven and, softly sobbing, read my first novel, brought home from the library: Hector Malot's *Sans famille!*

My early adolescence at boarding school was influenced by my strong friendship with a girl who was half Italian, a boarder like myself who went back to her coastal village every Saturday.

Together we discovered in the school library the correspondence of Alain-Fournier and Jacques Rivière, who were adolescents at a Parisian preparatory school before the First World War. This bookish and passionate friendship, dating from a half century earlier, became our entry (probably it was not just by chance that our tacit friendship was formed in the mirror of this dialogue between two young people from the past) to everything we later read. A wide-open realm, an expanded space…

We emulated them daily as the ten months of the school year unfolded and we read. During recess we had almost clandestine conversations about Gide's novels and about the theater, play after play by Claudel. Next I plunged into Giraudoux's short, clear, and cutting novels, especially because my French teacher had seen productions of his plays that year in Paris. Despite our intense nightly conversations, my friend and I had our differences: She made fun of my pleasure in finding Claudel's uncompromising heroines to be a reflection of something familiar, but what? My maternal culture, my tendency at the time to be religious? Our friendship intensified later when, after Rimbaud and Apollinaire, we were dazzled to discover the poetry of Michaux. And I suddenly began to seek out translations of ancient Arab and Iranian poems for my *pied-noir* friend.

I mention quickly our sharing of this first literary repast because it is connected with another day I still remember, the day that I was fourteen.

I had come home from boarding school. No one had thought to turn this first day of summer vacation (we were probably waiting to go to Caesarea shortly, to the family home) into a birthday celebration for me. My young brother had said ironically one day (or was this later?), "Celebrate a birthday? Just because we are neighbors with the French, does that mean we are going to adopt their customs?"

Why, ultimately, does this unforgotten day I turned fourteen come up? Because I decided to celebrate it alone with a new undertaking beginning—my journal. Maybe I thought, *Like Alain-Fournier, like Jacques Rivière!*

This is my life's project... at least until I am thirty.

I lifted my hand from the page. *After that,* I thought, *I shall be old!* I did not know how one was supposed to live after thirty, or if it was even possible to have projects...

But thirty years hence? I saw myself then as halfway through my life—or at least the life I believed worth living: in my reading adventure I completely disregarded the restricted space of the home in which I was growing up. And, in the same way, I had not yet been struck by the injustice of the confinement of the women in my family. I felt only their poetry, their warmth which was sometimes not without sadness; only the pride of my mother, an aristocrat in my eyes, in her stiff silk veil—like Zoraidé, of course, in *Don Quixote*, which I do not think I had read yet.

Consequently, though isolated between two extremes in this village established by colonizers, I did not think of myself as alone. *What should my life project be?* I asked myself grandly. I wrote, and even now I remember these words from a journal that was, moreover, very soon interrupted, and rediscovered by chance in an old pile of stuff. I read the lines again with amused indulgence, and the scene of what we might call "the first writing" rises up intact.

I want to obey, I wrote, *my own rule of life, the one I choose for myself today, at the age of fourteen, and I promise to do so.*

Behind me stood the poets who had become my friends over the last few months, backing me just as much probably as the acrid pride of Lla Fatima and that of her daughter Bahia, exiled for the time being in this village. Behind me, before I spoke these words of a juvenile vow, the familiar saints from past centuries made their presence known, the ones whose sanctuaries I had only rarely visited when I was very young: the Berkanis, father and son, buried side by side, and Ahmed or Abdallah, whom I had so long ignored… Behind me, but why did I stubbornly persist in looking "behind" my first commitment for ghosts who, the instant they were invoked, crumbled away into dust, or rotted there in neglected tombs. Why "behind," why not look for what was ahead, toward death in the distance, toward the last time one takes flight, the final departure?

I write. Beside me in the small living room my father talks at length with a neighbor, an employee who is "native" like himself and who has recently come from our city, Caesarea. My father is talking to this young man about the need to send "our daughters to school, all our daughters, in these villages and in the old cities as well, where traditions benumb them."

I wrote at the beginning of this journal (which had no sequel beyond the notes I took on my readings then) *I make this commitment, and to this rule of life I will remain faithful because I think it is the purest:*

> *"Never to wish for happiness, but for joy!*
> *Never to seek salvation, but grace!"*

The following year, this time alone, I plunged into mystical writings, Islamic ones as well as those I found in my reading at school: In the wake of Claudel's heroes, I moved to Pascal, then Francis of Assisi... Finally, thanks to having mastered ancient Greek, I landed in Greece, as if home at last!

These emotions kept me occupied while I was in boarding school but also when I was in the family harems in Caesarea the next summer, then for another whole year... Eventually an intoxication with poetry, a secret exaltation of sentiment, was all I retained of this. As a result soon afterward, and too quickly, I fell into love for the first time, absolutely. That lasted seventeen years...

Not happiness, but joy, I wrote in my youthful wisdom—and presumption.

More than twenty years later, when, just before turning forty, I leave my first marriage, the only part of this precociously written law that I have left is simple joy, thick of course and slow, joy in space each time it opens up, unscathed joy.

Even today all that I seek, far from "salvation" and for want of "grace," is the feel of passages—sometimes they are too slight, but even then, at least, they may be too narrow, but then, at least, they let my searching gaze arrive ahead of me.

Arable Woman VI

THE FIFTH DAY OF FILMING. The sun has returned; the light is delicate. I am not sure that the photography director can feel how it shimmers, like some questioning iridescence… How—seeing certain dim blues, with hints of gray in them, the flat green of leaves on Barbary figs that bring out sudden, overlapping nuances—one wants to cover up and at the same time to float, eyelids half closed in this winter radiance.

Early January in my country on the Mediterranean coast. Sensation of light on my body, a purely feminine sensation. As if I believed, in mid-winter, that I had left winter behind, this light felt like emerging from the darkness of the harem each time I felt it… I resign myself to the thought that the technical crew, being men, imposing their bodies on space, have not the slightest idea that one can slip through it softly and stealthily as if breaking and entering.

I stroll among them; I have pointed out a specific way to frame the landscape; I am going to lapse into sadness. I would have liked to tell them that this morning more than ever the space is not empty; something rare is happening here that one could try to look at really, densely. Nature this morning seems young; the shepherd children, now used to us, run freely around in the distance or among us—the biblical freshness of these images.

When will we make films with blind people propelled by the fierce desire to see truly? Expecting to show what is there in the first lull, in this first pause that is, if not esthetic, then pagan! Lesson of space first, then lesson of colors.

In the beginning it was a matter of knowing how to get silence. Making one want to enter space the way mimes do, their hands in front, body slowly floating and imperceptibly resisting. Yes, I ask myself again, when *are* we going to use the blind, or people who have been blind, to make films? Then I smile, thinking there is some hope perhaps, hope for the next century, for the decade to come. When all the many women emerging from all the harems, whose eyes have been too cramped in the shadows of walls, will take flight into the blue and want to melt into the light they have won back.

Feeling in this way the brilliance of dawns, the blinding weight of middays, feeling the wantonness of freedom. Freedom is not necessarily a path, it is an ether into which one plunges, where one sleeps on one's feet, where one dances either half bowing or scarcely bent without moving, where one merges with what was held back from ecstasy. Light fingering the whole body...

I will obtain none of this reality, not a trace, though it was not dreamed but intensely perceived. Must I be permanently saddened by this?

Full sunlight while we work on the location shots; in the picture this light ought to "develop" in the same way that Ali's view of Lila develops, and Lila's view of the places and faces that she discovers around her develops.

I turn now to this chain of seeing. Gradually I understand the constant presence of these gazes. In the beginning the story as it was written established the immobility of the husband in his wheelchair. Lila exists in relation to the gaze of the husband, a devouring gaze that is all the more so because it remains at a distance. This, then, was the first shot filmed on the first day: not a shot of the Arab woman but of the image of the woman for the Arab man. Almost a painting of a neutered man.

But this first point of view would have done nothing more than elaborate a path of alienation for the woman: shadow once again, turned into the pretext for anecdotes once again, as she is in almost all of masculine cinema, whether Arab or not.

Long afterward I discover what really sparked my search: Over and over again, a year before starting the film, I would lie in my bed, thinking alone. (Coming through a tight spot then, I did not speak, I mean I really did not speak to anyone, I did not confide in anyone, and moreover I did not write either for myself or for anyone else...) And, to myself, justifying a fierce desire for silence and enclosure, I would repeat this litany, always the same: *I speak, I speak, I speak, I do not want them to see me...*

I, the one not speaking, repeated to myself *I speak* three times; in the pride of *I do not want* I was setting myself free as if in complete refusal of some constraint. And always with this refrain the same image emerged: my head seen from the back against a white wall...

Feeling one's forehead against the coolness of a wall, head nodding gently against the stone because it wakes you up and sets you on guard against some possible surrender, against the danger of a river of tears inside you overflowing... However, even if alone in the room, even if you are sure you are alone, in the event that someone might enter by surprise, you are reassured: Nothing, he would see nothing of you, absolutely nothing. What would a head seen from the back against a wall tell him, your body does not even move, your hands barely tremble spread out against the stone. Barely. Don't worry, no one sees you. The film can begin, the camera can get started. Let it fix its huge eye, its venal eye. I murmur, "I speak, I speak, I speak… I do not want you to see me… truly!"

Of these shudders and of this refusal the camera will only have the brown hair barely swaying back and forth against a wall of dirty whitewash.

Firmly rooted in that time of my life, this was the beginning of the film for the character Lila. In shots 20, 21, 22, etc., filmed, it is known as the scene "of the bedroom."

There is some point of darkness hidden in this film, so that gradually the gaze rolls back to make you look at yourself. Suffering wells up; and proliferates; it is wildly vivid, but no less subtly presented than a mere scratch.

Other eyes watch the couple: Lila looked at by Ali, who is immobilized, she herself trying to free herself graduallly from this gaze where, of course, she is stuck and from which she only frees herself by beginning to look at others… The story of Lila's learning to look at others, at what is outside.

Throughout these months of groping after my character, I learned that looking at the outside in this way is simultaneously a return to memory, to oneself as a child, to earlier whispers, to the inner eye that has not moved from the heretofore hidden story, a gaze suffused with vague sounds, inaudible words and a mixture of various musics… This introspective, backward-looking gaze could make it possible to search the present, a future on the doorstep.

Learning to see, I found out, is indeed recalling. It is closing one's eyes to hear again the earlier whispers, the earlier murmuring affection; it is hunting for shadows one believed had departed… then, opening one's eyes in the watery light, questioning with an unflinching gaze, then bringing this gaze to rest, transparent and discrete, before the unknown; watching, finally, seeing the others move, live, suffer, or simply be, be in the most daily way, yes, be.

I remember certain moments in the film story. In sequence 2 Lila has walked the doctor back to his car. Before starting the engine he says to her, "Ali will get well quickly. But you, after this long absence, are you really here?"

She answers absent mindedly, surprised, "I am! Of course I am!"

The car drives off. Lila goes into the house, her head bowed. Maybe she is wondering, *why this question?*

We started by filming her return to the house at the end of the day, for the first time. She is seen from the back, arriving at the front of the house, noticing her daughter who is playing with the children next door, watching but not calling her, then entering the first room, the second… My only problem was the lighting of the rooms: the interior lights (a copper gong on the wall, a door opposite the first door and, in the same shot, a barred window with the sea behind it…).

I was going to ask that there be these numerous relations of half-light, of twilight: the brilliance of the gong, the fragmented gap of the bay, the almost imperceptible stripe of the sea, all these nuances, seen from where we stood—about fifteen feet from the façade in the spot where the doctor was talking before his car drove off.

I began to go around and around the house like one of the numerous village dogs constantly underfoot. I had chosen this house for its thick walls, for its bulk and its solid, earth-colored pillars, for its women inside, in the darkness.

Behind, approaching the black-barred window across from the bread oven, I made a decision. That was where Lila had to be seen from as she entered: catching her in the distance, from the front, with the two doors and behind her the road and the fields. Little by little Lila approaches; we see her leave the light, reach the first partial darkness, then the second… In the foreground, behind the bars, Ali dozes in his wheelchair.

The camera is no longer at her back, the shot no longer a gunshot. The camera waits for the far-away woman who is going to come closer. Then I wonder why such a shot is necessary. Who is looking? I think to myself, *Who is the camera?* A little girl stands there before me, twelve-year-old Zohra, the one who was just playing with Aicha and was now standing there against the hedge, watching us. She had only done walk-on parts once or twice, usually when Aichoucha suddenly found herself with too many ewes to tend… I called Zohra. "Look, go to the window and watch Lila come into the house… would you like to?"

Yes, she would like to.

When I called her she was far away. As she came closer, I noticed once again how gracefully she walked. (She was a natural dancer; I became more and more convinced of this later.) Coming toward me, she let her hand trail along the stone of the wall.

Long afterward I linger with the happiness of a new mother over the shot, beginning with a little girl next to a hedge; she has seen Lila in the distance, but we will only know this later. She bends down and begins to run furtively behind the façade. She goes to the window, her hand trailing along the rough stone; catlike, she presses herself to the bars; she does not move… Behind her we see Lila arriving at the first door, going into the first room, removing her cape and tossing it on the bed, appearing at the second threshold and stopping there.

A reverse angle, close-up: Zohra's face with her ravenous eyes, a close-up probably from the point of view of Ali in his wheelchair.

Then, a wide interior shot: Lila, who has stopped for a moment on the threshold of this second room, goes toward the window, wonders if Ali is asleep but catches sight of the child spying on her, who is intimidated and goes away. Lila closes the window blinds with her finger and moves toward Ali. He, very slowly, backs his wheelchair a few feet farther away. So is he asleep?

What is new is no longer the couple's silence but the suddenly established solidarity between the little girl and the woman: Zohra's curiosity watching the dreamy return of Lila as she enters the half darkness, stopping, then going closer to, Ali. Lila smiles at the child, who, intimidated, wants to leave. What connects these two are the worn wooden shutters still to be closed.

But though Zohra, who has been spying, goes away, she does not flee. Yes, I am sure of it, she is not frightened when she sees Lila: She recognizes her. They recognize each other for an imperceptible moment.

Up to now it has been Lila's gaze upon the others… During the entire time that Lila searches, searching herself while contemplating the others, she is also being looked at. Looked at as part of a couple. This couple seems strange to so many unsophisticated witnesses who, of course, have seen city people before but not for any length of time. Seeing, moreover, an image of a couple in which the woman is very much on the move fascinates them, which explains the little girl's staring. Zohra's look questions the present before Lila's does. I was generalizing: The eyes of all the children upon you, you, the couple who claim to constitute the "main characters" of the story. What gives you the right?

A film, a story, when all is said and done, ought to be this: characters gyrating slowly as they become "main characters"; during this entire time, multiple pressures, outside the frame at first, then gradually within the picture, challenging the roles granted a priori to the "heroes." What gives them the right?

Each person is looked at in his or her solitude, in his or her proud solitude. The camera calls itself into question to make this felt: the constant process of reality against fiction, of reality ever more present.

In this film a woman walking alone rests her productive gaze on other women. Throughout, we, that is the others of the film, you, we, others, are watching her and trying to make her feel that she is us… that we begin with the curiosity of voyeurs but that very quickly it becomes something much more, that we are affected.

Is she indeed real? Is she not rather merely our dream transposed?… This doubt is made concrete by the watching eyes of Zohra, the little peasant girl who should have been a dancer but for the time being is still illiterate, who moves with regal grace through space that, in a year or two, when they shut her up, will become constrained. Zohra, in her role as witness, makes this concrete. Her silent appeal to Lila: *No, don't be a dream, you at least, win this freedom of movement, to question, to see, that we will all envy you for afterward, myself first of all! Trace a path before us. I watch you; I support you; I close the window; I seem to leave you in your individual story, but in fact you are living for us all. As we watch you, not leaving you, on the road, in the paths, along the ditches, in the courtyards and behind a half-open door, all of us, we demonstrate our solidarity with you. Thanks to you we are not condemned!*

Thus the fiction, within the documentary, carries a symbol of hope.

SIXTH MOVEMENT:
OF DESIRE AND ITS DESERT

THE WOMAN WHO CONSOLES

So often during my childhood I saw the terrifying grandmother abandoned to her rages and her magical dances. Then, afterward, when she would reemerge from them, she was as much in cool control of herself as she was of her entire household.

I also saw her in the village when we lived there not far from the school. In the winter she would come visit us on her way to the capital to pursue her numerous lawsuits (disputes over land, allotments, inheritance). She used to come to consult her son-in-law, the only man in whom she had confidence. I would hear her muttering every evening across from my father, who was trying to temper the progress of her recriminations. I would end up falling asleep right there next to this hum. A virile grandmother with a bitter energy, whom I later begged for something, what exactly? Some "other thing," maybe also some other voice!

But no. When she would come to the village, or when every summer I would return to her city and her house, I, who was ten or a little older at the time, without a veil, grown up too soon, really became

311

something of a nuisance for her. Occasionally the old woman would examine my facial features close up and mutter caustically (why? about what? in any event with distrustful surprise and as if suddenly in the role of enemy), "Those eyes, ah, those eyes!" Then she would look away from me and declare, this time to my mother, "Well, so, are you perhaps going to make her be a boy?"

She was no longer talking to me but to her daughter, who smiled a little. And the little girl that I still was could see that her mother was somewhat ambiguous, almost embarrassed, because she was hesitating over what to do that would both avoid offending her own mother and at the same time defend her daughter.

As for me, I shrugged my shoulders, pretending indifference; then, without a veil, without a shawl, and sometimes even bare-armed, I went off to visit my paternal aunt. Ah! I only had to cross two tiny roads in the old city to find this green-eyed, sharp-faced aunt, tall and thin in a way that was both rustic and thoroughbred, and find all the love in the world! She embraced me, she welcomed me effusively, going on and on.

Above all, every other minute, she would start her sentences by calling me, "O daughter of my brother!" There was so much affection in the way she spoke that her voice still haunts me today, as if the secret vibration of the mother tongue, to reach me, had to pass through the love of a sister… "Mother tongue," I call it, but it is the quaver of this sisterly echo that I should evoke!

THE WOMAN WHO GUIDES

I finally understand that the pure passion that I first revived through words aimed at oblivion was for me a second birth. This began, as is often the case, at least for women finally reaching maturity, when there is a strong sense of feminine solidarity, when my mother first came to talk to me: seeming, in a single scene, to bring closure to this move I was making in my life.

So I had taken refuge at my aunt's house—this aunt was my mother's half sister; hers was the jasmine on the balcony that accompanied my daydreams during these days of transition and torpor. I slept opposite the balcony and the sky, to the sounds of the working-class apartments across the street. My aunt served me in silence, spoke very little, prayed beside my bed. It was only as we sat together in the evening that she would talk: detailed anecdotes about the women who were her neighbors and whose nagging voices sometimes reached us. In the evening twilight, just on the verge of falling asleep, I would recall the past affection of my aunt in Caesarea. She had been so vociferous, but still the reserve of the aunt who was present made me think of her.

One morning my mother came to find me. She came alone by car to the place where I was staying; she had learned to drive in the early days of Algerian independence and liked to set herself up as my chauffeur. She thought I was having a breakdown; she ate with us. I watched how full of energy she was and understood that she was preparing for combat, but in what battle? I left the aunt to go with my driver. Once outside, after she had begun to drive, and as she was slowly returning to center city, she asked briskly, "What are you going to do now with your life, your children, or…"

I was silent for a moment, then I forced myself to say what I was feeling: that my divorce was a repudiation on my part. She was startled by the Arab word, *repudiation*, that I had used!

"Irrevocable," I added, "because it was pronounced three times! I know. I am the one who made the vow!"

She went on driving. How, I thought to myself, could my decision, hard and straight as steel, be transformed into words for the others? We went along for a good while in silence.

"All I know," I said with difficulty, "is that I will not go back. Not at any price! If I did he might try to take away the children whom I would not give up! The children are growing up."

"What do you wish to do… to defend your rights?" She repeated these words *your rights*. Then she assumed the position of official adviser: She proposed to take me right away to a lawyer, either someone close to the family or someone else. I would talk to him privately. She would wait outside. She added, "There are laws in this country! Defend yourself!"

The whole time she was taking me to her friend, a woman lawyer who was the one we had to have, my mother was not looking at me. In fact she never got over her amazement: So here was her eldest daughter, whom she thought was thoroughly clad in armor, paralyzed and unable to speak. In a totally traditional modesty that feared the brilliant light of the sun on intimate things, this daughter wants to struggle and release herself but would rather do so in a half-light, consequently in confusion.

We arrived. She chose to wait for me nearby at the home of one of her cousins, a woman of almost forty who was pregnant again. "She is making babies at the same time as her daughter-in-law, and in the same apartment!" she commented disapprovingly.

My mother was my guide. She led me, outside, in the jungle of the city, in the minefield of new laws, without suspecting that this time it was the energy of her own mother, now departed, that had driven me forward, almost with my eyes blindfolded.

A few days later I appeared before the *cadi* for the scene known as "the attempt at reconciliation." I see myself seated facing the magistrate's desk; my husband, who came in shortly after me, is seated to the side. I feel him; I do not look at him.

The representative of the law spouted a long speech in a form of Arabic that is referred to as literary. All that I got of it was its stiffness and its hollow circumlocutions while the man's eyes, prying and suspicious behind black-framed glasses, goaded me. I take myself somewhere else: It is such a beautiful day, outside the window!

Then the husband and the *cadi* speak together, man to man: I am vaguely aware that this humming sound is a spider's web being put in place. The judge asks me one last question, which he repeats. I merely say *"Lla!"* ("No"!) because I have the ludicrous and in fact ill-timed notion that this is the beginning of the *chahadda*—according to them, the words of submission. So I will only say one word in their learned language: no, *non, lla!*

I also remember that my innocence as a woman finally dawned on me and seemed obvious: *I shall add nothing,* I decided. I erased this face of justice from my sight, and at once my heart flew far away, outside the window, like swallows in flight. I tried to contain the smile that was about to break out on my face. The *cadi* examined the beginnings of this glow relaxing my features, or he saw into it.

Then I told my lawyer, who had waited at the door, how I had maintained my silence and why. It was this shadow of a smile, she explained to me later, that justified for the magistrate a verdict of separation, ruling that the "fault was mine" as well. As for myself, when I left this *mahakma* at midday, all I saw outside was the sun. And a second later I felt its actual heat, its vibration almost exploding against me, right in the chest.

My mother went with me the next day to the airport: In Paris my young sister had just given birth.

When I entered the room in the Paris clinic, the first thing I saw was the baby: She was up and naked and her head was covered with curly hair. The nurse laughed heartily as she wrapped the blanket around her flushed skin. My niece was less than two days old. I did not dare touch her then or caress her... For the next week I slept list-lessly at my sister's. Forget everything. Especially do not discuss with her any of the upheaval in my life. My lawyer, whose sister, Djamila, is very close to my sister, had asked me, "Have you talked to your sis-ter about... about the night of the crisis?"

"Yes," I said. I had talked to her about it in an ironic manner. My face was not swollen anymore, my hands were out of their bandages, but how could one explain this on the telephone, from so far away? I felt only cold irony about my stupidity. Because we could not spend hours on the telephone, I had shortened the story. I tried to think of some novels we had read together, or one of us first, then the other, at home... I ended up explaining: "You know, without being aware of it, I started to act out the princess of Cleves with my husband! Well, everybody—and he first among them—believed that I had chosen to play the part of the domesticated shrew! A simple mistake of repertory!" Then I laughed.

I laughed for the first time, after having spent days waiting to recover, my body more or less intact, and my face where, thank God, my eyes could still see!

"I laughed," I said again to my lawyer, who ventured a more spe-cific question: "Your sister listened; do you know how she reacted afterward?"

"No," I said, "There was a long silence on the other end... I hung up finally; I did not want to upset her too much!"

"I found out later, through Djamila, who saw her in Paris. Your sister began to cry. Silently crying. She didn't have the strength to speak to you. She cried, she told Djamila, because of her earlier fear and also because she was relieved!"

I remained silent there with my lawyer: my new friend—she whose sister seemed so close to my young sister, who for the past two years had been happily married in Paris, now with a magnificent baby. It was then, I think, that I decided to go and spend a week with her. To reassure myself that she was happy.

Sisterhood: Would that be the hidden, but calm, and infinitely open, eye that waits beneath the silent tide of friendship?

Sisterhood does not mean being permeable to each other, and certainly not sharing each others gloom. No. It just initiates some friability of emotion, where emotion flickers in two places at once.

Hands, gestures, smiles are slow to speak. A resemblance that, despite kinship or a shared childhood, is gradually revealed, abruptly unveiled: a sun after rain.

The days in Paris were good for me, a brief spell in which I was always outside. Carefree and relieved to be free; above all happy to have kept my sight. Walking in the crowd and looking greedily, to the point where I forgot myself. The wonder and elation of knowing I, a woman, was an anonymous passerby, a foreign passerby! As a result of seeing new things, multitudinous things, the repetition of landscapes and faces, I become nothing but gaze!

I returned home. I decided to propose a "semi documentary" project finally, one that would feed on my investigations and my research with sound.

In the building where I had once worked for several months, I introduced myself and the twenty-page dossier I was championing to the man responsible for production.

"What title do you have for your outline?" the producer asked indifferently.

"*Arable Woman*," I replied.

THE WOMAN WHO GOES AWAY

Algiers once again, home base. Going somewhere else, and always coming back! On one of these later homecomings I recall the face of a neighbor, a young woman living like myself on the fringes of transience in this oblique city, this capital always on the brink of some fever.

Why would I suddenly linger over this neighbor, my only friend in the old days? The old days, in my other life, that is, before the breach introduced by this passion in the process of being obliterated (during which I was alone, but also so little receptive to others...). Swallowed up in my youth, that is, absent in some way, or distracted, or immobile: The only things I seemed to put myself into were the air, the clouds, the unknown faces floating before me! As if I had no roots, as if I never touched the ground, except at night, sometimes, and in the revived voluptuousness of love...

And yet this friend suddenly appeared. Hania, which means the peaceful or the pacified: anyhow she sought her peace however she could. Her round face with large, shining eyes, a thick short nose, high cheekbones, jet-black hair that hung to her waist or was arranged in two soft braids that her hands would play with; her always-questioning eyes... Hania could not forget her oasis near Biskra. Like André Gide, who was preyed on by temptations in an earlier time, she would return there regularly believing that only there was she really herself.

She lived in a crowded, low-rent building, where I would come for her regularly. She asked me about my life, and then about my work: photographing the peasant women from the mountains of my childhood, what was I going to do with that? she demanded to know. I tried to say how much I liked to look at the people, as if I were seeing them for the first time, when I came "home." "The people?" she said, looking at me with her devouring gaze.

"The people out there!" I answered. "Old people, children, little girls, adolescent girls, people who are out there, and outside this city with its incessant noise!" She listened to me.

I had to explain that, apart from my students and a few technicians, while I did my research during the past few months, I had seen practically no one. My parents. The children. Five or six friends, men and women. That was all. I felt I was living a full life.

"And all the others?" She made a face and a mocking gesture, her arm in the air.

I did not understand. She made the gesture again, a bit like a clown, suddenly so expressive.

"The people 'upstairs'?" I translated.

"The ones in charge," she said. "The ones who have *solta!*"

I smiled. I remembered the expression that was several centuries old. I said it in Arabic, its music resounding like steel. "*Dhiab fi thiab!* As el Maghroui said!" To myself I repeated, bitterly, *Wolves in men's clothing!*

She laughed for a long time. And with that she right away became my friend. And so she poured out her life story. All I can remember of it now is one detail that leaped in my face.

She gave birth regularly every two years, sometimes with even greater frequency than that. All her pregnancies wore her out; no, she would not have an IUD inserted, "a steel thread in my belly, oh no!" As for the Pill, she did not know how to count the days of her cycle. So, once again, she laughed, then suddenly stopped her shrill laughter, looked at me, finally unburdened herself:

"The nausea had just begun, I am in the second month, hardly farther along, I ask my husband"—(she said in fact, "I ask Him"!)— to go there, to the *douar* that is my home. He refuses: his mother also refuses, because with me gone she will have to take care of the children—four, soon five now! In the fourth month, or a bit later, without meaning to, I lose my voice! Oh, I am normal, I work, I face the work. It is only that, once my belly becomes heavy, my voice goes away… And I know what it is doing, it has left and gone to the oasis, ahead of me! The children cry because they can't hear me anymore; sometimes one of them refuses to eat, another gets sick. My mother-in-law is the one, finally, who pleads for me: 'Let her go back to the oasis long enough to give birth!'

"And every time it is the same thing: I leave this city, I go to my people; when I am there, I speak hardly at all, but my voice comes back like a trickle, a tiny, thin trickle. Above all, I give birth among my sisters, with my mother and my aunt at my bedside. On the seventh day, after having finally presented the baby to the day and naming him, we dance the whole night long beneath the palm trees near the *oued!* I revive! And the baby then is so beautiful, full of vigor. I come home full of confidence. Every morning I sing…" (She is silent.) "But hardly have I weaned my child—at six months or a little older—and feeling light hearted, when unfortunately, in no time at all, the nausea is back; I'm pregnant all over again!"

She was silent. She did not laugh anymore. She sighed.

"Next time," she muttered, her voice hard, "I hope to have a good miscarriage, or else to stay there and never come back to Him!"

In fact she had a miscarriage the next year. Three days later they carried her off, dead. Thirty years old and with five children already, all of them still very young.

She was buried in her village near the *oued.* Her face is the one surfacing within me; I hear again her inexhaustible laughter in the low-rent building where I find the mother-in-law who tells me what happened. I was not there in the city when the pallbearers took her away under a shroud, her face toward the sky. Her voice went ahead of her to the oasis, I am sure.

COMING OF AGE

Should one tell, O mother (why do I suddenly speak as if I were the one, the dead child, the child never mourned, the child buried without my knowing how to find any trace of it again?) yes, do you have to be reminded, O mother, that you were worried about me from the time I was twelve until I was fourteen, waiting for my blood, my menstrual blood?

In vain. I had a bloodless adolescence, a bloodless coming of age, the way one would describe a death as bloodless. Later, well after my marriage, the gynecologist explained that one legacy of this land was that very young girls contracted the tuberculosis bacillus without anyone knowing, and they would only find out later, sometimes too late, that genital tuberculosis made them sterile wives. I gladly accepted the verdict: I would therefore be miraculously sterile, available to be a bosom friend to children, all heart, and never any blood!

So my coming of age made my life easier, allowing me to think of myself as androgynous for a rather long time. A gift. One that I expressed in the ignorance and haziness of a mind steeped in mystical reading (a jumble of Claudel and Jalal-ud-din Rumi) that day I turned fourteen, when proudly, too proudly, I wrote out my life project in black and white, *Until I am thirty!*

So, intoxicated with space and motion, I dreamed my life; I danced my little life of an odalisque who has left the frame for good, at least until I turned fourteen… And ever since? Between shadow and sunlight, between my vulnerable freedom and the fetters imposed on the women of "my home," I zigzag along the frontier of a bitter, voracious land. I try my hand at living, that is at looking, one eye turned wide open to the sky and sometimes toward others, the other eye turned inward where it rediscovers, farther and father back, the funeral processions of yesterday, and the day before yesterday…

MATERNITY

Any number of interviews, meetings back to back, dozens of forms to fill out, questionnaires explained by the social worker, read by the woman in charge of children's services, put in order by the family counselor, all ladies with sweet expressions, but who move quickly, speak like inquisitors, are courteous and attentive, and are probably prolific mothers outside these offices. For the past three months Isma has been severely testing the high walls of her patience. After she and her husband had the same impulse at the same time and decided to adopt a child, they had found the bureaucracy trying. Now that is over with! This is the morning they will choose.

They are going together to the nursery where all the babies are, some, they have been told, only a few days old, and some already as old as six months.

Choosing a baby the way you choose a doll, a knickknack, a refrigerator, a dog in a kennel, a cat; no, not a cat, people give you cats—a ball of fur in the palm of your hand—or sometimes the cat comes in by itself through the garden gate, stops on the sill, rubs itself for a second against the doorframe, studies the half-light inside the home, and suddenly it lives there.

Perhaps the same is true for a toddler who gets lost in the street, who dawdles in a playing field, who seems distraught at the entrance to a market: The child lays its eyes upon you and will not withdraw them. The decision opens up inside you like a water flower on some inner lake: It is your turn to approach, look, keep the child... Ah, such a choice (who chose whom?) would be lived as some obscure abduction in full daylight.

Isma has dreams like this as she prepares for the encounter at the nursery. Adopting a child is moving toward a moment of slow seduction, or of falling in love. She moves into this imaginary space: prowling, visiting a friendly house, leaving it. Where would it be? In what place open to every wind would she find herself face-to-face with this child?

Three or four years after the end of this long war, in every city in the country, and sometimes in the towns on the plains, homes have been set up where dozens of orphans live; boys of ten, sometimes older. The summer before, Isma visited the children's houses in her region, one after the other. Once she forgot herself for an entire afternoon, playing with twins who were six or seven. It hurt her to leave them, and she made herself not go back to see them again. They had a paternal uncle, a peasant from one of the frontier regions, who was going to take them... The husband then came to a second decision: they would take in a child who was less than a year old, one of "the ones truly abandoned," he said. Isma did not object and no longer went into the villages. The autumn rains flooded the city; the wind and its icy squalls preceded the winter that would be sunny, but chilly, violet. Isma was silent for days at a time.

The government's positive response arrives: They are going to have a child.

The time to visit approaches. Isma leaves the house. She has dressed herself as if for an ordinary day. An hour later she meets her husband in front of a nursery in a nice neighborhood. A bright two-story building between gardens. They smile at each other uncertainly.

She makes the decision: "Let's go in!"

He takes her elbow, his fingers gripping the wool of the young woman's jacket.

A hostess greets them. Courteous reception; a few gentle phrases of small talk, a soft breeze of words murmured to swathe the beginnings of anxiety. The woman in charge of the nursery is introduced: she explains to them how the formalities will unfold, that was her word, *formalities.*

They stop for a moment in an icy corridor with a view of flowering groves. Outside, the sweetness of spring suffuses the horizon striped with rose and mauve.

The woman in charge points to a closed door. Her sharp voice pierces the silence that seems to have slipped in from outside:

"This is the room where our children sleep! Walk between the rows and look at them. There is a number on every bed. If you see one baby in particular…" Her voice is left hanging.

Isma keeps her head turned toward the door. "So go on!" the first lady says. "It's always up to the woman to get things going. Your husband will do what you do."

The husband lets go of Isma's elbow; he had still been holding it tightly.

"Here we go," she whispers.

And what if it's just a game? she thinks, beset by timidity as she pushes open the door.

A deep, bright room, where the first thing awaiting them is the hospital smell. An undefined smell, not medicine but rather the stench of enforced waiting. And the silence. A few pediatric nurses in white smocks, all of them astonishingly young. These women tread imperceptibly from one bed to the next; they hardly seem to be working. Even the rustling folds of their smocks, when occasionally they brush against each other, cannot be heard. There are also the little canvas beds; they are deep and hide their contents. Tightly clasped in these two rows lies something like an evanescent secret...

When Isma reaches the center line, however, she notices a murmur, then plaintive sounds, a bit farther a sort of gurgling, the beginnings of some monotonous chant, the consultations of the deaf or the blind in this vast place, haunted despite the brilliant daylight. The visitor, motionless, considers there before her the great distance to be crossed to the canvas beds that are occupied but closed in upon themselves.

To choose, she says to herself, *you have first to look at them, you know! Them!*

Thirty, forty children, from one week to a few months old, are in this room. Later she will be told that this is a common number of abandoned children to be gathered in one administrative district over a period of several weeks.

For the moment, standing there motionless, Isma's vision is clouded. The sounds, the crying, the purring, like mini-orchestras distributed among these beds as if they were many orchestra pits. She steps forward. No longer is she aware of anything except the room that seems to her both full of people and, at the same time, transparent—a lake of absence so far from the city. Forgetting her husband behind her, she walks cautiously.

Suddenly she is stopped by the arm of one of the nurses, who recognizes her and greets her with a smile. She says a few words; at first

Isma does not understand, then finally she realizes that this is a neighbor from her building. The woman boisterously reminds Isma of
meeting once and even of a conversation at the butcher's where they
both shop. She is a round woman with a puffy face; her red hair is
pulled back and her eyes are moist. Soft sweetness spreads from her
whole being, a sort of healthy freshness. She bends down beside a bed
and takes a child in her arms, perhaps even the one who was purring
like a kitten. She holds him out to Isma.

"This is my favorite!" she adds unequivocally.

Tense now, Isma avoids looking at the child she is offered. She
feels ashamed, pressured. The baby begins to wail, its spasmodic cries
more and more high-pitched. The nurse turns around and, just as
abruptly, returns him to his cradle. There is an unexpected languor in
the way she curves from the waist to do this, like a dancer rehearsing.
Isma smiles slightly, turns away.

She starts to walk again. She finds she is in the middle of the long
room. She has not yet come up against any child's face, not one
expectant face. She finds she is relieved; is she trying to avoid saying
no, being somehow strangely guilty?

There is no longer anyone in front of Isma, only the white beds,
hollowed out, two rows of pink splotches under sheets one can barely see. The nurses seem to have vanished. Isma does not even turn
around to make sure her husband is still following her.

Silence again. The invisible presences, curled up, urgent, down
inside each bed. She has decided to walk on: as if almost done with
an exam she is intent on passing. Suppose they, the motionless, wordless beings, suppose they are the ones who, in some imperious and
capricious aphasia, will decide?

Yes, she is sure of it: The magical and necessary choice is going to
be imposed from these beds, from all these many hollows watching

her intently. They are asleep, or they are awake, those presences, but certainly they are waiting. They are waiting for her.

Isma is almost at the end of the corridor. Facing her is a French door with a long curtain of blue-gray organza quivering in front of it, its long folds poured in an oblique wave moving downward. She stops; not knowing why, she turns her head: the last bed.

"She" rests there: Isma sees only her big black eyes, almost round, how they look out with the gaze of a peaceful woman. At the same time the gaze is full, so full that the deep bed is full, Isma thinks, and threatens to overflow. A flooding gaze. And yet its black water is clear, solemn, as if it were going to submerge the surrounding space. The little girl—"a three-month–old baby who always smiles," says a nurse who has returned to stand behind Isma—the little girl contemplates the morning visitor.

Fifteen years later I describe the moment for her: "You were waiting for me! All I saw was your eyes! You were the only one I saw! When we left that room, your father, like me, could only talk about you. The next few days, while we waited for me to bring you home to us for good, we met up with your eyes everywhere! There was an advertisement for powdered milk at the time, with a baby on the poster. The same eyes!"

The girl bursts out laughing.

Born for the second time in this room flooded with sunlight through which, a short time before, an unknown couple had walked, the woman first, the man walking behind her.

"My mother first, my father…," the young girl repeats.

All the years would go by like a lazy summer siesta, but how long it took to overcome the ordeal of crossing that room to choose, that

span of time. Walking alongside the peril and keeping a sharp eye out
not to be thirsty for it!

Succumbing, from that point on, to the lurking anxiety silently
beginning, I keep for myself the burden of this mystery.

On the sunny doorstep a young girl—my daughter—is preparing
to go out.

THE YOUNG GIRL

My daughter is twenty and lives in Algiers. Enrolled at the university,
she is waiting to get a room in the student residence halls.

The first days of October 1988. Suddenly she finds herself alone
in a friend's deserted apartment. In the city the young people, the
children, are demonstrating, marching, destroying things. The police
sound the retreat. The army is in the city. Tanks at night. Insurrection. Blood in the streets...

My daughter, alone... I take the first plane at dawn the next day;
when I arrive, the driver of the last available taxi at the airport con-
sents to take me.

Finding my daughter; we stay in this apartment on the heights,
hemmed in but together; every night we sit unmoving to watch the
city through the large bay windows—Algiers deserted and under curfew.

Two or three weeks later the young girl goes back to her studies.
Three years go by. Shortly before the heavily charged October
anniversary, she calls me on the phone: "They have just offered me a
teaching appointment in..."

She tells me the name of the city: her father's city, the one in
which women secretly refer to every husband, real or potential, as
"the enemy." How will my daughter be able to fall in love someday
in the midst of "enemies"?

I give a start. "Refuse," I advise her. "And take the next plane. Please. Come home!"

When she arrives, she decides to go on with her studies in the provinces, in Rouen. I tell her with a smile that at present there is only one place I am familiar with there—the prison. "So we will discover the Seine and the cathedral and Corneille's house, and…"

I was joking. To tell the truth, I had just understood that through my only daughter I was maintaining a tradition, barely outlined up to this point: with my grandmother (who permanently left the *zaouia* for the city) and my mother (spontaneously turning her back on the old ways and instinctively open to the new). Now I was making my daughter, who had been ready to settle into her father's country, into the latest fugitive.

Smugglers together from that point on, she and I: bearing what furtive message, what silent desire?

"The desire for freedom," you'd say of course.

"Oh no," I would reply. "Freedom is far too vast a word! Let us be more modest, desiring only to breathe in air that is free."

Arable Woman VII

WHILE FILMING THE LAST of the location shots I find myself up in a crane about sixty feet above a field with the cameraman. We are trying to get a long, panoramic shot of the Roman aqueduct that is still the boundary of the old area outside Caesarea.

The crane's platform where we are installed and where the cameraman is now attempting to work is not stable enough. It is an early morning in June, the light is full of nuance, brilliant in the distance...

"Are we ever going to manage to get a good shot?"

The camera moves: the cameraman grumbles. Suddenly from up high I see at my feet, way down below, near the truck controlling our movements in the sky, a stele almost exactly beneath our feet.

In the end we redescend. The cameraman wants to have it out with the man driving the crane... I go over to the tree, an oak, and lean over to look at the stele almost in its shadow. I read the Arabic inscription. The stele was set up a few years before: It marks the hundredth anniversary of the last insurrection here in these mountains during the last century, in 1871. In honor, says the inscription, of Malek el-Berkani.

I let my imagination go; I smile. Must not tell the crew that I am, through my mother and my mother's father (is that the most fruitful genealogy, one that intertwines the maternal network with that of one of the father's?) the direct descendant of this combatant. Though it is true that he, at the head of his three hundred mounted troops, was only able to hold out for two or three weeks, scarcely more, while the mountains of Kabylia were ablaze for months!

So I was there that morning, high up in the air in the crane, directly above my ancestor's body, and all I cared about was the horizon, the Roman aqueduct: focusing on this with a panoramic shot that would then open onto "the song of the city."

At my feet, while I sought an image in the sky, my ancestor must have been disturbed by my incongruous presence, especially by my being oblivious to his resting-place, the place where he is buried. Was I being faithless? No, irreverent and thoughtless perhaps, but seeing here, on the contrary, a return to what is truest, while poised precisely between heaven and earth, practically in a state of levitation—after all. That had been my choice the summer before, to go in search of the oral memory of the mountain ladies (including one very pious one, my great-aunt who fasts all year long enveloped in her veils of mauve gauze). These women had taught me how, during the final days of the last insurrection, my ancestor had advised them to protect the Christian prisoner, treat him as a guest, and in the end set him free, while he, our chief, went off for the final cavalcade and died in the last battle…

Buried in these hills, this act had never earned any written account because the new "learned men" go to the archives and consequently to reports, inventories, maps and sketches from the final impoundment; in short, they follow the traces left by clerks and notaries. During all this time, in hushed tones, the daughters of the granddaughters of the grandmothers, in the hamlets where folk wisdom, sometimes haloed with legends, still exists (but also a tenacious and determined memory, concentrated like the green of the leaves of a fig tree, like its starry thorns), these talking women pass on the shreds of their unoffical history...

"Do we have to redo the shot and go back up?" the chief cameraman asks me. The light will allow us fifteen more minutes of work. "One final attempt," he insists, without having noticed the stele on the edge of the highway.

He and I go back up on the crane. We are rising, my gaze and the camera's once again turn toward the tawny, age-old rocks of the aqueduct in the distance.

This time I cannot forget the ancestor who sleeps at my feet near the tree. I am sure that he is watching me, ironically or affectionately—I wonder. I also think about the Christian prisoner in 1871, set free just before the end of the conflagration, before the triumphant return of the French soldiers of that period. He probably went away, far from Caesarea.

I would like to begin the planned six minutes of the film about my city (that will be accompanied by a flute composition by Edgar Varèse, *Density 33*), with these stones that are twenty centuries old. Will this shot turn out? I suddenly feel it is impossible, and a month later, on the editing table I find this confirmed.

"The viewfinder moved again!" exclaimed the cameraman, exasperated.

Then he and I redescended.

I did not make the retort that perhaps my dead ancestor also had moved—in his tomb where he has been for a hundred years. Would he not have been offended that I, his great-granddaughter, in jeans and wearing a cap on her head, my face sunburned by working outside these past days on location, did not first bow before him, a few words of prayer on my lips, that I preferred (inadvertently in fact) to fly away up there in search of an image of stones that were even more venerable than he was?

SEVENTH MOVEMENT:
SHADOWS OF SEPARATION

THE MOTHER-IN-LAW

Was it the time that I was worried and went back to stay with my daughter in the midst of Algiers in revolt? No, I remember another homecoming, to a country still at peace, an opaque and illusory peace in fact: During that summer of 1988, just before the autumn when the tragedy came to life…

I see myself at the Algiers airport. A friend, a kinsman by marriage, had come to get me and take me to a distant beach to be with a family that was dear to me. The man greeting me laid out the whole plan they had made for one or two weeks of vacation. The summer promised to be scorching, and the village beside the sea, so far away, would have a deserted beach: a kingdom just for us!

"Come with me," he proposed. "I would like to say hello to a cousin of mine, despite this crush of people!"

He took my hand so that we would not lose each other in the jostling crowd. It was, in fact, unusually crowded; I quickly understood that the people congregating here were pilgrims, of both sexes but especially older people.

"The next plane is for Jidda! Booked entirely for the 'little pilgrimage'!"

I wanted to tell the friend, "I'm not following you! I'll wait in the cafeteria." But a loudspeaker began to shout, and an even denser crowd—many women in white *tchadors*, their faces flushed with quiet excitement or openly joyful, grouped together like convent-school girls on an excursion—swarmed over the spot where we were in just a few minutes.

I let go of my guide's hand. He found himself propelled farther along, but I did not budge. It was then that, trapped in the middle of the group, helpless at first, then resigned, I saw her, "her." About six feet away from me. Bizarrely, despite the earlier tumult, a strange empty space widened between us. Between the woman ("my mother," I was going to say, whereas of course this was not my mother) and me. I stood frozen.

Her. Now a little over sixty, the same tall silhouette but heavier, more massive... It was my mother-in-law, or rather, because my divorce had taken place two or three years earlier, my ex-mother-in-law. (Recently remarried, I had a second mother-in-law, this time in the principal city of the west.) I was really going to say "my mother." I had loved her so much and still loved her so much despite the estrangement. Here in this chaotic airport I discovered how much this one loss from the breakup of my marriage hurt me, the loss of this woman alone, her, the mother of my first husband.

It was her, and yet not quite. Her silhouette stopped in front of me, about six feet away. Dressed in a Moroccan *djellaba* of light beige; wearing a *tchador* in silky white muslin with folds framing her face. Her face had stayed the same, chubby and austere at the same time. (In the past I had confirmed very early, and thanks to this mother-in-law whose soul was so beautiful, that there was a law of sorts: True goodness is austere, almost invisible to the eye, sometimes even offputting, and rarely does it have the radiant appearance one might expect. Because what is most often radiant is the pleasure of giving rather than the thing that is rarest: the complete forgetting of oneself in the gift.)

That is how this woman seemed to me: on a first meeting not at all open-handed; above all, reserved, and with a rather severe face. A woman whose richness of heart and moral rigor combined with modesty, this I had experienced. The modesty of a humble believer. My mother-in-law, or the purity of Islam.

Now here I am facing her after four or five years of absence and silence. My heart pounds as if I were seeing a vanished lover reappear. Before thinking: *What shall I do? Greet her or not?*

At the same time I was paralyzed, there was something disquieting. *Her, but not her!* I thought to myself again, disturbed, ready to step forward. Because she was right in front of me. I could forget the proprieties, not take into account the burden of the recent past, forget her son; I could simply embrace her, her, speak to her, ask about her health (she was older), listen to her dear slow voice questioning me, then finally tell her that I missed her and the "old days" I used to spend with her (weekends, conversations on Friday evenings, the hours we spent at the baths). In short, I could throw my arms around her, at the risk of becoming emotional. But just as I was about to step forward, I was suddenly shocked to see that the sixty-year-old lady, whom I discovered I still loved like a mother, this lady in front of me did not see me: She was blind.

I did not move. Staring at the lady who was so dear to me, the brotherly, or rather the motherly shadow of my past. Was that when

I decided not to go up to her and make known my presence? Instinctively, probably out of cowardice, I stepped back.

Of course I should have simply kissed the palm of her hand (as I used to do every morning in my childhood as a sign of respect to my grandmother) and murmured, "I wish you a good pilgrimage! And pray for me there!" I would have said my name if she did not recognize me even after hearing my voice.

No, that was not how I did things. Or I could have taken the time (and mustered the courage) to speak cautiously. She was blind and she was going off to pray for her salvation and the salvation of her family!

Abruptly the shadow of her son raised a barrier, I think.

Even today I do not understand why. I can only confirm that there is something strange that recurs: When I leave a man, I have a hard time getting over the absence of his mother, or sometimes his sisters.

SIDI

During this same stay in Algeria I returned for the last time to Caesarea to pay my respects to an uncle, an aunt, and some cousins. Leaving the old city with my father, I went to visit Sidi in a country village not far away.

Sidi, the husband of my oldest maternal aunt, the only man that I would have called "Sidi," like this, "my Lord." He was a farmer, and a true model of his kind. An extremely corpulent man, he spoke rarely and humbly. We all respected him; as children we had been afraid of him, but because of his reserve, his calm haughtiness, and the familiar way he treated his horses and dogs, we found some mystery about him that reassured us. Later I learned how, during his youth, one characterized both by obedience and by a rebelliousness that was hard to hold in check, he had had to endure a maternal uncle who was the only means of support for his mother when she was too soon repudiated. This man acted as his father and rapidly became his oppressor. Rich, polygamous, and sterile, the uncle seemed to have it in for his nephew because, though the old man was constantly getting married, the boy was still his only heir.

Sidi came into his inheritance but never changed the austere life he led in the little village near Caesarea where I used to spend part of summer vacation. His sons had been students, his daughters had married: he had raised his family by his own labor and without ever counting on the miserly uncle.

My earliest memory of the country, farthest back in early childhood, is connected to Sidi. There he sits in the *barouche* in which I was taken with my girl cousins very early in the chilly halfdawn to one of the farms that would be the private world of our games and escapades. I can still hear, close beside me, the rhythmic monosyllables of his voice guiding the mare and talking to her. I am grateful to him for this vivid, undying sense of simply moving along, as if sailing above the road, in the fog, the cold, and boundless nature: "my Lord"!

Thirty, forty years after this sharp memory (the mare and the road before us, the voice of the reassuring coachman close beside me), now he is about to die...

The last time I saw this uncle he had just had the entire house whitewashed again: the façade, the numerous rooms, the two vast courtyards and the dovecote, even if the latter was empty now. My father, who was with me, remarked, "Sid Ahmed, your house certainly is beautiful!"

"Just clean, O Tahar. Clean and neat! This way, when it is my time, everything will be ready when people come."

We were silent. My father must have protested. And, filled with emotion, I stared at him. Since the death of his eldest son at fifty of cancer, Sidi, who was seventy-five, suddenly looked ten years older. He rose early. Took care of the animals. Made an appearance in the village. Returned home for his prayers. Came and went stoically.

"When it is my time," he had said. I did not see him again. One month later the men of the village went into the house that was so clean. They came to wash him, read the litanies, carry him away.

I learned about his last moments from his wife, my aunt, who had been more like our grandmother for twenty years, for all the boys and all the girls.

"He woke up at five in the morning as he did every day. I heard him vaguely in my dawn slumber. I faintly heard his prayer, his faint voice."

Suddenly she was silent for a moment, let a few tears fall from her nearly blind eyes, then with the same voice went on: "He stood near my head. 'Get up,' he told me, 'O Khadidja!' I sat halfway up, attentive. 'The time is come,' he told me. 'I feel it!'

"And right there, almost next to my bed, he went back to his prayer mat. He kneeled down again. I heard the beginnings of a verse... then... nothing more! I got up; I groped around. I found him crouched down; I touched him; I called him. 'God is great! God...' I said. He was dead."

Her voice shook, just one spasm.

"Your Sidi, your Lord is dead! In his dawn prayer!"

Why is it that I am determined to report Sidi's final breath? Why recount this very simple death? To open these our present days to the others, to the "dead who pull the earth to them like a blanket."

To recall that my uncle Sidi died like so many others, men and women of this period of silence, patience, and simply carrying on.

They watched the first oppression, the one in the first half of the century; then they saw the coming of oppression by their own people, their "brothers." They underwent the first with the distance guaranteed by their faith. They contemplated the second with disdain and deep withdrawal—harsh silence and poorly concealed surprise. The world of the *roumis* had not surprised them; it was too completely strange to them, in its iniquity as well as in its foreignness. Occasionally, almost as a miraculous exception, they would acknowledge some kinship, sometimes just one person, a man or a woman, whose value they tacitly appreciated, and they would then grumble among themselves: "This Christian, he's essentially a Muslim and doesn't know it!"

Now, with age coming on, in the midst of all these changes and the stridency of the public displays that followed independence, they were often isolated within their own family circles. Suddenly they witnessed different forms of dissension and new hatreds whose nature they did not understand... It was no longer the foreigners who had set themselves up there as masters, and now were gone, who proved to be foreign to them! The strangers were their own descendants, people they knew shared their blood and, they had thought, also their aspirations—these people were the foreigners, in huge numbers, a hybrid species; still, among them they could also find, though rarely, some innocent man, some innocent woman.

> *Copper is the style today instead of gold!*
> *The rooster rules the skies in the kingdom of the hawk*
> *While eagles are imprisoned in chicken coops amid dung*
> *When the dog takes himself to be king of the forests!*

Bards in the markets of the last century already disguised their despair and pronounced, "Everything is so upside down that scandal becomes normal!" They maintained therefore their reserve, their austere morality, and prickly distance. And like Sidi, who interrupted his prayers to announce that his time had come, they are dead. A purified, bloodless death. No blood, no murder. They left all that behind.

They are the men I want to write about—not the victims, not the murdered ones! Because behind each of the latter there are ten murderers, and I see, oh yes, I can make out the cascades of blood behind the one man, the one woman, assassinated today.

I cannot.

I do not want to.

I want to run away.

I want to erase myself. Erase my writing. Blindfold my eyes, gag my mouth. Or else, let the blood of the others and of our people swallow me up naked! Dilute me. Root me to the spot, a crimson statue, one of the statues of Caesarea that later, much later, will be smashed to pieces and fall into ruin...

Shall I call the narrator Isma once again? "Isma": "the name." In the mixing confluences of this evocation, out of superstition or fearing pagan omens, I would so much like to extract her from her earlier exaltation, after the emotions that shook her, the belated gust that blew as she approached her forties, to the shores of the lake of serenity! The serenity that is called *sakina* in Arabic: not the sudden transparency of being that, they say, shortly precedes the coming of death, no! but the serenity of passages that seem never to need to end. As they stream by, *sakina*—serenity—fills your heart and soul, reinforces you with liquidity, nourishes you with surfeit, while around you everything tips and capsizes and changes. And you have decided to go forward, eyes cast downward, to follow the path mysteriously traced out on the ground for you.

The *sakina* of a person who knows how to keep sight of the road, of a blind man who sees best at night...

But everything else, living and dying, the masculine (that is, the nationalist pride) and feminine (the lucidity that makes one strong or drives one crazy) natures of what I believe to be the soul of this land, the rest is draped in sheets of dust, in French words masking the unformed voice—the gurgles, the disowned Berber, and barbarous sounds, modulated melodies made Arab, and laments—yes, the multiform voice of my genealogy. How hard it is for me to free myself from it!

JUGURTHA

June 1993: I have planned a few days of peace in Copenhagen walking in the footsteps of Kierkegaard's ghost, or at least that of the Kierkegaard I dreamed of in my youth... Then, a painful piece of news reaches me, pierces like a knife: This very day in Algiers another of my friends has suddenly been murdered—not by bullets this time, not with his chest ripped open by a knife, no, this friend, the most upright, discrete, pious, is "sacrificed" according to a bizarre ritual—slowly drained of his blood while, next to his bed, three murderers surround him as closely as possible.

And right beside them in the room his young daughter hears her father's death rattle; a physician, she finds the strength to grab her doctor's bag; she throws herself upon the still-warm open body, the body of her father, alive but drained. Her agonizing cry occupies this house for ever now, this June dawn in 1993.

And I occupy my hotel room, I the traveler, the one spared. I cannot, I do not want to mourn my blood-soaked friends and family there; for this friend at least, what I am attempting to do is bring his last breath back to life. Approaching, for just a fraction of a second if need be, the extent of his martyrdom: in the hollow of reddened shadow...

With that the image of Jugurtha revived within me, for the days that followed and the days that followed them. And not as he is so often summoned up, by all those fine nationalist emotions!

He comes to me the way a clear vision of my young brother on the road to Verdun came over a great distance to the clairvoyant woman in the Roman theater in Caesarea. I, however, am only capable of raising familiar ghosts and inviting them to a selfish, egotistical celebration. Sometimes better able to experience my loves when I think they are erased, I feel they have only deserted me to unburden me, and I am now lighter because I am moving, running. It is not the friend gored in June 1993 that I summon (O M'Hamed, with the sweet name my tribe is so fond of, the same as that of my maternal uncle, assassinated just before 1962, whose kind-hearted nature is still proverbial among us). No, it is not the dead people who are close to me that I call up before me. Probably, alas, because their blood has not dried!

I see—yes, thanks to Dougga, thanks to the plundered stele that can only be read again by going to its kidnappers in London—I see— thanks to this commemoration of that yesterday (the yesterday, that is, of 138 B.C.E.)—I see a young man of seventeen who stands a few steps back to watch the ceremony. The notables, one after another, read or recite their speeches: one in Punic, the other in Libyan (no doubt the most unpolished and the proudest), and the third— because already this would be diplomatic—in Latin.

Before them and their retinues, Micipsa listens, silent and solemn; he is absorbed in the evocation of his father, the great Masinissa, whose "imperishable" (as each of the speeches reiterates) memory is being honored exactly ten years after his death.

The young man, alone, aged seventeen, is the one I see: Jugurtha in the sun, on the edge of the first row of zen oaks. I see him, a thoughtful spectator who is discreetly stepping back to go away... What road will he take? The one to Cirta of course, but then the one to Caesarea, my city, to go from there to Spain, where he will accept the invitation of Scipio, the generalissimo. Fighting at Numantia in the Roman army, the first in the world at the time, showing them how a Barbarian, a Berber, can combine bravery and intelligence with—what to call it?—a fierce personal reticence, silent, implacable. Already neither lend oneself nor give oneself, only ally oneself for the moment... and watch!

So I see this young man turning his back on the stele and its double writing. But then, immediately after, I see him twenty years later; what does he become once the dense fabric of his calculations, his strategy, also his ambition, sometimes his rages as a leader in fierce battles, has all played itself out? In the end, will it be treachery that was foreseen but not discovered, not escaped, and where will he collapse? Or will he fall from great heights, really the one murdered long after everyone else?

I see him again, this time "on the road to Rome," handed over in chains. "Rome, a city for sale!" he used to proclaim. He is conquered and taught a lesson. He is Africa's first Lumumba.

Does he remember his insult, appreciate the irony, when he goes into the "city for sale," where he is going to die slowly an extremely long and drawn-out death? A hard, dry death: of hunger in a dungeon in Rome.

Did I say I see him? No, I hear him above all. Because he is ironic. His guts cramped and emaciated, he voices an entirely unwarranted fervor: "So vast the prison," he murmurs in his next to last breath, while the memory of the Berber lament rocks him to his death and carries him away—"release"!

I hear him, of course, because the language is there. It cannot be erased: *"Meqqwer lhebs!" Meqqwer, meqqwer*—but then the word that means the scope, the vastness, of the murderousness reaches me and has its effect. Despite the distance in time, it strikes me.

"Lhebs?" says Jugurtha. No, it is not vast. Gradually, day after day, like the ogre from the mountains up around Cirta who is tricked and caught in stories, all his days run out in this hole. *"Tasraft!"* he murmurs, because he in turn has been caught in a trap. *"Tasraft,"* the trap that is, the dungeon, this hole in the heart of Rome where he will really die, where, worn to a shadow, he dies.

Unchanging, it is the word that crosses twenty-one centuries in the twinkling of an eye to bring to me Jugurtha's last life breath, right here.

Nothing will be written by or about him. The women will talk of course; a century later, the legend, impalpable, will be evoked but never set down. Nothing in the hand of the hero himself will reach us, not even in Libyan script. But, in fact, Sallust, then Caesar, will write—in Latin—of course, about this unforgettable man who was defeated. "They," in the alphabet belonging to them, think to perpetuate Roman victory, but they are the ones who will firmly set down Jugurtha's glory.

He died in a hole, in Rome. Narrow the prison, nowhere release! Thus his death by silence crumbled and spread across the land of sun from Dougga to Cirta, then on through Caesarea as far as Volubilis. In spite of that, or because of that, his shadow grows longer.

Oh, I see (or hear, I do not know which), I see those who have been longest dead—including my younger brother, though my only memory of him comes through the shaky voice of my father describing the sorrow of the orphan mother. I see these people who died long ago not because I claim any legacy from Lla Rkia, the sorceress (there is no brazier down around my skirts, nor will I ever go on a pilgrimage, no), but simply because in my country, these past two or three seasons, all the dead are returning indiscriminately.

We women are haunted by their desire. Each of us has been too long shackled within our bodies, or too often without our voice, as I have been. As my hand races across pads of paper, my voice is patiently wrested from me, or rather, and this is something I do not really understand, the sound of my heart is stripped from my body!

The dead return to us; what do they desire in this sudden desert?

THE WOMAN IN TEARS

A young woman of my country was taken regularly to Paris by her husband to be treated for advanced cancer. On their last trip, despite the husband's affection and precautions, the sick woman understood that the doctors were giving up hope.

She did not weep. She went home to her city on the coast. She picked up the phone to call her sister, who lived in a city in the interior. She spoke to her in the language of their mother.

"Daughter of my mother, a curse on you if you do not agree to what I shall ask now!"

"What do you want?" asked the other, knowing the state her sister was in.

"Listen, it is all over; I am never going abroad again for these treatments! I am going to bed this very day and I shall not get up again!"

"Don't say that. For the sake of your children at least! Don't say that! You must trust in God's mercy at least."

"I make one request of you. Agree to do what I ask before I even tell you what it is."

"Yes, dear sister!" (The woman wept as she later told me of their conversation.)

"Listen, I want… do you hear, I want you to weep for me, I want you to mourn my death now so that I can hear you!"

The sister did not know what to say. And the other one, the sister who was ill, insisted: "You say nothing, but you can sing! Listen, I know that I am going to die. Very soon I am going to lie down and never get up again. I beg of you, daughter of my mother, weep for me, mourn my death so I can hear you myself while I am living!"

The sister held on to the receiver, gripping it tightly, and for ten, maybe twenty choruses she went through the slow, heartrending threnody sung by mourning women in her village. She celebrated the young woman's too brief life, her marriage—first daughter of the widower who scattered his daughters too soon because their mother had died. She recalled the misfortunes of the young bride and the children that now she, in her turn, would leave as minors. Finally she keened to end it all, ululating one long breath of lament into the phone, until the woman listening on the other end could conclude, "Blessings upon you, O daughter of my mother! Now, do not come to see me before the funeral!"

That very evening she lay down. At dawn a few days later she died, and the next day, from the distant town where she lived, her sister was then able to come to her doorstep.

LAMENT

I thought that, by dint of writing about those who died last century in my country in flames, the blood of men today (the blood of History and of the opression of women) was rising again to splatter my writing and condemn me to silence.

Blood in my writing? Not yet, but voice? Every night my voice leaves me as I awaken the sickly sweet suffocations of aunts and girl cousins that I, a little girl, glimpsed and did not understand. Wide-eyed, I contemplated them, and later was able to picture them again and finally understand.

At the age of six, my mother turned her back on her dead sister. Annihilated her. Did not write about her. How can one write about her?

I relived the grief of my mother, banished from her childhood, just as I myself am by this very grief, the same as is described in the oldest of writings.

As if I were simultaneously Chérifa, dead at eighteen; Chérifa, the happy, expectant fiancée; Chérifa, her beauty shattered by the typhus epidemic in Caesarea that struck her down. As if I were simultaneously the dead woman dead too long because never spoken or written about and, at the same time, become again my stunned mother, a distraught little girl, taking this stroke of fate like a powerless old woman or an adult seeking in vain some way to rebel. Yes, the little six-year-old girl who stayed there, her mouth open and eyes dry (they did not show her the young woman's body, only the thin shape beneath the white sheet, onto which the shrouded girl's mother threw herself full length), and the little girl does not weary of her mother's trances, her mother's frenzied dancing and tearing of her cheeks—I am this little girl, an extra, an onlooker who wanders, voiceless, how long did you say, for six months? No, more, almost an entire year, until September, when the principal tenant farmer brings blanched almonds and jars of olive oil, just before the second tenant arrives with the lentils and chick-peas that have been harvested.

Chérifa the dead woman has returned. Onto Algerian soil the dead (men) are returning after so long. The women, forgotten ones because they have no writing, make up the funeral procession, new Bacchantes.

The dead (men) are returning onto Algerian soil. Is that the deepest desire of the men? The women? And would death be only "masculine," as I thought: old women and old men, mere slips of girls and male corpses, all of them forming only an asexual mass without tenderness, merged out of fear or resignation into something ghastly and impersonal?

I had thought this before already as I looked at my grandmother's body beneath its shroud, a body still possessing such a tenacious resentment, despite the lamentations and the verses of funereal poetry... I really thought that every death in Islam is experienced as masculine; because our proudest women in the end die as men so that they only bow before the greatness and the magnanimity of Allah.

And this recurrent dream that haunts my nights! In the bottom of my open mouth a soft, viscous paste, phlegm, stagnates, then gradually flows and I sink irremediably into this feeling of sickness.

I have to get this paste off my palate; it is smothering me; I try to vomit. What do I vomit other than a whitish stench stuck deep down in my throat? These last few nights the blockage in my pharynx has been worse: I have had to take a knife and cut some kind of useless muscle that hurts me, spit covering my vocal cords.

My mouth still hangs open; my persistent fingers are busy among my teeth, a spasm wrenches my abdomen—rancor or irresistible nausea. I do not experience the horror of this state: I have picked up the blade, I try to cut all the way down, slowly, carefully, to the bottom of this gluey stuff hanging under my glottis. Blood is all over my fingers, this blood not filling my mouth suddenly seems light, neutral, a liquid prepared not to flow out but to evaporate inside my body instead.

I perform this attempted amputation very carefully: I do not ask myself if I am suffering, or if I am wounding myself, and especially not whether or not I will remain voiceless.

Every night I am tormented by the muscular effort of giving birth through the mouth this way, this silencing. I vomit something, what? Maybe a long ancestral cry. My open mouth expels, continuously, the suffering of others, the suffering of the shrouded women who came before me, I who believed I was only just appearing at the first ray of the first light.

I do not cry, I am the cry, stretched out into resonant blind flight; the white procession of ghost-grandmothers behind me becomes an army propelling me on; words of the quavering, lost language rise up while the males out in front gesticulate in the field of death or of its masks.

PART FOUR
THE BLOOD
OF WRITING

"You say that suffering serves no purpose.
But it does.
It serves to make one cry.
To warn against what is insane.
To warn of disorder.
To warn of the fracture of the world."

—JEANNE HYVRARD
La Meurtritude

"They say that after a long wait,
the stone lying beneath the earth
turns into a ruby.
Yes, I believe it—but it does so
with the blood of its heart."

—HAFIZ

YASMINA

YASMINA IN THE DITCH… Precisely at the moment that I bring this journey to a close (mourning so often friends killed in the preceding days—sobbing every morning, but continuing to walk, dancing at night with a hardened heart—days of exile, mauve, streaked with blood…); a young girl, who went to school with my daughter not long ago, has been killed…

A week before she was with her family, there, behind the door her voice still resonates, determined: "I cannot live outside Algeria, no! I am definitely gong back!" She went home. In Paris she kissed her father and her French mother. At twenty-eight she refused exile.

Yasmina, a young teacher, but also a proofreader for an independent newspaper.

That day at the end of June 1994 she was with a foreign visitor—a Polish woman. This friend was resigned to cutting short her trip because they could not wander in the streets and roads together or swim peacefully on the nearby beach. "There is danger everywhere, invisible but everywhere!" a neighbor told them, alarmed at seeing them so young and full of life. He added, and probably regretted it later, "Danger has a smell now on this earth!"

Yasmina drives her friend to the airport. Halfway there she stops for gas and finds police searching people. They are in fact fake police; they take the young foreigner away to "the station."

Yasmina does not let go so easily: She follows the so-called police and suddenly, in open country, they take a shortcut. Yasmina—who by then must have recognized the "smell of danger"—does not give up. She feels responsible for her friend. She does not hesitate, harrying the kidnappers, honking constantly, not losing the trail, in the name of the sacred duty of hospitality.

The armed men—there are four—stop. Yasmina confronts them. They encircle her. They search her; and seeing her press card, it occurs to them that a woman journalist is a much better catch than a mere foreigner!

They set the young Polish woman free, taking in exchange their new prey. In their ultimate performance that is all caricature, they condemn her to death behind a clump of trees. Then they go after the friend she rescued.

The young Polish woman—will I ever speak to her?—left Algeria the same day, freed and voiceless: she runs away, she will run, I feel it, to the four corners of the earth. But before vanishing she testifies—a few brief words; this woman for whom another woman spontaneously gave her life—testifies that Yasmina, to the end, thumbed her nose at her murderers, insulted and defied them with her last breath. The only thing that cut short her angry voice and impotent pride was the death rattle, beneath the knife! This voice, the voice of Yasmina—Jasmine Flower—I shall hear it in all four corners of the earth...

Yasmina, whose mutilated body was found the next day in a ditch.

Yasmina, who every day of her last year carried the *kalam* in her hand.

"I cannot live outside of Algeria, no!" she had decided.

Algeria—blood.

THE BLOOD OF WRITING
—FINAL

TODAY, AT THE END of a year of dark, incomprehensible deaths, defiled deaths, in the shadows of fratricidal conflict.

What can we call you now, Algeria!

Luckily I am not in the middle of it all, the scene in which, as Kateb Yacine saw forty years earlier,

Men shot down pull the earth to them like a blanket
And soon the living will have nowhere left to sleep!

In the middle of it what can one do other than be dragged down by the monster Algeria—and do not call it a woman anymore, unless it is a ghoul (which is feminine), or a voracious female centaur risen from some abyss, no, not even madwoman.

Sucked up by the monster, what was there to do except plunge my face into the blood, smear myself with it, scald myself with it, in trances, hallucinating—the performances of Sidi Mcid, described by the mother of the poet in those carefree days, before there had even

356

been a May 1945 (and the blood of Guelma, Tébessa, Sétif) to drive her insane.

In the middle of this scene, above all not crying, nor improvising funeral poetry, nor contorting oneself in stridency—the dances at Nador ravine but also at the sanctuary of my childhood at Sidi-Brahim, facing the sea, with its pebbly beach reserved for the deeply religious, little girls, and beggars...

Because from now on the dead we think we bury today will fly off. They are the lighthearted ones now, relieved, lightened: Their dreams sparkle while the gravedigger's mattock is at work, while the mourning is filmed, projecting their revived grief to the four corners to repeat this procession of shrouds!

We think the dead are absent but, transformed into witnesses, they want to write through us.

Write how?

Not in some language or some alphabet? Not in the double one from Dougga, or the one of the stones of Caesarea, the one of my childhood amulets, or the one of my familiar French and German poets?

Nor with pious litanies, nor with patriotic songs, nor even with the encircling vibratos of the *tzarlrit!*

Write, the dead of today want to write: now, how can one write with blood?

On what Koranic board, with what reed reluctantly awash in vermilion red?

The dead alone are the ones who want to write, and "with the utmost urgency," as we like to say.

How can one inscribe with blood that flows or has just finished flowing?

With its smell, perhaps.

With its vomit or its phlegm, easily.

With the fear that is its halo.

Writing, of course, even a novel...

    About flight.

    About shame.

But with blood itself: with its flow, its paste, its spurt, its scab that is not yet dry?

Yes, how can one speak of you, Algeria?

And if I fall someday soon, backing up into the hole?

Leave me, knocked over backward, but open-eyed.

Do not lay me either in the earth or at the bottom of a dry well.

    Rather, in water.

    Or in the wind's leaves.

That I may keep on contemplating the night sky.

    Smelling the grass quiver.

    Smiling in the streaks of every laugh.

    Living, dancing feet first.

    Rotting gently!

Blood for me remains ash white.

    It is silence.

    It is repentance.

Blood does not dry, it simply evaporates.

I do not call you mother, bitter Algeria,

    That I write,

    That I cry, voice, hand, eye.

The eye that in the language of our women is a fountain.

Your eye within me, I flee from you, I forget you, O grandmother of bygone days!

And yet, in your wake,
"Fugitive and not knowing it," I called myself,
Fugitive and knowing it, henceforth,
The trail all migration takes is flight,
    Abduction with no abductor,
    No end to the horizon line,
Erasing in me each point of departure,
Origin vanishes,
    Even the new start.
Fugitive and knowing it midflight,
Writing to encircle the relentless pursuit,
The circle that each step opens closes up again,
Death ahead, antelope encircled,
Algeria the huntress, is swallowed up in me.

                Summer 1988—Algiers.
                Summer 1991—Thonon-les-Bains.
                March–July 1994—Paris.

GLOSSARY

aïd: a religious festival.

bachagha: in Algeria, a chief who is the *caïd's* superior.

baraka: luck, a favorable destiny; also a benediction.

bey: the representative of the sultan of Constantinople in Tunis. Although the sultan grants him this office, the bey functions, in fact, rather independently. In Algiers the same officer is referred to as the dey, and his independence was so notorious that the French referred to him as the "king of Algiers."

brasero: see *kanoun.*

cadi: a Muslim judge with both civil and religious jurisdiction.

caïd: a North African chief who served as a representative of the French government for purposes of taxation, policing, and other administrative duties.

chahadda: the first verse of the first chapter of the Koran. It begins with the profession of faith.

chatter: someone who is tireless.

the Dahra: the back regions of the mountains.

djellaba: a long, loose Moroccan robe.

douar: an Arab hamlet of tents or more permanent structures.

fatiha: the Koran verses containing the profession of faith.

fellagha: an armed partisan of independence.

hadja: a woman who has made the pilgrimage to Mecca.

hadj: a man who has made the pilgrimage to Mecca.

hammam: the ritual baths.

hand of Fatima: the image of a hand used to ward off the evil eye.

hanéfite rites: rites practiced by the Hanafiyah, one of the smaller Sunite sects of Islam.

imam: a Muslim priest.

Kabyle: the people inhabiting the mountainous regions of Algeria. They speak the Berber language and have maintained ancient Islamic customs.

kalam: a pointed reed used to write on the Koranic tablet.

kanoun: a small container for hot coals used to heat a space or for cooking.

kharidjines: young men who have come of age.

koubba: the tomb of a local saint and the sanctuary associated with it.

Lla, or *Llalla:* address of respect for a woman: "My Lady," the equivalent of *Sidi* for a man.

mahakma: the judge's chambers.

mamané: a term of affection. Its English equivalent might be "granny."

marabout: a Muslim holy man who has devoted his life to ascetic contemplation.

la Mitidja: the fertile coastal plain southeast of Algiers, presently a hotbed of religious fundamentalism.

mokkadem: the current representative and direct descendant of whoever the saint in question may be—whether Saint Ahmed or Saint Abdullah (our equivalents might be Saint Peter or Saint Paul, Saint James or Saint John, and so on).

Moriscos: the Spanish Moors, descendants of the Muslims expelled from Spain at the beginning of the seventeenth century. When they arrived in Algeria, they were given the name Andalusians because of their most recent provenance.

Mourashidien: the "well-guided *imams*" were the first four caliphs, abu-Bakr, Omar, Othman, and Ali (the Sid Ali referred to by the old aunt). The term is only used by Sunite (Orthodox) Muslims, who consider that, following the schism prompted by the death of Ali, they and not the Shiites represented the legitimate continuation of the line under the guidance of Muhammad himself and hence, Allah.

muezzin: the Muslim priest who sings out the prayers at fixed moments in the day when the devout stop whatever they are doing and face Mecca to kneel and pray.

noubas: Andalusian songs retained as part of the "classical" music of the Maghreb.

oued: a temporary water source at an oasis (*wadi*).

pieds-noirs: French colonists in Algeria.

raïs: a pirate.

Ramadan: the ninth month of the Islamic lunar year, during which Muslims fast, practicing strict abstinence from sunup to sundown.

rebec: a bowed musical instrument derived from the rebab and having a pear-shaped body, a slender neck, and usually three strings.

roumi: Christian.

sakina: serenity, particularly the moment of illumination experienced at death.

sarouel: the loose pants worn by women.

Sidi: a term of respect used before the given name of a man, because of either his age or his station. In North African cultures it is more or less equivalent to "my Lord."

solta: unbridled power.

sura: a chapter of the Koran.

tchador: the face veil worn by Muslim women.

tzarlrit: a traditional musical form of Berbero-Spanish origin composed of five distinctly different movements.

yaouleds: the sons of workers: lower class.

zaouia: a community built around a sanctuary where noble families descended from the local saint live.

zen oak: a type of oak typical of the Mediterranean coast.

ABOUT THE AUTHOR AND TRANSLATOR

ASSIA DJEBAR won the prestigious Neustadt Prize for Contributions to World Literature in 1996 for perceptively crossing borders of culture, language, and history in her fiction and poetry (previous winners include Max Frisch, Francis Ponge, and Gabriel García Márquez) and the Yourcenar Prize in 1997. She is a novelist, scholar, poet, and filmmaker who won the Venice Biennale Critics Prize in 1979. She writes in French and her books have been translated into many languages; those currently available in English are *A Sister to Scheherezade* (1993), *Fantasia: An Algerian Cavalcade* (1993), and *Women of Algiers in their Apartment* (1992).

Algerian with Berber roots, Djebar was educated in France and in her homeland. She is currently Director of the Center for French and Francophone Studies at Louisiana State University. She lives in Paris and in Baton Rouge, Louisiana.

BETSY WING is the author of *Look Out for Hydrophobia,* short stories and a novella and has published in *The Southern Review* and other journals. Her translations include Helene Cixous's *The Book of Promethea,* Didier Eribon's *Michel Foucault* and more recently *The Governor's Daughter* by Paule Constant as well as poetry and essays by Edouard Glissant (*Black Salt* and *Poetics of Relation*). She lives in Baton Rouge, Louisiana.